# The Principle of Life: Deciphering the Code

The Principle of Life, Volume 1

Erika Kane

Published by Erika Kane, 2025.

This is a work of fiction. Similarities to real people, places, or events

are entirely coincidental.

THE PRINCIPLE OF LIFE: DECIPHERING THE CODE

First edition. November 21, 2025.



ISBN: 979-8993761213

Written by Erika Kane

# Table of Contents

This map loosely represents Kude Island and is not drawn to scale.

"My brain is only a receiver; in the Universe there is a core from which we obtain knowledge"

- Nikola Tesla

# Chapter 1: The Afterlife

"Hey, we should definitely stop by Arcadia after this," Detective Skeeter suggested. He stood five feet and six inches from the ground. A pudgy man with rosy cheeks and a patchy beard. A few slicked strands failed to hide the bald patch at the crown of his head. He clutched his foil wrapped burrito like it was a weapon in a robbery.

"Hm." Detective Piquette clenched the steering wheel, refusing to look at Skeeter's greasy eyes. His breath smelled of chip grease. She let out a deep, strained sigh.

Skeeter continued to speak, inhaling chips from the greasy paper bag, crumbs accumulated at the corners of his mouth. "I heard they've got brand-new items." His eyebrows rose, turning toward his partner. "Wouldn't that be fun, Piquette? Can we go?"

Without taking her eyes off the rocky path or loosening her grip, Detective Piquette replied flatly, "Yes. We can stop by Arcadia if that makes you happy."

Detective Safina Piquette was a woman of silence. She rarely showed emotion and kept to herself. Her doe eyes graced her face with beauty, despite her icy stare. Dark ginger hair tied in a low ponytail, barely brushed the nape of her neck. Although not old, lines already marked her face. The best detective on the Force paired with Skeeter because he wasn't the fittest. Training for the Force was brutal, but she graduated top of her class in Defensive Skill, Tactical Response, and Adaptability. Skeeter, for his part, was a savant with evidence—blood spatter, footprints, molecular residue. His uncle, a high-level detective, kept him useful.

Skeeter grumbled. "I only want to go if you think it would be fun."

After a few moments of silence, broken only by Skeeter's obnoxious chip-crunching, he fussed, "Are you sure we're going the right way?"

Detective Piquette didn't respond. Her mind was far from the dirt path ahead, tangled instead were the details of the case that had consumed the entire island.

A'Kierra Jones, sixteen years old, had vanished without a trace after last night's Afterlife championship game.

The championship was especially chaotic. During each round, the maze itself shifted unpredictably, even the stadium lights pulsed and changed color, amplifying the frenzy of the crowd and adding the dramatic effect.

But this case was bigger than the game.

A'Kierra was the daughter of a respected banker and a lead engineer at PortMaster, the company behind Earth's teleportation network known as Blink Stations.

As much as she wanted to believe otherwise, a gnawing fear lingered in her chest—a fear that it was her own father. Long missing and suffering from Cognitive Deviation Syndrome, also known as a cogger. She was afraid he might somehow be involved. He'd disappeared into the mountain ranges years ago, and a recent report placed a strange man dragging a body the night A'Kierra vanished.

Piquette needed to be sure it wasn't her father. Because if it was, she didn't know whether she'd run to him or run from him.

She used to believe he could get better—that the treatments would work, that some piece of the man who raised her was still in there.

But every year, his mind slipped further into the abyss. His anger and delusions grew dangerously violent.

Piquette felt trapped between control and love. The cruel ache of wanting to save someone who no longer wanted saving.

She was just almost at the door when the Chief stopped her in her tracks.

"Take Skeeter with you!" he yelled.

It took every ounce of restraint not to ball her fists and explode right then and there. She had no choice but to bring him along and now she had to figure out a way to get rid of him. He was oblivious to the hard stares and cold shoulder.

No one knew this part of the story, not about her father. And she intended to keep it that way.

Her mother died at birth, leaving her to be raised by her father in the slums of Belgae. He made his living as a factory worker until an injury left him out of a job. When her application for Kude Island was approved, Piquette thought joining the Force for the benefits would be a good idea. It's been them ever since.

Her memory flashed.

It was just before sunrise. Shouting echoed outside their apartment. It was her father once again.

She stumbled into her slippers and rushed out, her sleep clothes brushed against the cold, wet pavement. Light raindrops tapped against her shoulders. A couple stood on the corner, the woman trembling, the boyfriend gripping a knife and breathing wildly.

"I told you to get away from her!" he barked. "He tried to grab my girlfriend, he's a cogger, isn't he?!"

Piquette dropped to her knees beside her father. Blood seeped through his shirt where the blade had entered, his eyes unfocused.

"I'm okay," he wheezed forcing a smile even as pain twisted his face.

"No... you're not." Her heart hammered. The streetlights flickered in time with her panic.

"He needs to be locked up!" the boyfriend shouted.

"No!" Piquette screamed before she could think.

"I—I have gold. Please. Just... just wait here." She held up her finger.

She sprinted back inside, grabbed three gold coins, nearly everything she owned, and hurried back out.

She shoved the coins toward him with shaking hands.

"Here. Take it. We're good, right? No need to call anyone."

He stared at the gold—knife still half raised.

Slowly his shoulders dropped, his jaw unclenched. The knife lowered.

"Yeah," he muttered. "We're good."

"Come on, babe," he said, pulling his girlfriend away. The clicks of her heels faded into the distance.

Piquette wiped the blood from her father's chin.

"Those damn kids," he grumbled, confusion twisting into bitterness. "They don't respect me..."

"I know, Dad," she whispered, slinging his arm over her shoulder and helping him up.

"I've got you."

Since that day she put a tracker on her father and kept finding him wandering about the mountain ranges. Then one day the tracker disconnected, and her father was gone for good.

Driving through the rocky landscape, the vehicle cut through the dense green until the trees swallowed the road. Piquette parked her standard issue Force vehicle, a Mauve X6 designed to resemble a jaguar. Black and low to the ground. Oversize fan wheels, and a tear drop shaped dome. Its headlights glowed with a predatory gleam, and the adjustable tint shifted with the surrounding environment, camouflaging the vehicle almost perfectly.

"We're here," she sighed at last, stepping out and inhaling the damp forest air. The silence was a relief, anything was better than listening to Skeeter chew. After three years of partnership she still hadn't gotten used to his childish ways, but she still couldn't find it in her to lash out at him.

"Wait... where are we?" Skeeter asked, brushing burrito crumbs from his shirt as he tried to clamber out of the car. "This isn't even an actual road. It's just a dirt path!"

He used the roof to haul himself up, wobbling once as his boot hit uneven ground. Limping forward, he pushed up his sliding glasses and crouched. His joking façade faded away as he focused.

"The dirt isn't disturbed enough for a body to be dragged through here," he noted, brushing his fingers over the soil, "If someone hauled a person, we'd see deeper grooves—boot trails, torn roots, compressed soil."

He pointed to the small prints heading towards the trees. "And these here are fox footprints."

"Yeah, well," Piquette shrugged, starting up the trail. "These are the coordinates. Someone must be here."

She didn't look back, but anxiety tightened in her chest like a fist. She was very close to the truth.

Skeeter groaned but followed. His hunger outweighed his curiosity.

A'Kierra thought it would be a good idea to take James to the game; she wanted them to escape their parents' constant arguments for one night.

But A'Kierra made the biggest mistake of her life.

The night was breezy and slightly chilly. A'Kierra and James were leaving the arena. The arena levitated above the tip of a mountain called Olympus. Cords and wires hung from the bottom, surrounded by mist. The only way up was through the tunnel-covered escalators.

Players and workers, however, had a separate entrance at the base of the mountain.

A'Kierra was still buzzing with excitement her team, the Red Pythons, had won! She was rubbing the victory in James' face as they rode the escalator down.

"Did you see Zean? Man, he moved like a lightning bolt! Grabbed the token just in time to make it across!" A'Kierra pumped her fists, a wild grin lighting up her face.

Afterlife wasn't just a sport. It was a brutal, computer generated holographic maze where two teams battled not only for victory but for survival. Offense had thirty minutes to push through traps and collect tokens, each one unlocking a new path forward. Defense had one job: stop them, by any means necessary. Traps, ambushes, even death—nothing was off limits. Most players were veterans of a broken world. Ex-soldiers, trauma survivors, people who had nothing left to lose and everything to gain.

When they reached the ground, the siblings joined the crowd of people heading back toward the city. They could have taken the Skyway, but A'Kierra wanted to walk, to be seen. A soft glow spread across the crowd as tall, skinny lava lamps lined the path.

She walked side by side with her brother as they recalled the best plays of the night when someone called out her name. "A'Kierra!"

She turned, and her heart dropped.

Violet Viller was calling out her name.

One of the most prestigious girls at their private school, thanks to her father, who owned one of the largest coin banks on the island. Violet wasn't just rich, she was a descendant of one of the original Founding Scientists on her mother's side. And Violet let no one forget it. Many of the founders' families controlled most of Kude's technology and its economy.

Violet waved for her to come over. Beside her was her usual posse, and with them stood Luke, the boy A'Kierra had been quietly crushing on.

A'Kierra pointed at herself in question. Violet laughed and nodded as she fiddled the chewing gum with her tongue.

A'Kierra kneeled beside her brother and grabbed him gently by the shoulders. "Hey, I'm going to go say cheers to my friends over there. I'll be right back."

"But Mommy said to not ever leave me alone," James cried.

"I'm not leaving you, silly. I'll be right over there." She pointed towards Violet.

"Is that the girl you said was always mean to you?" he huffed.

James had always been too smart for his own good.

A'Kierra rolled her eyes, ignored the question and forced herself not to get frustrated. She stood and left him behind, convincing herself that he'd be fine.

Their parents might have been well off, but they were still toxic people. Their mother was addicted to Gerthuim, a drug made from crystal dust, which had many side effects, including hallucinations. A'Kierra and her family had moved from Ameris to Kude Island, the Island of the Future, to get a fresh start. Their family had been on the wait list for two years, and her father's engineering skills were the only reason they'd gotten accepted.

Despite five years on Kude Island, A'Kierra had a hard time adjusting to this society, and she would do anything to prove that she belonged.

"Ouch!" Trinity cried as her milkshake slipped from her hand.

She'd been trying to keep up with Cy and Isis through the busy crowd, but A'Kierra stopped her in her path. Trinity already had a long night. Isis had forced her to sit between her and Cy, she felt like an adopted child out with new parents trying too hard to impress her. They had painted her face with a red python and given her a laser light. Isis always made her feel small, treating her like a child. The only reason she had agreed to come was for the milkshake. Olympus had the best desserts.

Trinity froze, staring as her vanilla smoothie seeped into the cracks between the stone tiles. A chorus of oohs rippled through the crowd. Heat flared in her chest; she clenched her fist; arm still raised in the air.

A'Kierra's eyes widened as she gasped. "Oh, I am so sorry!"

Trinity met her gaze, and the tension in her chest softened. There was something heavy in A'Kierra's eyes—sorrow and shame. Trinity felt in her energy she was truly embarrassed. *Except for the straight hair me and her almost look identical.*

"No, it's okay. I should've been watching where I was going," Trinity admitted. And it was true she was dazed, watching Cy and Isis hold each other as she trailed behind them.

A'Kierra shakily pulled a gold coin from her pocket, pressed it into Trinity's hand, and closed her fingers around it. "Here. Take this. It'll buy you a hundred milkshakes." She glanced at Violet, who was too busy chatting to notice. "I've gotta go. Sorry!"

Trinity reached out, wanting to give the coin back, to tell A'Kierra it was only an accident, and she shouldn't have felt ashamed. But A'Kierra was already hurrying off toward her group of friends.

Envy prickled through Trinity. *I should be with friends like that. Instead, I'm stuck with my stupid aunt and Cy.*

"Trinity!" Isis's voice cut through the crowd.

Trinity winced.

"Now how did you manage to spill your milkshake? I swear I have to keep a better eye on you."

Trinity closed her eyes and drew in a deep breath. She was almost home.

"What's up, guys?" A'Kierra approached.

"Oh, nothing! We were just headed to the kissing booth. Do you wanna come?" Violet asked, smirking.

A'Kierra's stomach twisted with nerves as she glanced down. "Umm."

"Aww, she's scared." One of Violet's friends mocked and laughed.

"What's wrong, A'Kierra? Scared of the tree man?" Violet teased, trailing her fingers along A'Kierra's arm, making her blush.

A'Kierra quickly shook her head no, accidentally catching Luke's beautiful brown eyes.

"Oh, I see," she purred, reaching forward to pinch A'Kierra's cheeks. "Aww, come on, A'Kierra. I'll give you seven minutes in heaven with Lukey-bear."

"Ooo!" Violet's friends hooted, delighted by the idea.

Luke chuckled as his friends continued to tease him.

A'Kierra smiled nervously and tucked a strand of hair behind her ear. "Okay, I'll go."

"All right, then. Let's go." Violet's grin widened as she looped her arm through A'Kierra's and led the group away.

A'Kierra looked back at her brother and mouthed, "I'll be back."

Sadly, A'Kierra never returned.

The "kissing booth" turned out to be nothing more than an empty clearing bordered by trees—a popular spot for teens to drink, dance, and sneak off together. Violet and her crew were already tipsy, laughing too loud, stumbling over one another as music blared from a portable speaker. A'Kierra kept her distance, sitting on a stump and sipping from a cup as she exchanged shy glances with Luke. One by one, couples began disappearing into the bushes.

"You! Come with me," Violet commanded suddenly, grabbing A'Kierra by the wrist behind some trees. "We need to doll you up to make an impression on Luke."

Violet's eyes swept over A'Kierra's outfit with open disdain, and a hot blush crept up A'Kierra's neck.

"Ugh, let's get you out of these raggedy clothes." Without warning, Violet stripped her of her sweater and shirt, leaving her in a thin pink vest.

A'Kierra shivered. *This is so vexed. Why am I letting her do this to me? I just want to go home now.*

"Are you sure Luke will like this?" A'Kierra asked softly. She wished she stayed with brother.

"Okay! We are missing one more thing." Violet leaned forward and kissed A'Kierra on the lips to transfer over her lip gloss. "Now, let's blindfold you to make it extra special." Violet pulled out a handkerchief and tied it tightly, covering her eyes.

A'Kierra's chest got tight. "Violet, I don't think I like this." She frowned, a soft quiver in her voice.

"Ugh, don't worry. Luke is like my best friend. He loves this stuff! He's such a freak."

A'Kierra listened as Violet's footsteps rustled through the leaves. She sat and waited eagerly, shivering while listening to the music that was still playing.

Moments went by, then suddenly the music cut.

"Umm, guys?" she called, but there was no answer.

With her fingers trembling, she pulled off her blindfold and circled the tree. Her eyes scanned across the empty field.

Everyone was gone.

Her eyes filled with tears as she wrapped her arms around herself disappointed. Embarrassed and alone, she began her lonely journey home.

Walking through the thick forest, she followed the constellation Orion, a trick her father had taught her, to guide her back toward the city. Each step crunched softly against the earth.

Then her shoe brushed against something thin and metallic.

A tripwire released a cloud of spores into the air surrounding her.

She coughed violently, doubling over as her throat burned. The effect was immediate.

Her heart rate increased. *What was that?*

Her legs trembled, strength draining from her muscles, and she collapsed to her knees. Gasping for breath, she clawed at the air, lungs refusing to obey. Her vision blurred, eyes bulging as panic surged through her body.

The forest tilted sideways, her fingers still reaching for something, anything to hold on to. Darkness crept in from the edges of her vision, and with one last shuddering breath, her eyes fluttered shut.

A'Kierra's eyes snapped open to darkness. The air was hot and stale, heavy with dust. For a moment, she couldn't remember what happened until her knees hit something solid just inches above her chest. Her heart skipped a beat. Her hands discovered she was surrounded by wood.

The coffin was narrow and splintered; its jagged wood scraped her arms whenever she tried to move. Sweat trickled down her skin, and every shallow breath made the space feel smaller. Somewhere beyond the wooden trap, a television played.

"Please find our daughter! A'Kierra means so much to us. Let us know your demands and we will accommodate you. Please, she is our only daughter. She's our baby. Just give her back!" A'Kierra's mom sobbed.

Her father took over the conversation. "We appreciate all efforts being put into finding my daughter. Thank you to everybody who has shown us support and love, but for right now, please respect our wishes for privacy. Thank you, and that's all." His voice cracked on the last words.

A'Kierra sobbed quietly as she heard her parents' cries on the TV.

"Get me out of here!" she yelled, banging on the coffin's lid, but it didn't budge; the lid was glued shut. Her tears fell harder.

Her captor laughed, creepy and childlike. "No one's coming for you, my dear."

"—16-year-old A'Kierra Jones has been missing for over 24 hours," the TV proclaimed.

"She was last seen at the arena with her six-year-old brother, James."

A'Kierra's heart sank when she heard her brother's name. *How could I be so stupid?*

Then came another sound from a distance. A low metallic growl followed by a sudden roar of a chainsaw.

Her survival instinct kicked in. A'Kierra knew she had to escape.

The wood in the coffin was old and brittle. She pressed her trembling hands against the coffin. There was enough room to throw a punch. Fueled by survival, she hurled her fist up with all her strength, adrenaline drowning out the pain. The wood cracked. Again, she threw her fist with all her strength.

"Ah!" she cried, clenching her teeth. Her skin split and blood gushed out, but that didn't stop her. Splinters started raining down around her.

Detective Piquette and Skeeter had been walking along the dirt trail for seven minutes. Seven minutes of Skeeter babbling about anything and everything. Piquette tried to ignore him while her mind calculated every outcome of what they might find ahead.

"Hey, Piquette! Are you even listening? Did you hear a word I said?" He huffed, trying to match her pace.

"Mhm," she grunted.

"I was talking about that space program." He continued.

"Oh, you mean the one where you sign your life away? No thanks." Piquette scoffed.

"Oh, come on! It's not that bad. The perks are insane free housing, free food, state-of-the-art gear, and the crush ray!" he mimed firing a weapon. "You know, the gun that shoots invisible pressurized energy? It crushes you on impact. What a brutal way to die... but man, I'd love to fire one."

Piquette raised an eyebrow. "You don't say?"

"Ha, I knew you'd like that. Anyway, rumor is they're recruiting intergalactic travelers, people to explore space, set up human stations across the galaxy."

"I was more interested in how that gun works," she said dryly.

"Oh! Well, imagine I shoot you in the chest. Wherever it hits, the force crushes your body like crumpling paper. Energy conversion tech from some gazillionaire genius."

"And you know this how?"

"Remember, my cousin Ralph? He got citizenship at Stone Wall. Lucky bastard. Been up there two years now."

Piquette glanced up at the smooth black ring that orbited the Earth.

Stone Wall. Home to the extremely wealthy, the ones who abandoned the planet long ago.

"Greedy punks," Skeeter muttered. "I heard they don't even use currency anymore. Everything's coded to DNA. They live in luxury while we're down here cleaning up their mess."

"Now you're making up stories." She scoffed. "It's funny how—"

A rustle in the trees cut her off. Piquette raised her hand for silence and scanned the shadows. Something, someone was stumbling toward them. The figure broke through the bushes, limping and covered in blood.

A'Kierra.

She was sobbing, staggering toward them. "Oh, thank God! Please, please, you have to help me!" she stopped to gasp for breath. "A lunatic—he kidnapped me!"

"Hey slow down, deep breaths. This man—what did he look like?" Piquette quickly asked, her voice steady despite the adrenaline coursing through her. Each thump of her heartbeat hit against her chest hard.

A'Kierra took a deep breath to focus, swallowing hard, "His hair was red and his body was all skin and bones. I was able to get a quick glance as I was running." A'Kierra fought through the sobs as tears streamed through the blood on her cheeks.

"Okay, calm down. I'm Detective Piquette, and this is Detective Skeeter. We're here to help. Back down the road is a Force vehicle. Wait for us there. My partner and I will find this man and subdue him." She gulped. *Red hair. It's him. It must be. I have to protect him.*

Piquette draped her jacket over the girl's shoulders, gently guiding her past.

A'Kierra sniffled a thank you and hobbled down the path then turned back and grabbed Piquette's arm.

"You *have* to catch that man. His underground bunker is like a maze. I ran through so many hallways, and I don't think he saw me escape. But the walls." Her eyes wandered off as she recalled the horrors.

"The walls were covered in blood as if he painted them with it. And the smell." She began to cry.

Piquette glanced down at A'Kierra's bloody hands. Flashes of her father's suffering came to her. She couldn't come to grips that her father was the monster A'Kierra was describing. Piquette had to see it for herself. She couldn't live with herself if he was put through more suffering. If it was something she could do about it. A wave of darkness clouded over her, absorbing the last of her restraint.

"I understand, now head to the vehicle." She ordered her once more.

As A'Kierra began limping down the path, Piquette's fingers brushed the gun and twitched as she placed her thumb print on the biosensor that unlocked it from the holster. There was no turning back. Her chest heaved and sweat trickled down her face.

She let out one last sigh.

Then, before Skeeter could even process what was happening. Piquette drew her gun.

Two sharp blasts shattered the silence.

A'Kierra's body dropped to the dirt, lifeless. Blood pooled beneath her.

Skeeter froze, horror flooding his face. "What are you—"

Two more blasts rang out. His body hit the ground with a heavy thud.

Piquette's vision blurred red. Now in the bunker, she paced back and forth, thinking about her next move. Then he laughed again. She spun toward her father, who was crouched in the corner.

"Shut up!" she screamed.

He bounced cheerfully, circling the corpses with childish delight.

"Hehehe! Look at them sleep..." he whispered, head tilting, closing his eyes, pretending to sleep with them.

Piquette pushed hair from her sweaty face, staring down at Skeeter and A'Kierra's bodies. She dragged Skeeter up the path, then returned for A'Kierra. The moment she saw her father she was questioning if she made the right choice. The blood on the walls was exactly as A'Kierra described. Thick with blood and stained in repulsive smell. But none of that even came close to the heartbreak she felt when she saw her father for the first time. He looked like a completely new man, unrecognizable as the father who raised her.

Her father clapped like a toddler that received a new toy. "You did it! You fixed it! No witnesses!"

"Do you have any idea what I just did?" Her face hardened, lips curled with rage.

He didn't hear nor did he care. His attention drifted to the blood pooling from the bodies, his giggles rising again.

Skeeter's face had turned blue, lips darkening, death settling into his features.

Piquette stood there, unable to breathe as a panic attack was settling in.

Then she broke. Her own fist began beating on her head as she screamed in pain.

"Stupid! Stupid! God, I hate you!" she shouted.

"I hate you." She whimpered, "I hate what this island did to you..." a tear fell down her cheek.

"They made you worse. When they were supposed to be helping you."

# Chapter 2: Shadow Land

Isis sat at her table of living vines. As she enjoyed her breakfast, the strands of roots softly flowed. The vines shifted, molding around dishes, cups, and utensils as natural placeholders and beautiful decor. They recoiled when a dish was too hot and stiffened when a dish was too cold. The chairs, also woven from moving vines, reshaped to fit a person's size and posture.

Sometimes, Cy would fill the vines with fireflies, their soft glow transforming dinner into something warm and romantic for Isis. The table bloomed with life as it corresponded with the seasons. In winter, crystalline frost dangled; in spring, colorful flowers bloomed; in summer, dark green leaves coated the table; and now, as they were approaching fall, the leaves were dying off, fading into shades of amber, crimson, and brown.

Isis wore fluffy brown pajamas, silver bracelets with charms and colorful beads as she ate her breakfast. Isis had copper skin with full lips, high cheekbones, and alluring siren eyes. Hair jet black, smooth and shiny. Even now, with a few strands pulled out to frame her face, gathered into a messy bun. To keep her hair fresh and vibrant, Isis got it washed and pressed every half-moon cycle. She loved having voluminous layers as it resembled the sea.

With her fingers, she picked up a strip of turkey bacon off her plate and pinched it. It vibrated lightly as another piece of bacon formed and fell onto the plate. She continued to eat as she smiled. Isis had the power to double anything she wanted. Being an alien was cool enough, but being an alien with a superpower made Isis feel untouchable. Having the gift to double anything with just a squeeze. When she first realized her powers, she made copies of everything. She even grew her hair twice its length in less than a second. There was barely a need to grocery shop because Isis had that covered, and having rubels would never be an issue. Though as Isis was maturing, she found herself using her powers way less.

"Good morning," Cy called, emerging from their bedroom across the hall. Next to their bedroom door was a conversation pit that served as a living room. He had to walk up a short flight of stairs and through the hallway to reach the kitchen.

Cy greeted Isis with a kiss as he entered. Dressed in gray sweats and a Synthix silver shirt made of chromium. He wore silver-framed diamond earrings and a thin silver chain with small nanonite diamonds that he never took off.

Synthix was a clothing company that had discovered how to slice crystals so thin it could be worn like fabric. Their clothing was exclusive to the island only.

He was a shade darker than Isis. Stood 6'3 and had a slim, muscular build. He styled his hair with low-cut caesar waves. His face held together with beautiful almond-shaped eyes that matched his full face, including his chubby cheeks.

Isis loved his laugh, he reminded her of a chipmunk.

Isis and Cy's apartment had a futuristic Bohemian theme. Burgundy Synthix drapes with evil eye dots made of blue agate. Sun catchers of different-sized pendants captured sunlight from windows, filling their apartment walls with colorful patterns. The conversation pit was U-shaped with a white fur carpet and filled with a burnt orange couch piled high with cloud-shaped pillows. Across the pit lay a wall made from a screen. They painted the ceilings and walls dark teal.

Cy and Isis were almost inseparable. With communicators inserted in the backs of their left ears, they were never out of touch.

"You should conjure me up some breakfast." Cy teased taking a seat next to her.

Isis giggled. "I'm an alien, not a witch. There's more food on the stove." She pointed.

He sighed as he stood to make himself a plate.

Trinity had been up all night. Her thoughts refused to let her sleep. *One day, I'll find the truth—the truth about why I'm here, and what all of this means. Ugh, I wish I knew. I wish I knew what I'm missing. It doesn't matter now.*

Staring at the ceiling she listened to Cy and Isis as they prepared breakfast. The clinking of utensils against the sink. The crash of pots and pans colliding had woken her up before the sunrise bells. It brought her some comfort that she wasn't alone anymore. *I don't want to go. But I must. Having a job will take my time away... but at least it will give me productive something to do. But will it truly make me feel free?*

Trinity often felt cursed—not by fate, but by consciousness itself. Her thoughts were chains, binding her to emptiness and solitude. She longed for something deeper, something meaningful, but she didn't know what it was or how to reach it. It was as though her soul was crying out for a door that didn't exist, desperate for an escape from a cage she couldn't see.

She'd woken up early because Med Inc. was having a job fair. Trinity didn't want a job, not really. But she was tired of Isis treating her like a child, and she figured the only way to prove her maturity, and independence was to get one. *Last night was so embarrassing. Isis was trotting me around like I was five. All my friends were at the tournament. Ugh, I hate her so much. And that girl, I don't know why but I feel bad for her, something about her, it was like she was filled with sadness. Maybe will cross paths again and hopefully we can be friends.*

She let out one last sigh before climbing out of bed to prepare for her trip to the Twin Cities.

"Hey, Trin," Isis greeted as Trinity entered the kitchen.

Trinity wore all black, her signature style. Black pants, a Synthix tourmaline shirt, and a black leather jacket with a matching black leather shoulder bag. She wore a silver chain, with matching rings and bracelets. All encrusted with diamonds. Her long, curly, jet-black hair was in a slick bun. Like Isis, she had high cheekbones and siren-like eyes, but they were more of a cat shape. Her baby face made her look younger than she was.

In fact, people often mistook her for Isis and Cy's daughter. Initially, it was really embarrassing, but now they'd gotten used to it.

"Headed to another job interview, I see!" Isis's eyes followed Trinity as she walked through the kitchen. "You look beautiful." Her voice rose an octave.

The kitchen had many built-in ovens, stoves, sinks, dishwashers and gadgets. If Cy could not find the right kitchen tool, he would build it. He had three slide-out freezers, one of which held a secret, slide-out computer screen. It was the only place cold enough for his quantum computer chips. All apartments included a built-in water filter in the kitchen. Garbage chutes were also built-in to separate plastic, paper, and food. But food never went to waste there. Cy loved to cook. The robot dystopian scene painted across the ceiling was Cy's favorite part.

"Thanks," Trinity muttered. "Hey, Cy!" her voice perked.

Cy gave her a slight nod. Trinity grabbed a Lytora from the cooler—a genetically engineered fruit made from a dragon fruit and a lychee—and peeled the soft, snake-like scales from it. Dark red bits flaked from it to land on the counter, revealing the juicy and creamy meat within. The sweet-tart innards made it worth the inevitable mess.

Most fruits on Kude Island were a product of genetic engineering and bio-technology. Nowhere else on Earth could you find the new breeds of fruits and vegetables that were grown there.

"You should sit down and have breakfast," Isis suggested.

"No, thanks. Running late," Trinity responded as she headed for the built-in cooler rack where they kept their shoes. She wanted to leave as fast as possible.

Said rack wasn't originally part of the apartment, but Isis had Cy build it in because his feet constantly smelled wretched.

Isis rolled her eyes. "You know you don't have to work, right? I don't know why you keep going to interviews. It's not like you're ever gonna land a job," she scolded. But she instantly regretted the words she had just spoken. "Sorry, that came out wrong."

Trinity huffed. *She just can't help it.* "I can't depend on a reformed criminal for my future, now can I?" Trinity threw on her black boots and went out the door.

"Hey, Trin! Don't forget we're having a family dinner tonight, so be back before dark!"

Cy shouted as the door slammed shut.

She returned opening the door. "Of course! Anything for you, Cy," and then slammed it shut once again.

Isis's lip twitched at the corner. *Brat.* "I can't believe that girl. Did you even see what she was wearing? Who wears all black for an interview? She looks like she's casing the place." Isis continued to eat her strip of turkey bacon. "I've been taking care of her all her life, and you see how she treats me?"

"Well, she is becoming her own person. Can you blame her? Plus, you haven't been taking care of her *whole life*. She has her own plans, Isis. You do realize that?" Cy pointed out.

He returned to the table with a plate filled with smoked eggs, a fruit berry tart, turkey bacon, and a citrus lytora lemonade. Isis took a sip of her chai tea to help calm herself as Cy scarfed down his food.

Isis sat there deep in thought, contemplating what her next move should be.

At tonight's family dinner, she had promised to tell Trinity the truth about their past. They weren't from Earth, but Trinity had been too young to remember. Now the questions were piling up, and Isis was too afraid to answer. She wasn't sure how Trinity would take the news. Things had been hard for both; Isis had been home for almost a year, and their relationship was still rocky. There was more anger than trust. It felt like betrayal was the head of this family, and Isis intended to fix it.

"Oh, don't forget I have a meeting with my probation officer after work, so I can't pay the leasecode. Today is the last day," she stated, pushing her nerves aside.

"Mm-hm," he grunted his full mouth.

Trinity walked down the hallway, passing by the small kitchen lobby on her floor. She headed for the beacon, a cordless magnetic elevator, and went down six floors. Trinity took her Tabs out of her pocket; when she pulled the two oval shaped magnets apart, a screen appeared between them, as if it was an electric scroll. The device stabilized in the air wherever you placed it. She double-checked her interview time.

The beacon doors opened to the main lobby. The warm hues of sunrise inspired the lobby's color palette. Mixed with soft shades of amber, gold, and rose gold, to cast a gentle glow across the space. Ancient pillars and tall monstera plants growing from golden vases filled the corners. The floor was marbled with sand that flowed like a river. The lobby had a bar, a garden tearoom, a café, and a few resting pods.

When she stepped outside the golden sliding doors, the fresh fragrance of earthy soil, sizzling oil, and faint burned food hit her. This is the Shadow Land smell she'd grown to love. People from every corner of the world migrated to Kude Island, turning it into a melting pot of a wild mashed-up of languages, food stalls, and fashion experiments. Hologram outfits shifted with every step—dragons breathing fire across jackets, ocean waves rolling down pant legs—while 3D-printed clothing flickered like living art. Then there were body modification artists: glowing tattoos, chrome limbs, gemstone lenses and other cosmetic upgrades that pushed the realm of human creativity. It reminded Trinity of the holiday Halloween she studied during lessons.

The island was divided into three distinct cities. Shadow Land, built on the ground and cloaked beneath the mountain's shade, was home to Level One and Two citizens. Built into four living quadrants. Above it, connected by a winding trail dotted with trinket shops and cafés, were the Twin Cities—the electric Blue City, alive with glowing circuitry and luminous flora, and the fiery Red City, its twin. Finally, high above them all, stood the domed City of Light—a shimmering beacon of progress and power.

She loved living in the Third Quadrant. It was calm compared to the rest. Even the hologram ads seemed quieter here. But to reach the Skyway, she'd have to pass through the bustle of Quad Two, where everything was louder: the food markets, the floating salon drones, the rows of rent-a-bots hustling services. But the further you wandered into the living quarters, the quieter everything became—just the hum of crystals and the occasional rent-a-bot rolling past. If you knew the right name to whisper, secret clubs opened to the underground like trapdoors to another world. The only real downside was that no aircrafts were allowed. Too many people, too much risk.

Trinity turned up her music in her earpieces drowning out her thoughts and began her descent.

It took nearly thirty minutes to trek across Shadow Land and reach the winding trail curving up the steep hill toward the city gates. Thankfully, public transit on the island was free. So, she joined the line and waited for the Skyway—a cable-rail transport that spread like spider legs to different points of the island.

The legend says that a Septrillionaire, who wanted to build the world's first tech paradise, bought Kude Island almost a century ago. Initially, only scientists, doctors, and engineers could enter. But one by one, they died under mysterious circumstances. No one questioned it, they considered their deaths to be inevitable tragedies of science.

Now, the island has officially been open for seventy-five years. Powered by an endless supply of crystals, ensuring crystals were an everyday part of life.

Trinity stared out the window as she glided across the clouds. She watched the skyscrapers and air traffic. Reaching the stop at the top of the hill, she couldn't resist that savory, burned smell of spices and dough. She had to stop at Patties & Coco's Bakery before making her way to the gates. It was the only shop on top of the hill. Everyone loved Patties & Cocos, a bakery named after the owners. Pattie & Coco were Jamaican women whose families had opened the restaurant about 50 years ago.

It was a small, square diner with pink, diamond-patterned stitching on the furniture. Trinity opened the glass door to an establishment full of people screaming and shouting orders above blaring music. Even though the diner was open 24/7, people always packed it. Everyone loved this place—the business executives, dope boys, tech nerds, and even people from City of Light came out just for the food. It was the only place on Kude where one could see the different parts of the city merging. That and Afterlife.

Trinity waited in line. "Two chicken patties on coco bread and a HypeFizz," she spoke to the screen before placing her Citizen Card on the scanner.

Upon arrival on Kude Island, every citizen was gifted ten gold coins. Most of the island's wealth lived deep underground in fortified crystal vaults, managed by a banking system.

The currency itself was carved from real crystals. Quartz coins for pocket change. Silver rubels for bigger buys. And gold coins for status and power. Four quartzes equaled one silver rubel. Ten silver rubels equaled one gold coin.

Some people even had coin slots ingrained into their skin to carry wealth on them—a weird flex Trinity would never do.

Still, hardly anyone used physical coins anymore. With a simple tap of your Citizen Card, the system handled everything for you.

A chime dinged.

The screen opened with a HypeFizz, their signature drink, ready for her to grab. It had a luminous glow, and starlike sparkles floated inside. The powder they fused with chemicals ensured it was always cold. Suckleplum Blue was her favorite flavor.

When one of the staff called her name while holding up a bag, she collected her food and left, wondering if she should eat now or after her interview. Savory chicken baked inside two slices of flaky, fluffy, sweet bread... *I don't want to go in smelling like patties. I'll just eat one now and one later.* Trinity tucked a patty away in the side compartment of her bag and devoured the other.

The gates surrounding the Twin Cities were tall and pointed upwards, active with a blue light circuit board. There were five doorways: three to enter—that had extra human guards to prevent forced entry—and two to exit. Every single person had to have a Citizen Card to enter.

The guards wore Force combat uniforms: cream-colored compression shirts with dark olive panels down the ribcage, materialized-light helmets that shimmered faintly with shadowed visors, heavy utility belts built with pouches that contained light restraint cuffs, dark olive cargo pants, matching combat boots, and blast rifles in hand.

Trinity waited in line, hands on her hips, huffing when the old lady in front of her hesitated to swipe her card. When the card contacted the machine, it buzzed in error, turning red.

"Oh! Umm, I'll try again," the old lady quavered to the nearby guard. She quickly placed her Citizen Card on the scanner again. It flashed red a second time. She frowned as her hands shook.

"Look, your card is not working. Go see your local press." the guard whined.

"Please, sir. I am a Level Two citizen; I just earned the points yesterday. My granddaughter needs medicine from inside," the old lady begged, tears building in her eyes.

The guard just shrugged keeping his finger on the trigger, "Nothing I can do."

Trinity avoided eye contact as the old lady sadly walked away, shaking her head in grief.

Citizen cards were a thin sheet of clear acrylic infused with tiny fragments of crystals boxed in a bulky metal frame. Thin rays of light streaked across the frame. The front displayed an identifying photo, citizenship level, badges, and the citizen's age. Each level of citizenship had a color assigned to it.

Citizens could customize their badges, rearranging the icons for work, education, and security privileges however they wanted—as long as the system approved the order.

Trinity was Level Two, and Isis used to be Level Three until she got arrested. Neither had any badges. Showing up for the interview would give Trinity five points, as that would count as a task that proved she would be an outstanding member of society. Hiring her would give her 25 more points. She only needed 3,435 points to become Level Three.

Trinity looked down at her badgeless card and placed it on the scanning device. At the same time a tiny spark zapped her hand. Slowly, the gate lights started to dim, a surging hum filled the air as energy drained.

*Crap. Not again.*

Trinity's eyes darted around as she slowly took a step back. Whispers rippled through the crowd as people inched forward with curiosity.

"Hey, everyone just back up!" the guard yelled, raising his rifle. "We've got another blackout. We should get things back up. In the meantime, everyone can scan their cards on our Tabs." He pulled his Tabs from his pocket and stabilized it in the air.

Trinity scanned her card again carefully as she held her breath and this time no sparks, and the screen turned green.

"You're good, go ahead." the guard ordered.

At the same time another guard opened the back of the scanner. A green octahedron crystal barely kept afloat. A faint hum lingered, and its light was completely out. He drew a small device from his utility belt and pointed it at the crystal. With the click of a button a red laser emitted, striking the crystal battery at its center. Faster than he could blink, light flooded the crystal as it rose. And just like that the gates were up and running.

Trinity checked over her shoulder as she kept walking, making sure no one was following her. When she saw people using the scanner again, she breathed a sigh of relief.

Ahead of her was the Blue Lagoon, the most famous spot in Blue City, mainly because it was the first restaurant in line. It had glass-box balconies, so it was always possible to see what was happening on different floors. Its own lake also surrounded it, making it a premier location to visit.

Everyone had a unique way of dressing in Twin Cities, which was Trinity's favorite part of the island. She loved the creativity and how everything was so well thought out and put together. Colors, patterns, shapes, bags, belts, accessories. It was all so innovative. The crystals intertwined with the city dazzled her, and she admired the different constructions of almost every building, including the skyscrapers. There was a building with holes and a building built like steps.

Even with all the distractions of the island, Trinity's mind was always elsewhere. Her job interview was at Med Inc., which was in the heart of Bluc City.

"Cheers, would you like to—" Isis cut herself off and forced a smile as she was ignored, yet again, by another customer. Holding a pink-chrome, heart-shaped perfume bottle, she tried the next person who walked by. "Hello, do you care to try our—"

"No, thanks," the lady frowned as she passed.

Isis was wearing her best suit today, but she still couldn't get a single sale.

She saw a lady eyeing a perfume bottle in her department and gave her some help. She skipped happily with a smile. "Cheers! I see you're eyeing our new Opient by—"

"Oh, no. I'm not buying," the lady interjected with a weird accent.

Isis sulked back over to her perfume stand. She worked at a perfume store on the 15th floor of The Grand Mall, a circular, thirty-three-story building in Blue City.

"Don't worry, girl," her coworker Angela said, "We all have our days."

"Yeah, girl. Tell me about it," Isis replied. There was so much on her mind. *I could be on my planet, resting peacefully among the stones. How'd I end up here? I feel like a failure.* She was dreading dinner so much, she was trying to sabotage it. An accidental fire, a freak accident—anything to keep her from attending dinner.

"Isis? Isis!" her manager yelled.

"Yes, Mr. Toby! Sorry," she snapped out of her trance.

"In my office now," he declared walking off. Mr. Toby was a fair-skinned man. Tall and broad, with big shoulders and a slim waist. A head full of thick black hair. Sweet but stern. It was always hard to tell if he was in a good mood.

She dragged herself to his office and sat down at his desk.

"Look. I signed your papers since you've been doing good work around here. I'm very proud of you." He expressed with an emotionless face. "I'll give your probation officer a good report," Mr. Toby assured her. Isis sat there with the same look, annoyed by having to hear the same script again.

"Is everything okay?"

"Oh, yes, Mr. Toby," Isis responded, forcing a fake smile, "I'm sorry. I was just drifting off."

"Good, just sign here," he instructed tossing her a pen.

She happily signed the paper and went on her way. Isis's initial sentence was seventy years at Kude's correctional facility, Gravity Grave. After finding her guilty of fraud, the use of false identification, identifying as a Force operative, entrapment, assault, grand theft, forgery, false entitlement, and much more, the judge luckily had a change of heart and sentenced her to four years at the harshest school for girls.

The headmistress was an evil lady, heavily abusive and had a dozen henchmen who did anything she asked.

Isis hated it there. The best thing about that situation was Cy, because that's how they met.

Trinity reached the halfway point on the stairs to the top of the building, where they would conduct the interviews. Med Inc. was a U-shaped building, and the stairs curved along the outside.

Kude Island usually had warm weather even in the chilly season, so people didn't mind waiting outside. There was a massive water fountain carved out of rubies, inside grew bonsai trees, some of which stretched almost to the sky.

The court was full of people. Some were stopping at the Med Inc. café, chatting by the water fountain, or watching the huge TV in the middle of the center. Med Inc. was the number one supplier of healthcare, medicine, and—most importantly—medical robot assistance.

An infomercial with fake smiling people and a medical android played repeatedly. "Hello! Welcome to Med Inc. You love us. We heal your wounds and provide you with assistance when no one is there."

In the two hours she'd been in line, Trinity had memorized the words to every commercial and now she mouthed them alongside them. The job interview was for a new branch of the company. They needed people to document faulty machines and the causes and then document the people who did the initial report.

It paid well. Trinity would be silly not to take this job if she got it.

Trinity was hoping to make a good impression. She desperately needed this job to get away from Isis and make a name of her own.

She was thinking about her other patty when the screen started to glitch, capturing everyone's attention.

An old, bald man appeared on the screen, accompanied by a dark, grungy background. His eyes were missing; nothing but skin filled the sockets. His nose was missing as well, nothing but flat holes.

In that moment, it felt like the air stood still. Trinity glued her eyes to the screen. *What is this?*

The chatter of conversations died down; people stopped in their tracks to listen.

"We don't want war," the man spoke. His teeth were full of plaque, and his black tongue seemed too big for his mouth.

Trinity took out her earpieces, stunned. *Hacking Med Inc. is a big deal. Who would do this?*

"Oh, hell no, girl let's go!" a young woman grabbed her friend by the wrist and pushed through the crowd rushing down the steps. Others quickly followed.

"You can't own a soul, and you can't harvest consciousness. Our lives aren't yours—you can't just suck out the very essence that makes us human. We are not afraid, and we want them to know that we are the ones who run the world! And we know their secrets!" the eyeless man snarled. He started laughing uncontrollably.

"You think your machines heal people," the man hissed. "But we know what Med Inc. really does with the minds it collects."

The sound of propellers slicing through the wind grew as an enormous, run-down blimp cut through the air.

Trinity froze with anticipation. She felt a tight knot in her stomach.

As the blimp moved with speed, people started panicking and screaming. Its shadow engulfed the sky.

"Run!" someone shouted.

Trinity tried to run down the stairs, but it was pure chaos as everyone began shoving, trying to fight their way to safety. People fell over the rails as the traffic clogged the staircase. Trinity couldn't get through. The screams of the people falling left scars in her ears.

She panicked as the blimp closed in, and the old man's laughter made everything worse.

"Go!" she cried. Panic coated the surrounding voices as well. The lady next to her gave up and started praying.

Trinity had no choice but to witness the blimp slam into the giant screen, erupting in a blast of green flames.

The railing behind her groaned and snapped free from the structure.

Trinity felt her stomach drop and she began free falling. Her hands wildly swung in the air.

Screams from the people falling around her filled the atmosphere, adding to her terror as they all plunged hundreds of feet toward the ground.

# Chapter 3: Smoke Clears

"Isis, did you see the news?" Cy asked as he sat on the couch with a bowl of cereal and cotton milk, a creamy drink made from a cotton-like plant that contained a sweet sap in its thick fibers.

Isis glanced down at her CuBE—a square, transparent flip phone that became fully visible when opened and glowed with projected controls. It could cast its screen into the air or transfer it to another device, depending on her needs. She loved this edition. Everyone else used Tabs, but Isis preferred her CuBE; the Tabs were too easy to lose, and besides, the CuBE had sentimental value.

"Didn't have to," she answered, checking her nails, "I'm at the Force. I heard the explosion."

"Did you know Trinity had an interview there? They're calling it a DeathStar attack."

"Wait, where?" Concern cloaked her voice. "She didn't tell either of us where she was going." A hard lump formed in her throat as her leg began to bounce.

"She told me. It's the place where they sell the Med-Bots. Med Inc."

"Oh, no..." Isis whispered, her voice trembling. "Have you heard from her? Or from anyone else?" *Of course the one interview she goes to, and it blows up.*

"No, not yet. And really? Do you think anyone would call here?" Cy questioned.

"No," she whined, rubbing her eyes. "Mr. Waters left and never came back. I'll wait here and keep you updated." Isis buried her face in her hands. This was the very last thing she needed.

DeathStar was a known terrorist organization, one believed to have originated in Ameris. They were infamous for their ruthless attacks and elite-level hacking. No one had ever traced their location. Five years ago, they carried out their first major strike on China. The explosion of a chemical plant that filled the skies with toxic gas for months.

Kude Island had never suffered an attack before. Today was a life-changing event for everyone.

# Chapter 4: Poisoned Pact

Piquette's leg wouldn't stop bouncing. Sweat beaded her temple as she sat biting at her fingers. *Papa's bunker showed that he has intelligence, he's still there, I know he is. I had to. I made the right choice. I know I did. I will find a way to save him and get his mind right. There must be a way.*

This was her last resort. The only place she knew he'd be.

Gravity Grave.

Gravity Grave rose at the top of a hill at the very edge of Red City. A black steel structure that looked like an ancient cathedral crossed with a Hindu temple. Towering turrets twisted upward in geometric spirals, carved like a processor harnessing power. The entire facility was a machine—a square foundation of long hallways and secluded towers, each section fitted with exposed mechanical gears and crystalline conduits that pulsed faintly. Guarded by Skinner's task force, the Grave Diggers.

The Grave Diggers worked separate from the Force, although most still held deep respect for Chief Studd.

"Ma'am?" the secretary, Melody, called. "General Skinner will see you now."

General Skinner's office was located at the end of a maze of hallways, only a few knew how to get to.

Piquette stood, forcing her lungs to exhale steadily. The door opened into a chilling office—cold metal walls displaying rifles, medals, and mounted animal heads. Jars of floating eyes lined dark shelves that moved as one. Piano music played softly, eerily, from hidden speakers.

Skinner sat with his back to her. When he finally turned, his eyes slid over her like a predator evaluating prey. He was old, with saggy pale skin and a face lined with scars he refused to remove. He never wore anything but his olive general uniform, decked with golden medals and his general hat.

"I know you," he said, voice like gravel. "One of Studd's rats."

Piquette swallowed. "General Skinner." Her voice cracked slightly as she stepped forward. "I need your help."

"Oh?" he leaned back leisurely. "And why would I lift a finger for you?"

She forced the words out. "My father is... a cogger. He's getting worse. I've tried to protect him, to do what's right, but—"

"No need for the sob story." He chuckled. "I can spot a dirty conscience from a mile away."

Her fists tightened on her knees.

"What did he do? Kill someone? Rob someone? Hurt the wrong person?"

"With respect, sir... I'd rather not say." Her voice shook despite her fight to steady it. "But it could all trace back to me. And my partner... he's gone. Because of me."

Skinner exhaled slowly through his nose, studying her.

"You're asking for a lot," he growled. "Especially for someone who let a fellow detective die on her watch."

His grin spread—not with sympathy, but with hunger. He saw leverage.

Piquette's breath hitched. "Please. I'll do—anything."

"Anything?" His eyes gleamed. "Good."

He unlocked a drawer and pulled out a small glass vial filled with wriggling, glowing blue organisms.

"This is a sleeper agent," he explained, rotating it between his fingers. "Set it on his skin. It dissolves instantly. It will put him under for twelve hours. Long enough for you to get the job done. Just don't make direct contact."

She reached for it, but he held it just out of reach.

"In exchange," Skinner purred, "I want you to come for me. As an agent. We are exploring whether to open Kude's borders. There's a place I need you to survey. You'll collect intel and report it directly to me. And only me."

Piquette nodded without hesitation. "Yes, sir."

"Good girl." He finally placed the vial in her hand. "Now... what was your partner's name?"

Her stomach clenched.

"Officer Caster Skeeter," she whispered.

Skinner smiled wider.

"A shame," he sighed. "Accidents happen."

The sound of an explosion awakened Piquette. Her alarm blared and projected a simulation of the blast while the words CODE 1114 scrolled across the screen. She shot upright, heart pounding.

This was it. This had been the moment she'd been waiting for.

Skinner's words echoed like a curse: *You'll have to plant evidence to make his death look like an accident. That part I can't help with.*

Her hands gripped the edge of the bed until her knuckles whitened. Closing her eyes didn't stop time.

She had no other choice.

She already accepted her role, and Skinner was sending her to Skeletor Island to prove her loyalty. She forced herself to move.

Her apartment, cold and colorless, offered little comfort. Minimalism was her lifestyle. Identical clothes, one toothbrush. One block of cheese and an apple in the fridge.

She dressed fast: dark jeans, a dark sweater, boots, and a leather jacket.

Then came the part she dreaded. The freezer door creaked open. Skeeter's finger, frozen in a small evidence bag. Her breath hitched as she removed it and set it into the warmer.

"I'm sorry, Skeeter," she whispered sadly. *But my father comes first.*

She tucked the evidence bag into her coat pocket and slipped out the door.

Piquette lived on the edge of Red City, near the back borders. With Med Inc. a few miles away, she chose her cycle—a one-wheeled motorcycle—and cut through the back roads to avoid traffic.

Security on the island had doubled. Med-Bots stood on every corner. By the time she arrived in Blue City, chaos reigned. Smoke filled the air, and screams echoed. A dome light shield covered the whole wreckage. She reduced her speed as the crowd grew bigger. After parking and locking her wheel, she flashed her Level Four Citizen Card to push through the frantic bodies.

"Excuse me, detective coming through." she declared.

Every muscle in her body still ached from the night before. Skeeter's body took a lot of energy to drag.

"Please, my baby is in there, please help me find my baby!" a distressed woman clung to her arm.

Piquette looked at the bewildered lady for a moment and snatched her arm away.

"Please!" the lady cried. Unwelcoming glares followed Piquette through the crowd.

At the barricade, the eagle symbol on the card identified her as a detective. The Med-Bot scanned it and stepped aside.

Air rushed into her lungs as she broke free from the crowd. She walked through the shield with ease.

Just as Piquette had hoped, it was a disaster. Bodies lay scattered. Pieces of skin glued to shards of glass from a once tall building. Bloody water spewed from the ruptured water fountain.

Most importantly, the detectives were overwhelmed with taking statements. Med-Bots were tending to the wounded while scanning fingers and unblemished parts of faces for identification.

All she had to do was act normal and make sure Skeeter's finger was "found" among the dead.

Piquette moved like a woman on a mission, took statements, talked to the other detectives, and searched for clues.

"This machinery is old?" her eyebrow furrowed in confusion. The wrinkles on her forehead pushed together.

"Yeah, it's a blimp. You know, the ones used during the early war times? Like the Second World War, I think," a fellow detective answered.

"You think they're trying to make a statement?"

"Could be. DeathStar is known for using old war gear, like TNT and C4. We are not sure why. We didn't even know they were here. The last thing I heard was they were in Ameris."

"Hmph and where's Studd?"

"He was the first on-site about an hour ago, he left I think he was headed back to the office."

"I can't believe I slept through the explosion." Piquette said now that she was realizing she was late on the scene.

"Apparently, they used some type of sound blocker hoping to slow down rescue, those damn bastards thought of everything."

"Hmm, alright then let's get to work."

While searching for evidence, Piquette found a secluded corner filled with rubble; she kneeled beside a mangled heap of bodies and forced her breath to slow. She glanced over her shoulder to ensure no one was watching. Then, her gloved hand slipped into her jacket and came out with the small evidence bag.

For a heartbeat, her stomach clenched. Taking another look around, she crouched down and pretended to inspect the dead bodies and shook the finger out of the bag and into the pile, angling it so the Med-Bot scanner would find it, then stepped back as if she'd just arrived on the scene.

"Scan that pile I thought I saw some missing fingers," she ordered the nearest Med-Bot, voice steady. She watched as the blue light swept over the bodies until the scanner settled on the finger.

The first part of her plan was done.

# Chapter 5: *Reunited Bonds*

Isis would never forget the day she finally became free from Miss Thorn's School for Troubled Girls, a place that was supposed to reform her but had instead carved deep scars into her spirit.

The girls of the house gathered in the small common room, their eyes swollen with tears, clinging to one another as if this were the last time they'd ever see her.

"Oh, Isis! We're going to miss you so much," one of them cried, pulling her into a tight group hug.

"Girls, stop. Please. You know this isn't the end," Isis whimpered, addressing the room with a shaky smile. "Every one of you made the time here fly by like a speed train. It wasn't easy, but we got through it together. And I'll always carry those memories with me."

One by one, she hugged them all goodbye before turning to face the headmistress, Miss Thorn.

Miss Thorn was a striking woman with ageless skin and long, jet black hair. Sharp hazel eyes framed by lashes like spider's legs, all set against warm, tan skin. Her beauty was something all the girls admired. Isis always thought her attire was strange, even by Kude Island's standards. Most of her clothing comprised traditional robes, silk skirts, and corsets with flower prints and ruffles. Clothing similar to the kind once worn by royalty in humanity's earliest eras. But it was her cold presence that had always unnerved Isis.

"Isis Rose," Miss Thorn spoke, holding out her hand. "As of today, you have completed your four-year sentence at Miss Thorn's School for Troubled Girls. We will notify the Force of your release. You are to report directly to them to be assigned a probation officer."

A thousand dark thoughts flooded Isis's mind—those hands had caused her so much agony and punishment for four long years. With just a squeeze, Isis could crush her bones into dust.

She swallowed hard, forcing her trembling hand into Miss Thorn's grip. After a shake and a fake smile, she was finally headed to the front door.

Her heart jumped into her throat when she spotted a figure through the stained glass—*Trinity*!

*Oh, my stars. She has... boobs.* Isis gasped softly and chuckled to herself. With a deep breath and nerves fluttering her insides, Isis opened the door to freedom.

The first gust of wind felt like a rebirth. The city sounded livelier than before, the sun seemed brighter, and the people looked more alive than she remembered. Isis had a brand new perspective on life.

"Hey, welcome home," Trinity welcomed her with a shy smile.

Before Isis could think, she was sprinting forward, wrapping Trinity in a crushing hug.

"Oh! Umm..." Trinity patted her awkwardly on the back. Four years apart had turned Isis into a stranger.

"Promise me you'll never get yourself locked up like I did," Isis stressed, gripping her niece's shoulders tightly. She needed Trinity to understand her deep sense of urgency.

"Yes, I promise! Goodness, Isis." Trinity blushed.

This was the most affection she'd received from a female figure in a long time. It felt foreign and uncomfortable—part of her wanted to pry Isis's hands off—but she pushed her insecurities aside. She understood how overwhelming it must feel to come home after four long years and see family again.

"Good," Isis said with a grin releasing her grip, "Now turn around and let me look at my all-grown-up niece."

Trinity rolled her eyes but obliged, doing a quick spin. Isis squealed and slapped her playfully on the butt. "Whew!"

Trinity jumped with laughter. "Isis, stop!" She couldn't stop grinning, her cheeks felt warm, so did her heart.

"My, my... look at you! You've grown, haven't you? What are you now fifteen?" Isis slung an arm around Trinity's shoulders as they began walking toward the city. The school she'd spent four years at was tucked behind a brick wall in a back alley of Red City. They walked through the narrow, damp corridor together.

The last time Trinity has seen Isis in person was at her sentencing. At the beginning they would be on the phone or holo calls for hours. But over time the phone calls reduced in frequency and length. Over time Trinity's tone got sadder. Isis had never blamed her for not visiting during family days. She thought that was how Trinity processed things.

Unbeknownst to Trinity, Isis visited her a handfull of times. Sneaking out at night just to view her from her bedroom window. But life in the girls' schools took a turn for the worse and Isis eventually stopped visiting. Before she knew it they went over a year without communicating. They had just gotten back in contact weeks before Isis's release.

"Fifteen. Yep, that sounds about right." Trinity wrapped her arms around herself as she blushed. She felt happy, unlike any happiness she felt before. It was like she discovered a hidden gem after deep cleaning her room. She couldn't stop smiling, the overwhelming feeling of completeness overtook her. Her cheeks hurt from the stretch of her smile. *Maybe I should've visited Isis.*

"Oh, stars, Trinity, that place was hell. I'm so happy to be free. You *have* to catch me up on everything and I mean everything. They didn't allow us any tech after our riot. No Tabs, no holograms, not even Med-Bots. It was so primitive. I don't even know who last year's Kude Island Talent Girl was."

"Oh, that reminds me." Trinity pulled out a transparent square from her pocket and handed it over.

"You got me a phone!" Isis squealed, her eyes lighting up.

"Yeah. It's a new model. Completely see-through the controls light up when you open it. It's called a CuBE."

Isis planted a loud kiss on her niece's cheek.

"Ew." Trinity laughed, quickly wiping it off.

"We have to stop by to see my probation officer first," Isis noted, "but after that, I'm taking my beautiful, generous niece out to eat. Deal?"

"Deal." Trinity nodded.

The two walked side by side toward Force headquarters. Isis rambled on about her school friends and mostly about Cy. Trinity kept on a front with a smile, but inside, she was panicking. She hoped Isis wouldn't ask too many questions about the placement homes. Every time the word home or place came up, she changed the subject. Eventually, they reached the Force and her nerves skyrocketed.

"Hello. I'm Mr. Waters, and I'll be your probation officer," the man said as Isis entered his office and took a seat. His voice was flat, his face unreadable, and the office eerily sterile. Not a speck of dust or smudges on the surfaces.

"I received your release form from Miss Thorn. Congratulations on your freedom. Now, let's review your routine for the next three years." He split apart his Tabs, the screen filled with a long list of rules.

Isis sighed, rolling her neck. "Are you kidding me? I just spent four years with the Duchess of the Ether, and now I have three years of probation?" The corner of her upper lip rose in confusion.

"You do realize you're getting off extremely lightly, considering the crimes you committed," he stated, raising his bushy eyebrows.

"Fine. Just... get on with it." She waved her hand.

"As I was saying, you'll be promoted to Level Two citizenship but won't be able to advance to the next level for six months. The system will hold any points you accumulate during this time. You must find a job within three months, and your employer must sign a weekly review confirming you're following the rules—which they'll send to me. Now, I've set you up to stay in Quadrant Four of Shadow Land."

"Quadrant Four?" Isis yelled shooting out of the chair. Quadrant Four was the worst part of Shadow Land, crime ridden, full of drugs and rogue bots.

"Even the school had better conditions than Quadrant Four." She fussed to herself.

"You're free to live in any other part of Shadow Land once you have the money, legally, to move. Until then, Quadrant Four." he cleared his throat; she sat. "Now, let's go over Little Miss Trinity." he activated a hologram with the wave of his hand, showing a long list of offenses. "Your niece has been busy these past four years. She's been through six placement homes, and in that time, she's racked up assault charges, minor offenses for disrupting the peace, breaking curfew. Even a suspect in a murder investigation."

Isis's chest tightened. *Oh no, six? And murder investigation? When was this? I had to pay some placement parent off for another incident, I was lucky to catch wind of that, but murder? I knew Trinity gave trouble I didn't think it was that bad. Boy did I have her underestimated. Looking back, I could have paid someone to keep an eye on her. Shit, how could I have been so blind. Shit... Maybe I just wanted to overlook it.*

"We had a bet going that she'd beat your record for most citations, but there must be a god watching over you both because she received pardons and her case file is sealed. So, to keep her out of trouble, you'll officially be her guardian since you're of age." he smiled, interlocking his fingers on the desk.

Isis sighed with relief. "Oh, thank the particles in the sky!" she shouted, clasping her hands together. *Even if her cases are sealed... why does he know about them? Maybe because he works Compliance. Maybe he was the one responsible for transferring her from home to home and knew the details firsthand. Either way, he's bound by secrecy. Anyone who reveals sealed case files could face the death penalty. Hopefully he's the only one who knows. I couldn't bear for our secrets to be exposed.*

"Just be sure to keep an eye out for her. We have bigger planets to destroy. Anyway, here are your ten silvers to get you started." He handed the roll of silver and the Tabs. "Sign here and you'll officially be free. I'm also sending you a regulation list, so you know your responsibilities."

Meanwhile, Trinity sat anxiously in the hallway. Sitting on a bench, she watched detectives stride by in their tailored suits. Every time she saw someone she recognized, she quickly dropped her head. The Compliance Department was colder and quieter than the rest of headquarters—all sterile walls and paperwork. And it wasn't her first time there.

*What if they're telling her about my crimes? They wouldn't do that. Right? I mean, they never officially charged me. Crap. Isis is going to think I'm a terrorist. I'm so done for. What's taking her so long?*

Her hands fidgeted, her legs bounced, and she bit her fingernails as panic built in her body. She was terrified someone would burst through the doors, arrest her, and throw away the key.

Finally, after what felt like forever, Isis stormed out of the office.

Trinity jumped to her feet. "So, what did they say?"

"Calm down, Trinity. Did crystal dust fly off a cogger and up your nose?" Isis teased, irritation seeping through. She was annoyed, just released from jail only to feel trapped again.

"Oh, no. Sorry. Just wanted to know." *There's the Isis I know. That didn't take long.*

"Look, I'm sorry. Let's just eat. There's a restaurant I've been dying to try in Red City called Ruby Palace."

## Chapter 6: Red Resurrection

Trinity woke with a splitting headache and a metallic taste in her mouth. Her eyelids drifted apart to the blur of a dim blue light. As her vision cleared, panic clawed at her chest, she was sealed inside a medical pod.

*Why am I here?* The question ricocheted through her mind until the memory struck—the explosion, the screaming crowd, the fall. Her lungs took a deep gasp. "I... I survived?" she whispered. "Holy void..."

It made little sense. She remembered the impact, concrete rushing up to meet her, yet here she was alive and whole dressed in Recovery Center clothing. She was able to move her body fine, no broken bones or bruises. Not even a scratch. She stared at her reflection in the pod's glass, searching for some visible reason, some explanation for the impossible.

The chamber was lined with soft blue padding, designed for trauma patients. Condensation fogged the glass as she banged against the glass.

"Hello?!" she shouted, her voice trembling. Rows of pods surrounded her, each housing motionless figures. But no doctors came, no nurses answered her calls. Only silence, the kind that pressed against her skull and made her heartbeat sound too loud.

Eventually, exhaustion dragged her under again. She drifted in and out of foggy dreams until a sharp bang on the glass jolted her awake.

Two detectives stood outside, watching her closely. The first—tall, dark-skinned, with sculpted features and a practiced calm—pressed a button. "Hello," his voice echoed through the intercom. "I'm Detective Jontray Wright, and this is my partner,

Detective Romain Pillar." He nodded toward the second man, pale and stone-faced, his gaze unreadable. His head, full of light brown hair. "You're being held under suspicion of aiding a terrorist attack."

Trinity's eyes widened in disbelief. *Aiding?* Her mind reeled. "Are you serious? I was a victim! I—I almost died!" Her voice cracked, the words spilling out too fast. "Please, just let me out of here. I'm feeling claustrophobic."

"Remain calm," Wright said evenly, holding up a syringe. "This is Cinnaide. It will help you stay relaxed while we transfer you for questioning."

"No! This isn't right!" Trinity pressed against the glass. "I saw the explosion—I was there! I didn't do anything!" But fine mist cut off her protests as it hissed into the pod. Her vision blurred, her words slurred. Thoughts slipped through her head like water through a crack.

The chamber hissed open. Wright held out her wrist, and Pillar placed a small levitating metal ball between them. With it set in place, materialized light projected as cuffs and sealed around her wrists. Together they hauled her to her feet. Her legs felt weightless, she could barely pick up her feet.

Time moved fast for a little while. Before she knew it, she was stepping out a beacon to shouting voices, panicked cries, detectives shouting orders. None of it loud enough to overpower the sound of her beating heart.

Reaching the detective quarters she was somewhat regaining consciousness, detectives tapped on what looked like blank, transparent boards. But through their Force-issued glasses—a neural-lens system synced directly with their optics—streams of data and classified reports became visible, layered like holograms over the empty boards.

She's never been on this side of the Force. Every time she was brought in she was taken to the juvenile halls, this was for the big-time criminals.

They guided her down a narrow corridor into a cold interrogation room. It was empty but for a steel table and two chairs. They sat her down and her body almost collapsed. A beam of light from the cuffs linked to a port on the table.

"What did you do to me?" she croaked, reaching for her temple only to have the light beams tug her arms back with force.

"Don't worry," Detective Wright said calmly, almost too calmly. "The effects won't last long. We administered only a small dose."

He'd been the only one to speak. The other detective, Pillar, stood silently behind her—his expression cold, his gaze sharp and watchful, like a hawk circling prey. Trinity turned to him, her voice trembling, tears swelling in her eyes.

"Please... if I could just call my aunt, she'll explain everything," she whimpered.

Pillar didn't respond. He didn't even blink.

"It's no use," Wright clarified, almost with a hint of amusement. "Pillar doesn't talk." he pressed a button beneath the table. A hologram activated in front of her.

The sudden burst of light stung her eyes. When they adjusted, she realized she was looking at ariel footage of the explosion.

"The red zone has a ninety-nine percent fatality rate because of the point of impact," Wright explained, gesturing to a section of the screen. "Now, if you look here..." His finger circled a figure caught in the chaos. "This is you, Ms. Trinity Rose. Let's play it back."

The footage rolled. It happened just as Trinity remembered. Panic swept through the crowd as the blimp entered the atmosphere. People scattered, screaming, clawing over one another to reach safety. Bodies rushing down the stairs swallowed Trinity's silhouette and then the blimp made impact. She saw herself fall over the railing.

She remembered that moment—the terror, the wind tearing past her ears, the certainty she was going to die. She closed her eyes shut, trying not to burst into tears.

"As the blimp collides," Wright continued, "everyone is crushed, burned, or thrown from the structure. But you... you fall hundreds of feet, and you survived without a signal injury. Care to explain that?"

The corners of his lips twitched upward, not quite a smile—more like disgust wrapped in suspicion.

Trinity stared down at the table. She knew if she said anything, it would only make things worse. *He's lying! Don't believe him!*

Wright leaned in closer, "How does a sixteen-year-old girl survive a terrorist explosion in the deadliest sector and walk away without a single broken bone?" Wright threw up his finger. "But here's the odd thing—you landed on a woman. And her body was crushed from the impact with the concrete, *and* from the force of your body dropping on her. Doctors said it was as if a boulder fell on her."

"You're lying!" Trinity snapped, "You're a damn liar! I don't believe shit coming out your piss poisoned mouth!" her lips trembled in fear as she shouted. *Shit, Trinity you should have kept your stupid mouth shut.*

A slow grin stretched across his face, "Pillar, I think we should watch the holo again."

Wright replayed the footage repeatedly. Each time Wright changed angles, enhanced the sound—every shriek of life ending cries echoed in Trinity's skull.

They were trying to break her.

She squeezed her eyes shut, forcing herself to think of anything else.

But the time stretched on. Her legs couldn't stop bouncing. She bit down on her lip so hard the skin almost broke. Her mind was heavy with exhaustion.

"We can do this all night," Wright taunted, his voice dropping to a predatory growl. "I could leave you here until you give us something useful. Just tell us why you would kill all those innocent people Trinity? Hundreds of lives lost because of you."

That was it. Trinity couldn't keep quiet anymore. Her eyes locked on to Wright but this time there was no fear, it was as if another person stepped inside her. Wright tilted his head in curiosity.

"When my aunt gets here, she's going to rip your throat out and make a stew with your collagen." Trinity was shocked at her own words, bewildered they even came from her, but it was too late to stop now. She slowly rose to her feet and slammed her hands against the steel table.

"Let me go now!" Her neck stretched so far it felt like it could tear from her body.

"You got some damn nerve." Wright rested his hand on his hip and cocked his head. Getting yelled at by suspects was a normal day for him. "Sit your ass back down, we ain't done yet." The words rolled off his tongue as if he was saying grace, his demeanor calm and cool.

Trinity slowly sank back down and planted her face in her hands. Wright wasn't shook, not even in the slightest. I can't believe this is happening. *Isis, please get here, please save me.* She could feel it, the heat around her neck like it was wrapped in barbwire. The tension in her chest, Trinity was close to her breaking point.

"I don't understand why you won't let me through!" Isis's voice thundered through the hall.

Two detectives blocked the entrance to the detective quarters, their stances rigid under her glare. She had been waiting for hours, she knew Trinity was inside, and she wasn't leaving without her.

The Force—Kude Island's elite Security and Intelligence Agency—comprised of thousands of service men spread across specialized divisions that monitored and protected every sector of the island.

The Force detective building served as Force headquarters. The detective division wore standard uniforms, casual or business casual suits, a deliberate choice meant to keep their presence unthreatening and blend them seamlessly into civilian life. Suits were embedded with gold chrome swirls only seen under special light. Fabric strong enough to stop a bullet and resist fire.

If Med-Bots detected imminent danger or if they had to go into combat they changed into their combat suits and a strike team would mobilize in minutes.

"I'm sorry, ma'am, but as I said, you'll have to wait. The quarters are busy," the secretary called from behind a glass shield.

"Lady, I don't give a quantum curse about what you said," Isis hissed, words seeping from her clenched teeth. She stepped closer until the glass reflected the fire in her eyes.

The secretary took a sharp gasp as her head jerked back.

"My niece is in there. So, you'd better let me through, or this Force will meet a real one."

The officers exchanged wary glances. There was something about the way the air shifted around Isis; it was heavy, charged, as if the room itself was holding its breath.

"Well, look at that. If it isn't Isis Rose herself."

An older man, average height and bare of hair, descended the stairs with deliberate calm. Once, muscle had made up his physique, but now soft flesh formed his belly instead of hard abs. Skin looked as if it had kissed the sun. Detective Arthur Studd, Chief Inspector of the Force and all divisions, regarded her with a mixture of caution and amusement. Dressed in his usual attire—a green puffer jacket, dark blue jeans, a black t-shirt, and black boots. The guards instantly hit the salute. Fist pounded in front of their chest and elbows out.

"Just stellar, Detective Studd. What a surprise," Isis sneered, folding her arms. "I should've known you were behind this."

Detective Studd lazily raised his hand to the saluting soldiers to relieve them.

"What? Are you joking? I don't have a clue what's going on. They paged me about a lady terrorizing my poor secretary." Studd offered a half smile to the secretary.

Then a scream broke through the atmosphere and the lights shut down one by one.

Isis froze. *Trinity*. Immediately she broke her way through the guards.

They glanced at Studd for the approval.

With chills climbing up his spine and looking around his dark building, he raised up his hand, "It's fine. Let her through."

Something in her presence unsettled even him, "Someone get these lights back up!" he barked.

Isis moved quickly, heels striking the floor with purpose as she stalked through the detective floor, searching every corridor and doorway. She knew the place too well.

"You scrap heaps of oil waste better not have harmed a single hair on her head!" she snarled, her voice echoing down the hall.

"Isis, I'm in here!" Trinity shouted in relief, rising to her feet.

"Be quiet!" Wright barked, shoving his finger in her face.

Following her voice, Isis forced the interrogation door open with enough force to rattle the hinges. She froze just long enough to take in the sight: Trinity handcuffed, two detectives towering over her.

"I know you people are not interrogating a minor without an adult present!" Isis's voice sliced through the room. "She's under nineteen! Uncuff her. Now!" the veins in her neck throbbed.

It took every ounce of restraint not to tear the place apart. Her fists trembled at her sides, and the faintest hum of power buzzed beneath her skin.

"Who are you?" Detective Wright inquired.

"It's okay," Studd remarked, stepping into the room behind her. "She's with me. Uncuff the girl."

Detective Pillar pressed his fingerprint to the ball between Trinity's wrist, releasing her instantly. Trinity bolted forward, throwing her arms around Isis and burying her face in her stomach.

"You'll be hearing from my lawyer," Isis snapped before leading Trinity out of the room, clutching her tight.

"Chief—" Wright started, but Studd cut him off with a look.

"That is not how we do things," Studd gnarled. "Questioning the underage family member of someone I put away? Think, Detective. Ethics aren't optional."

Wright squared his shoulders. "With respect, sir, that 'underage family member' is the only known survivor from the red zone."

Studd stiffened.

"The red zone has a ninety-nine percent fatality rate," he stated. "That's why it's called the red zone."

"Yeah well, she didn't *die*." Wright tapped the table as the hologram still played "There she is, Trinity Rose. As the blimp collides, she's swept over the rail. The fall should've been fatal. But when the bots scanned her. Clear lungs, normal vitals, no augments or injuries. And that's not the only thing. She crushed a lady a death just with her body weight." His mouth tightened. "Something's up with that family. Let me find out what."

*With her body weight?* "Just do your job," Studd ordered. "Go talk to the people on the streets. I want to know why DeathStar has the bright idea we are harboring minds. And call me when you have facts. I need you sharp. The both of you..." He glanced at Pillar briefly.

"Especially you, Wright. From now on, we are running a tight ship. And don't worry I'll talk to our lawyer to get this situated."

Wright's jaw tightened, but he hit his salute and marched out of the room with Pillar following behind him.

"With just her body weight huh?" the thought couldn't leave Studd's mind, so he decided to investigate.

Back in his office he called for his AI, "Search up Trinity Rose and tell me what you can about when she was found after the attack." He ordered, slipping on his glasses.

"Hello Chief Studd... Looking up the records for Trinity Rose and the attack on Med Inc.... Trinity Rose was located in the red zone with no fatal injuries." Images of the aftermath and location around Trinity bloomed with statistics and data.

"Yeah, yeah I know but the person underneath? What happened to them."

"... From the scans taken it appeared that the victim that was found underneath Trinity rose was crushed to death."

"So, the impact from the fall didn't kill them?"

"It is hard to say but it is likely with a seventy percent success rate that the impact made from Trinity's body killed the victim. Would you like for me to pull up the victims autopsy Chief Studd?"

"No, seal this file. No one read this without my permission."

"Yes, Chief Studd... file is sealed."

# Chapter 7: Quantum Rift

"Who was that guy? He looked familiar," Trinity asked as they pushed through the growing mob in front of the Force. Her hands wouldn't stop shaking, she was still trying to suppress the emotional toll the interrogation left, not to mention the fact she killed someone. Outside, a sea of people demanded answers about their loved ones. Trinity's chest tightened as she scanned their faces. *I had nothing to do with this. Anything I did was just an accident.*

"That was *the* Detective Studd," Isis answered, glancing at Trinity. "You know, the guy who arrested me, stormed into Mother June's, and took me out in handcuffs?" Isis clinked her wrists together.

Trinity had a flashback to that day—it was one she would never forget. Early one morning, dozens of detectives burst into the house and raided everything before taking Isis. They'd pointed rifles at her face and destroyed her room. She was enraged, however, Mother June calmed her. Isis put up a major fight and tore up the house in every way. Trinity swore she saw Isis smile as they flew her away.

"I don't understand. Why would they think I had something to do with DeathStar?" Her voice quivered as she refused to let go of Isis's arms.

The sky darkened as thunder and rain crept in.

"I don't know, Trin, okay? It makes no sense to me either. Look. We'll talk about it when we get home," Isis whined, anger stepping in. *It's always one thing after another; I can't take this right now.*

"Oh, wait. My stuff—my bag! Isis, he has my bag!" Trinity eyes widened, panicking. All her essentials were in there, and her leftover chicken patty, "No, Isis, we have to go back! To get my bag, and my clothes." She yanked Isis back so hard she almost got whip lash.

Isis pulled away. "Trinity, we'll get it another time. I'm not going back in there now. The crowd is getting bigger. Come on, let's go before it pours." She removed her blazer and used it to cover her hair. Then she took a double take looking at Trinity. *Ugh, who can resist that pout.* She removed her blazer and covered Trinity's head and crouched down to her eye level.

"Look I'll come by tomorrow after work to get it okay. Right now, let's just get home Cy is waiting. And those recovery center shoes look like they will degenerate at any minute. The secretary gave us your Citizen Card, that's all you need for now." She offered a slight smile and Trinity returned one back.

Isis stared into her puffy, red eyes. *Something bad happened, really bad.*

"Hey," Cy flashed a grin and threw a head nod to Isis as they walked through the door. He immediately wrapped his arms around Trinity and squeezed her tight, picking her up a few inches off the ground. Isis's heels fell from her feet. Isis gave them to her when the recovery center shoes started to break apart.

Trinity sunk into his arms for a second and then pulled away. "You don't have to worry about me. I'm fine." She said wiping a tear. Cy set her down and she made haste to her room.

His words followed her as she ran away, "I know. I'm just glad you're okay!"

"It smells good in here," Isis commented, removing her wet clothing.

"Yes, I'm cooking family dinner, remember?" He walked back to the kitchen.

"Of course." *Oh vex* "Let me go shower and change."

Isis retreated to their bedroom. With her soaked hair, her body collapsed on the bed. She closed her eyes and took a deep breath. Going over the day's events in her head. After a few moments, she found the strength to drag herself into the bathroom.

Cy and Isis's bathroom rendered a winter-lodge theme, always kept cold and dusted with light layers of artificial snow. A hollowed tree trunk served as the shower, and a steaming hot tub was in the center.

She opened her cabinet in search of her healing salts. Pushing bottles and vials out of the way, her fingers froze. There, tucked behind a jar of salts, a single galaxy-swirled pill twinkled as if it were winking at her.

Her pulse quickened.

*Just one would quiet the noise and make me feel fine.*

Isis swallowed hard.

"No," she barked to herself.

She shook her head, fighting off her dark thoughts, the screams she kept locked away. Instead, she grabbed her bath salts and oils, clutching them like a lifeline.

"Pull it together," she muttered, slamming the cabinet shut. She feared the temptation might leap out after her. There was no way she was turning back. Not after the hard work she did climbing to sobriety.

She added lavender oil, healing salts, lava rocks, and a mixture of crystal dust to the water and dipped in.

She'd laid back in the soothing hot water and used this time to meditate. Dreaming of a life with Cy in a house of their own, swimming with children.

She smiled, sinking deeper, blushing at the thought.

Trinity entered her bathroom avoiding every surface that showed her reflection. She couldn't bear to look at herself. Not after what the detective said. *You were covered in blood.* It was all she could think about as she stood in the shower with the hot water soaking her hair.

The tears just wouldn't stop flowing. She covered her mouth to hide her loud sobs in fear Cy would hear her. She wanted to stand under the shower all night, but she knew eventually someone would come looking for her.

After rinsing out her hair, and stepping out of the shower, she finally gathered the courage to face the mirror. The swollen eyes staring back at her made her want to cry even more. *God, I look destroyed.*

Once in her bedroom, she sat at her vanity. The soft lighting did little to lift the heaviness. Tears kept streaming down her face as she tried to focus on her skin routine—applying lotion with trembling hands, wiping tears away, starting over again.

Her mouth downturned as she fought the sniffles. "You're not a monster." Her voice cracked. "Nothing was your fault. It never was."

The scratchy feeling in her throat began to ease as she closed her eyes and took deep breaths.

*If anything, it's Isis's fault. I know, I just know she's hiding something from me. How, just how was I able to survive that accident?*

She removed the towel wrap from her head. Her fluffy curls came puffing out, dropping down her back. She parted her hair into four sections and began with the back.

Rubbing a combination of castor oil and aloe vera gel between her curls, she began brushing her hair softly.

As she looked in the mirror, she stared past herself—at all the memories and bullying she'd faced during the placement homes. Then the detective's words came again. *You smashed her head. Her body was crushed. Killer.*

A frustrated breath burst from Trinity. She slammed her silver brush against the vanity, the handle snapped clean in two.

She froze as her fingers twitched. She teased at a thought that had been clawing at her mind all day, all her life more like it. She took the sharp edge of the broken handle and without hesitation dragged it along her arm. The pressure was there, but the pain was almost dull. She dug the handle deeper with all her strength.

*CLINK!*

It snapped.

Trinity's lips parted as her eyebrows rose. "That... shouldn't be possible." she whispered.

Panic pressed as she jumped to her feet. She began pacing the room with deep thought. *Am I augmented? No, wait, I would remember something like that. What... am I? I don't know what to think. Right now, I don't want to think any more. This whole day, my whole life is just a disaster.*

Trinity thought back at all the awkward moments in her life, her failed attempts at making friends, her inability to find a home. *Why am I thinking about this stuff now?* She laughed as she took a seat at the vanity, continuing to brush her hair. *I guess what everyone said is true, I am a freak. I am a monster.*

After getting ready for dinner, Isis met Cy in the kitchen. Dressed in a purple silk pajama set and purple slippers with the matching purple jade bangles. Cy was still keeping busy preparing dinner.

Shadowthorn was a spiky, fleshy fruit that grew deep in the forest where sunlight was scarce; the plants had to adapt to low-light environments, which made their taste more potent. They came in different colors—even tie-dye, although that was rare. It tasted sweet, tangy, and juicy, and had meaty flesh. It was Kude Island's national fruit, and Cy used it as a base for all his fruit smoothies and lemonades.

"Oh, babe, it smells so good!" Isis planted a kiss on his cheek as his focus stayed glued to the stove. Isis knew Cy did not like to be disturbed when he was cooking, as it was his oasis away from the world and its problems.

"Don't worry," she continued. "I'll get out of your way. I'll tell Trin the food is almost ready."

The hallway attached to the kitchen led to Trinity's room. To the right was a closet, and next to it, her bathroom.

Trinity designed her room to be like a forest oasis, and everything was in shades of green. The bonsai tree in the corner of her room stood hollowed out for a waterfall with patches of moss. She painted the walls to resemble a leafy, vine forest with roses. Dark green sheets like grass covered her tree-trunk bed. Sheer green tie-dye drapes covered her bed from above. There were floating holographic butterflies and a spray of lavender water every time the door opened. She called it "cleansing space."

Isis knocked on the door before entering. "Hey, I'm coming in." Isis walked in to see Trinity sitting at her vanity, which was carved from jade. Isis had gotten it specially made for her after one of their horrible fights.

Trinity sighed as she continued to braid her hair. "What do you want, Isis? Is dinner almost ready?"

"Yes, dinner is almost ready, but I also wanted to talk to you." Isis took a seat on her bed, "Tomorrow, you will go to see a lawyer. What they did to you was unfair and against Kude Island law. I'm sorry that happened to you. You were at the wrong place at the wrong time; that's all. Your arrest had nothing to do with me, but it doesn't help that we are family. The lawyer is good, stellar actually, so I expect him to get justice swiftly," Isis watched as Trinity ignored her, not even making eye contact.

"Hello, earth to Trinity. Do you not hear me talking to you?" she scoffed.

Trinity rolled her eyes, sighed, and snapped her neck. "Yes, Isis, I hear you talking. I always hear you talking, but you don't seem to say the right things!" she snapped.

Trinity and Isis's relationship had been rocky since her release. Their communication was off, and both had lost trust in people, including each other. They often argued about their traumas and family history. Isis just wanted to go back to how things were before she got arrested. It was hard for Isis to bear the burden of the secret, hiding the truth from society and Trinity. Trinity missed her parents and felt like she and Isis were drifting away.

Isis rose to her feet and approached, hands up. "Hey, whoa, Trinity—what's going on? Talk to me. What happened? Did they hurt you back there?" She got on her knees and placed her hands on Trinity's leg. *Goodness, now she's mad at me.*

"No, Isis. I'm fine." She continued to braid. "Let's just get through family dinner, okay?" Her voice perked flashing a teary eye smile through the mirror, hoping Isis would see the pain in her eyes. *Hopefully I can score some sympathy points.*

Isis's mouth twisted, she was at a loss for words. *Shit, she didn't forget.*

Isis stood to her feet and wiped her sweaty palms on her legs. "I'll just, uh, meet you at the dinner table."

Isis sat quietly at the dinner table staring absent mindedly into space. Her body reflecting her thoughts as her legs bounced frantically and her teeth digging into her nails.

"Trin! Dinner's ready!" Cy shouted causing her to twitch.

Trinity swallowed hard, staring at her flawless skin—at the evidence that her entire life had been a lie. She stood in her yellow silk pajama set and headed off to dinner.

Cy cooked pan-fried duck, braised in a white wine butter sauce sauteed with garlic, shallots, capers, chives and dijon mustard and a side of creamy mashed potatoes and heartgreen salad. For drinks, he served raspberry-peach lemonade to wash it all down.

Cy, Trinity, and Isis got so lost in the food's flavor that they forgot they were even supposed to be talking about the day's events. The meal almost saved the night from any awkward conversations.

Isis kept shooting quick glances at Trinity, pretending to adjust herself whenever they made eye contact.

Trinity responded with eyes rolls and deep sighs.

*Dammit Isis say something, the girl looks so destroyed.* "So, you're taking Trinity to go see the lawyer tomorrow," Isis stated, breaking the silence.

"Aww, man, what? I hate that guy. Remember when y—" Cy coughed as he caught Isis's expression. Her burrowed eyebrows hit him like daggers. "Never mind, he's a nice guy" He cleared his throat. "What time are we going?"

"At Sunrise, Cy, when his place opens."

The island mainly used sundials to track the sunrise, midday, and sunset. Bells rang to notify the citizens. Clocks weren't common on Kude Island, since most citizens measured the sun's position. But old habits were difficult to break, and people liked the extra clock measurements.

In front of every other building stood their own design of a sundial. The sundials rest on six-foot platforms carved from limestone with a hologram displaying its image hovering above.

"Trinity, how do you feel? I know you had a rough day," Isis probed as she glanced across the table.

"Oh, umm I'm fine you know," she sulked. *She's spent this whole dinner in silence, it's clear she isn't going to tell me anything. Oh no I can feel it, the tightness in my throat. I need to leave before I burst.*

Trinity stood to her feet abruptly, "On second thought, I'm not that hungry. Thanks for dinner Cy, I'll finish the rest tomorrow do you mind cleaning up for me?" Before Cy could answer Trinity turned away.

"Sure, no problem kid." He answered while watching her slowly retreat to her room. Once she was out of sight he confronted Isis.

"Y'all need to sort this glitch out," the tone in his voice hardened.

"I know, I know." she whined smacking her forehead "I just don't know how or when. I clearly can't tell her now with all this. Just look at her she's practically lost it."

"There will never be a right time Isis. You went away for four years and missed out on important parts of her life. You owe her the truth at least, and it might even set you both free."

Cy was always the voice of reason. Even Trinity came to him repeatedly, sometimes just to cry or ask for advice. Trinity would never admit it, but she loved Cy like the missing father figure in her life. But admitting she loved him would admit that she thought Isis had made a good choice—but nothing Isis did made sense.

"I mean, she just literally survived a terrorist attack. Don't you think she's becoming suspicious?" Cy questioned.

"She's been suspicious all her life, Cy. Now she's demanding."

Once dinner was over Cy knocked on Trinity's room door, "Hey Trin it's me, mind if I come in?"

Trinity couldn't find a way to smooth her unwavering voice. "I'm—I'm fine Cy. It's okay I'm just getting ready for bed." She called. There was a moment of silence. *Please, please don't come in.*

"Alright, I'll see you in the morning."

After dinner Isis snuggled in bed, wrapping the cotton sheets tightly around her. The warmth of Cy's body gave her the comfort she needed. *Tonight my dreams will have the answers.*

Forcing the day's events out of her head she shut her eyes tight and drifted to sleep.

Trinity stayed awake most of the night. She often had battles against her own mind; sleep didn't come easy. With her head on her pillow, she was deep in her thoughts. The gentle sounds of the water flowed from her earpiece. *I would do anything to live a normal life. Why did I have to be there during the explosion? More importantly... what is my survival telling me? Is this fate? Am I a med bot experiment gone wrong? Just what am I? A monster? A freak?*

## Chapter 8: *The Bully*

The round hooded vehicle rolled to a stop outside a wide three-story house, Trinity's new home. For a moment she just stared out the window unable to move. She just wanted the day to be over.

"Here we are!" The woman in the driver's seat turned to her shooting a beaming smile. Her hair was frizzy despite brushing it back dozens of times, and there was a stain on the collar of her shirt that looked older than Trinity. "Don't worry sweetheart, the children are going to love you. They always love the newcomers."

Trinity didn't answer. She'd been picked up from Force headquarters that morning, not the usual place a placement mother would retrieve a kid, but nothing about Trinity's case was usual. She climbed out of the vehicle ready to get things over with.

The house mother gripped her shoulders the second they were through the front door, her hands greasy against Trinity's skin. "Everyone, come round, come round! Meet your new placement sister, Trinity Rose."

A dozen kids scattered throughout the living room looked up and not one of them so much as blinked.

"Oh, don't mind them," the woman said waving them off, ushering Trinity down the hall before embarrassment could hit her. "They'll introduce themselves eventually. Let's get you to your room."

Trinity's room sat on the second floor. The hallways seemed to stretch on forever.

As the placement mother helped Trinity unpack, she used this time to study her. It was clear to see this placement mother was burned out and overwhelmed. The bags under her eyes looked related to a lack of sleep. But this placement mother wasn't cruel, and her cooking, Trinity would learn, was some of the best she'd ever had. Eventually Trinity realized her fingers were always greasy because she used her hands to fry food. Coating them in shea butter helped with the burns. And she cooked everything from scratch.

A few moons later Trinity was still adjusting. Speaking still felt like a task Trinity hadn't fully relearned. She'd gone mute for months after her parents died, and even years later the words still couldn't escape. The other kids took notice fast. Trinity would open her mouth to speak then close it immediately. "What's wrong you got mute mouth or something?" onc of the kids teased. Mute mouth became her new name for a while until the placement mother put a stop to it. Sometimes the kids would even joke that her last placement family had sold her voice to a demon processor.

Although most placement siblings of hers made her feel out of place, there was one boy who didn't. Zion barely spoke either, and kept to himself the same way she did—though the girls in the house adored him for it, convinced his silence made him mysterious.

Zion found Trinity in the hallway on her day. Her headphones plugged in one ear, hoping one of the kids would call her to play.

"You're the new one," he said coolly.

Trinity's face lit up as she nodded. The way his body was outlined in golden light, like he had the aura of a god. *He's so cute I never actually looked at his face before.*

"Don't worry, they'll stop in a week." he shrugged like his own advice didn't matter and kept walking. It was the first thing anyone had said to her that felt genuine. She blushed as he left. Her grin stretched wide across her face as she bit her bottom lip. She relished that moment the whole day.

The next week Trinity had to start her schooling.

"Hello, Trinity." The wall above her desk rippled to life, dots of light gathering into a screen. "I will be your learning model. Would you like to design a human model for your educator, or would you like me to customize one for you?"

"Customize," Trinity answered.

"Excellent. Please select your preferred choice from the following topics: colors and shapes, texture, patterns, designs, and habitat."

She took a moment to think. "My choices would be pink, cubes, and silk. I don't like patterns, I prefer solids. And for designs... formal, I guess, but skulls and bones are cool. And for habitat, the arcade."

"Good choices! Thank you. Now, please choose your favorite learning curriculums."

Trinity scrolled the list of choices: music, philosophy, history, technological advancement, math, arts, media, astrophysics, astrology, quantum bending, chemistry, biological science, plant science, earth science, language, and physics.

"Easy. I'll choose philosophy, music, and astrology."

"Curating your education professional now."

The screen rippled again, and a man built himself out of pixels. Blue jeans with dark chains printed as designs, a white shirt under a blue sweater that turned orange when flipped, hair spiked black, shoes white. His eyes were hard, but his smile was friendly. A tie hung loosely around his neck.

He sat on a game console that served as his desk. Behind him on chalk board drawings of musical notes, flowers, quotes, and constellations.

"Risings, Trinity. I'll be your educator Mr. Aster, it's a pleasure. We'll touch on everything from that list eventually, but we'll spend most of our time on what actually keeps you interested."

Trinity smiled. She never had a learning system like this before. She could ask Mr. Aster all the questions she wanted to and he would never grow tired of her.

Trinity had officially been at the placement home for almost a moon cycle. She learned every full moon the whole house spent the day on the beach. The children also had to earn days to spend outside with chores and learning assignments.

Usually, she ate alone during meals but today was different. After getting his plate Zion walked past the table he usually sat alone at and joined Trinity's table without saying a word. He hadn't spoken to her since that day. She glanced up and watched him sit and eat as if he didn't make a life changing decision. Instead of saying a word she just smiled quietly and continued as if his presence didn't make a difference. The other kid's eyes cut toward them all at once.

Zimbria's eyes cut hardest.

She'd hated Trinity since the day she walked in, and now she had a valid reason. It didn't take a genius to see the crush Zimbria carried for Zion. She was always desperately trying to get his attention. Tripping in front of him or always running to sit beside him at group therapy. Which Trinity hated. Group therapy was held twice a week. The therapist tried to force Trinity to talk but she didn't budge. Every time it was her turn to speak, she'd wish to disappear.

Zimbria sighed loud enough for everyone to hear, "Looks like the freak show gained another clown."

Trinity heard what Zimbria said, everyone did. Her eyes turned to Zion and didn't have a care in the world. He picked up his chicken leg and took a bite.

A few days later, during a coding session in the study room, Zimbria approached her, "Trinity! I can't believe you!"

Trinity looked up from her Pixel device, "What are you talking about?"

"Don't play dumb." Zimbria gloated. She had gotten one of the other kids to hack into Trinity's Pixel and the screen bloomed with images that weren't hers, "Look Trinity's watching nasty stuff!"

She looked down at her Pixel, "What? No, I'm not!" Trinity slammed both hands over the screen, but the laughter was already spreading, kids leaned in for a closer look. Zion immediately stood and tried to remove the images.

"I saw it! Don't lie!"

Then Trinity felt it, a rage she hadn't felt in a while. The type of rage she would lose herself in.

"I said I wasn't!" her fist came down on the table so hard it cracked. Every Pixel in the room went black at once.

The laughter stopped. The room went so quiet Trinity could hear her own heartbeat. The only person who didn't react was Zion, he gave her a side eye but continued to remove the images.

"Good Vex." Zimbria said, her voice now brittle and small, "Calm down, you freak." Her words trembled as she clutched her chest.

Trinity snatched her Pixel and left before anyone could see her hands shaking. Zion ran behind her, cutting his eyes to Zimbria as he shoulder checked her.

All eyes were on Zimbria as she stood in embarrassment, "What... what are you are staring at!"

Then things took a turn for the worst on farm day.

A man arrived with a trailer full of animals for the kids. Trinity sat cross-legged in the grass with Zion beside her, and within minutes the rabbits the farmer let loose had abandoned everyone else to pile into her lap. Animals always liked her, she didn't know why.

She watched one twitch its nose against her palm. Her mind wandered absently. She questioned if the rabbit knew it was free. If it was happy. If it understood anything at all. It couldn't tell her either way, so in the end it didn't matter—she just let it climb over her knees while Zion laughed along with her.

She never saw Zimbria coming behind them.

Zimbria tipped a glass container over her head. Dozens of them, spiders slipped into her hair, down the back of her neck, into her clothing.

"Get them out!" Trinity shouted, springing to her feet. She shook her head so hard the world blurred.

"Get them off of me!" she wailed, shaking her body frantically. Spiders clung to her curls as they whipped through the air.

Zimbria stood there laughing silently.

Zion moved before Trinity could even blink. Without a word he walked across the yard to the pig pen and scooped a fistful of poop and feeding. Everyone was too distracted by Trinity's yelling to notice what he was doing. Zion marched straight to Zimbria and launched the repulsing goop across Zimbria's face. Her head flew back from the force.

Every gasped. The silence was considerably loud. For a second Trinity forgot about the spiders when she heard Zimbria scream. Then she broke out in wild laughter, the kind that made her tear. Zimbria stood frozen in embarrassment as the other children laughed. Zion stood there with a perfectly straight face, wiping his hand on his jeans like it was nothing.

The panic drained out of Trinity all at once when she saw him. And the spiders followed suit. They dropped from her body and hair one after another, hitting the grass and scrambling off in every direction, as if something invisible had told them to flee. Trinity held up her arms and watched them drop down from their webs.

She never forgot that day, it was the day Zion became her first boyfriend.

# Chapter 9: Faces Revealed

The next morning, Piquette sat at her desk, trying to keep her composure while her fellow detectives scrambled around like ants around a destroyed colony. Her expression was blank as she pictured the future and her plans to come.

She'd got home late, so she couldn't visit her father. He was lingering in her thoughts.

"Piquette!" an officer yelled, slamming his fist on her desk. "What the hell is wrong with you? Are you deaf? I said Chief Studd wants you in his office. Now!"

Piquette snapped out of her daze and headed to the second floor.

"You wanted to see me, Chief?" she asked as she stepped in his office quickly hitting a salute.

"Uh, yes. What was I—? Oh, right." Studd pinched his nose. "Unfortunately, I have some bad news. Your partner, Skeeter... his remains were found at the explosion site. We concluded that he was a victim in this massacre. I'm sorry for your loss."

Studd hadn't been home since yesterday's attack. The explosion had everyone on edge. By now the words came out like a script he'd read a dozen times too many.

"What the hell was he even doing there?" Studd mumbled, then raised his voice.

"Anyway, you are free to take bereavement leave."

"Actually, sir... I have some more unfortunate news," Piquette took a step forward. "I'm resigning from the Force."

Studd clenched his jaw. He locked eyes on her. "Are you being serious? You're resigning in the middle of this mess?

Come on, Piquette." Studd exhaled a weary breath slamming his hand down.

"You're one of our best detectives!" *Why would she quit? Why now?*

"Aren't you even interested in catching the people who did this? Who's responsible for your partner's death?"

"I've already sent my resignation to your email. If you could just sign, please." Her tone was even. "It's been a pleasure working here, but my time has ended." She held her head high with her hands behind her back, fingers unable to keep still.

Studd was at a loss for words. He lounged back in his chair, mouth agape, as he rubbed his temple. "I guess I can't say no, can I? I'll be honest, this is coming as quite a shock and a disappointment. You've been on the Force for ten years. Why leave now?"

"I don't feel valued here, sir. The attack put things in perspective. As you mentioned, I served on the Force for ten years, and they honored me only once during that time. I solved most, if not all, of my cases with at least a seventy-nine percent satisfaction rate, but you never considered me for the position of your second in command." Her voice stayed steady, the truth plain and sharp.

"The first terrorist attack on the island and your first thought is to quit because you don't feel valued, huh?" he knew he had no choice but to accept her decision. "Well, it's been a pleasure, Piquette. Best of luck." *I'll play along for now, although I don't buy her pathetic excuse.*

He reached his hand across the desk with a forced smile.

Piquette didn't hesitate to grip him back firmly. "Thank you, sir, for all your hard work, I hope our paths cross again." With her last salute Piquette slipped out of his office sighing a breath of relief.

Studd slid on his glasses and stood at his board opening Piquette's email. He exhaled in relief as he signed.

"There was no way she was going to be my second in command."

"Chief!" Wright yelled at the door.

"Yeah, come in!"

"We got him Chief he's in interrogation room three." Wright said peeking his head through the door.

Studd turned to him, "I'll be right there." He glared with a smile.

Studd helped detectives interrogate dozens of suspects by the time the midday bells rang. He was able to gather small clues but nothing that truly satisfied his revenge lust. But he had a feeling this new suspect would change that.

He strolled into interrogation room three with his chin held high, ready to engage in another battle of words. Wright stood behind the suspect with his arm crossed, a calculated look smeared on his face.

Studd walked over to the table slowly and perched a seat on the edge of the table, "Switch, long time no see. How ya been?" Studd asked voice flat.

Switch sat with the light cuffs almost burning his skin. A silver bar pierced his right eyebrow, and empty hole pierced his other. Hence his name. Switch, an eighteen-year-old delinquent who spent his time moving product, dealing with information and living in the shadows. Sweat beaded on his terra cotta colored skin. His hair styled with a fade covered in razor designs. A sharp jawline attached to his long face. He stared straight forward with his down turned eyes. Dry blood smeared across his full lips and the corner of his eye. He put up a fight with the Force when they invaded his bunker.

"I saw you took a few trips to Ameris a while back care to tell me what that was about?"

Switch stayed silent.

"Look kid I don't have time for this I have a meeting in about fifthteen minutes so either I can leave you here all day while those cuffs burn your arms off or you can cough up something."

Switch's eyes shoot towards Studd like daggers. He spit a mouth full of blood on the table, "Curse you and this vexed Force!" he shouted.

Before Switch could blink Studd slammed his head against the table, wiping the blood with his face. Studd leaned in to whisper in his ear, "Listen you paradox born fuck, I want to know how DeathStar was able to infiltrate my island without anyone hearing a peep. So, you better start talking." His whisper sent chills down his spine, there was something sinister in Studd's voice.

Switch struggled as Studd's grip got tighter, "Look I swear I don't know anything, I went to Ameris for research purposes only."

"Research for what?" he yelled, Studd's eyes stretched open so far, he even gave Wright the chills.

"Ahh man you're crushing my face!"

"Answer the damn question!"

"Okay! Okay! There's a rumor that some scientists were able to transport people to another dimension, so I went see if I could break into the facility."

"And what did you find?"

"Nothing I couldn't even get close. Every time I thought I was, I somehow ended further back or in a different place." His words pushed from his clenched teeth, pain surging from the pressure of Studd's hand pushing his head into the steel table.

"And what about DeathStar? Did you hear anything about them?"

"Yeah man, everyone in the dark streets know them. DeathStar likes to trade with government factions across the world. I'm not sure what their game plan is but from what I heard they act as government hitmen. They take jobs from the highest bidders."

Studd released the boy from his grip and took a step back. "What exactly is being traded?"

"Polar vex man I think you broke my cheek bone." the boy cried as he lifted his head, blood dripping from his cheek.

"We can worry about that later. What is being traded?"

"What do you think, high grade accelerators, weapons, laser beams, stuff like that." Switch fought his hardest to hold back his tears.

Studd stood in silence and nodded to himself, this was the information he needed.

"Get him to the recovery center and then get to the meeting." Studd ordered Wright.

Wright knew exactly what those words meant. He'd been working under Studd for the last seven years. Learning the hidden clues in his speech, how he handled every scenario they came across. He knew Studd as if he was his personal CPU.

Studd didn't have time for pleasantries, his only job was getting answers, and he was willing to do anything to get them. One lesson he learned throughout his life was sometimes you need to get stained by blood to help the people who bleed. As for right now, Switch was the only gap between him and DeathStar. Switch had a talent for not only staying hidden but for constructing the finest devices the island had ever seen. He built hacker systems from scratch, processors from scraps, and energy weapons from salvage. Between Switch and Isis Studd couldn't choose which one gave him the hardest time.

Wright followed orders and guided Switch to the Force's Recovery Center. Each city had a Recovery Center, but Force headquarters had their own attached to the building.

"Wait here." Wright scolded placing him in a medical pod, "A lawyer will be with you soon." On his way to the meeting Wright sent a message to one of the Force's lawyers. *Potential informant, medical pod seven. Vital.*

In the meeting room were high level detectives. Nexuses of the nine Force detective squads. Also in the room were directors of the other Force branches.

Darrell Phillips, director of the Cyber Force. Xeric Rain, director of the Land Force. And Orion Asteria, director of the STAR Force and Studd's close friend dating back to their training days. Pillar was also in the room as a documenter.

Studd stood in front, eyes studying the tired faces of his subordinates. The weight of yesterday's chaos still hung heavily in the air.

"First and foremost, I want to thank everybody for their hard work. Yesterday's events were nothing short of catastrophe. Our island will never be the same. I don't need to remind everybody that it's our duty to prevent this from happening again. With that being said, let's get down to it."

Studd put on his glasses and the rest of the room followed suit. Studd waved a hologram to life of suspects' faces arranged in a pyramid.

"So here they are. The people we believe to be connected to DeathStar," he began, voice firm. "From what I've learned they're not only a terrorist organization, they're also a resistance—one that trades in weapons, circuitry, and human lives. And yesterday, the resistance showed its hand. As some of you may know, this isn't DeathStar's first attack. They have been terrorizing other parts of the world. Manly enterprises and industry titans. Sadly, were just their latest victim."

He let the words hang for a beat before he continued.

"Right now, we're keeping things cool. We don't want to rush in and give away our composure. There's no way they're getting off this island. Air control has doubled, Med-Bots and security androids are patrolling the grounds, and we've already deployed a search team into the mountain ranges and Quad Four. But that's not enough."

Studd stepped closer, his gaze sweeping over the room.

"I want every one of you to keep an ear to the streets. Talk to informants. Lean on your contacts. If someone breathes DeathStar's name, I want to know. Find out who's connected to who. What's moving and why. If there's an anomaly in the system, we find it and break it. I want each of you to crack down on your team and have them crack down on their informants. Get me some vexxed answers,"

The detectives, galvanized by his words, nodded in agreement.

"And if you hit a wall you come to me. No one gets left in the dark. Also, I'm expecting STAR Force to keep me updated with the city life above I don't go up there as much as I'd like to." Studd spoke directly to Orion.

"Now, if no one has any questions. Let's get out there."

Once the room was cleared Studd gave explicit orders to Wright and Pillar.

"Listen, it's vital you keep a close eye on the Roses. I don't need to explain why this is our number one priority, do I?" He fixed his eyes on Wright with a hard stare.

"No, sir. We're on it," Wright declared, tapping Pillar on the chest, determination burning in his eyes. "Let's move."

Switch sat in the attorney's office. Face and cheek bones completely healed, but his anger still vibrant.

"So, Mr. Pearson, during your interrogation with Chief Studd you admitted to crimes you've committed overseas—"

"What? That's crude! You people storm into my den, crash my shit and bust my lip. Then Studd's fat ass damn near broke my neck. I was in that medical pod for hours. This is entrapment yo." Switch argued, but it had no effect on the lawyer. She sat untouched by his words.

"As I was saying, during your interrogation you've admitted to your attempt to break into a government building. Not only that you lied on your travel visa claiming your trip over seas was for family." The lawyer sighed as she removed her glasses. A headache started seeping in. "Look Mr. Pearson the Force is making an offer, we won't extradite you to Ameris if you're willing to work for us."

"I ain't no damn snitch." He argued.

"I think it's too late to be making those claims. You have two choices, either leave this island or help with our investigation. So, which is it?"

Switch sucked his teeth as he looked around the room in thought, "What do I have to do?" he threw his hands in frustration.

"The Force will implant a tracking chip that can record all your senses. Your sight, your smell, anything you can think of. You will head back to Ameris and continue your... extra circulator activities while gaining more intel on DeathStar. In exchange for corporation, you will be given a hundred and fifty gold coins, and your criminal record will be wiped clean."

"A hundred and fifty gold coins." He scoffed, "You know I can I make that in a day, right?" His finger banged on the table with each word.

"I'm fully aware Mr. Pearson but I would argue nothing is more valuable than your freedom. There are two detectives outside my office so it's safe to say they won't leave until you give me an answer. So, what is it?"

# Chapter 10: The Living Dead

"This chip you say... it can control minds?" Skinner pressed curiously as he studied the hologram of Crypt Cane.

"Complete neurological override," Cane replied. His voice crackled slightly through the transmission. "It takes a little time to sync, sometimes days. But once bonded, the subject's body responds only to the one holding the frequency key."

Skinner's brows lowered as he calculated his thoughts.

"Chip the girl," Skinner said.

"Already done," Cane grinned slowly, menacing.

Piquette hiked up the now familiar trail to the cabin, eyes tracking the dry blood spots she tried to scatter the night before. Every step tightened the knot in her stomach.

She needed to see her father off before she left for her mission.

Inside, she sat him gently on the couch, gripping both his jittery hands.

"I have to go away for a little while," she spoke softly. "But I'll come back. I promise."

She slipped on a glove and took out the vial Skinner gave her. Her father giggled, excited by anything new. Unaware of the true danger he posed.

"This medicine... it's going to help you feel better. But you must finish all of it. Okay? So if you wake up just do as I am doing."

A single blue organism writhed against her fingertip as she turned the vial over. Placing the organism on his boney arm, it dissolved instantly. His body reacted quickly. His eyelids drooped and his giggles slowed.

His body fell limp onto her arms. Flashbacks of when her father was a healthy man entered her mind. What was once a normal man in his fifties, with a sharp mind, was now a hunched-over cogger made of paper-thin skin and a thirst for murder.

"Please, Papa... keep taking the rest until I return." Piquette gently lowered his body to the couch. She cuffed him to an exposed pipe in the walls and left the vial in his lap.

"I found you and I won't ever lose you again."

After planting a kiss on his forehead, she forced herself out the door without turning back.

Piquette sat strapped inside the single-pod craft as it descended through a suffocating layer of storm clouds. The world below slowly revealed itself—a jagged wasteland of black stone and spiked mountains. Lightning didn't strike down from the sky here, it erupted upward.

Skinner had seen her off at the border checkpoint, entering a dial sequence to part the invisible dome shield protecting Kude Island. The shield was made of millions of plates, each one functioning like a dial pad, its camouflaged steel surface linked seamlessly together.

The pod eased onto the terrain with a metallic hiss. The hydrogen blasters made for a smooth landing.

A man in a flowing purple silk robe, layered with yellow trim stood waiting a few feet away. A glowing flower-shaped insignia rested on his chest—the flower of life. His robe whipped violently in the wind.

The pod hatch lifted and Piquette descended the steps onto the rocky terrain wearing a Grave Diggers uniform. A helmet made of hundreds of mini lightweight metal plates, with only a slit across the eyes and mouth. They were dressed in black cargo pants and tight-fitting long-sleeve shirts fused with cotton and leather, along with utility belts and heavy black boots.

She removed the helmet, leaving it in the pod as breathing was already hard enough. Her boots crunched against the shattered crystals and dirt. She approached the man with caution and offered her hand.

The stranger clasped it briefly. His skin felt too cold for her liking. She tried to pull away but he opposed her action, pulling her in closer.

"I am Reven, envoy of Lord Cane," he greeted. "Welcome to Skeletor Island."

Reven stood hairless, with yellow crystals dotted where his eyebrows should be. His long chin and small teeth didn't help his case. And his slanted eyes made her more uneasy.

She nodded with a nervous smile, "Pleasure, I'm Digger Piquette."

Her gaze drifted to the impossible sight a few feet ahead:

A steel citadel perched atop a wide industrial platform, strung with cables and thick transparent pipes filled with flowing black fluid.

Beneath it, half a dome protruded—inside, trapped orbs churned and hurled themselves at the barrier, releasing arcs of violent lightning.

Her hand brushed against her utility belt ensuring her blast gun was still in place. "So... what is this place?"

Reven gestured for her to walk with him as he took a few steps forward. She made sure to stay just close enough to hear, but far enough for an escape.

"Skeletor Island is not just an island," he boasted. "It is an invention. Lord Cane comes from an ancient bloodline. Scholars of the Great Dark Arts, masters of forbidden science. When his father died, he inherited this island and its... potential."

"Hmph, and what exactly do you do here?" Piquette inquired, eyes sweeping over the exposed machinery.

"We produce the rarest oil on Earth. A resource unlike any other."

His tone was almost cheerful. It made Piquette's skin crawl. The whole place had a dark and gloomy atmosphere. As if there were a dark barrier turning the sunlight grey.

As they reached a support beam, Reven paused and turned to her.

"Before we continue—you're not prone to nausea, are you?"

Her brows tightened. "Why?"

He rested his hands lightly on her shoulders, too lightly. She tried to roll them off, but he gripped her tighter. They locked eyes for a split second.

A paper-thin chip, swarming with circuitry, clung to his fingertip.

Lord Cane had given one order: *Chip the girl.*

A sudden burst of blue light detonated around them, swallowing them in a blinding flash.

He took the opportunity to stick the chip on the back of her neck so she wouldn't feel anything as they disassembled at the molecular level.

For half a heartbeat, reality tore. The man's figure splintered into ribbons in front of her eyes, warping and stretching through space—and then Piquette was somewhere else.

Her boots scraped metal as she stumbled, the world spinning. She braced her hands on her knees, trying to steady the nausea that rushed through her. The steel beneath her vibrated with a deep, mechanical pulse. Above her towered a massive fortress of dark steel, its spires like jagged fangs tore through the sky.

"Transportation complete," Reven spoke calmly, already ahead of her as if nothing had happened.

*Dammit, why do I feel so dizzy.*

She rubbed the back of her neck before she forced her legs to move, following him across a bridge of metal fused with bones.

Inside, black palm trees bored the edges of the room. In front of them, the upper half of the glowing dome pulsed violently.

Inside, trapped orbs hailed lightning bolts in the sky.

"Skeletor Island sustains itself through soul energy," Reven explained. "Our reservoirs supply oil across the world. Fuel for cities, medicine for the sick, purification for poisoned lands."

He gestured to the dome.

"The lighting from the souls strikes the earth and the sky. We then process the dirt and rain into an element we call liquid pureness. A miracle only Lord Cane can create."

"And the people?" Piquette inquired with disdain. "Where are they? Who supplies the souls?"

He smiled, "The souls are offerings from our devoted members or people who were deemed too vile for their society. As for our citizens. Well, there are no living citizens... not anymore."

Reven guided her to the elevator doors. He pressed the button and stepped inside. Piquette hesitated to follow.

"Come now, I hear you have to hurry back."

Piquette swallowed her pride and stepped inside the elevator. She and Reven were now just centimeters apart. *He is the strangest person I have ever come across, this place has such dark energy. I can feel it in my bones.*

Reven's eyes monitored her closely. He reached across her to press the down button. She took a quick step back watching his movement, brushing her hand against her gun.

Then the elevator descended under the earth.

When they reached the underground level, the doors opened to a dark cave.

Instinctively she retrieved her blast gun, pointing it straight ahead. Reven lowered her hand.

"What the hell is going on?" she pressed.

Then his flower insignia shone a bright light. Piquette's breath hitched at the sight in front of her.

Hundreds of corpses shuffled aimlessly in the dark, their chests stood still beneath torn rags. Mouths open in silent screams. Eyes hollow.

"Behold," Reven proclaimed. "Our workforce."

He nudged one of the corpses. They showed no reaction, not even to the light.

"Harmless... until commanded." He smiled.

Piquette stepped back, eyes wide in horror. *This... this is madness.*

She raised her weapon towards him, the weapon pitched as the beam filled with energy. She quickly pressed the button to bring them up, eyes refusing to break contact with him.

"I assure you there's no need for such hostility, everything we do is for the greater good." Reven smiled.

Once the doors opened, she retreated backwards. One foot behind the other, weapon still raised. Her grip tight around the handle.

Once she made it outside, she inhaled a deep breath trying to come to grips with the reality she just saw. *What did I get myself into?*

"As you can see," Reven spoke, his tone thick with pride as he snuck up behind her.

"Our island provides far more than the world understands. Kude Island is a marvel of its own but joined with us?" His lips curled. "We could become unstoppable."

"If you stand on the processor it will send back down. Tell General Skinner that Lord Cane sends his regards. And his interest."

He paused and gave a slight bow.

Piquette hurried to the spot where she landed and stood on the processor symbol. Before she knew it, she was reduced to her molecular level and back on the rocky terrain. Without turning back, she marched to her pod and wasted no time putting distance between her and the island.

Only once she was alone in the craft did she let out a gasp, clutching the back of her neck.

The skin there burned beneath her fingers; a rash was forming.

She moaned in pain. *What is that?*

# Chapter 11: The Fine Print of Fate

"Okay, Trin. Now, remember you are innocent." Isis said cupping Trinity's cheeks with a slight squeeze. "You did nothing wrong, and that's exactly what you're going to tell him." Trinity could feel her warm breath. The warmth coming off her body. Isis smelled so good.

Trinity nodded, swatting her hand away. She sat on the couch, anxious energy radiating through her leg as it bounced against the coffee table. Avoiding eye contact, she softly asked, "Then why do you keep acting like I'm guilty?"

Isis's comfort was pleasant; Trinity wished every moment were like this.

"I know, baby, I know. We just have to be extra careful." Isis crouched low, forcing Trinity to meet her eyes. "We don't want detectives sniffing around." She raised her voice loud enough for Cy to hear the warning from the kitchen.

Trinity gazed away absently, twirling her fingers in her hair. She had nothing left to say. Isis gave a sad nod and walked off. After gathering her things and a purple pineapple smoothie Cy prepared, she kissed his cheek and headed for the door.

"Love you, guys! Cy, don't forget to call me after." After she made her exit the tension in the air dissolved.

"Damn, she never shuts up," Cy joked from the stove, steam rising from the pan.

"She really loves to hear herself talk." Trinity grinned as she rolled her eyes.

"She does, like she's the queen of this household or something. Anyways the food ready."

Trinity wasted no time reaching the kitchen.

Cy made creamy scrambled quail's eggs cooked in duck fat, turkey bacon, and deep-fried potato balls stuffed with cheese and herbs, served with a side of horseradish-basil tomato sauce.

"Now listen," Cy elaborated as she ate, "This lawyer is a slick man. Does nothing unless it benefits him. It's important to make sure he learns nothing he can use against you. Me and Isis used to work for him back in the day. He's cool, but you *always* have to watch your back."

"I'm getting really tired of everybody knowing what's best for me even though none of you can spare me the truth."

"Look, Trinity. That's between you and your aunt, and I'm not getting into that. Now finish up. We've gotta be there in an hour."

Cy felt bad. Their story began long before him and would continue long after he was gone. All he could do was offer support.

After breakfast, Trinity dressed in a black cotton sweater dress, wrapping her waist with a loop chain made of onyx. She undid her braids, framed the hair to her liking and misted it with rose water.

Gazing at her reflection in the vanity, she tried to have a different attitude than last night.

Cy preferred simple fashion: a crisp orange tee shirt with white 3D lettering, dark blue baggy jeans, dark brown boots, and golden grills for the bottom of his teeth. His genuine sense of style came through his tech-infused jewelry—massive chains and watches, each with its own unique design and hidden features.

He slipped on his diamond encrusted silver necklace and his circuit board watch to complete his look.

The lawyer's office was at the edge of Blue City, right on the divide where Red City began, a place known as the Dim Light District.

Trinity and Cy hiked up the trail to the city gates and used the FastTrack, a levitating train capped at 250 miles per hour for safety reasons.

The energy of the island had shifted. A massive hologram floated above Med Inc., displaying the faces of the victims. Med-Bots stood stationed on every corner scanning the streets for any hint of danger. Trinity could feel that weight pressing on her chest. Her nerves were a wreck. She'd been in trouble before, but seeing a lawyer made her feel terrified.

After getting off at their stop, Trinity followed Cy until they reached a two-story building with the words LAW FIRM written in cracked gold. Towers surrounded it twice its size. It was easy to miss, yet somehow hard to overlook once you found it.

"Alright this is it. Just keep your answers short and to the point," Cy advised.

Opening the door, allowing Trinity in first, she stepped inside a narrow hallway stretched into darkness. A single light glowed at the end. Inside the light was a hologram of a woman who seemed to be working tirelessly. Trinity didn't know it at the time, but it was the lawyer's security system.

"Uh, what do we do now?" Trinity whispered, glancing at Cy.

"Follow me," he directed moving ahead.

Cy ran his fingers along the back wall until he stopped and pressed on a hidden panel. A soft click followed, and a secret door opened. Behind it, a brightly lit staircase that led to another door.

As they climbed her stomach turned with each step. The air was dry, without a single distinct smell.

The door opened to waiting room with tan-colored carpet, white walls, folding chairs, and a couch. There was a lady in a clear enclosure, but this one was not a hologram. She had dark red hair with the matching color eyebrows and eyelashes. She wore red-framed glasses. Her skin was smooth, with an oak-like complexion. She wore a lot of gold rings and had small rubies that bordered under her eyes.

Without asking, Trinity knew the crystals were rubies. She and Isis had a gift for knowing the names of crystals without being told. When they were younger, they would go hunting for crystals using their senses. Then they read all the books they could find detailing the name and descriptions of crystals. As Trinity grew, she realized not everyone had that gift.

"Cheers Jill," Cy greeted, approaching the enclosure.

Jill pointed at the door without looking up from her work.

Cy nodded and then turned to Trinity. "You ready?"

Trinity gave him a crooked smile, unsure how to answer. For her first visit to a lawyer's office, this seemed doable. She unwound her shoulders and took a breath out as Cy opened the office door.

A man with his back towards them gazed out the window to the view of a brick wall. He turned at the sound of the creaking door. "Well, if it isn't the handsome stud himself!" The lawyer was a man with tan skin and slicked-back hair that still managed to be fluffy. He spoke quickly, but his pronunciation of every word was clear as quartz. Trinity could see he had a view of the city's back streets. He reached from behind his desk to shake Trinity's hand.

"Greetings, I'm Maverick Beech, Top Attorney on Kude Island. I will be handling your case."

Trinity shook his hand raising her eyebrows from his strong grip.

"Please have a seat," he instructed. Beech sat, pulled out a larger version of Tabs from an invisible cabinet above him. He stabilized it a few inches from his face and began his speech.

"So, your aunt told me that you were an innocent bystander who was wrongly accused of aiding a terrorist attack. Your case file from the detective's report states that you are the sole survivor of what is called "the kill zone," also known as "the red zone." The scanner only detected your heartbeat, and after further examination at the Force's Recovery Center, they determined you had no injuries. I don't know what that's about, but that is pretty freaky." He didn't wait for a response.

"Anyway, it also states you were under the influence of Cinnaide for a period of time, which is what we are going to focus on. It's something that could help us. We can rule that your legal and personal rights were violated. You were drugged and then detained. That alone can cause an uproar because they took you without your consent while you were under the influence. And since you are underage, they shouldn't have questioned you without your legal guardian, and doing so was unlawful. We are going to file misconduct against the detectives who did this to you, so you have nothing to worry about. Just sign here, and I can start your appeal as soon as possible."

He took his Tabs out of stabilization and handed it over to Trinity who didn't hesitate to sign. Using the pen on his desk, she signed her name, Trinity Rose, next to the big X at the bottom of the document. *He's right. They violated my personal rights. Those damn rockeaters.*

"Just slide that over to Cy so he can sign as your guardian." Beech instructed while he was distracted by another screen.

Trinity turned to Cy and gave a hesitant smile as she handed the pen to him. She looked at his face, looking for a tic or an expression of annoyance, but there was none. Cy didn't hesitate to grab the pen and slide the Tabs towards him. He even pressed his lips together to mock a smile as she stared. It gave Trinity comfort. It was the first time he had been called her guardian out loud. She hadn't given it much thought. To her, Cy was just a guy she moved in with because he had money and he was Isis's boyfriend. Now that she thought about it, Cy had always been there. Even when Trinity was in the placement home Cy was there in all of Isis stories.

Cy signed his name under hers, Cyrus Shakur.

"Ah, great. This kid is going places. She didn't even say a word!" Beech chuckled. "Now, I'm going to submit these to the Appeals Department, and given the state of your case, we should hear from them soon." He reached out his hand for Trinity to shake again.

"As for you, Cy, we've got business," Beech smirked.

Cy dropped his head. "Of course we do." He sighed. "Trin, would you wait for me in the waiting room?"

"Sure."

As Trinity sat in the waiting room, a wave of uneasiness washed over her. A nauseous feeling climbed her throat. Her head was dizzy, her vision blurred, her breathing became rapid as she hunched over for breath. Sweat began beading on her nose. *Jupiter's rainstorm not another one.*

"Hey sweetheart, maybe you should go outside and get some fresh air." Jill recommended.

Trinity heard her, but the words were jumbled. She caught one word, air.

She pushed off the chair and wobbled down the stairs, one hand trailing the wall for balance. At the bottom, she searched for the door. *No handle, of course.*

She hit the seam where they'd entered, shoulder first. It clicked and swung open.

Once outside, she took a deep breath of cool air and leaned back against the building, eyes closed. A shadow fell across her eyes as it blocked the sun. She opened them to find a man approaching, arms spread wide.

"If it isn't my beautiful niece," the man cheered. His voice was deep and smooth like a cello, cloaked with a slight British accent. A navy-blue suit covered him. He wore a white button-up underneath but had no tie. Instead, he had a thick gold chain and a gold wristwatch to match. Diamond earrings weighed down his ears. His hair cut low, skin a dark chestnut brown, and his teeth were white like clouds on a sunny day. His cheekbones were prominent, which paired well with his almond eyes.

*Who the vex is this?* Trinity stared at him, silent. She wasn't in the mood for any street actors today. She straightened her posture and turned her body so her back wasn't against the wall.

"Ah, that's okay. I don't expect you to remember me. I haven't seen you since you were a little girl," he chuckled, brushing her off with his hand.

No one had ever said that to her before. It caught her attention. "Excuse me, do I know you?" she pressed.

Tilting her in question, she took a step closer. *He seems oddly familiar.*

"Well, yes and no. Trinity, I'm your uncle," he disclosed.

Her stomach sank when he said her name. "Wait, who are you? How do you know my name?"

"I'm guessing your aunt didn't tell you anything about me?" He fixed his cuffs. "That's fine, I guess. I'll reintroduce myself now. Trinity, I am your uncle from your mother's side." He stopped talking to admire her. "You have her eyes, but you grew to look like your father. Nevertheless, I am very pleased to meet you." He grinned.

Trinity stared at him blankly. He was putting her on edge. She was at a loss for words. "Then you know the bad news. My mother is—"

"Dead, I know. She passed away when you were a child in a horrible accident at the Recovery Center. Gosh, I miss my sister dearly." The stranger shook his head with a look of grief.

"Okay, now you're beyond my comfort protocol. Who *are* you and how do you know that?"

Her tone grew serious, which left him confused. *She really doesn't know who I am. Though I look different, I thought Isis would've told her all about me.*

"Who's this?" Cy prodded coming out the door.

She turned to look at Cy. Before Trinity could think of what to say, the stranger spoke again.

"You must be the great Cyrus Shakur!" the man gleamed, reaching out for a handshake. His smile grew wider.

"And you are?" Cy frowned, ignoring his hand.

"Me? I'm just an old friend of the family," he responded.

*Why is he smiling like that? Why did he just lie? He said he was my uncle.*

"I was just walking by and happened to see Trinity, but I'll let you guys be on your way. It was nice seeing you again, Trinity." Her uncle reached for Trinity's hand and bent down to give it a kiss only to be pushed back by Cy.

"Uh huh." Cy said slapping his hand to his chest.

"Oh, my apologies." the stranger said.

While Cy was distracted, her uncle slipped a small business card in her hand.

She blushed as the arches in her eyebrows rose. She immediately gripped the card tight, then took a quick glance at Cy to see if he'd caught the exchange.

"And nice to meet you, Cy. I'm a big fan." Her uncle walked off, disappearing into the crowd of people.

Cy was a celebrity among some. In Ameris he had a best friend named Titanium, or Ti for short. Cy used to joke that Ti's bones were as strong as titanium, even without enhancements, and that his heart was made of steel.

Both their fathers were high-ranking military men, and the boys had followed in their footsteps as soon as they were of age. Ti was a weapons engineer who fought in the field against rebel groups, while Cy, a computer whiz, who fought his battles with a keyboard.

Ti died in a horrific bombing weaponized with a new chemical called Sulfurioxde—its flames burned light green and teal. The gas was the latest weapon in chemical warfare. It scorched the lungs from the inside, and the heat it produced was strong enough to melt bones.

Cy did everything in his power to hunt down Ti's killers. He traced the rebel group responsible, the Chemical Agents, and found a secret faction of military commanders who funded them and sought control over what remained of Ameris.

When the government covered it up, Cy snapped. He fell into a deep depression that neither his father nor Ti's could pull him out of. In his grief, he hacked into military networks across the globe, shutting down weapons systems, communications, and power grids.

During his rebellion he was injured from an explosion that literally blew his brains out, and only then was he caught. He received reconstructive modification surgery so that seventy percent of his brain was now cybernetic—he also now had a full robotic skull, and robotic eyes that glowed light blue when he would "channel himself" he called it. Any time he used his brain to hack, he called it "working the machine from the inside."

Cy also had his own language; one he'd built from ancient texts and symbols. It was the only language he ever coded in. Even Isis had a hard time learning it.

News outlets plastered his face all over because of his crimes. Many people called him a maestro. After receiving amnesty on Kude Island, they punished Cy at the reform school for boys.

"Um, that was off sequence," Cy remarked. He was the nonconfrontational type, so he didn't think too much about the conversation, plus people noticed him on the street all the time. But one glance at Trinity's bulging eyes and the pulse of her heartbeat let him know the interaction was far from harmless.

"Come on Trin, let's get some ice cream before we go home."

# Chapter 12: *Fate's Black Hole*

Isis sat in her room at the edge of her bed. She buried her face in her hands. Tears flowed down her wrists as she gasped for air through the gaps. She winced every time a disturbing image flashed in her head. The forty-eight hour torture session was brutal.

*What's the worst that can happen? I'm indestructible.*

Blending in was the hardest part of living on Earth for Isis. It took her years to learn how to control her strength. Hiding her full power felt like burying herself alive and she hated it.

She came straight here after registering at Force headquarters. Miss Thorn's henchmen locked her in a featureless padded cell, strapping her wrists and ankles to a steel chair. Cold patches attached to wires pressed against the sides of her head. An oversized mouth guard was forced between her teeth.

After making sure she was secure, they exited. Silence engulfed the room and Isis couldn't hear anything beyond her heartbeat.

Her eyes darted from wall to wall, searching for anything other than anticipation.

An hour turned into two, then five. Her mouth ached from the guard that kept slipping loose, forcing her to bite hard. She tried fighting off sleep at the sixth hour, but her eyes were heavy with exhaustion, closing despite her will.

Then a deafening alarm jolted her awake and it didn't stop.

Her first instinct was to cover her ears, but the metal straps tightened with each movement.

After a few moments the lights went out. Then still shot images were projected on the wall, grotesque and disturbing.

A man with six arms and a head of bleeding eyes.

Burning bodies as a city collapsed into ash.

Her sister falling into an endless pit, head smashing against an invisible shield.

A rip through the fabric of space time and darkness seeping through.

Isis shut her eyes in terror. Just as she did a jolt of electricity seared through her body. Her body convulsed in pain as her teeth broke through the guard stabbing through her tongue.

"Aaah!" she moaned in pain.

She could have stopped it. Broke free to reduce the chair and the room to splinters. But she didn't. Relinquishing her power was the only choice that mattered.

Just when she thought things couldn't get worse muffled screams filled the room and the chair slowly lifted from the ground.

Another shock ripped through her body. The pain was unbearable. Slowly, her tears changed direction as the chair rotated in a circle. Sobs escaped her bloody mouth as she continued to keep the guard in place.

Every time she closed her eyes another shock came. Hours strolled by before the images vanished. The chair still hovered in the air then after what seemed like a day it finally lowered to the ground.

By this time Isis' body trembled, her breath shallow and uneven. Hair clung to her damp skin, swaying with each exhale. Hours passed as things returned to normal. Then the process was repeated.

Twenty-four hours later, she was past her breaking point. Her eyes were hollow; her body was limp. Her brain fried beyond belief. Her spirit was utterly shattered.

Finally, the henchmen returned and carried her to her room like a rag doll. Her limbs dangled lifelessly. To her, it felt as though months had passed.

The moment she touched the bed an outburst of shrieks left her body. *Why? Why did it show? My sister?* The image of her sister falling replayed in her head for hours as she cried until she managed to fall asleep.

By morning, she couldn't move her body. *I can't believe I'm stuck here for four years. This is just madness, pure madness. I hope Trinity is having a better time than me.*

Outside, laughter echoed from the hallway. Girls chatted and joked as if nothing in the world could touch them.

*How can anybody be happy in a place like this?*

She buried her face in her pillow and cried silently until there was a knock at the door.

She shot upright, wiping her face dry and clearing her throat. "Come in," she called, her voice unnaturally high.

"Hey, Isis, right?" A girl peeked inside. "I'm Zya—one of the OGs around here. I make care packages for the new girls."

Zya stepped in with a warm smile. Olive tan skin, with a face dusted with freckles. Short curls framed her face. "I brought biodegradable absorbing pads, a juvica face mask, and a few other goodies." She paused, then grinned. "Also—for the record, a few girls and I are big fans. We've been following your case since the beginning. The way you had a copy of the judge's Citizen Card and tried to break into his office? Total badass move."

"Thanks." The corner of her lip managed to move. *I forgot I did that.* "So, are we gonna discuss what that was?"

Zya snickered. "That was Miss Thorn's initiation. The images are based on your fears and memories. The chair reacts too—it reads your brainwaves and creates a simulation. Basically, we all tortured ourselves for forty-eight hours."

"Great," Isis muttered. "A device that can see my secrets. Just what I need."

Zya smiled sympathetically. "You'll get used to it. Anyway, be prepared for a lot of manual labor. We do city maintenance and anything workers are too lazy for. Last week we picked burning sap plants for five hours." She rubbed her thumbs together, grimacing. "My fingers were covered in welts! But at least we can choose our chores. I work in the infirmary, but you can pick from the kitchen, gardening, cleaning, laundry, repairs, or the boutique."

"There's a boutique?" Isis asked with disgust. Her eyebrows rose wrinkling her forehead as her bottom lip upturned.

"Yeah, Miss Thorn is a stickler for fashion and hygiene. The boutique sells clothes that she designs. You can buy stuff with the credits you earn from chores. Every full moon we get the day off which was two moons ago. Tomorrow, we're doing some landscaping in the mountain ranges. So, make sure you work hard because if we don't meet our quota or have an accident, they add time to our sentences. And if you really mess up... you get sent to the chamber."

"The chamber?" Isis asked warily.

"Oh, nothing major," Zya said with mock cheer. "Just a time distortion room that makes a few hours feel like years. So, don't get sent there."

"How long have you been here?"

"Just shy of ten years," Zya said casually.

"My goodness! What did you do—kill a Council member?" Isis asked, half-joking.

Zya hesitated to speak, then nodded slightly.

"No," Isis whispered, eyes widening. Her jaw dropped when she realized Zya wasn't joking.

"Yep," Zya said, popping the p. "When I was ten, I hacked into his home interface just to scare him. Ended up electrocuting him.

Who knew he'd be in the bathtub?" She shrugged, showing no remorse.

"That was you?"

"Yeah, my parents were beyond heated. But technically, he wasn't a council member yet—just running for it. And I've got a hearing coming up, so maybe I'll get out soon. Plus, the age cap here is twenty-two."

Isis stood to take the package and grinned. "Thanks for this."

"We're having lunch at midday. Don't miss it we only get three meals a day, one for each bell and you'll need the energy." Zya smiled, "So I'll come back in a few to show you tour?"

"Yeah, sounds good."

Isis took time to look around the room and what Zya said started to make sense. The lamp beside her bedside was beaded colorfully. The Persian carpet and its intricate patterns were soft beneath her feet. Even the bed frame was carved from expensive wood.

She opened her drawer to find a simple grey cotton sweater and pants. In the bathroom closet was one towel, a washcloth, and a bright blue soap bar. The sink came with a costume teeth flasher.

Isis showered quickly, ran a comb through her damp hair, and dressed without bothering to dry off fully. When she stepped out of her room, she found herself on a mezzanine corridor overlooking the open first floor below. Last night she'd barely been conscious enough to register anything. Now, fully awake, she took it in. High ceilings, Persian carpets coating the floor, walls painted a deep tan with patterns barely visible, a railing of dark oak curving the edge of the platform.

She couldn't believe how beautiful it was. Two girls in lace dresses passed her, giggling. She leaned over the railing and spotted more of them below, trading gossip in small clusters. A small drop of water fell from her hair. Her sweater was sprinkled with droplets. *Oh, great now my hair will get frizzy.*

"Oh, cheers!" Zya jogged down the hallway toward her. "I see you made it out of your room."

"Yeah. I had to see what all the giggling was about."

"Stellar, then let's start he tour." Zya led her toward the stairs. "You're lucky, by the way—your room's right above the main lobby."

They came down onto the first floor, and Zya pointed as they walked. "That tall steel pod is the chamber I told you about—every house has one. And that's the boutique." She nodded at a glass door with a closed sign in the window. "Only opens when we get our day off, or if there's a festival coming up"

She led Isis past it, down a hallway lined with more doors. "We got more rooms down here. Some of them have multiple girls in the room. We've got about two hundred and sixty-five girls total."

At the end of the hall was a heavy wooden door, with two more hallways branching off on either side. Zya pressed her palm against it; a soft blue glow outlined it. Then the door slid open revealing a wide stone veranda.

Isis stepped out and gasped. "Solar plex. This place is like a resort."

"Ehh, sort of. We don't actually get much access to any of it. Like I said only on days off, or festivals, that's it."

"What's all this festival talk?" Isis asked, crossing her arms.

"Instead of celebrating the changing seasons like the rest of the island does, Miss Thorn throws her own festivals. They're something to see." Zya continued leading her across the veranda toward the next building. "This house we're in is the antique house. This next one is the relics house."

She pressed her hand to the door, and with the blue outline around her hand the door slid open. "Only a handful of us can open the outside doors. It cuts off just before the sunset bells. You have to earn through years of credit building. Otherwise, it's the indoor doors between houses for you."

The relics house turned out to be another Victorian building, though the rugs were different and the hallways not as wide. It was less open than the antique house. As Zya led her through, she waved and smiled at nearly every girl they passed.

*She must really be liked here. No wonder she talks like she owns the place.*

"As you can see most of the hallways connect into squares," Zya said, rounding a corner. She gestured toward another door as they passed it. "That one leads to the younger girls' school. Wouldn't go in there unless you absolutely have to, they're vicious." She said dropping her chin and her tone.

The next hallway was wider, with no doors except a set of double ones at the far end. Zya pushed them open, revealing a cream-colored room—three long oak tables, candles, tall windows, and a few girls scattered around reading. Stone flooring and walls. Flowers hung upside down from the ceiling.

"This is the eatery," she said gesturing with her hands. "The kitchen's through the back. Every room's got a tea and water dispenser too, so you're never far from a drink."

Isis managed a flat smile, her arms still crossed for comfort. It was a lot to take in all at once, but she welcomed the distraction—anything to keep her mind off her sister and those images. They left her deeply traumatized, having to relive the death of her sister again.

Zya kept moving: the garden stood outside, just past the eatery. Then a quick tour of the heirloom house, where repairs were done. After that Zya led her down a hallway that looped them back to the antique house, past the laundry room, which she pointed out without breaking stride.

"You've noticed by now all the houses are connected," Zya said. "We're free to roam when we're not stuck with chores, though chores eat up more time than you'd think. Once you've earned enough credits, you can make phone calls, holo calls, whatever. I'll show you the communications room when your credit system is set up." She took a short pause and eyed Isis up and down, tongue rolling in her mouth as if she had something mysterious to say. Instead, she said "You've been quiet this whole time. Got any questions?" Zya squeezed her knuckles waiting for a response.

Isis was still registering her new life for four years. "No,jJust taking it all in." she sighed.

"Fair enough. I've, uh, got another newcomer to show around, so I'll catch you at lunch—I'll come get you at the midday bells?"

"Yeah, Zya. See you then." Isis didn't really want her to come back, but she didn't want to seem dismissive. Zya had been nothing but nice.

With a nod and thin smile, Zya trotted off.

Isis lingered for a bit. Taking in what would be her new home. She walked to the boutique door and peeked inside the dark room. Then the sniffles of a young girl caught her attention. Near the chamber a girl cried quietly in the corner.

*This place might be all glitz and glamour, but it's still a hell hole. First thing I need to do is find out where the henchmen sleep.*

Two weeks later, Isis had settled in. Adjusting to the routines and her housemates, though she missed her freedom and Trinity terribly. She still couldn't find any means of escape.

One night, she walked behind her friend's group of laughing girls, their arms linked as they enjoyed the night air. Even surrounded by them, Isis felt lonely. She'd been distant since she arrived. Maybe that was what drew people to her, her mystery.

That night, her housemates begged her to sneak out to meet the boys from the reform school. She cared little for boys, but she needed to get out of that house. Tonight was the night she'd cave in. Although her and Zya grew close, this was a secret she couldn't tell her about.

"Hey, what's up?" one of her housemates called greeting the boys, then turned to gesture at Isis. "Guys, this is Isis—our new roommate. Isis, meet the guys."

"Cheers," Isis pressed her lips together and whispered. She gave a shy wave.

A chorus of greetings followed. Then the two groups merged.

Cy noticed her immediately. Like Isis, he was a loner. All his friends had someone, but he'd always been content to stay solo. No one ever felt right. No one ever matched him until now.

And for reasons he couldn't explain, from the very first moment he saw Isis she felt like home. It could have been how her hair flowed gently in the wind swiping across her sad eyes. Or the moon's light casting on her cheek bones and lip gloss. Or maybe it was the way she carried herself with grace and attitude. One boot stomping in front of the other as if the street was her runway. What impressed him most was her style. Baggy black cargos lined with pockets, they fit loosely around her waist showing the waist band of her briefs. Her abs showing due to her black crop top. He smiled, straightened his posture, and approached with his hands clasped behind his back.

"How you doing, I'm Cy," he approached, unable to contain his smile.

Isis glanced up, and instantly he drew her in. As soon as their eyes connected, she felt an undeniable spark. A warm feeling coated her and all the noise in the background dropped.

"Cheers, I'm Isis." She flashed a grin, offering her hand.

He took it gently and kissed it, taking in the smell of her perfume. "Like the Egyptian goddess."

"Cosmic," she teased, "do you sniff and kiss the hand of every girl you meet?"

"No," he answered throwing his fist in his palm. "Just you."

She laughed, biting her bottom lip. "Ugh, boy, please."

"I'm serious," he said, leaning closer. "You caught me off guard—I had to think fast."

"And you thought of a kiss?"

"It's better than a regular handshake."

Isis couldn't stop looking into his beautiful brown eyes. With the streetlight shining above—it all felt like a scene out of a romance film.

"You'd better be careful with that one," one of her housemates teased. "He's trouble."

Isis raised a brow. "Oh, really?"

"Yep," she giggled. "Cy's the reason we can sneak out."

"Is that true?" Isis asked, turning to him.

He nodded proudly. "It's all up here." He tapped his temple. "Both schools use weak security systems. It's easy to hack them to make it look like the windows are locked when they're not."

Cy impressed Isis. She hadn't expected her night to turn around like this.

# Chapter 13: The Last Lie

Isis stood there in her pink pantsuit. She matched her blush and eye shadow with her outfit and glued two pink gemstones on the corners of her eyes. Despite her colorful curated outfit, the day was painfully slow. Hardly anyone was around because of the previous day's events.

Even so, her mind was fixated on last night's dream. She and Zya were assassins. Really good ones. She couldn't remember clearly but there was a family of assassins that were either their target or their prey. Throughout the dream her and Zya had to fight the family of assassins and during that time both of them fell in love with the brother who eventually joined their side. But Zya and Isis didn't compete over him instead they pushed each other to pursue him like a funny game.

Isis thought hard of what the dream was trying to tell her. *The dream definitely conveyed the theme of teamwork and love. But I was hoping to see a reality of me and Trinity not me and Zya. What could this dream be telling me? What am I missing?*

"Hey, there's a man here to see you," her boss said as he approached her. "I'll have Angela cover your part of the floor, so hurry—he's up front."

Isis jumped slightly as he startled her, "Okay," she responded as he walked away.

*Ugh. What now?* Isis rolled her eyes and stomped toward the entrance.

The last few years of her life had been a nightmare. She just wanted it all to end. There was always an unpleasant surprise or an enormous problem waiting around the corner. No matter what she did, life always turned against her.

As she approached the front, she spotted a tall man watching her. The way he stood made her uneasy. Crossing her arms, she shifted into a defensive stance. The closer she got, the more familiar his face looked—but she couldn't place him.

"Can I help you?" she pressed, assuming he was from the Force, another detective sent to badger her. But then she noticed the jewels, the sharp tailoring of his suit, the way the fabric shimmered in the light.

*He's certainly not dressed like a detective.*

The man didn't answer immediately. Instead, he studied her with an unsettling smile, as if measuring every breath she took.

"Why haven't you told Trinity about me?" he asked at last, tilting his head like a curious predator.

Isis let out a dry chuckle, more disbelief than humor. "Excuse me—who the hell are you?"

"I can tell you've done a piss-poor job raising her," he spoke calmly, stepping closer. Her shoulders stiffened at his step.

"She looked like she hadn't slept in days when I caught her leaving the office and worst of all—she's wasting her potential."

"Potential?" Isis's scoff almost turned into a laugh. "You've got to be kidding me. Potential—"

The word stuck in her throat. Her laughter died instantly.

*Potential.*

Her breath caught. The scent in the air, the familiar pull of his presence—no disguise could hide that from her. Balling her hands into fists, every muscle in her body tensed.

"It's... it's you," she stammered.

"Yes, Isis," he smirked, voice low and deliberate. "It's me. Your dear older brother. And I've come for Trinity. She doesn't belong to you."

"What?" Isis snapped. "Trinity isn't property and she sure as hell doesn't belong to you."

She hadn't seen him since the explosion at the Recovery Center, but deep down, she'd always known he wasn't dead, just hiding. His scent had haunted her for years, a ghost she tried to forget. Now, the ghost was standing inches from her.

"Well," he said coolly, "that's for her to decide. Goodbye, Isis."

He walked past her slowly, close enough that their shoulders brushed. The contact was electric, a spark of tension she refused to flinch from.

Isis stood frozen. The weight of the encounter pressed down on her chest.

Then it hit her like an arrow—*him*! The creep who used to linger outside that one placement home. The one she'd dismissed as a random stranger. He'd changed his face, disguised himself so thoroughly that she hadn't recognized him until now.

Unbeknownst to them, he had been keeping tabs on them. Watching from across the street. Following Trinity on late-night walks to the arcade.

The last time Isis had seen him, she had been in her early teens. Trinity was still a child.

Trinity had gotten into a fight with a bully from their placement home while Isis was out running errands. When Isis returned, she found her sitting on the stoop pale and panicked.

"Trinity... what's wrong?" Isis dropped her bags and ran to her.

"They're kicking us out!" Trinity screamed. She sobbed so hard she could barely breathe.

Isis had never seen her like that, shaking violently, her shirt soaked in tears.

She burst through the front door to find the housemother crouched beside an unconscious boy while a Med-Bot scanned him. Kids huddled around, whispering.

"What's going on?" Isis asked, her voice barely steady.

The housemother looked up, eyes wild. "What's going on?" she repeated, her voice dripping with rage. "This is the fifth incident that little girl has caused! First the Delorys boys, and now this. He doesn't even have a pulse, Isis! I can't take it anymore. You and your niece monster need to go. Now!"

Isis knew the housemother would lie to the Med-Bot. She wouldn't trigger an investigation. The woman had too much to hide; she was a criminal herself and had taught Isis much of what she knew. They'd lived there for a little over three years.

"You know what? Fine! We don't need you. We don't need any of this!" Isis shouted, storming out. As she turned, she saw him across the street, watching. Their eyes only met for a second.

"Get up, Trinity. Let's go," she barked, running down the steps. "And we'll be back for our stuff!" she urged over her shoulder as Trinity followed.

But they never went back. That night, everything changed.

Isis cried quietly in the bathroom of a Stay Room, clutching their last few rubels while Trinity slept on the bed. The sound of cartoons barely masked her sobs. She remembered the gnawing hunger for safety and control.

Her fists clenched tight... and then, without warning, coins spilled from her palm, clinking against the cold tile. She stared at them in shock.

In that moment, Isis was reborn into someone who could provide, who could create, who would never be powerless again.

After her shift, Isis returned home to the pleasant smell of Cy at work. The scent lifted her mood instantly.

"Hey," she greeted, kissing him on the cheek.

"Hey, baby. How was your day?" he asked puckering kiss lips for a second kiss. Isis did as she as commanded and kissed him softly.

"It was, um... surprising. Unexpected. How was the Beech visit?" she responded, quickly pushing the topic aside. Sitting at the table, Isis leaned back as the vines gave her a massage, molding around her body.

"It went well. You know he's going to do his thing—but can you believe that starfart asked me to do a job for him?" Cy scoffed.

"What, really? What does he want now?"

"Let me correct myself—when I said me, I meant us. But you know, I told him we're not into that life anymore. I didn't even give him a chance to state his demands."

"Hmm, that's interesting." The touch of the vines softened her voice.

"But something strange did happen," he added.

"Oh, yeah?"

"Yeah. There was this weird guy talking to Trinity outside."

Isis shot up. "A weird guy?"

"Yeah. He said he was a family friend, but I wasn't buying it, so I did a quick facial scan. Get this—that guy was Malcolm Booker, a money man for Nova Financial."

"Interesting." She grabbed a drink from the fridge, doubling it to make a replacement. "What else did your scan say?"

"I don't know. His file is sealed. I'd have to use the station to dig up more dirt if I can, but this dude was cosmic—had a gold chain, one of those reflective suits made from snake scales, and a fade. I mean, this dude was keen."

"Mm, so he... he spoke to Trinity?" Isis inquired, taking a quick gulp to soothe her dry throat.

Cy turned. "What are you hiding, Isis?"

Cy always knew when Isis was lying—or trying to get something out of him. Her heartbeat was different. He usually didn't pry and read vitals unless he felt he needed to.

"What? Nothing, nothing. You're paranoid! I've just got to be careful, you know. A lot of people could be after Trin." She laughed nervously, then began massaging his shoulders, hoping to distract him. "I'm going to wash up before dinner." After planting another kiss on his cheek, she was off.

Crawling to the bathroom, Isis peeled off her teethwraps and stripped off her uncomfortable suit. Throwing her hair into a messy bun, she sank into the tub filled with warm purple bubbles, closed her eyes, and dreamed her favorite dream.

The smell of spices filled the air. Tonight's dinner featured panoplies—Kude's new species of onion. Cy's version of jollof rice with a whole head of panoplies, served with pickled cabbage and carrots. The main dish, poul fri chicken along with bush tea lemonade.

Isis kept stealing awkward glances across the table while Trinity sipped her lemonade slowly. Cy didn't care what tension lingered; his poul fri chicken was wonderful, and that was enough. Silverware scraping against plates were the only sound that dared to interrupt the silence.

Eventually, Trinity had enough. She would say something tonight. She'd tossed and turned in bed most of the day once her and Cy returned home. She only woke once Isis returned home. It was as if her body could sense Isis' aura. There hadn't been time to think about the stranger she'd met—she'd just have to wing it.

"A man stopped me on the street today and told me he was my uncle." She said as she scooped a spoon full of rice in her mouth.

"He said he was your uncle?" Cy's spoon clattered against the plate. "Isis, I thought you said your only brother died."

A deep breath escaped Isis as her eyes closed—this was the moment she'd been avoiding. *I wish I had the power to freeze time.*

"Yes, he did die. At least, I thought he did." Her tone softened, eyes opening slowly. "It's about time you knew this, Trinity. There were more of us. I'm the youngest... of five."

"Whoa!" Trinity shouted. "You said my mother and your brother were the last family we had. Now you're telling me there's more? So, you lied?"

"Alright, first no. I didn't lie," Isis shot back. "I *thought* he was dead. He was in a freaking explosion, for crying out loud!" A nervous laugh slipped out, thin and brittle. "And it doesn't matter. All my siblings are gone, Trinity. All except him, apparently." She reached a hand across the table, but Trinity pulled back, her face hardening.

"Trinity, I don't understand why you're so upset," Isis cried. "They died a long time ago, long before you were even born."

"You're such a spawn of dark matter, do you know that?" Trinity's chest heaved as her anger grew. "How could you not know your own brother was alive? How could you lie to me about my family history?"

"Do you really think I kept our past hidden to hurt you? I did it to protect you. Our family history is a nightmare. Believe it or not, I did what I thought was best. You don't need to know everything, and you should watch your tone while you're at it. We don't want to start throwing insults around."

"We've been alone as long as I can remember. I thought we were abandoned. No history, or story of our lineage. I always knew something was missing—and you knew what that was. How could you not see how angry that would make me?" Her throat scorched with anger as she began to shout.

"I bounced from house to house alone while you had family. You knew about *my* family and never told me. Isis, you've been lying to me my entire life. I was alone with memories of parents fading away. And then you left me to fend for myself." Trinity shot out her seat with force.

"That's it! I want to know where we came from. And now he's here. He can tell me everything. I don't need you anymore!"

"Fine!" Isis stood, her voice turned cold.

"I'll save you the trouble. My siblings are dead, just like your parents. So, grow up and get over it. You *always* want someone to feel bad for you. You're not a lost little puppy. Stop acting like one." The dishes on the table rattled as her fist came down. She hadn't realized she was out of her chair, towering. Cy's wide eyes reflected the shock everyone felt.

"I think we should all calm down." Cy spoke up.

"You're a low-life thief who only thinks about herself. Mean, selfish, and conniving. Everything you touch rots, Isis. It should've been you, not them."

Isis rounded the table before she could think. Her vision blurred with rage as she slapped Trinity across the face. The sound whipped through the air and the light flickered. A sharp breath caught in Isis' throat the moment she saw blood on Trinity's lip. "Trinity, Trin! I'm so sorry, I didn't mean—"

"Don't touch me!" Trinity shoved her back, tears streaming. "I hate you, I've always fucking hated you!" She fled to her room.

Isis looked back at Cy, who sent her a look of utter disappointment.

Then a bang on their door. Cy stood to answer it.

"No, it's okay. I'll get it!" Quickly raising her hand to stop him. She wiped her tears and forced her teeth to show.

Isis opened the door to her neighbors.

The older gentleman cleared his throat. "Hello, Isis. Sorry to interrupt. We know that you are—"

"Oh, save it, you protocol prude," an old woman snapped, cutting him off. Mrs. Ivy was the grouchy neighbor who complained about everything. She and Isis had once been close until they realized they were too much alike. "This is the third night this month you've kept us up with that racket."

"Mrs. Ivy, it's not even sunset," Isis frowned. "Please, go tend to your cats and take a sleeping pill."

"Look, Isis," the man interrupted, trying to smooth things over. "What Mrs. Ivy means is... we understand how hard it is raising a teenage girl. Trust me, I know—I have three daughters. But enough is enough. Your fights are affecting our lives. Your voices echo through the walls. You're the only neighbors we have this problem with."

"And don't forget the electricity going haywire every time you argue! Show her the form," Mrs. Ivy ordered, slapping his shoulder.

With a disappointed look, he handed Isis his Tabs.

"A petition to kick us out? But... that's not fair!" Isis whined, snatching it from his hands. "I watched your daughters for free when your wife died. And you—" she turned to Mrs. Ivy, voice shaking, "I sat with you when you were on the verge of tears because your daughters never visit. How could you guys do this to me?" she whined.

The man sighed. "Look, I appreciate everything you've done. But when you first moved in, there was arguing almost every night. Now my daughters think it's normal to fight like that. We just can't take it anymore. I'm sorry, Isis. We'll give you one more chance... but after that, I'll have no choice but to file the petition."

The band of neighbors slowly wandered away.

"And get your monitor fixed, you cheap!" Mrs. Ivy added.

Isis fussed and slammed the door.

"Ugh... can you believe that girl? I've raised her, sacrificed everything for her, and this is how she repays me? Like I'm the villain? Like I'm the one who ruined her life?" Isis paced in the bedroom, too furious to sit still.

Shirtless and ready for bed, Cy sat at the edge as he listened to Isis ramble.

"Why didn't you tell her about your other siblings? More importantly, why didn't you tell me?" Cy somewhat felt offended since they shared everything.

"Cy, it's complicated. What's the point of dredging it all up now? They're gone, all of them. And him? He's not a good man. If he's after Trinity, it's not out of love."

She finally took a seat, Cy rested his arm around her. "Malcolm Booker isn't even his real name and that accent's fake too. I know they died in that explosion. Him and Trinity's parents. I've replayed that night a thousand times. The flames, the screams. Their faces..." Her voice cracked. "I'll never forget the way they burned."

She swallowed hard, trembling as the memory burned behind her eyes. "But... somehow, my brother survived. And I remember one thing."

"What?" Cy asked.

"Someone grabbed me, pulled me away right before the blast could get me."

"And it couldn't have been him? Your brother?"

"No. It couldn't. I saw him in the room when it happened."

"And where was Trinity?"

"She was in another room being examined, while the other doctors spoke to her parents. I sat on the bench and saw everything."

"He can't be in two places at once," Cy noted with a shrug.

Isis pondered. *It couldn't have been him who swiped me away. I saw him in the room with Trinity's parents before the explosion happened. Who whisked me away?*

"Can we go to bed now? This mystery is frying my circuits." He sighed collapsing back.

Crawling onto Cy's lap, Isis wrapped her arms around him. He mirrored her embrace, pressing a soft kiss on her forehead until she melted in his hold.

"Look," he fessed, "you don't have to talk about it—but giving me a heads-up about a sinister brother who apparently evaded death would've been nice. I have a family to protect."

Isis blushed, burying her face against his chest. *I'm sorry Cy, some secrets you just shouldn't know.*

Across the hall, Trinity screamed into her pillow as loudly as she could. Her cheeks burned with rage.

Her life felt like a cage. *I'm not her puppet. I'm not a project she gets to fix.*

Tugging the covers over herself, her thoughts drifted to Mother June—the last person who'd truly felt like family. She missed that woman's soft voice, the smell of her herbal garden, the way peace clung to that house on the hills of Eden.

Then the memory hit her like a jolt—*the business card!*

Springing from bed, she dug into her dress pocket until her fingers brushed the edge.

*Let's have a chat 082-757-9328.*

Heart racing, she perched on the edge of the bed, and split open her Tabs then dialed the number.

"Hello. Thank you for calling," a robotic voice chirped.

"Uh—hi, I—"

"Please say yes if you would like to have a chat."

"Yes?" she answered, unsure.

"Excellent." A soft chime played. "Would you like to have dinner at the Ruby Palace?"

Her heart skipped a beat. "Yes!" she answered in a cheerful whisper.

"Estimated arrival time: forty-five minutes. Would you like me to arrange transportation?"

"No!" she blurted then lowered her voice. "No... no, thank you."

"Your reservation has been confirmed for 9:00 p.m. Please give your name to the host."

The line went disconnected.

Trinity stared at her screen. *Could this finally be my chance to know the complete truth?*

She knew exactly what she'd wear: black leather pants draped in diamond chains. A brown and black snakeskin corset and the matching purse. For her feet, black platform boots. Jewelry for the night, onyx earrings with matching bracelets and necklace.

Fully dressed, Trinity tiptoed to the front door, hovering her hand over the handle. With just a step out the door everything could change. Maybe she'd never come back.

She exhaled and slipped quietly into the night.

Isis had a long night of thinking ahead of her. Long after Cy fell asleep, she dragged her feet into the bathroom feeling defeated. Trinity's words struck her hard. *It should have been you.*

Isis cried harder than she ever did in her life. She sat on the bathroom floor with a massive weight of guilt crushing her chest. *I can't believe she would say something like that... to me. We always had our differences, but to wish death on me? It's... it's unforgivable. How dare she! She has no idea what I've been through just to keep us together.*

After crying for what felt like hours, Isis finally crawled back into bed.

But Cy was awake the whole time, listening to her smothered sobs. He knew this was a pain she needed to feel on her and he would be there to comfort her when she returned. He wrapped his arms around Isis and buried his face into her neck. The warmth of his breath, the steadiness of his heartbeat, and the smooth touch of his hand rubbing across her thigh put her right to sleep.

# Chapter 14: One-Man Council

Studd's day had been nothing but grief.

He'd spent the morning visiting families and issuing condolences. A'Kierra Jones's home was the worst so far. Piquette's report stated that their findings were inconclusive. Studd knew better; he needed to see the truth himself. He wasn't going to let DeathStar attack overshadow this missing case.

The aura he felt in that house was dark. He could feel the gloominess creeping up his neck like cold, bony fingers.

He knocked on the family's door and the father answered almost immediately. Studd was met by his grizzly appearance. Patches of hair were growing on his face, his eyesblood shot red and heavy with bags.

"Council man Studd, or—sorry Chief Studd please, please come in."

"Thank you, Mr. Jones. How you holding up?" he asked as he entered eyes sweeping the interior of the cluttered home.

"I'm hanging in there." Mr. Jones led Studd to the living room, "Please have a seat I'll get my wife. James!" he shouted, "The Chief is here!" Then he slipped into a room.

Moments later the father returned guiding out his lifeless wife by her shoulders. Her skin was pale, and her face was lifeless. Eyes vacant of any emotion, her mind had gone somewhere inside herself where no one could reach. At the same time James emerged from the kitchen carrying a tray of water and assorted meats.

James walked as steadily as he could, but a bit of the water spilled. The sound of the water splashing on the floor caught Mr. Jones' attention as he sat his wife down.

"Dammit James you need to be careful!" he barked marching over to him taking the tray from his hands, "Go get the rest of the food." He scowled balling up his lips.

Studd watched in disappointment as Mr. Jones brought the food over.

"Here you are Chief. These are some of the foods the local restaurants have been sending over please help yourself."

Studd looked at the tray then back at Mr. Jones, who seemed disturbed he couldn't keep still.

"Uh, my son will be right out with the rest of the food. James!" the father shouted again as he fidgeted. His arms kept changing positions as he paced the room.

Seconds later James emerged from the kitchen with another tray and set it in front of Studd. Studd watched as the sad boy refused to make eye contact with him.

"Thank you, kiddo." Studd said, but James ignored him by taking a seat next to his lifeless mother.

"So, Studd any news?" the father asked refusing to take a seat.

"Unfortunately, no, I have some bad news. The detectives on the case are no longer available. One detective was a victim in the attack and the other... well the other decided the job wasn't for her."

"W—what does that mean? So, no one is looking after her case? No one is looking for my daughter?"

"No, I didn't say that I have personally taken over this case over which is why I'm here. I just need to ask a few questions."

"Okay, great, stellar, go ahead."

"Well, for starters who was A'Kierra close to?"

"Uh, you know, uh A'Kierra didn't have many friends did she James?" Mr. Jones scratched his head.

James slowly shook his head while staring at the ground.

"Yeah," the father raked his finger through his hair, "I—you know I'm sorry Chief I just find this a bit ridiculous. Kude Island is supposed to be the city of the future. Yet you're telling me with all this super high grade tech you have zero leads on my daughter?" he began nibbling on his fingers.

"No sir that's not it at all I just need to gather all the necessary information most likely the people close to her would have vital information."

"I—I wouldn't know Chief. Uh I—sorry." He sighed pinching his nose, "You know what we... uh... we are going to have to cut this meeting short as you can see my wife is not doing too good. Please let me escort you out." He said already marching to the door.

Studd stood and glanced at the wife who hadn't moved an inch.

"Yes, Mr. Jones thank you for your time I'm sorry I couldn't be of much use, but I promise I will find your daughter." Studd followed behind him.

At the door he held out his hand, "Look Mr. Jones if there is anything you need you come talk to me you understand." Studd's voice swirled with concern and command.

Mr. Jones gripped his hand tight, "Yep." He responded voice breaking.

As Studd walked to his vehicle he felt a tug on his coat.

He turned and looked down; it was James holding up a to go plate.

"Hey kid what are you doing?"

"I saw A'Kierra go off into the woods with Violet and her friends," the boy whimpered. "A'Kierra said Violet bullied her."

"Violet? As is Violet Viller? Don't they go to the same school?"

James nodded, "Promise not to tell A'Kierra I said anything... She'd be mad."

"I promise kid," Studd responded taking the food, "Now hurry back and get home before your dad gets worried."

"My dad doesn't care about me, now that A'Kierra is gone."

Studd sighed and bent down on one knee, James still refused to look him in the eyes, "Look kid if there is anything you need to talk about you call up the Force headquarters and ask to speak to me you got that? The code word would be dragon scales okay?"

James nodded quietly.

"Okay pal now head back home." It was clear to Studd that the dad was on Gerthuim, but without proof or a complaint there was nothing he could do.

He knew of Violet Viller because of her family. He also knew the powerful Viller family wouldn't step foot inside Force Headquarters. So, he went to them.

The Viller estate laid beyond the Twin Cities. A neighborhood of extreme wealth that stood hidden behind a gate of trees beyond Red City.

Studd parked outside the towering gates of the Viller estate. He walked up to the intercom and lifted his Citizen Card to the camera, then pressed the button. "Chief Studd," he announced. "I'm here to speak with Violet Viller regarding a missing person investigation."

Without a response the gate buzzed and opened. The path leading to the front door felt like a mile.

The Roman style mansion stood flawless, guarded by towering limestone pillars and a wide staircase that led to an arched entrance. Pale stone tiles paved the courtyard in intricate patterns.

Before he could knock on the polished doors, the door swung open. Mrs. Viller greeted him with a seductive smile, her silky white robe hanging loosely over a matching slip dress trimmed in lace. Glossy black hair spilled down her back and over her shoulders.

"Well, hello, Chief Studd," she purred.

He cleared his throat, straightening his jacket. "Afternoon, Mrs. Viller."

"Please... call me Iris." She extended a perfectly manicured hand "Do come in."

Iris always had a thing for Studd. She thought he was the epitome of a man.

Studd took her hand briefly, then stepped past her perfume cloud. "Is Mr. Viller available? I'd like to speak with both of you, if possible."

She pouted. "Oh no, he's at work. It'll just be us." Her smile sharpened. "Come in. Sit, I'll fetch Violet."

The interior felt like stepping into the renaissance. Arched ceilings stretched high above. Polished marble floors reflected the glow of polished chandeliers, while towering bookshelves curved along the walls. The staircase, carved with swirling designs, headed upward to the upper floors.

Iris led him into the living room, which reminded him of royalty. At the center of the room sat a massive oak table. It rested between two silk-upholstered couches, imprinted with a shiny damask pattern, their frames carved from gold.

Studd sat on the pristine couch, eyes drawn to shelves of crystal décor and framed photos of Violet at galas and competitions.

"Violet!" Iris yelled up the stairs. "A detective is here for you!"

She returned, crossing her legs as she sat across from Studd. She poured water from a tiny vase into two crystal cups, making sure he noticed the movement of silk and skin.

He pretended not to. His eyes darted across the room, finding other things to focus on.

"This wouldn't be concerning the missing girl I saw on the news now, does it, detective? A'Kierra?" Iris presumed.

"Unfortunately, yes, it does," he answered.

Studd smiled cautiously, and he could tell she had taken a few sips of Pollen Port, an alcohol derived from pollen.

Moments later, he heard footsteps. Violet drifted down the stairs in pajamas and pink slippers, chewing gum, expression untouched by fear. She didn't greet him. She didn't even sit close to her mother. Instead, Violet flopped at the end of the couch and stared.

Studd didn't waste time.

"Hello Violet. I won't introduce myself because you already know who I am. Witnesses say A'Kierra was last seen sneaking off with other students after the Afterlife game. Do you know anything about that?"

"No," Violet answered flatly.

Iris shot her a warning look.

Studd leaned forward. "If I ask Luke, will he tell me the same?"

Violet's jaw twitched, anxiety rippled through her confident posture. It was easy for Studd to look up Violet's media pages to see who she was with the night of the championship game.

"I don't know what Luke would say," she muttered. "Ask him."

"Violet," Iris snapped. "If you know anything about the girl disappearing, you better tell the detective. Do you understand?"

"I said I don't know!" Violet's eyes watered, but the crocodile tears fooled no one.

Studd's tone softened. "I just came from A'Kierra's home. Her family isn't doing too good. James, her younger brother, can't even speak without breaking down. Her parents, I couldn't even begin to explain." He shook his head. "If you could just think of them."

Violet looked away, arms folded not knowing Studd already knew the truth.

Now, here he was watching Violet lie through polished teeth.

Iris stood abruptly. "Thank you, detective. As you can see, Violet has nothing further to add. Perhaps your source was... mistaken."

The warmth vanished from her demeanor. She tightened her robe, ushering him to the door with a firm hand between his shoulder blades as he stood.

"If you have more questions, do return... Preferably when my husband is home."

The door slammed behind him before he could respond.

After a short break and another meeting, Chief Studd rode the private beacon to the top of the court building, his tughra pinging him through each floor. The Council chamber opened: low light from hovering orbs, dark oak everywhere, and a long table veined with tiger's eye and brown topaz. Chairs curled like open hands rounded the table. At the far end, a dark pillar held a woman's holographic head—Aurora—eyes closed, waiting to be summoned.

The Council was composed of seven of Kude Island's most trusted citizens, elected by the people to serve a five-year term. They oversaw the island's legislators. The legislators are chosen by the people to act as their voice. They present the Council with data, statistics, and any complaints by the people. Eclipse Enterprises handle business operations and currency flow. The legislators worked closely with both parties.

In the corner of every Council Member's Citizen Card, a golden tughra burned with shifting fire, the royal insignia of the island's Founders. It represented authority.

For City of Light citizens, a radiant sunburst rested in the corner instead, it represented status and privilege. Only Level Five citizens could live in the dome-capped city and hold the symbol.

Eclipse Enterprises status was represented with a golden bar with three slits. As for legislators, they were depicted with the image of Maat, the goddess of law.

"Okay, everyone—emergency session is taking place," Studd started, taking his seat at the head of the table. "As you know, a terrorist attack killed eight hundred and eighty-six civilians and crippled Med Inc. We're here to decide how to move forward and how to fund reparations."

Edith Kimble lifted her chin proudly. "I've already compensated families with lifetime stays on Kude and two thousand gold coins."

General Skinner barked a laugh. The gold badges on his hat gleamed in the dim light. "Did you replace your brain with a rust bucket? Lifetime stays? Two thousand coins? You trying to paint blood on our doors?"

"Watch it," Studd cut in. "Drawing blood is your lane, General. Show some respect."

Athena Gray folded her arms, cool as marble. "Edith, I love the intent, but lifetime residency? We can't even grant that to ourselves. It's not legal, and it sets a precedent we can't defend."

Athena Gray. A sharp, formidable lawyer best known for winning the landmark case against the Canadian government when Kude Island stood accused of harboring fugitives. In her now-famous defense, she declared, "Kude Island is the land of the lost. It is where people fled after their own governments tried to kill them. We harbor the sick, the homeless, the needy, and the hurt. If the Canadian government believes we are harboring fugitives, then what does that say about them—are they a government or an anarchy? Are we harboring fugitives or prisoners of war?"

That single speech earned her a seat on The Council by popular vote. Athena, a height of 5'6" (5'9" in heels), always dressed impeccably in tailored suits. Golden skin with flawless, layered hair and a signature sweet scent that announced her presence before she spoke. Prim, precise, and commanding, she also served as counsel during Cy's case.

Garth McMallian cleared his throat. “The gesture’s noble, Doc, but if word gets out that tragedy equals a forever home, you’ll have people staging tragedies.”

Edith held their eyes, with her voice steady. “People are devastated. Money won’t bring anyone back, but it can keep their lives from collapsing. We need to show we value our citizens more than our ledgers.”

Skinner’s lip curled. “Newsflash, people die every day. Handing out treasure makes us look soft to the sharks circling our borders.”

“That’s what we want them to think,” Edith shot back. “Soft on the surface, steel underneath. We need to show the people and the world that we are one.”

Studd exhaled. “I agree with showing up for our people. But not with lifetime residency. No one gets that, not even City of Light. We also don’t rewrite foundational law in a panic.”

Athena nodded. “Agreed, let’s scale the stipend down. Create a relief package we can defend in court and on the streets.”

“I agree. Nothing lasts forever. No need to give people false light if we’re already in the abyss.” Lupe added, eager to leave.

“Two hundred gold per family. Six months rent-free where they already live. Free counseling through the Recovery Center. I think that’s something we all can agree on.” Studd scanned the room as the Council members nodded in agreement.

Studd glanced towards the pillar. “Aurora, record.”

The holographic head brightened, eyes opening. “Recording Council man Studd.”

“Let the record state that the year is 3147, moon cycle is waning. This is a vote regarding the care package for the families of the tragic Med Inc. explosion. All in favor of providing families two hundred gold coins each, no amnesty extension, and six months of free housing plus counseling through the Recovery Center—raise your hand.”

Hands rose around the table one by one except Edith's.

"Aurora?" Studd called.

"Motion passes: six to one," Aurora announced.

Edith met Studd's eyes, and he didn't look away. He searched her expression, trying to read the energy beneath her calm exterior. Desperate to understand what she needed from him. More than anything, he wanted to do right by her, to make choices that would earn her respect. One day even her heart.

"Anything else?" Zean Pierce asked from halfway down the table, quiet but firm. His blue-silver prosthetics peeked beneath the cuff of his jeans. "If not, my wife's on a rare night off. I'd like to catch bedtime."

Zean Pierce. The captain of the Red Team, a decorated war veteran from Ameris whose bravery had become legendary on the island. Years ago, he'd saved five children from a shark attack by throwing himself into its path, losing both of his legs in the process but killing the beast with his bare hands. The beaches of Kude Island were closed for many moon cycles after his incident. The shark's massive head now hung proudly on his wall, a reminder of both his sacrifice and his strength. Dr. Edith had performed the surgery that gave him his prosthetic legs. Despite his heroic past, Zean remained laid back and soft-spoken, preferring to avoid the spotlight.

"Adjourned," Studd announced. "The monthly session will resume on the full moon, unless we call another emergency."

Chairs scraped. Athena vanished down a side beacon. Garth clapped Zean's shoulder and left along with the other members. "Good game, Zean," Garth chipped, "Had a lot betting on you."

Edith lingered. Skinner did as well.

The general slid up to Studd, voice low. "Try not to let the good doctor's perfume fog your judgment. You're here to uphold the law, not chase a crush."

General Ivan Skinner. Beyond his role as warden, he served as Chief advisor for the island's tactical defense operations, often shaping policies that balanced on the edge of morality and necessity. Skinner was infamous for his ruthless discipline methods: physical labor was mandatory, and the island's farms and recycling plants thrived on inmate manpower. The approach, controversial as it was, boasted a 62% rehabilitation success rate—one of the highest in the hemisphere. Still, whispers followed him everywhere: rumors of humiliation rituals, sensory deprivation, and mind-altering compounds used to "break" the most violent offenders. No one ever proved any of it, but the haunted eyes of those who left Gravity Grave said a lot.

Studd smiled without warmth. "Says the man leashed to Malcolm Booker."

Skinner's eyes glittered. "Someone sounds jealous I took their best worker."

Studd's smile faded. "What are you talking about?"

"Oh, she didn't tell you?" Skinner's grin was slow and ugly. "Piquette came down to Gravity Grave and begged me for a job. I don't need her, but I found room. Conditions on your Force must be unbearable. Don't worry she'll fit right in."

Studd's jaw tightened. "The grave isn't a transfer. It's a demotion."

Skinner shrugged, leaning in. "Not when it's a stepping-stone. As Chief of Defense, I take it upon myself to do whatever's necessary, even if it means contacting ghosts."

"Ghosts?" Studd's brow furrowed. The word sent a ripple of unease through his chest. *Whatever that meant, it meant nothing good.*

Skinner had certain privileges in his position, but even he couldn't make a move without approval from the Council. This raised suspicions in Studd.

He narrowed his eyes at Skinner. "Get out of my chamber, General."

Skinner left with a grin carved across his face, the heavy thud of his boots echoing on the oak floor long after he was gone.

Edith stepped in as the echo died. "Thank you," she said softly. "For the package and for not letting them turn this into numbers."

"Someone had to keep the floor from falling out," he chuckled, studying the tired brightness in her eyes. "Dinner?"

For a moment, silence stretched between them, a silence that said more than either of them dared to. Their bodies spoke the words their mouths didn't. His eyes lingered, searching hers for a sign.

With a slow smile, she finally replied, "My place. You bring the wine. I'll bring the view."

"Done," he beamed. As they walked toward the beacon, their hands brushed for the briefest second neither of them pulling away.

By the time Studd hit street level, he was already in motion, jacket zipped, mind shifting lanes. Eclipse Enterprises headquarters tower rose like a black blade. A handler in a razor-cut suit waited in front of the building.

"Chief Studd—this way."

Studd didn't bother with pleasantries. Security gates parted for them as they strolled through the halls; the beacon spat them out on the twenty-first floor into a boardroom that smelled faintly of sweat. Dozens of investors, all shine and nerves, turned as one when he stepped into the room.

Studd groaned the moment he stepped into the boardroom, a wall of suits and expectant eyes staring back at him.

"Oh, you've got to be kidding me," he snarled, slapping his knee in exasperation. "I thought this was a briefing, not a stockholder circus. We could have done this over holo."

"Chief Studd," one investor stated nervously, "the board is... concerned. They just want to discuss the future of business on the island."

"Business?" Studd barked a short, humorless laugh. "Business hasn't changed. We're still a functioning island with almost two million people depending on us." He stepped forward, addressing the room with authority. "Med Inc. is down yes, but I'm meeting with its owner to discuss next steps. All operations remain internal, as they always have. PortMaster will continue for travel, but for now, keep trades as low as possible for Med Inc.. Honestly, we should extinguish all trades with the company until we sort this mess out. For right now let's boost small tech companies and metal shops. Get creative. I'll send some detectives who are pros with business to help out."

A murmur rippled through the crowd, but their anxious expressions softened into something closer to relief. Studd took that as his cue to leave.

"Good. Then we're done here," he said, "I have more important matters to deal with."

# Chapter 15: Ghost Veins

Piquette staggered from the pod, barely conscious. The border shield opened upon her arrival in the same spot Skinner saw her off. She mounted her cycle, gripping the handlebars with trembling fingers. Somehow with pure instinct she made it home.

By the time she reached the stairs to her apartment, her body was drenched in sweat. She was starving, an animalistic hunger, and her mouth was bone-dry despite the sweat dripping down her lips. Every nerve screamed.

She placed her thumb on the scanner; it buzzed twice due to the sweat. she broke the door open with her shoulder. Her vision blurred in and out of focus. She tore off her jacket, stumbling toward the bathroom.

"Aaahhh—!"

The yell ripped out of her as she collapsed.

She crashed into the carpet, clutching both sides of her head. A shrill ringing screamed inside her skull, like metal scraping inside her brain. Her teeth clenched so hard, her jaw almost cracked. She spat out saliva, trying to keep from drowning in her own spit.

Darkness swallowed her. As she fell into a deep sleep, the dead approached her.

A'Kierra's hollow eyes stared inches from her face. Then her voice came.

"You did this...You killed me...Why?"

Ghost-like hands reached for her. Then she heard her mother's voice, a voice she hadn't heard for years, and it sounded the same as it did in the home videos. Then a deafening screech broke free.

Piquette jolted awake.

Her heart thundered. Nightclothes clung to her skin from the sweat. The blanket was neatly draped over her. She stared down at her shaking hands.

"How did I get in bed?" her words slurred.

She turned to her clock; she'd been asleep for hours but her dream lasted seconds.

A sharp pain stabbed the back of her neck.

She gasped and pressed her palm there. There was a cyst that felt hot, and swollen with fluid. But even worse she could feel something moving, like tiny worms swimming beneath the skin.

"No..." Her voice broke in horror.

Pulling the blanket off, she rushed to the bathroom.

She stared into the mirror. Her hair was wild, her pupils blown wide. Pulling out her med kit from the cabinet, she grabbed a scalpel. Her breath stuttered. Steadying her hand, she reached back and with a deep breath she pressed down with the blade.

Blood and pus spilled. She dug her finger in, screaming in agony until she felt it: a chip. Fine metal wires curled into her veins like parasitic roots.

She yanked, grunting in pain as the wires tried to stay latched.

"Ahhhh!"

And with a violent snap the wires tore free.

She collapsed forward, panting, the chip writhing in her palm like a mechanical insect desperate to live.

It slithered out of her hand into the porcelain sink.

"No, no, no." she panicked.

She slammed a glass cup down on it again and again until it was dust.

Blood dripped down her back, staining her waistband. She stumbled for her bandage kit, hands stained with blood. Inside she grabbed an antiseptic bio-foam.

She sprayed it directly on the wound.

"Hhh—AAAH!"

The foam sizzled as it sealed the wound, burning hot like fire.

The pain was too intense, causing her vision to blur. She slid down the wall fighting to keep her eyes open.

# Chapter 16: *Pretty Bars*

It had been a while since Isis's release, and freedom felt like a costume. She and Trinity were now living in a one-bedroom apartment in the slums of Quadrant Four. Trinity got the bedroom, and Isis slept in the living room. Though most nights, sleep didn't visit her.

Tonight, the terrors came early. The heat under her skin and static in her ears tortured her. Her eyelids wouldn't stop twitching. She couldn't remember where she'd put her last pill. The apartment looked like a tornado hit. Drawers pulled wide open, blankets flung, chairs were flipped.

Luckily, Quadrant Four had one reliable kindness. You could always find something to numb you.

She threw on her jacket and cracked Trinity's door. The girl was fast asleep. With that done, she headed out into the night, where Quad Four truly came alive.

The streets glowed with dark purple and blue lights, which matched the gloomy atmosphere. Peebles shook to the base of the music as she strolled through the streets. The smell of deep-fried food filled her nose. She pulled up her hood to hide her messy hair and sweaty, pale skin.

Her destination: Ripe Whispers. The club rose like a black pyramid, its metallic blades shining under the moonlight. A holographic eye floated above, blinking as it watched below.

Tonight, the line was long, but as a club member, Isis could walk right in after pricking her finger with her special knife and placing a drop of blood on the biometric sensor.

Inside, the lighting was low, with streaks of teal and purple sweeping through the crowd. The floor panels bloomed with black petals under every step. The music roared through her body; her heartbeat matched the thumps.

Prism's section sat at the back, roped off with light. He wore an all-black Synthix tux, posture loose and eyes dark as obsidian. Thick, predatory brows framed his face, which was carved into a permanent scowl. His oak skin, oiled with moisture.

Rumors said the third floor was a revival chamber where he staged death and rebirth on a loop for anyone who crossed him. The rumors felt right.

Isis approached with caution, slipping on an earpiece from a glass bowl. The noise of the club went dull.

> "Prism. I need another dose," she stated tugging her hood lower.

He signaled for her to come over with his finger. Isis kept calm and climbed over the light beam separating him and the crowd. She sat next to him, leaving some space. He closed it and wrapped his arm around her shoulder.

"You know what I find strange?" He inched closer to her face. "Last time I saw you was over a month ago, and you only purchased two sleeping pills... I know you're not buying from my other competitors because... well, I would know. So, how do you stay medicated if you're not constantly re-upping?" His thumb skimmed her sweaty jaw.

Her words scattered as she flinched, "I—uh. I—"

"My formula is hard to recreate," he went on. "It's a one-in-the-universe kind of drug. And the devil knows I hate a thief." His lips pursed together.

He studied her long enough to make her bones itch, then palmed a clear capsule from his pocket. The substance inside looked like a trapped galaxy.

"Before I give you a refill, I want you to be the test bunny for a new substance." Prism said, easing the tension in his body.

"Oh, no. Prism, I just came here for—"

"I'm not asking." He pressed his palm against her skull.

Isis knew she had no choice; she wanted more sleeping pills. "What does it do?"

"Take it and find out, but let's get something straight: if I find out you're buying from someone else or trying to recreate my formula, there will be death to pay."

Isis took a moment to contemplate. Snatching the pill from his hand, she tossed it back. It dissolved into a fizz that coated her gums and lit her nerves on fire. Warmth spilled down her throat, then weightlessness took over her body. Invisible threads clinching around her skull like they were clinching every thought. The club shifted planes.

People unraveled into geometry—bodies became colored shapes, faces turned to patterns and spirals. A yellow triangle pulsed at the edge of her vision and spoke.

"Breathe," the yellow triangle vibrated. "In. Out."

Her own thoughts went thin, then vanished. She tore out the earpiece and lurched to her feet, colliding with drifting hexagons and rolling spheres where people should have been.

She moved through the streets with her kaleidoscope shaped vision. She felt the floor thump with the Earth's heartbeat. Colors she didn't have names for twisted in the air. Every few steps, the world reassembled itself differently.

When the comedown finally found her, she was face down in a puddle of water. She clutched her skull and screamed in agony as a Med-Bot approached, lights soft.

"Your pain receptors are ignited. Shall I arrange transport to the Recovery Center?"

"No," she rasped.

"Noted. Distressed citizen #4027 declined medical attention." The bot pivoted away.

She staggered home, skimming the walls for direction and support. Sweat soaked through her sweater. She pushed into the apartment sinking to her knees. She crawled to the bedroom door and weakly reached for the handle opening the door. Her stomach sank at the sight. Trinity's bed was empty. She gasped as her eyes widened in fear.

Reality set back in and her symptoms took a back seat. Isis tore through the apartment complex, checking every stairwell and shadowed corner. She then moved on to the usual teen hangouts. The café and game room, still no Trinity.

At last, she spotted Trinity at the Quadrant Lagoon, lounging with a pack of kids. Her toes skimmed the glowing water as she sipped a bottle of catnip—the island's mellow, citrus-tinged alcohol. Laughter echoed across the lagoon as hoverboards drifted over the water's surface. Music roared from a portable speaker.

"Trinity," she panted approaching the group of teens. "You... need to come home... now."

Their conversations faded away. Trinity went still. For a beat, she pretended not to hear. Her aunt looked wrecked. Glassy eyes and sweaty, a dead giveaway she was high, or coming down from one.

"Now, Trinity!" Isis found the strength to throw her voice.

Whispers trickled through the group. Trinity stood barefoot, grabbed her shoes, brushed past Isis with her shoulder. Isis stumbled into a bow, "Performance over kids."

Trinity marched barefoot back to the apartment. Each stomp was harder than the last. Isis trailed along in a much better mood now that she had located Trinity.

"You just embarrassed me in front of all my friends!" Trinity cried, hurling her shoes to the ground.

"Oh, please. They aren't your friends." Isis scoffed weakly. "You have no friends." Clinging to the walls for support, she collapsed on the couch.

"And you're high, again!" Trinity threw up her hands.

Isis hunched over and projectile vomited on the floor. "Ahh... Not anymore." She smiled weakly, wiping her mouth.

"Are you okay?" Trinity rushed over to her side.

Isis nuzzled her back. "I'm fine." She stood trying to steady herself.

"In fact, I'm feeling much better. I don't want you hanging out with those kids anymore. They're no good."

"The last person to give a lecture is you. You're gone all hours of the night but then want to lecture me about hanging around the wrong crowd," Trinity spoke softly. "You think I don't know what it is you do when you're gone?"

"I don't care, Trinity!" Isis exploded. "Goodness! Look, the next time I see you hanging around those kids, I swear to everything on the planet I will lock you in your room until you're fifty! Now, go to bed!"

As long as Trinity was away from anything that could cause her trouble, Isis didn't care. Someone had to be the bad guy. Trinity was too vulnerable. The last thing she needed was for her to get locked away; that would probably expose their secret. *Trinity can't become uncontrollable.*

Trinity's eyes twinkled with tears. Heartbroken, she slammed the door shut and turned the lock.

Isis shuffled to the bathroom and stripped for a long, hot shower. As she undressed, a small capsule slid out of her sweater pocket and clinked on the floor tile.

She reached down. *One sleeping pill ...*

Trinity stared out her window, watching her friends laugh and giggle as they lit small rockets and used luminous rocks to make crude energy beams. She couldn't help but to laugh—the property manager would come storming out any minute now to chase them off. But the smile faded as quickly as it came.

After being caught sneaking out again, Isis installed laser beams on the windows and locked Trinity's bedroom door with a puzzle lock that activated at night. Though she was free to leave during the day, she still felt like a prisoner on borrowed time. If she wasn't home before the sun dipped below the skyline, Isis would go ballistic.

The relationship they once had no longer existed. Now their conversations were reduced to dull exchanges—"Hi." "What's for dinner?" "Can I have token money?"

No laughter or warmth. It was soul crushing. Trinity didn't even have the energy to argue anymore. She just let Isis take control.

At least Isis wasn't home as much now that she had a new job. But even in her absence, Trinity often found herself trapped inside, unable to leave her room most days of her own will. The psychological weight of Isis's rules had settled deep into her bones.

In the last few weeks, however, Isis had been more upbeat. At dinner one night, she made a big announcement.

"I know we've been stuck in a dark pit for a while, but I have some good news," she smiled with delight.

Trinity didn't lift her head. She just pushed the food around her plate.

"Cy is being released in the next few weeks!"

Trinity's stomach sank. *Oh, no. Not him. Cy is all she ever talks about.*

Isis saw a lack of enthusiasm on her niece's face but pressed on. "And guess what? He bought us a new place in the Third Quadrant."

"What, really?" Trinity glanced up. For the first time in a long time, a flicker of hope returned. *The Third Quadrant? That's like City of Light for Shadow Land.*

"That's right, baby. I know I've been keeping you cooped up, but trust me—it was for your safety. But now that we're getting out of Quad Four, I promise you'll have more freedom. You've grown a lot, and I trust you to make the right decisions."

Color crept back into Trinity's skin, and the corners of her mouth twitched upward.

Isis made hard choices, choices that had cost them their relationship. But she still believed they were for the right reasons.

"Trinity," she declared, gripping her niece's fingers tightly, "we're going to be a family again."

# Chapter 17: Split Tails

Although this wasn't her first time at Ruby Palace, the excitement buzzing through her veins was undeniable. She had visited once on a field trip, but they had only allowed them on the first floor. Another time, she'd come for Isis's birthday dinner—they'd sat on the third floor because according to Isis, anything beyond that tasted dreadful. Then of course she came upon Isis's release.

The building itself was carved as a palace six stories tall, carved from mahogany and ruby stone, its surface streaked with veins of dark crimson acrylic. Gold cursive writing spelled "Ruby Palace" above the entrance, glowing under a warm light.

A grand staircase, lined with golden railings, led to towering red double doors framed in intricate gold trim. The copper handles shined from the light poles on either side of the door.

Trinity grabbed the handle and stepped inside, instantly surrounded by the tantalizing aroma of exotic spices. A dark crimson carpet stretched toward the host desk, encircled by round tables draped in black cloth and enclosed by elegant wooden railings.

"Cheers, I have a nine o'clock reservation. Name's Trinity," she told the hostess.

"Yes, right this way, Trinity," the hostess replied with a warm smile, dressed in a dark red suit.

She led Trinity to a beacon and pressed the button for the sixth floor—a gold, cursive 6 etched into the panel. Trinity's fingers trembled with anticipation. The higher they ascended, the stronger the fragrance grew.

The beacon dinged. When the doors opened, her breath caught in her throat.

The sixth floor was breathtaking—a heavenly realm on Earth. Floor-to-ceiling windows framed in gold stretched across the walls, adorned with flowing red silk curtains. Angels adrift in space, gliding through swirling gold clouds, painted the ceiling. Ruby chandeliers hung linked with ruby chains.

Enormous, white feathered fans waved gently in the corners of the room, and rose petals drifted down from above, vanishing before they touched the ground. The kitchen was fully visible behind a glass wall, chefs moving like dancers in a culinary ballet. A piano played on a short stage.

At the center of it all stood a towering statue of a female centaur wielding a spear, frozen in mid-charge. Tables surrounded it, their conversations in low elegant chirps.

The hostess led Trinity past the crowded main floor and up a set of stairs to a raised, round platform by the window.

And there he sat, the same man from earlier.

Time slowed as her heartbeat quickened. She wiped her sweaty palms on her thighs as she approached.

He sat waiting with a bottle of wine, two crystal glasses, plates, napkins, and an assortment of silverware. When he saw her, he rose and extended his hand.

"Hello," Trinity said softly, placing her hand in his. She suddenly wondered if she'd dressed too casually for the occasion. His dark blue suit screamed high class. She hadn't expected to be seated on the sixth floor.

"Enjoy your meal," the hostess called as she departed.

"Hello, Trinity. It's so nice to meet you again." He gave her hand a gentle squeeze before they both sat down. "Tell me, what made you decide to come see me?" he queried, smoothing the wrinkles from the tablecloth with practiced grace.

Trinity inhaled deeply before answering. "I've never met any family outside of Isis and my parents. I'm eager to see who you are and maybe learn more about where I come from."

He chuckled warmly, though something in his gaze flickered beneath the charm. "I'm at a loss for words. I wasn't expecting you to be so eager, Trinity." His voice softened. "I'm here to tell you the complete truth about who you are, and about our family."

His eyes glistened as he placed a hand over his heart.

A tall man dressed in a tuxedo with a golden Synthix vest and matching gloves approached the table.

"Hello, I am your server for the night. Appetizers will be right out. May I get your preferred drinks?"

Trinity wondered which part of the world he was from, his thick accent sounded French to her guess.

"Yes, I'll just have water with Lyris," Uncle ordered.

"I'll just have a watermelon cherry fizz with nitro ice, please," Trinity ordered. "But may I have a menu?"

"We don't have menus on the sixth floor, madam. This fine gentleman chose a theme for tonight's seven-course meal: Sea Breeze, which means all your meals will be seafood-based. Your first appetizer will be fresh shrimp with a spicy curry-basil dip and crispy citrus chips. I will bring that along with your drinks." He bowed and walked away, stiff but swift.

"I haven't had the Sea Breeze menu in a very long time," Uncle asserted. "I thought sharing it with you would be refreshing."

"Yeah, that works out great. I haven't had seafood in a while. Cy usually only cooks duck or turkey."

"Oh, really? Why is that?"

"He believes other meats are obsolete." She grinned at the thought of Cy.

"Would you say that you're happy at home?" Uncle probed.

Trinity felt awkward. *Why the vex is he asking that?* She'd come here to get a break from Isis and her badgering. She could still feel the sting of the slap. The cut on her lip had vanished without her realizing.

Taking a sip of water from the glass already on the table, she answered. "Uh, yeah. Mostly." *Right now is not the time for a sob story.*

"Really? And how's Isis? She's grown so much since I last saw her."

Trinity traced the rim of the glass with her finger, avoiding eye contact. "I really don't want to talk about *her* right now." She sulked.

"Why don't we talk about you? What kind of business do you do, and are you really my uncle?" Her voice leaned into curiosity. Getting as much information was vital, who knew how long he'd stick around.

The server returned with a tray, his accent even thicker. "'Ello, madam and monsieur. Your Lyris water and watermelon cherry fizz." Mist trailed from the nitrogen ice as he set down Trinity's drink. "Your appetizer for tonight," he stated, setting the plates on the table.

Cracked with gold, the plates were deep red. Shrimp whiskers decorated the rims, making the plate rresemble a cage. The food rotated slowly as hot smoke rose in a small tornado.

"This is super fancy," Trinity beamed, eyes twinkling as she clasped her hands together, gazing at the dish like it was a pot of stardust.

"Trinity, I know all this must be confusing, but trust me when I say our family has always had it hard. I was always away doing business, and now that I've become successful, I finally have the freedom to come back for my niece and my sister." Uncle couldn't take his eyes off her. He marveled at how much she'd grown—and was surprised she hadn't died yet.

"Are you going to answer my question?" Trinity asked as she picked up a massive shrimp dripping with sauce. "Jupiter's rainstorm—this is cosmic! You've got to try this." She lost her train of thought mid-bite.

Uncle chuckled. "No, thanks. This entire dinner is for you."

There was a moment of silence as Trinity devoured shrimp after shrimp.

"How about this?" Uncle suggested. "For each meal, you can ask me one question. And I get to ask you one back."

"Okay, deal." Trinity immediately covered her mouth. "Does the appetizer count?"

"Yes. And you already asked me a question. You asked what kind of business I do."

Before she knew it, her plate was empty, and the second appetizer was on its way.

The server presented the next course on a clear plate. Inside, flower petals shaped like hearts floated in a clear liquid. "Appetizer two: flower salad composed of sunflower, hibiscus, roses, and teressed, served with an apple-and-pear champagne vinaigrette."

Teressed was a small, round green flower. People classified it as an herb similar to fennel because its tiny seeds were edible. The flower had a zingy, earthy taste.

Trinity didn't want to scare Uncle away, so she kept her questions vague.

"So, where's the proof that you're my uncle?"

Uncle's face brightened as he shifted his body. "Of course. Your mother, Liberty—she was the oldest. We had another sister, Angel, and Isis was the youngest. Our parents didn't plan for Isis; she kind of just happened, a surprise to us all. Your mother became pregnant with you not long after. Our mother, your grandmother, her name was Neffi. And we also had a brother named Jah, born after Liberty," he outlined, still refusing to eat. "Our father, Ka, was an astonishing man. Everyone admired him."

Astonishment washed over Trinity. Her mother's name *was* Liberty. Her mother used to tell stories about her father, Ka. It was one of the few memories Trinity had of her parents. *Isis said mom had been a daddy's girl, spoke about him every chance she got.*

"Oh, and how could I forget." Uncle pulled out a tiny metal box from his jacket pocket, opened the lid and pressed a button on the side. A hologram appeared—a photo of him, Liberty, Trinity's father, Isis, and baby Trinity.

They were on a rocky mountain. The background was eerie, full of mist. Liberty was holding baby Trinity in one arm and Isis's with the other. Isis grinned widely and wrapped her arms around Liberty's leg. Trinity's father's arms were around Liberty, and beside them stood Uncle. Oddly, he was in a suit while everyone else wore drape-like clothing. It fueled her curiosity.

"Oh, heavens!" Trinity yelped. "I've never seen this photo. Aw, they look so young! We all look so young." Her eyes darted across the image, studying every crevice. *We all look so happy. What happened? Where were we?*

"Keep it. It's yours." He closed the box and placed it on the table. "How long have you and Isis been on your own?"

Her expression shifted as she tucked the box into her purse. Her smile flattened. She cleared her throat. "After what happened to my parents, they sent us to placement homes. We bounced around for a while. Then Isis spent four years at the girls' school because she went on a crazy crime spree. When that happened, they took me away from our last placement mother. She was the best one I ever had. But the Force decided that since Mother June allowed Isis to commit crimes under her care, she wasn't a good fit. I felt so bad—Mother June was so heartbroken. Anyway last year, Isis became my guardian after her release."

"Trinity, I'm sorry you had to go through that."

"It's stellar. I'm over it now. Those days are behind me. And honestly? It wasn't all bad. I had some fun and met some friends."

The server returned to refill Trinity's drink, then came back with the next course.

"Meal one: lobster claw sliders braised in lemon and herb butter on a brioche bun, spread with caviar garlic aioli and served with a side of purple pepper fries all presented in a large clam shell."

Kude Island was home to over 150,000 native species of plants, herbs, flowers, vegetables, fruits, and trees. No meal ever tasted the same. Balancing flavors always challenged the chefs, but Ruby Palace delivered dishes that were complex yet never overcomplicated.

"How did you find us?" Trinity pursued, picking up the bun and taking a bite. "Oh, my—" She closed her eyes as the food sent her into a trance.

"Seeing that I am part-owner of Med Inc., I can find anybody. After a lengthy recovery from the explosion, I tried to track you girls down but had no luck. Then I had to travel overseas. When I returned to the island, the Force wouldn't release any information. But finding you again... it's as if fate brought us together. Your mother would have wanted me to find you," he affirmed.

"Wait," she said between bites, "you never answered my first question. What do you do for a living? Being part-owner of Med Inc. is prestigious. But lots of people have investments in that place."

Trinity didn't mean to sound insensitive, but it was true. Med Inc. was a strong branch in the financial system.

"Let's just say I give people the resources to build the future they dream of. Sometimes they succeed, sometimes they burn out. Either way, I make sure their potential doesn't go to waste," he stated.

"Interesting. So, you're some kind of rich System Saver who helps people and whatnot," Trinity joked.

"I guess you could say that. I try to give people the opportunity to build and create. This new world has so much potential."

The server approached again once Trinity's clam was empty and presented the next meal.

"Meal two: shrimp gumbo poured into a hollow crab shell, rich with wine and spice. The broth is steaming with the scent of the sea. The dish includes whole grain rice, turkey sausage, orange corn, purple carrots, and garlic croutons." He bowed as he set the shells down.

"This smells like perfection," Trinity happily sighed, closing her eyes and following the steam with her nose. She took a spoonful of gumbo and instantly melted. The warm broth coated her insides, and she felt at peace.

"This food... it feels like it's healing all my problems."

Uncle finally took a sip of soup himself. Both ate in silence as they savored the flavor and the moment.

"You didn't want to attend any higher mastery schools?" he asked.

"No. I finished mandated schooling though." She dabbed the corners of her mouth with a napkin. "When Mother June took us in, she tried to teach us chemistry and plant science, but we just enjoyed playing in the fields of flowers." She chuckled, remembering herself and Isis running through clouds of pollen. "I just decided school wasn't my thing," she added, returning to her food. "What else do you own besides Med Inc.?"

"For starters, you're in one of my fine establishments right now."

"Seriously? You own Ruby Palace?" Her spoon clattered against the shell. *My uncle's a golden goose.*

"Yes. I also have some clubs in Red City and other investments that would likely bore you. As a silent partner, my ownership is unknown. I'd like to keep it that way." He pressed a finger to his lips.

After they finished their meals, the server presented the next course.

"Meal three: seafood pizza with lobster and shrimp on a lobster-oil-and-quail-egg-infused dough, served with squid ink tomato sauce. From now on, I will serve you on edible gold dishware." He bowed.

Uncle could see Trinity was more relaxed now—the perfect time to strike.

"Trinity, this next question is very important," he phrased carefully. "Trinity... what if you didn't have to go back home? Would you consider living with me?" He pressed his lips together, hands clasped, his plea soft but deliberate—reeling her in.

"What?" All the noise in the restaurant vanished, and Trinity's smile disappeared. *Is he mental?*

"Would you like to live with me?" he repeated softly.

Just then, the alarm on Trinity's Tabs went off. "Oh, vex!" she fumbled, pulling them out of her purse. It was a special alert that triggered when she'd missed too many messages from Isis.

She stretched the screen open. Four missed calls. One voice message. Twenty unread texts.

She clicked one.

*"You better bring your butt home right now, Trinity, and I mean it. You think this is some sort of game? What the Pluto pit of ice is wrong with you? I hope to whatever gods are out there you better not be where I think you are. Come home. Now!"*

Her eyes widened as panic set in. The words on the screen blurred, every missed call stabbing her in the chest—reminders of how easily Isis had control over her. But Isis's control felt like a leash tightening around her throat, a constant reminder that no matter how far she ran, she was never truly free and that was far more terrifying than any threat.

"I have to go," she whispered, slowly rising to her feet.

"But wait just one second," he pleaded, reaching gently for her hand.

She pulled away. "I... I don't know. It's just a lot right now, sorry. And I mean I can't just move in with you. I barely know you," she stammered. *What a whirl the last moon has been, an unexpected second chance of life now an uncle. This must be too good to be true.*

"Please, just—you're already out, so you might as well stay for the full course meal. Trinity, you're old enough now to make your own choices, don't you think? Isis should know that by now," Uncle said, trying to convince her to stay. He knew that was the only reason she was leaving so suddenly.

Her instincts screamed, leave now. But curiosity whispered louder. *Maybe one more question. Perhaps dessert. If I stayed a little longer, I could finally understand who I am.* Reassuring herself, she slid back into her seat.

"Sure, whatever. What's the worst that could happen?"

*For now, Isis can wait. But could I really trust a stranger?*

"Dessert one," the server announced. "Colorful candied coral."

The coral was bright pink and red under a coat of burnt sugar.

"Candy coral? I thought they banned this stuff!" Trinity beamed.

"No, not banned. Just very hard to find." Uncle's shoulders relaxed slightly, though his posture remained tense.

"Tell me about Isis. How was she like as a baby?" Trinity wondered, crunching on the sweet coral nuggets.

"Ah, everybody adored Isis. She *was* the baby of the family." Uncle tapped his finger on the table as he stared into the past, grinning. "Everyone always spoiled her and put her on the throne. Dad gave her anything she wanted. She was a good listener and followed instructions well. She would've been a wonderful leader," he proclaimed, adjusting himself and crossing his legs. "But she was always quiet, it's strange. I remember one time I left her in my room while I went to my studies. I had forgotten all about her, and when

I came back hours later, she was still in the same spot. She hadn't moved an inch."

*Why is he talking like that? Throne? Leader? There is no possible way. It must be code for something.* Trinity had checked out a while ago. The conversation was mentally draining. Her head ached, and the thought of Isis waiting for her at home made it hard to focus.

She flagged down a passing server. "Actually, I think I'll take my last dessert to go. I want to request the Golden Frost Delight, please. Oh—and some extra candied coral on the side. Thanks."

"Listen, Trinity," Uncle perched, leaning in. "Before you go, I want you to know this—I want you to live with me because I want my family back. I would invite Isis, but she doesn't seem like the type to react positively to the idea. Think about it; I can open so many doors for you. I know it's a lot to take in but just think about it."

He reached into his jacket pocket and pulled out a small, thin rectangular stone. Carved in the center was a compass.

"This is a key to my personal home. The compass will guide you there. Go to the end of the forest; past Olympus, there is a path. Start there and always follow the red arrow, it will guide you." He pointed.

The compass-key was heavy and cold. It pressed into her palm. Whatever path it pointed to, there would be no turning back. She stared at it; it could either be a key to her freedom or destruction. Trinity slipped it into her purse and waited for dessert.

"Hey... what's your name, anyway?" she inquired.

"Booker. Malcolm Booker."

# Chapter 18: *Can You Stand the Rain*

Trinity had now been at the placement home for almost a year, and things were finally feeling normal. The children stopped teasing her. Zimbria barely even looked her way. Her relationship with Zion grew as they spent every waking moment together. He began speaking to her more, telling her stories about his previous placement homes and why he was always so quiet.

"I don't know, talking to people who aren't important seems like a waste of time." He told her once.

Like every other night, Trinity laid in bed thinking of him as it rained. Trinity loved the rain, especially thunderstorms. The soothing sound always put her to sleep. She would close her eyes to the howling sounds of the wind and patter of the raindrops against her window. Instantly she would fall asleep.

Tonight was a special one because the lightning bolts spelled her name in the sky, at least that's what Trinity saw. With no one around to confirm she wasn't sure her eyes were telling the truth. With her happy thoughts she fell into a deep sleep.

The same night Zion tossed and turned in his bed. It took a few hours to fall asleep and once he did, he experienced a vivid dream.

He and Trinity were empaths, set out to save the world from an impending doom. A demon made love to a human, the result: an evil egg. He and Trinity were the only ones who could locate the egg. Because of their power, a secret government agency was after them, using them to be lured to the egg. Zion and Trinity were successful in their hunt. But Trinity was taken captive by the agents and told Zion if he wanted to be with Trinity again, he would have to give up the egg. Trinity pleaded with Zion through their empathic ways for him not to.

Zion raided the agents building and caused chaos until he reached the thirtieth floor where Trinity was held hostage. That's when a gas was released to stop him in his tracks. Thanks to the smell of the egg Zion retained his consciousness. Surrounded by agents he knew he had no choice. He stuffed the egg down his mouth with results not of his death, but his rebirth. His body literally became mother nature and transformed into thick vines. With his new power he used it to rescue Trinity.

Then he woke up. He didn't know why this dream came to him or what it meant. He brushed it off as his brain trying to configure to his insecurities about love and being loved. He lay wake, string at the ceiling unable to fall asleep. Then from the corner of his eye, he swore he saw a familiar shadow crossing his window. Then the curtain swayed as if the wind blew, but his window was sealed.

He threw back the covers and stood. He slowly pulled back the curtain, allowing only one eye to peek through.

And there she was. She looked like an angel for a fleeting second.

Trinity stood outside on the roof, in the pouring rain; her arms open as if she were sacrificing her body to the sky gods. Zion stared in awe and disbelief. He inched closer for a better view. *There's no way that's Trinity.*

Then a lightning bolt struck her body. Her head snapped in his direction, their eyes meeting.

Her eyes glowed bright white, the veins on her face glowed. Zion gasped and instantly scrambled under his covers in terror. *No this can't be true, it just can't be.*

He was shaking so badly he could barely breathe. He stayed awake the entire night, too nervous to sleep. Only when the sun rose did his eyes finally close. Just as he drifted into sleep, he was suddenly shaken awake.

"Zion!" he heard a voice call.

It was Trinity. He peeled back the covers to see Trinity standing beside his bed. At the sight of her, he wasn't sure how to react. He wasn't even sure what he saw was real. He just stared at her as his thoughts swirled.

"Zion?" Trinity said softly.

"What's wrong? Did you have a nightmare?" she asked, placing her hand on the edge of his bed.

Zion looked down and pulled his legs away unintentionally. Trinity instantly frowned and took a step back.

"Uh, sorry. Yeah, I had a bad nightmare. Spooked me something crazy." He scoffed.

"I just don't want to talk about it."

"It's okay. You don't have to," she said gently. "Anyway, I came to tell you breakfast is ready."

Trinity could see the look in his eyes, one she had seen before. He wasn't afraid of a nightmare. He was afraid of her, she just didn't know why, and that was the worst part.

"Cosmic," Zion said nervously. "I'll be right down."

After what he saw last night, he had a new theory. His dream must have been a cryptic message.

He always thought Trinity was special, like superhero in comic books. The way animals flocked to her. Her undeniable strength, but she was oblivious to all of it, so he let her grace in her ignorance. He wasn't sure if she remembered last night and was contemplating if he should bring it up.

Trinity sat at their table already starting on her breakfast when Zion finally joined.

"Do you feel better?" she asked as he took a seat.

"Yeah." He answered flatly.

Trinity rolled her eyes as the pair ate in silence. But the silence was undoubtedly filled with pins and needles. The pair have been in disagreements before. Like when Trinity ate the last of his snack bar, or when he earned an extra free day and left her in the house. Or when Trinity would cause trouble at the arcade. But this was different. An unwavering feeling of tension pulled at her heart.

"So, are you not going to speak to me?" she finally gained the courage to ask.

"Trinity just eat your food." He responded with a deep sigh.

Zion was disappointed. He didn't want to think negatively of Trinity, but he couldn't come to grips with what he saw last night. And wondered if anyone else noticed her on the roof. He didn't care if Trinity wasn't normal, he just didn't want her to be evil.

His words felt like daggers in her chest. *Trinity just eat your food? What does that even mean?*

She sat frozen and watched as he ate as if the words he spoke had no effect.

The sound of her fork clattering against the table caught the attention of everyone around. Then her aggressive leave from the kitchen sparked whispers.

Zion sat feeling defeated. He could feel all eyes on him as if they had a magnetic charge. Trinity and Zion didn't speak for the rest of the day. As badly as he wanted to talk to Trinity, he knew it would make things worse.

It was raining again that night. Worse than the night before.

Zion laid awake in his bed, unable to sleep. He knew that if he looked out the window again, something horrible might be waiting for him.

Then a massive flash of lightning lit up the sky. The bright light filled his room, only for the shadow of a body to make an appearance.

Zion jumped out of bed and rushed to the window, pulling the curtain back.

His heart sank at the sight. *Trinity!*

Her body being hit with dozens of lightning bolts.

Zion forced the window open, breaking through the safety lock.

He grunted through the pain as his hands bled. Once there was enough space to fit his body he climbed out.

"Trinity!" he screamed with his hand reaching for her.

He lost his footing and slipped. His body rolled over the wet, slippery surface toward the edge of the roof.

At the last second, he grabbed the ledge with both hands.

"Trinity, help!" he cried looking up towards her.

But she didn't hear him, she didn't even look his way. Zion lost his grip and fell.

The placement mother found him the next day as she prepared to water her garden. The screams that escaped her made the birds stop midflight.

"Oh, god!" she whimpered as she dropped to her knees. A pool of blood puddled around Zion's head.

"Mother Prim." One of the children called out from the front door, rubbing his tired eyes. When he saw the horrible sight before him, he froze in shock.

"No! Sweetie, back in the house. Now." She rose to her feet, her maternal instinct screaming to protect her other children. She grabbed the child by the arm and pulled him inside the house.

More of the children came running down the stairs. She tried to keep everybody inside, bracing herself against the door.

"What happened, Mother Prim?" someone asked.

Mother Prim didn't answer. Her head shook violently as she clutched her eyes closed, whispering no over and over again.

But the news traveled fast.

"Zion, he's dead!" Trinity heard one of the kids say in the hallway. "I saw his body out the window."

Instantly, she ran to the front door, where the placement mother awaited her arrival.

"Let me see! Let me see!" Trinity fought, trying to push her aside.

"Trinity, baby, no. I'm sorry. I'm so sorry." The mother cried, trying to avoid Trinity's swings

Trinity stopped and saw the look on her face, felt the sadness oozing out of her. It's true.

"I fucking hate you!" Trinity yelled.

The kids parted as she ran back upstairs and locked herself in her room. She sat with her back against the door, knees pulled to her chest and released violent screams.

When the detectives came, they could hear Trinity screaming from almost a mile away.

"I don't know how this happened. I have alarms on all the windows just in case the safety lock fails. I don't know why." Mother Prim cried. But the detective wasn't moved. "Get a Med-Bot down here, quick, and cover the body," he said to his partner.

"Who was Zion closest to in the house?" the detective asked turning back to her.

She was taken aback by the question. "What? Aren't you going to check the surveillance? Question the neighbors, even go see his room? What does it matter who he was closest to?"

"Ma'am, please don't question me on how to do my job. Last I checked, I don't have the body of a teenage boy splattered on my front lawn."

Mother Prim gasped and took a step back, clutching her chest.

"A name, ma'am. Who was Zion closest with?" The glare in the detective's eyes scared her, knots tying together at the pit of her stomach. Something was awfully wrong, yet she couldn't prove it. There was a dark presence around the detective.

Her instincts were pleading with her to protect Trinity, but she was just a placement mother with a child deceased under her care.

"Trinity, sweetie." Mother Prim lightly tapped on the door. She could barely keep her hands still as the detective didn't let her out of his sight for a second.

Mother Prim could hear the sobs of Trinity.

"Baby, the detective is here and wants to speak with you." Her voice cracked.

Trinity stood and faced the door. "No! Go away! I hate you, I hate all of you! I fucking hate this house! Leave me alone!" Her scream was so loud, so powerful, the door cracked.

Mother Prim let out a gasp. The detective didn't move an inch. He placed his hands on his hips and cocked his head.

"I—I think it's best we leave her alone. There's no reasoning with her when she's like this."

The detectives lingered around but there was barely an investigation. After the Med-Bot scanned the scene, Zion's body was taken to Force's Recovery Center. The detective concluded the placement mother was guilty of neglect, without a trial, due to the Med-Bot's determination. She lost her placement privileges for good, and all her children were placed in new homes.

Weeks later, Mother Prim threw on her finest floral dress. Her brown leather gloves with the matching clutch, a suede coat and hat. She found herself knocking on the placement door of Trinity's new home.

"Oh, cheers, um, Mother Prim." The housemother answered, slightly closing the door at the sight of her.

"Cheers," she smiled hesitantly, "I—please. Do you think it's possible I can speak to Trinity."

The housemother frowned. "Mother Prim, I don't think—"

"Please." Mother Prim's throat started to swell as she held back tears, her eyes desperate for a yes. It took her so long to build up the courage.

To her relief, the housemother agreed.

Trinity and Mother Prim sat on the porch, Trinity played with a holographic puzzle cube that kept her attention.

"So, Trinity, how are you holding up?"

Trinity didn't take her eyes off the cube. "I'm accelerating," she smiled. "This housemother is okay, but her cooking isn't like yours." She shrugged.

Mother Prim giggled. "Well, that's good to hear. Is there anything you want to talk about?"

"Hmm, like what?" Trinity twisted and turned the cube, the light danced in her eyes.

Mother Prim's face twisted. "About what happened at my house Trinity. About what happened to Zion?"

"What do you mean? He's back in Ameris. He's living with his grandparents, remember?" Trinity turned to her and flashed a toothless grin.

Mother Prim looked deeply into her eyes, unable to understand. "You're— you're right. How could I forget?" Her words trailed off. "I—I should be going now. I have someone waiting for me." She smiled.

"Okay, Mother Prim." Trinity stood and kissed her on the cheek. "It was nice seeing you," she called as she went back into the house.

Mother Prim sat with her confused thoughts for a moment, when she glanced up, that's when she saw the detective car.

# Chapter 19: Fork in the Road

As Trinity reached the front of her apartment building, she replayed the night's events in her head, remembering fragments of their conversation and the picture of a happy family she didn't remember. A small grin tugged at her lips before fading as reality crept back in.

"Time to face the consequences of my actions," Trinity whispered to herself. She scanned her thumbprint, and the door unlocked with a soft click.

It was dark. Trinity removed her shoes and tiptoed inside and made it halfway through the kitchen before the stove light flickered on.

She froze like a deer in headlights wincing at herself. *Fuck.*

"And where exactly were you dressed like the hottest star on the planet?" Isis said, hissing from the corner of the kitchen table, hiding in the shadows.

Trinity turned slowly. "You're not my mother. I don't have to explain anything to you." The words slipped out of her mouth before she could stop them. She wasn't in the mood for a fight. Dinner had left her in a good mood.

"Wait, sorry. I didn't mean it like that." She frowned, but the damage was already done.

"Oh, really? The law and the fifty gold coins I had to pay to bail you out says something different," Isis snarled, voice tight.

"Isis, please stop acting like you're doing me a favor with this piss-poor parenting style." Trinity shot back, "Please I'm tired I just want to go to bed."

Isis remained in her seat, calm, remembering the words Cy had said to her earlier: *Just let her vent. You're the adult, and she's the child.*

The visit from the neighbors also echoed in her thoughts. *Don't lose control.*

"That's the point, Trinity. I'm not your parent—I'm your guardian. So yes, I am responsible for you. You are so ungrateful! I never asked for any of this." *How dare she go behind my back.*

Trinity scoffed. "What and I did?" Trinity stared at her with an intense glare as she inched closer. "Let's not forget who helped you off the floor countless nights cleaning up your puke."

"Oh yay, let's give you the Kude Island Noble Citizen Award." Isis mocked, "Let not forget who had to clean up your shit in the homes."

Isis pushed her chair back, vines shriveling from her power. "There needs to be some level of respect. I'm the adult, and you're the child. It's time I set some major boundaries."

The two were inches away from each other. Trinity's jaw tightened, Isis refused to blink.

"Only one thing—I'm not a child. And I don't have to listen to what you say." Trinity gritted, the words cutting through like shards of glass.

Trinity pulled the tiny metal box Uncle had given her from her pocket and set it in her palm. With the flick of her thumb, the lid opened. And with the tap of a button the holographic photo sparked to life.

Isis's eyes widened. She stepped closer, voice barely a whisper. "Black hole blasphemy... Trinity, where did you get this?" she whispered in a soft tone, inching closer.

Trinity's chin lifted, refusing to look away. "Does it hurt, Isis? Knowing that I have pieces of the truth now?"

Cy crept out of the bedroom, eyes heavy with sleep. "What's going on?"

"Trinity, you are so stupid it's not even cute anymore," Isis muttered, "Do what you want I don't even care anymore. Just know this man in the photo is not the same man who you saw today. You're father would be so disappointed in you."

Isis saw the damage those words caused to Trinity. The soft gasp she let out, the tears gathering in her eyes. Isis didn't care; she wanted Trinity to feel the same hurt as she did when she wished for her death.

"Nothing, Cy. Let's go back to bed," she added through gritted teeth, brushing past him.

"Yeah! Run away, you... you bitch!" Trinity barked before wiping her tears.

Escaping to her bedroom, she threw off her fancy clothing and slipped into something she could move in—a pair of gray sweats and a sweater would do the job. Essentials were stuffed in a duffel bag. With trembling hands, she was off, climbing down the fire escape. She didn't care what time it was. Kude Island was always awake.

Pete's Diner in Quad One, a restaurant designed to look like an old, broken-down rocket; its 1950s-inspired interior filled with nostalgic charm. A true Kude Island staple, it was more than just a place to eat. The nostalgic environment brought her comfort.

The diner's front lawn looked like nothing from Earth. Instead of grass, fine orange dust swirled gently in the breeze, catching the neon purple light that poured from Pete's glowing exterior. Giant crystalline spires jutted from the ground in irregular clusters, humming quietly.

At night, it felt like a distant planet. A perfect place to disappear.

Opening the swinging doors, she headed to the prompter to see which tables were available. It was just her luck that her favorite spot, the second-floor window view, was free. She reserved it by entering her name and then made her way upstairs.

The diner was spacious. Checkerboard flooring, strobe lights, a towering jukebox, and cursive lettering that snaked across the walls. It was retro in the best way.

Trinity walked over to her booth, entering her name to unlock the light-shield doors. The touch screen table served as menu.

Full from dinner, she ordered a cup of mushroom-scallion tea. As she waited for her tea to arrive, she scanned the room. People watching was her favorite pastime. She wondered what their lives were like. Were they normal? Did they have secrets like hers?

She pressed her head on her palm, studying each table carefully—the couple arguing in hushed tones, the old man eating alone while scrolling through holo-memories, the group of teens laughing too loudly.

Her thoughts drifted back to her own childhood, but the memories only brought sadness. Then she remembered the friends she'd made along the way. She burrowed her face into her sleeves, cheeks warming as she thought of Zion. *I hope wherever he is, he is happy.*

Then she got an idea.

Splitting apart her Tabs, she searched: *Age limit to be independent*. The Island's doctrine was the first result.

"Citizens under nineteen are considered minors and must remain under the care of a parent or guardian. Those seeking emancipation must meet the following requirements: Level Two Citizen status, the Badge of Honor, and a clean mental health evaluation. Any minor with serious criminal charges is required to resolve their case through Force Headquarters before eligibility."

Trinity snapped the Tabs shut.

"Dammit!" she hissed then slammed her fist against the table.

The diner fell silent as eyes turned toward her. She sank lower into the booth, cheeks burning.

After finishing her tea, restlessness crept in. Sitting felt impossible with too many thoughts swirling in her head. She needed noise, lights, something to drown it all out. The Blue Moon arcade was the perfect place to disappear for a while.

Placing a silver coin on the table, she was off.

Trinity approached the moon shaped building.

"Would you like an arcade buddy?" the hologram attendant asked her when she stepped through the doors.

"No, thanks," she replied, waving it away.

She stopped at the coin exchange station near the entrance. The arcade only accepted its own custom tokens—small, glowing blue coins forged from a rare crystal called Jadnotite.

As always, the arcade was full. Familiar with every curve as if it were her home, she hurried to the second floor. She walked by the girls who dressed up a virtual model and skipped past the white room for laser tag. She quickly thought about entering the puzzle room, where moving pieces built the entire space, but she didn't want to stress herself further.

Creatures and Chaos was her destination. The room was dark blue and covered in grid lines. She sat at the black steel table and the interface activated. A medieval landscape bloomed to life full of magical beasts, enchanted creatures, sword wielding knights, strolling skeletons and scattered treasures. The dazzling lights lit up her face as her smile grew. The table gave her a bird's eye view of the game's map, letting her control the action from above, while the room itself transformed—its walls pixelated into a full, immersive view from her character's point of view.

Trinity loved that Creatures and Chaos let her choose from hundreds of games. She played a few games of The Phoenix and the Castle Crypt. A game where a phoenix had to navigate through alternative worlds to find clues to answer a cryptic riddle. Then she played Lost Catacombs, a game where you had to navigate through the catacombs as a skeleton and perform rituals, find treasures, and defeat demons to earn back your life.

Frustration was easing at her temple. She played for hours and couldn't get past the first few levels of each game. Part of the reason she loved playing, even the easy levels were hard to beat.

The next destination was Light Leaf Café in Blue City, a 24-hour teahouse where guests could brew their own blends straight from the plants that surrounded them. A three-story leafy architectural building, with dim and dreamlike lighting; most of the glow came from the bioluminescent plants and mushrooms.

It was the early morning hours, and the streets below were quiet but above, the sky buzzed with air traffic.

Trinity walked to the cashier and ordered a small cup of hot water. As she wandered through the garden, she plucked petals from flowers and dug up roots, dropping them carefully into her cup. Once the mixture had steeped, she found a bench and sat down.

She took a deep breath, tilted her head back, and closed her eyes. The warmth of the tea eased the knot in her chest.

The thoughts burned deeper with each sip. *Maybe... just maybe, he's the key.*

Her eyes opened slowly, the decision already forming in her heart.

After a few more cups of tea, she wandered over to a small theater nearby and watched a late-night film—a story about two robots who fell in love against all odds. It was sweet and melancholic, and for a moment, it made her forget how heavy her decision was weighing on her shoulders. Before the sun started peeking over the horizon, Trinity stepped out of the theater with her path was clear. With a steady breath, she started began her descent to Olympus.

## Chapter 20: Secrets in the Summits

Trinity followed her uncle's instructions precisely. It took her almost an hour to hike around Olympus, but once she did, she retrieved the compass and began to follow the red arrow until she reached a thin path. She wouldn't have pointed it out if she didn't know what to look for. From her pocket, she also retrieved a small sundial watch. Inside its glass dome, a miniature sun orbited above a tiny sundial, mimicking the real one in the sky. As the sun shifted, it cast a moving shadow, allowing her to keep track of time—each line it crossed marked an hour.

Trinity wasn't exactly thrilled about a hike through the forest. She didn't know what to expect, she never step foot past Olympus. No one did, it was rumored life in the wilderness was full of horrors. Creatures, mystical beasts, mad scientists, coggers, the list went on.

As she followed the path she came to a halt facing a thick wall of trees. Her eyes danced across the view of the soaring trees, thick roots, and overgrown vines. Nothing but darkness extended past.

She couldn't propel herself forward as she stared into the abyss. Her foot lifted from the ground but refused to take a step. Instantly, her lips quavered as tears escaped her eyes.

Turning to her back against the forest and crouched down in panic grabbing her head. *No, I can't do this. What am I even doing? Going off with a random man who claims to be my uncle... that's ... that's just mad. Even madder than surviving that fall? Crushing a human with my body? Why, why can't she just tell me? Why Isis? I should just go back... I should just...No wait. Isis didn't even flinch when I mentioned him, nor even deny it. She didn't even ask for proof. She just accepted it as truth, which means she has something to hide. But why is this so hard, why am I so scared?*

"Universe please. Please give me a sign." She sobbed, "What am I doing?"

Trinity planted a seat with her back still facing the dense jungle. She sat absent mindedly tugging at the roots in the dirt, waiting for a sign that she should push forward. Moment later, that sign came.

A black and blue butterfly flapped its wings across the horizon of her eyesight and landed on her lap.

As Trinity gazed at the creature, words came into her head. *Follow me*. She heard.

Then the butterfly slowly took off and without hesitation Trinity stood and followed.

Entering the forest, it wasn't as dense as she perceived it to be, or scary. She felt a bit embarrassed of her timidness to nature. Trinity followed the butterfly; it would periodically stop on a tree to ensure she wouldn't get lost.

"It's alright, I'm not losing sight of you." She assured it.

Taking a few glances at the compass, the butterfly and needle were in sync. This was enough confirmation that Trinity was on the right path. She also noticed the elevation of the land was rising higher.

Thirty minutes felt like seconds for Trinity when the butterfly led her to its intended destination.

An open field of trees coated in moss and wrapped in vines. Thousands of butterflies and moths swarmed the air.

"Cosmic." was all Trinity could manage to say as she stepped into the crowd of wings. The trees looked as if they stretched to the sun. The grass grew with a vibrant green. The flowers glowed with magical aura. Bunnies hopped over her feet. Boulders coated in moss stood guardian of the flowing river. It was a kingdom of wildlife.

Trinity stretched out her arms and took a deep breath. The sunlight bathed over her. An overpowering feeling of peace and tranquility washed over her.

*Is this happiness? I feel so full of resolve and completeness. I want to feel like this forever. I want my life to be mine. I want to live for myself. I want so badly to experience freedom, truly freedom. I feel so bound by my thoughts and human experiences. I don't know how much longer I can go without my questions answered.*

Focusing back to the compass, she realized it was now guiding her west. With newfound confidence Trinity found herself eager for what awaited her.

Two more hours of hiking gave way to rolling hills and steep, jagged mountains. The arrow guided her toward the edge of a massive cliff. At the edge, a carved path that snaked along the cliff side, every few miles were a short flight of steps.

A hard gulp pushed down her throat. After the explosion, she had a fresh fear of heights. The rail formed of stone gave her some relief.

Trinity tiptoed towards the edge to peek her head over and flinched upon collision. "Ouch!" she cried, her head hitting an invisible force field.

*At least I don't have to worry about falling over.*

With the path leading straight ahead, she tucked the compass into her pocket for the time being. She took in the view, the sunrise spilling gold over the mountains and valleys below. The vastness before her felt both humbling and terrifying, a reminder of how far from home she really stood. *I didn't even think we had mountains that stood this high. This part of the island has a higher elevation than I thought.*

After a steady breath, she continued her descent down the narrow path that clung to the cliff's edge.

Three hours passed and her impatience outgrew her excitement.

*I would have invested in a sky vehicle if I'd known the hike would be this treacherous.*

This was the farthest she'd ever been outside the city. Beneath her boots the dirt shifted red. This was the Red Mountains, a place where the sand transformed into a light hue of red.

Finally, she faced the last flight of steps. It brought her to an opening that showcased a valley of red mountains.

Then, an eerie tone stabbed her ears.

"Aww!" she cried.

She hauled the compass out of her pocket and watched as the arrow spun erratically.

"Ah!" She dropped the compass to cover her ears, but to her surprise it didn't touch the ground. It levitated, then slowly started to drift forward.

As she began following it, it picked up speed and so did she. Her chance for freedom would not outrun her.

> Without warning, the compass suddenly blasted off ahead like a stone comet.

"Oh, no!" She cried, sprinting faster. Minutes later, she skidded to a halt. The compass hovered in front of a towering mountain, as if it were waiting.

Upon inspection, a narrow slit with a blinking light caught her eye. It matched the size of the compass perfectly.

She reached toward the key to grab it from the air, but it had a strong force attached to it. Adding more of her strength she yanked it from its position.

With a tired breath she slid the key in. The slot sucked it in with a magnetic force. A green flame flashed, the stones on the ground shook. Then the mountain wall parted, breathing out a gust of cold air. A darkened room revealed itself.

"Hello?" Trinity called, stepping in. Not even an echo called back.

Reacting to her presence, lights shone on a room-sized beacon with transparent walls.

The mountain wall sealed behind her. On the walls glowed strange symbols, symbols that she recognized.

*Why do these symbols look so familiar. Why can I read them? Hmm... I am sure this one mean living quarters.*

Assured of herself, she pressed the symbol and it pulsed.

After a moment and a loud hiss, the beacon bolted forward. Trinity gasped as she braced herself, holding out her arms for balance. Next, the beacon rocketed up.

Quickly, it came to a halt, and the side of the beacon on her left opened, revealing an all black living room.

The floors were transparent, trapped inside, lava flowed like a stream between rocks, giving off a faint orange red glow. Icosahedron dressers hovered a few inches off the ground, and black jade lamps with geometric holes filled the room with light. Overhead, a round, glass chandelier filled with red sand that defied gravity. Swirling around in mesmerizing patterns as if it were listening.

A long, thin window ran the length of the room. From here she could see the dense jungles, The City of Light, and the faint line where the ocean began.

She ventured deeper and found tucked behind the living room sat the kitchen. Black on black with gray, marbled countertops—botswana agate. An encapsuled lava stove, with heat-adjusting knobs capped at 605 degrees. Cabinets blended into the walls for a flat, invisible, sleek look.

Next to the kitchen was a rocky staircase that led to a higher floor. Across from it lay another. Trinity wondered where they led and almost made it to the first step when a voice spoke from behind her.

"I see you found me," Uncle greeted.

Trinity jumped. "Oh, my heavens! You scared me." Hands to her chest. "Your place... its ecliptic." She gawked.

Uncle stood dressed in a suit, yet somehow the clothing didn't surprise Trinity. *A suit at home? Doesn't he know how to relax?*

"Oh, you like it? I just had the kitchen redone. Walk-in refrigerator and freezer, touchscreen stove, and lava oven. You're welcome to cook. It looks like you had a long journey," he eyes trailed her muddy footprints in disdain.

"Uh, yeah. It was a long journey." She glanced down at her dirt covered boots, embarrassed.

"Hm. It's all right. IO will clean it up," he assured. "IO!"

"You have an IO?" Trinity blinked. "I heard those don't come out for another five years."

"The first model. Co-founder of Med Inc., remember?"

A white-and-silver box rolled in from a hidden room behind the beacon. The box was wrapped in tubes and glowing blue liquid. The hidden wheels gave it a floating effect. Reaching Uncle's feet, it unfolded into an eight-foot humanoid robot with a face of rippling blue liquid.

"You called, Master?" the bot spoke.

"This is my niece, Trinity," Uncle introduced. "Trinity, this is IO."

"Whoa, it's huge," Trinity radiated, gawking at the machine and its many intricate parts. She'd never seen such a perfectly crafted android.

"I kept the first as a memento. There is nothing more perfect than the first," he stated. "IO, clean those mud tracks."

"Of course, Master." IO did as it was commanded and placed its feet over her muddy prints, erasing them as it stepped.

"Shall I show you to your room?" Uncle asked but didn't wait for an answer. He led her to a door that faced the living quarters and opened it eagerly.

Trinity stepped into the room and felt the cool air from the vents. This wasn't just a room—it was a temple of technology. Royalty and robotics fused together. For a fleeting moment, she forgot all her worries.

A massive bed with pink drapes embedded with diamonds caught her eye immediately.

Her mouth fell open in awe as she slipped off her muddy boots before crossing the threshold, each step on the cracked gold stones pulling her deeper into this new world—a world built to impress and seduce.

Her fingers trailed over the bedframe, carved from gold and traced with intricate swirls beaded with gemstones that pulsed softly with adjustable light. She sank her hands into the fluffy bedding, and the gold-trimmed pillows stacked with geometric precision. The comforter shimmered with a diamond pattern infused with actual dust diamond dust; it twinkled like a night sky frozen just for her.

On either side of the bed, two slender pillars supported levitating glass orbs, each swirling with an eternal thunderstorm—clashing clouds, flashes of lightning trapped in miniature worlds. The ceiling above was a living galaxy, a breathtaking simulation of a distant planet, pink and purple swirls orbiting under the gaze of three bright stars. The walls glimmered in reflective gold, and across from the bed, a massive circular frame encased a still water fountain.

For a moment, Trinity let herself believe she was in heaven. A reward, maybe for surviving everything life had thrown at her. But then the thought crept in. She'd seen this before. *How many times had luxury been a leash?*

She ran her fingers along the water display, mesmerized by the seamless flow. Buttons on the side revealed their hidden nature as a screen.

Her eyes landed on a regal throne carved from pure white opal, pulsing gently as if alive. Her heart skipped a beat when she remembered when Uncle mentioned the word throne at dinner... *Is this a part of my family's legacy?*

She sat down grinning. The chair fit her perfectly, "I heard storm balls are only found in the City of Light."

"The perks of being who I am," Uncle happily replied.

*Yeah, I wonder who that truly is.*

More icosahedron dressers showcased the latest gadgets—some she didn't even recognize, "This room is stellar."

"Yes, well. I'm glad you like it." His mouth flinched with a slight smile. "This room is yours, Trinity. Think of it as a gift for all the birthdays I missed. I would like you to stay, but don't overthink it. Give me a definite answer when you're ready."

"No static. I guess I'll probably stay a few days until things cool off," she bounced, trying to hide her excitement. But her smile spread wide.

"Cool off?" Uncle raised an eyebrow.

"Yeah, me and Isis got into a bit of an argument." She waved it off with a thin laugh. "We argue all the time, but don't vex it."

"Ah, okay. I see. Well I must get going. Duty calls." He fixed his cuffs.

"Tonight, I'll bring dinner, and we'll talk more. IO can get you settled. Two quick things: the rocky staircase *opposite* the kitchen is off-limits—my private quarters. Otherwise, enjoy your new home."

"Cosmic." She hesitated, one practical question slipping free. "Where's the bathroom?"

A soft chuckle escaped his lips. "I'll let you figure that out." With that, Uncle slipped out, the door closing behind him.

Outside, Uncle's voice drifted through the hall. "IO, give her whatever she needs. She'll be my second in command."

"She's with him. I know she's with him," Isis paced in the living room.

Cy sat on the couch hunched in a VR rig, headphones on. The Afterlife video game blinking across his visor. "Look on the bright side," he sighed. "Maybe he'll tell her something about her past."

"Oh, good one Cy. Hilarious." She mocked.

He slipped the visor up. "You say you don't want her near him—but you won't tell her the truth. What's so bad you can't say it out loud?"

"You don't get it, Cy." She dropped beside him. "Our history is deep. Messed up intergalactic reality TV drama."

"Yeah? Well, keep that intergalactic drama over there." He nudged her teasingly. "I want nothing to do with your alien toxicity."

"Oh, shut it." She shoved him back, letting a laugh slip. "You love my alien toxicity."

Then, his next words landed wrong. "I think... maybe it's good she went."

He winced at himself. "Sorry. I didn't mean it like that."

He did though—at least a little. He loved Trinity, but the constant crisis felt like an incompletable task.

Isis didn't comment back in fear of saying something she couldn't take back. *Cy doesn't know my brother. He's a devious demon with bad intentions. Hell bent on power. He mustn't get to Trinity.*

"Look," Cy offered, softening his voice, removing his VR gear, "I'll run him on the dark net."

"Aww, thank you! Thank you!" Isis squealed, clutching his arm.

"Yeah, yeah. Give me an hour or two. If he's what you say, he left footprints."

"I want her back, Cy. This isn't a job. I need her away from him." They fell into a deep glaze. Isis pulled him closer, pleading with her eyes. "I'll tell you the whole truth soon." Maybe, if she could drag it out of her own head. Flashes of memories were all she had. Arguments, yelling, a tall shadow in a cold room. Then the memory slammed shut again, her brain refusing to revisit.

Cy went into the kitchen and pulled out his workstation from a wall slot. His fingers flew and his code unraveled.

They'd been infamous once, back when the boys' and girls' schools were supposed to keep them in place. Most kids snuck out once or twice a week for the bar or a rooftop party. Cy and Isis? Almost every night they snuck out. They robbed gangsters, blackmailed criminals, broke into labs for weird substances, and traded stolen weapons. Isis always had a way of making jobs find them.

Cy loved her madness. After their time, he chose quiet, she chose him. They both chose out.

Throughout the two hours Cy spent searching through the dark net, Isis kept herself busy with organizing and doing a deep cleaning of the whole apartment. Deep cleaning was her favorite task. She would purposely leave corners of the apartment untouched so spiders could accumulate.

She crouched low and held her mouth open wide. With a soft push of air, a high frequency spilled out. The spiders would dance, swinging legs as they hopped side to side. It tickled her.

After she couldn't occupy herself any longer, she met Cy in the kitchen to discuss what he discovered.

"Malcolm Booker is the son of Alwin Booker," he began, throwing a hologram in the air of Alwin's young and polished face. "Alwin died in the Recovery Center explosion 13 years ago."

"Yes, that's him." Isis's voice sharpened. "My brother, the one I knew. Yes, Alwin *was* his name." A thin smile came behind her realization. "So, he faked his death and pretended to be his own son."

"Left himself all his wealth, too. He's the richest person on the island, maybe the richest. Tech, supply companies, Med Inc., Ruby Palace. Works at Nova Financial, Chief of the financial division." Paperwork bloomed on the hologram. "He holds citizenship in City of Light and Stone Wall."

"Of course he does. Why wasn't he on our radar?" She stood next to Cy as she studied the information.

"I mean, we only just got our freedom recently, and Booker doesn't push his name out there. Instead, I think he boosts social status of other analysts to keep them in the spotlight. With everything happening on the island, it wouldn't be surprising if he deliberately kept under the radar." Cy swiped to show her other articles.

"But this name keeps surfacing: Valskey Grunn. A bioengineer and plant inbreeding specialist." Cy dug deeper, unearthing a buried article. "Grunn accused your brother of unorthodox and immoral practices. Claims he stole his research to sell to corrupt leaders for mind control. Somebody tried to bury this. *Deep*."

"This is the juice," Isis grinned, rubbing her palms together. "Does it list where to find Grunn?"

"There's no address. But there's an old lab he ran with your brother—a school for medicine called The Painted Jewel. It shut down years ago."

"Great. Pack a bag. We're paying that bioengineer a visit."

The duo never ran without supplies: extra Tabs, tiny particle guns, x-ray detectors, crystal batteries, slime-coated nanites, nano-fiber gloves, laser rays—the basics. Tonight, they added the G48—an ovular sky vehicle modeled after a ladybug. Metallic plates overlapped each other, tires hidden, so it glided even on ground. To top it off, it came with invisibility mode.

After dressing in matching sweatsuits, the pair head to the underground garage. The opening was big enough for them to slip in and out with ease. Isis pressed her thumb to the scanner and the doors slid up. Inside sat a three-point steering wheel and screens that coated every surface, even the windshield.

"G48 on," Cy commanded from the driver's seat. Displays blossomed into life. He punched coordinates. "An hour by air," he stated, toggling invisibility.

The G48 rose with ease and eased towards the exit. It shot up the sky, skimming tree lines headed for the mountain ranges. STAR Force—Sky Traffic Advanced Riding—watched everything above a certain altitude. Cy kept them low, weaving through branches, lakes reflecting their invisible shadow.

"So, what exactly is Trinity's power?" he questioned, eyes narrowed on stimulated flight paths.

"I don't know," Isis admitted. "Sometimes her eyes have a faint glow. I've never seen her at full power. I'm sure it isn't harmless. Energy manipulation? Maybe she can harvest it."

"Basically, you guys are like Superman."

"Yeah, but I'm not a superhero." She paused. Sulking, she rested her head against the window. "She... she loses memory every time she uses too much of her power."

An awkward silence pressed in the air. Isis saw it again:

In their old placement home before Isis got her powers. Trinity played with the other house kids in the backyard. Isis was making sandwiches in the kitchen when she heard a loud bang. A chorus of screams followed. Trinity stood there, covered in blood, her face expressionless. There was a boy huddled in the fetal position on the floor, crisscrossed marks across his back. He was motionless.

"Trinity! Trinity!" Isis shouted frantically shaking her shoulders. "Talk to me!" she cried. Trinity was unresponsive, she stood there completely unfazed by Isis' yelling. There was a light in Trinity's eyes that were fading away. "Trinity!"

Trinity took a deep gasp, coming back into realization. "What happened to Griffin?" She mumbled. "Isis—blood—there's blood on my hands. Why?"

Isis hugged her tightly, tears falling down her face. "It's okay. It's okay. I'm here."

The housemother came storming out. "What is going on?"

"Griffin!" Isis lied fast. "A wild animal attacked him. She tried to help!"

The other kids trembled in fear and kept their mouths shut when the Med-Bots came. Within weeks, they shipped Trinity and Isis to a new home.

"Dark heavens," Cy remarked. "And you never told her powers or memory loss."

"I will. I promise I will." Isis waved her hands frantically. "It's just, when she pushes too far, she short-circuits. Dumps memory to save... power? Space? Something. But she's not safe with him. With his reach? He can manipulate her with a sim card and a smile."

"Don't worry. We'll get Trinity back." Cy assured.

"Anything else on Grunn?" Isis asked, wanting to forward the conversation.

"Yeah." He opened a file and placed it on the dashboard. "He and your brother started gene manipulation—new plants, animal species, new drugs. Grunn says your brother sold to the highest bidder and then cut funding. After that, Grunn went dark—no

Citizen's Card pings. No digital footprint, he just went ghost." Cy shook his head. "Your brother must be tainted."

"You don't know the half of it." Isis watched lakes slide beneath them, hands gripping each other tight in her lap. Trinity was so easily influenced—especially with the holes in her memory. Keeping her close had always been the strategy. Now "close" meant chasing her across the island.

# Chapter 21: Tilt the Crown

Booker sipped his hot tea as he glided through Blue City towards the tallest building in the city.

He stepped into the exterior beacon, a glass vein that ran the height of the tower. Built for top executives at Nova Financial, a sleek building carved from obsidian and covered in blue circuits. The city fell away beneath his shoes. His reflection revealed a calm face and a steady hand. A body he had grown to like. But the ghost of his former body haunted him. He longed to be reunited with his true body, his true existence.

Booker's job was to oversee the business deals, seek potential clients, maintain the flow of trading with approvals or denials, and calculate costs. He had an office on the forty-fourth floor, which he shared with five other executives. He designed his office as a sophisticated dark cave with emotion sensing panels that changed color depending on his mood. Blacked out windows that could turn clear with the flip of a switch. As for his desk, created from an obsidian slab and imprinted with a biometric command system, one that responded only to his touch and voice.

He sat and with the wave of a hand, he activated the holographic controls that hovered above the surface and issued a simple command: "Start the meeting."

Within seconds, the room transformed into a virtual boardroom. Several faces blinked into existence on hovering frames; all members of the task force he'd assembled—their sole mission: dismantle DeathStar.

"Good morning," greeted Skinner, filling the largest central frame. "As Chief of Kude Island's Defense Unit, I've called this emergency session to discuss the latest developments. DeathStar continues its coordinated attacks—the latest at Solar Bay and here on our island. This brings their total death toll just shy of a million. Each of their strikes gets bolder than the last. We believe another may be imminent. Special Agent Lyonel, share your report."

"Thank you, sir." Lyonel adjusted his tie before speaking. "As we know, Ameris is dominated by three massive organizations—The Fallen Stars, Legion, and the New Law Republic. I was stationed at Solar Bay, which falls under the jurisdiction of The New Law Republic. As far as we know they have no ties to DeathStar. While there, I obtained intel on the group's nexus. A local informant—a schizophrenic streetwalker named Begger—claims to have seen the man 'walk through a brick wall. He identified him by a distinctive eyepatch and short, wavy hair. Begger said this man recruited him from the future. He also said a lot concerning Gravity Grave. Which I will mention in my report."

"Any neuron-interface visuals?" Booker questioned, his tone clipped and professional.

"No, sir. The subject's condition prevented a clear neural imprint."

"Send that report only to me." Booker commanded.

The meeting continued for another hour, report after report filling the air with speculation, half-truths, and uncertain leads. Booker remained silent, his expression unreadable, but every new piece of data pressed a little harder against the back of his mind.

When the session concluded, Skinner cleared his throat. "Our next steps are clear: we locate their Ameris base, infiltrate, and bring them to trial. Everyone is dismissed."

The boardroom dissolved, leaving Booker alone in the quiet hum of his office.

The silence of Booker's office didn't last long. A hologram flickered on, shifting from blue to an ominous red as a new meeting window forced itself open.

He frowned. *I didn't schedule anything else.*

"Is he ready?" A deep, rasping voice asked before the feed stabilized.

A man appeared on-screen—heavyset, his pale skin coated with boils, bald head glistening under the low light. Colored crystal rings weighed down his fingers, and a silver cane carved into a coiled serpent rested in his lap. His name flashed across the corner of the frame: Crypt Cane—though most in the underworld knew him by another name: The Reaper.

Booker's posture stiffened. He knew Cane; most political leaders of the world did. A tyrant from Skeletor Island, a fortress-nation sealed from the public.

Another familiar face materialized beside him. Ivan Skinner. "Booker," he said with a toothy grin, "allow me to make an introduction. This is Crypt Cane, a valuable ally and potentially—a partner."

Booker clasped his hands, concealing the irritation that flared in his chest. The hue of his room went from a dark yellow to red. *Skinner. Always playing his own game.* "Ah, yes. The infamous Reaper," Booker said coolly. "To what do I owe the pleasure?"

Crypt Cane's voice came like gravel being poured through a metal pipe. "The pleasure is, of course, mine. I have heard so much about your... special island. And your recent scientific breakthroughs."

Booker leaned back, unimpressed. "Flattery's a poor opening for a negotiation."

Cane chuckled—low and humorous. "Very well. Our islands grew from the ashes of war. We were fortunate to obtain such rich lands. You stand on what used to be South Africa, and I on South America. You've heard the talk. The 'invisible forces' aboard my fortress. Those stories are no myth. While you chase immortality, my work concerns the opposite. They're captured spirits. Once men and women... now eternal soldiers under my command."

Booker's brow creased. *Impossible.* And yet, the way Cane said it left little room for disbelief.

"What do you want?" Booker asked, his tone flat.

"Isn't it obvious?" Cane's smile widened, revealing a row of rotted teeth. "Seventy percent of the world's gold and crystals flows from Kude Island. Imagine our power—my army and your resources, united. Together, we could bend the new world order to our will. The war between the U.S and Russia that happened all that time ago gave us an advantage. Wiped out most of the world's population, giving us a fresh start. And I've heard of your little problem. DeathStar is becoming more of a pest. World leaders are trembling at the thought of another global travesty set by their hands. But together... we could end them." His voice hardened with intent.

"As fascinating as your little necromantic side project is," Booker gritted, "Kude Island has no need for ghost armies or spirit-slaves. I'm going to decline your offer."

Cane's smile remained, but the edges hardened. "I wouldn't be so quick to refuse. I know about your black hole facility... and about your private mines hidden beneath the city. How do you think the other leaders would react if they learned about your endless reservoirs of gold and crystal batteries? Better yet—how would DeathStar react?"

The threat hung heavily in the air. Booker's jaw tightened, his pulse rising. "You've overstayed your welcome," he seethed, severing the call with a flick of his wrist. The holograms dissolved into nothing.

The room darkened, walls bleeding to a deep crimson—a reflection of his spiraling thoughts. *How did they breach my network? How much did Skinner tell him?*

"Prad," Booker called.

A small crystal orb wrapped in black mesh rose from the surface of his desk. "Online." it pulsed.

"Run a complete security sweep. Look for breaches, reroutes, anything abnormal."

Moments later, the orb responded. "No data leaks or network intrusions detected in the last twenty-four hours."

"Hmm. That will be all." *Skinner, he must have found a back door.*

Booker leaned back in his chair, fingers steepled under his chin. He had assumed for years that DeathStar's attacks were coincidental, unfortunate accidents connected to his businesses. But now, with enemies knocking directly on his door, the pattern was impossible to ignore.

It wasn't by chance. The messages from DeathStar were clear. Booker is their target.

He worked for the rest of the morning. Traders floated into his queue; he approved, declined, and budgeted. Potential clients pitched technologies he had already built in secret. He filed data, corrected figures in margins others never read, and answered communications in a tone people mistook for warmth.

Humans fascinated him—yet he despised them. To him, they were flawed, primitive prototypes of what higher beings became. A planet brimming with potential, ruined by hatred, greed, and shortsightedness.

On his home world, there was true unity. Every being intertwined. The word "memory" lay absent from their language. Their collective existence wove in vibrations. Time reshaped into a spectrum they could see. Past, present, and every future branching from the light inside their consciousness. All timelines ever present. Rigorous training took years as they learned to control their tunnel vision to avoid being blinded by infinite outcomes.

Humans acted blindly by choice. They stumbled through life without ever seeing the certainties in front of them, reacting to possibilities instead of inevitabilities. It made him wonder if even tunnel vision—the gift his people had mastered—might itself be just another variable.

In his early years on Earth, Booker had devoted himself to understanding humanity. He studied everything: history, religion, holidays, crime, occult magic, anthropology, psychology, cinema, even their obsession with technology. He wanted to learn how they thought, how they built their world—and then improve upon it.

Kude Island was his attempt to do just that. He tried to model it after Earth's golden age but with purpose and precision. Time measured by shadows and the movement of the sun and stars. Moon cycles controlled the thirteen month calendars. A colossal sundial stood in the heart of the Twin Cities, its bell ringing at sunrise, midday, and sunset. He reimagined old traditions to align with nature, and replaced religion with technology. There was no Christmas, no Thanksgiving, no New Year's. Seasons themselves became sacred—celebrated with grand festivals at the turning of winter, spring, summer, and fall.

Under his vision, Kude Island thrived. He had built one of the most transformative inventions in human history: Blink Stations—instant teleportation hubs that reshaped global trade and travel. They became the economic backbone of the island, a monument to his intellect. Next would be Med-Bots, the pinnacle of medical evolution—if only DeathStar didn't destroy almost everything.

What dawned on him most was Cane mentioning his black hole facility. It was true. At one time Skinner and Booker created a particle machine that tried to create the density of a dying star to create a controlled black hole. But with trial and error they failed, so he put the project on the back burner.

When the day thinned towards evening, Booker left the tower and crossed to Force headquarters to see to a minor errand: the insurance policy on Med Inc. The building was a block of stubborn concrete with ambitions toward sleekness, and a lobby that smelled of paper and disinfectant. He ignored the front desk enclosure and headed straight up to Studd's office.

He knocked only once.

"Enter," Studd's voice called—irritable and heavy with exhaustion.

"Detective Studd," Booker addressed as he stepped into the room. He extended his hand. "Always a pleasure."

Studd hesitated, then shook—the reflexes of a man who trusted respect even when he did not trust the person. "Let's keep it simple, Booker. Sign here," he exhaled, shoving a stack forward. "I'll send it to the insurer."

"A shame," Booker spoke with sorrow, glancing at the top page, "about the casualties. Almost a thousand."

"Yeah, almost," Studd repeated. He searched Booker's face for guilt. "We have no new leads yet. You'll know when that changes."

Booker skimmed until numbers caught his eye. "Fifty thousand gold coins to the corporate account upon settlement," he read. He lifted his gaze. "Pen?"

Studd dug through the papers and tossed one across the desk. "Use this."

"We have holograms, Chief," Booker said lightly. "It is the thirty-second century."

"I have little trust in light that acts like paper," Studd clarified. "The weight of the written word is something I like. I wrote the Retention Law for a reason—some things you hold, not swipe."

"Of course." Booker signed with a flick that looked careless, though it wasn't. "Most of that compensation will go to the families of the dead," he explained, still writing. "The rest to rebuild the island's most profitable enterprise." He set the pen down.

"Remember who supplies your task force with its bots. Commerce and justice do share a spine."

"Hmph." Studd's eyes narrowed.

The man had theories about Booker—an entire gallery of them. Booker had seen himself on the detective boards: a son with a dead father who had once run the Recovery Center; a fortune inherited with a blast; a string of allegations about worksite abuse and bribery; whispers about disappearances tied to Alwin Booker. Experiments on the people of the island. None of it ever stuck. Evidence was a god, and Studd prayed poorly.

"There's something else," Studd confessed. "We should talk about anything relevant to the DeathStar attacks."

"I assure you," Booker stated coldly, "there is no need."

Studd's jaw flexed. "Why so you can beat me to it? Look there was something that man said before the explosion. Something about mind transfers? And consciousness hacking? Whatever it is just know nothing walks past without me seeing its shadow."

Booker grinned, kind and empty. "You've already lost the race, Chief. You just haven't heard the gun. I promise Kude doesn't divulge in what was naturally given." He slid the papers back across the desk. "Submit immediately. Call me if you have any issues."

He stood to leave and headed for the door.

"Booker," Studd called to his back.

"Why is it that death follows you everywhere you go? What, you owe it a soul, *your* soul or something?"

Booker paused in the doorway. "Death owes me nothing," he said without turning. "Fortunately, I already have the prize."

Studd leaned back in his chair, eyes narrowing. "I've been doing some digging into DeathStar," he reported. "And it seems they follow a curious pattern. Most of their targets connect to you—a business deal here, a partnership there." A thin, knowing smile crept across his face.

Booker cracked a faint smile, his back still facing him. "Coincidences happen, Chief. And in a world full of enemies, I attract more than most."

"Mm." Studd's tone sounded skeptical. "And yet... it's interesting. I can't shake the feeling you've made someone very vexed." He hesitated, then added casually, "One more thing—does the name Crypt Cane mean anything to you?"

Booker's voice didn't waver. "No," he answered evenly. "Should it?"

Studd studied him carefully. "That Skinner—he's a slippery one, isn't he?" he countered, watching for any reaction.

Booker only shrugged. "Slippery men fall hardest," he replied, tone menacing.

"Booker, this may be your island, but they are *my* people. Don't make me clean up another one of your messes. And how long before these blackouts are fixed?"

Booker huffed, "As I said before it's an energy core issue we are dealing with, but I assure you it will stop soon." Booker slammed the door shut.

The door had barely clicked shut behind Booker when it swung open.

"Studd!" someone called out.

"Solar spirits, what now!" he barked, slamming his pen onto the desk. He looked up.

Detective Armand Grayson stormed into the office.

His eyes were bloodshot red, his jaw tight and beneath the anger was something deeper: desperation.

"I want answers, Studd. My sister's tearing herself apart and I have nothing to give her. Not even a body. Just your word that

Skeeter was in the blast." Grayson hunched over his desk, knuckled down.

"We're still cataloging remains. Many people... didn't make it home. I don't mean to sound harsh, Grayson, but at least you have a finger."

The words tasted bitter as they left his mouth. Constant exposure to grief and fury was taking a toll on him, but the last thing he needed was a suspicious death on his watch—especially a Force member.

"Don't insult me." Grayson snapped with a finger pointed at him, "Skeeter wasn't involved with Med Inc. He had no reason to be near that building. And now he's gone."

"What are you implying? That a Force detective death is my fault?" Studd roared, veins burning beneath his skin. He shot up from his chair, meeting Grayson's eyes with rage, knocking his finger down.

Many people thought Studd had a hand in Booker's innocence. He acted as an inside man, and the fact he was promoted to Chief didn't sit well with some people.

Grayson faltered under the weight of his gaze. "Look... you're right, Chief. I'm sorry. I just—" He swallowed hard, sadness overtaking him, fighting back tears he refused to let fall.

Studd sighed, the anger draining from his shoulders. "No. I'm sorry. I shouldn't have yelled at you." His voice softened. "Look, just take a day off, okay? I'll see you at the parade."

He reached out, resting a heavy, sympathetic hand on Grayson's shoulder, a gesture that felt more like pity than comfort.

Grayson nodded silently and turned to leave. But as the door clicked shut behind him, a knot tightened in Studd's gut.

Something told him this wouldn't be the last of it.

# Chapter 22: Celestial Treaty

Studd made his way to the research department, where a team strictly assigned to Switch's covert operation waited for him.

"Sorry to keep you guys waiting," he said, stepping into the room.

At the table sat Switch, his assigned Force lawyer, Mrs. Greyson, and one of the nexuses of the research department, Zakari Elliott.

Mrs. Greyson sat with her Tabs stabilized in front of her ready to record every word of the meeting.

Switch's expression read with regret. He sat perfectly still with his head low, gaze focused on no particular spot on the table.

"Proceed," Studd ordered taking his stance in the corner of the room.

"Yes, Chief. Switch, you are to use Blink Station as your means of transport. When you arrive, you'll head to the designated location and wait for your assigned Force detective, who will arrive after three moons. You and the detective will formulate a plan to get as close as possible to the research facility. From what we gathered, these scientists you mentioned must be distorting the electric field, teleporting people who who come too close. You'll reach that spot only once, and we'll collect data from the chip inserted in you. From there, we'll conduct research while you continue getting intel on DeathStar."

"And how long do I have to stay?" the words escaped as a low grumble.

"Until I say you can come home," Studd proclaimed. He slowly approached the table arms crossed. "You are our key to this mission. You play a pivotal role. These people, whoever they are, are dangerous. We don't know what they're capable of and we need to prevent the next attack. Your job is to lay low while collecting intel. We're sending you with some of our best tech to help you with the black market trades. Don't worry, the detective I'm sending is a natural born killer. You'll be perfectly safe. You shouldn't be out there for more than a moon cycle."

Studd nodded to Zakari to continue. Unaware of the glances Zakari and Mrs. Greyson were sharing.

"Yes, as Studd said, we shouldn't need more than a moon cycle to collect intel. Your transport takes place in a few hours. Do you understand everything that is being discussed?"

"Yeah, I understand." Switch cleared his throat and fixed his slumped position.

"Good. Don't forget—you're going to be a hero, kid. You pull this off, I'll get you any job in any sector on this island. You understand?" Studd asked.

"Yeah, I understand." Switch didn't want a job working for any sector on the island. He didn't even want to be working undercover like this. He was being forced to cooperate in a war that he couldn't care less about.

"Detective Morrison should be making his appearance soon to introduce himself soon. Zakari, I expect updates as their happening."

"Of course, Chief."

Once Studd stepped out of the room the tension in everyone's shoulders dissipated. Zakari's shoulders dropped the hardest.

"I don't think we need to inform you that trying to remove the chip will automatically renounce your citizenship here." Mrs. Greyson flatly said, tapping across large blue squares.

"I figured." Switch responded.

"Switch is there any more information you could tell me about this facility like a name or which faction it falls under?" Zakari asked.

"I don't know the name, and I'm sure they don't work under any faction, if they did DeathStar would be the least of our worries."

"Oh? How did you hear about if it's so secret?" Mrs. Greyson stopped typing and looked up from her Tabs.

"That's my job lady, to know things. A guy paid me to sneak in the facility to gather data. I'm guessing he either used to work there or was paid from someone else to get a lackey." Switch explained as he bounced a small rubber ball between himself and the wall. Zakari had given it to him prior to the meeting.

"From what I understand The New Law Republic often donates to research directly tied to scientific progression so it's possible they could be the one funding this lab. But without any critical information I can't say for sure." Zakari thought out loud.

"I have some contacts I can reach out to, maybe they can get us some useful information."

"That would be helpful Mrs. Greyson thank you."

Just then, Detective Axium Evander entered the room. Axium stood almost six feet tall, muscles bulging through his white button up. His jaw muscles flexed below his hollow cheeks. Veins streaked the sides of his face. A scar ran from across his face like an unfinished x. Running from the top of his head across his nose down his cheek. His large knuckles were covered in scars. When he stepped into the room, a demand for respect came with him.

Switch quickly swept Detective Evander's body before looking away. He clenched the ball with frustration. *Of course they gave me the fucking terminator.*

Zakari stood immediately to shake his hand, "Detective Evander, I'm Zakari Elliott a nexus for the research department, this is Mrs. Greyson, although I'm told you two already met," Zakari gestured to her. Evander gave her a slight nod, "And this is Switch."

Evander stared at Switch, studying his demeanor. How he anxiously played with the ball. How Switch was staring back from the corner of his eyes. Evander only had one thing on his mind. To seek retribution for the lives DeathStar took by any means.

"Fill me in." Evander spoke with a gruff voice.

The team spoke for an hour going over the particulars of the operation. Once everyone was in agreement on how Operation Blackhole would take place. Only Evander and Switch were left in the room.

An awkward silence filled the space as Evander sat in thought, "You wanna have lunch kid?"

Switch remained apprehensive throughout the whole meeting, refusing to make eye contact with Evander for more than one second. Giving his attention to the stress ball than to the adults in the room.

"Sure." He shrugged.

"Stellar follow me, I know a great spot."

Evander led Switch to the Force vehicle garage. He drove a Force issue Mauve X6. This issue of the car was the standard model of jaguar, but Evander made a few upgrades. Sliding doors, swivel seats. A curved glass dome tinted the darkest black Switch ever seen.

Switch stood in awe as they approached the vehicle, "This you?"

"Damn right it is, hop in the diner isn't too far."

The door slid open and Switch took a seat inside. The interior was lined with panels and a sleek curved dashboard. A panel on the dashboard opened and two curved frames emerged.

Switch didn't want to show it, but he was astonished at the tech that was built into the interior.

The ride to the diner was quiet, but Evander could see Switch's demeanor changed since they left. He hadn't played with his stress ball the whole ride. Once the pair sat at their table and their burgers came Evander started to pry.

"I read you're file, you're real talented. Care to tell me how a kid like you ended up living underground in Quad Four?"

"That's none of your business." He said mouth full, adding another fry to the mix.

"Fair enough." Evander threw up his hands, "There's a reason Studd chose you for this mission, granted his ways may not be... ethical, but deep down but I'm sure he saw the potential."

"He didn't see vex but a willingness to take advantage of the weak." Switch's eyebrows hardened. "Look I just wanna do this job and get it over with. It's bad enough I'm working with the Force but now I'm hunting down DeathStar." He scoffed in disbelief, "This is a trip man, I've got to say."

"It would make one hell of a story, could even boost your rep in the streets."

"My rep?" Switch laughed.

"I guess my jargon could use some work." He took a quick glance at his watch, "You have another hour or so before your departure. Let's go over the plan one more time."

# Chapter 23: *Magic Mush*

"Hands up! Hands up! Put your fucking hands up!" Studd yelled.

He was in the basement of a run-down science lab in the mountain ranges. When the strike team busted in, Studd was separated from his team as he chased the perpetrator down.

His rifle light stayed on the perpetrator who was huddled in the corner. The man's flesh was white as a cloud, his veins surged with black liquid, the same substance spilled out his mouth. His fingertips were black with frostbite dying. His skin was flaking off like garlic peels.

"Please, please, no—you—you don't understand. He told me to do it. Please." He whimpered. His words quavered from his chittering teeth. His eyes told a story of horror and fright.

"Shut up! Shut up!" Studd yelled, inching closer, his heart beating a mile a minute, sweat trickling down his face.

"Please, you have to understand. It—it wasn't me!" the breaths he took between words got deeper, like it was harder from him to breathe.

"Studd, what's going on?" his Force mate asked through the comms.

"It's all good. Subject contained."

Just then, a fast shadow went by the corner of his eye. The shatter of glass startled him. *What was that?*

Studd turned his weapon sharply, shining the light towards the sound in a swift motion. Finger on the trigger he turned on his heels slowly. On the ground, he saw tiny bloody footprints.

He followed the prints with his light until he saw a bony hand wrapped around the edge of a steel cabinet. The hand snatched away.

He huffed as he walked closer and closer, rounded it—and froze.

Six skeletal children, thinner than twigs. Their cheeks sunken so deep it seemed their jaws were floating, eyes bulged out further than their noses. The same black gooey substance seeping from their eyes.

Some were toppled over, appearing dead, chest's barely moving.

"My God." Studd cried out.

He turned back to the man and hauled him up by the shirt with one hand. "Why? Why would you do this?"

"I—I didn't mean to. He made me! He made me! I swear!"

"He? He who?"

"The...the...the voice in my head, man. It's like someone cast a spell on me, making me do those horrible things. I promise, man. I promise it wasn't me." He wept.

"There was no spell, you sick bastard. What did you do to these children?" Studd barked with an intense fire in his eyes. His body became hot with rage.

"Studd! Stand down!" Chief Goodwin came running down the stairs just in time.

Back at Force headquarters, Studd sat in the Chief's office. Chief Goodwin stood behind his chair gripping the top so tight his fingers were turning white.

"Look, Studd, I understand your dedication to this island and the Force, but you can't just go off and tackle things on your own. You are the only nexus that doesn't work well with their team."

"Come on, Chief. I told you before—I work better alone. And like I said, I saw the perpetrator run, so I took pursuit." His shoulder shrugged lazily.

"That's just not how we do things around here!" the Chief snapped. His voice was loud enough he was heard in the detective quarters.

Studd wiped his nose to conceal his smile.

"There is an order of command here, Studd. You can't just go around questioning things and running off on your own." He lowered his head and softened his voice, "Studd, please—I value your presence, for your own life's sake. Just learn to stay in your place."

"Oh, like how Booker keeps you in yours?" he pressed.

"You are out of order, detective. Leave my quarters now!"

Studd rose and hit his salute, trying his hardest not the smirk.

Chief Goodwin couldn't even look him in the face afraid of what he might do to him.

Back at his desk Studd sat as his eyes fixated on empty space, processing what he'd just seen. The sad, soulless eyes of those children. The black goo smeared on the walls. The tiny bloody footprints. Each image that flashed across his mind enraged him more. *They were so weightless, lifting them felt like I was going to break a bone. Can't believe that damn guy, there weren't any damn spells, just his psychosis.*

Then he heard it. That voice, that familiar voice. His eyes shot up to Malcolm Booker walking past the detective quarters, making his way up to see the Chief. He rose to his feet eager to follow. Then, he stopped mid-stride.

*No. Not here. I'll follow him when he leaves.*

"Chief, so good to see you. I suppose you caught the perpetrator," Booker said, taking a seat.

Chief stood with his back towards him. "I can't keep doing this, Booker. You and these goddamn experiments. You have this island riddled with people who think they can defy God and the laws of nature and look. Look at the outcome. Six children who were almost starved to death were found in a facility under your name. They're in such bad shape we're going have to lie to their parents until we can get some weight on them." He turned to look at him sternly and pointed. "Let this be the last time we ever find another tragedy under your name."

There was a moment of silence.

Booker lifted his eyebrow concealing a smirk. "Are you done?" He rose to his feet.

"May I remind you, who used to partake in these experiments themselves?"

The Chief's eyes widened, "That was a long time ago, and that was different. We were building soldiers for this island's defense."

"Same pot, different burn, Chief. Your hands are just as dirty as mine. Let's not forget the fifty gold coins that hit your account every month, or the—"

"That's enough!" Chief yelled, fingers curling in rage. He had reached his limit. "The next time this happens, I swear to the high realms above, I will bring you down and this whole island with it."

"Good luck with that Chief."

Studd stood outside Force headquarters waiting for Booker to make his exit, hood on and boots strapped. *That son of a bitch has got to pay. His name has been mixed up in far too many cases like these. And Chief always turns his nose. Not this time. I won't let him off that easy.*

Studd tailed him for the whole day, following him to different parts of the city. Different financial buildings, tea shops, even a trip to Gravity Grave. His last stop was at the Nova Financial building. Studd stood waiting in the alley till late at night. Booker finally exited the building and began walking toward the suburban side of Blue City. Studd tailed close behind, not taking his eyes off him. He inched closer until he knew the coast was clear. Waited until the perfect moment. Then he ran up behind Booker and pushed him into an alley between two buildings with his shoulder, then grabbed him by the collar and pushed him against the wall.

"You're going to tell me everything you made that man did to those children, and you're going to tell me right now." Studd's voice dropped an octave. His eyes fixed with an intense stare. He pressed on his tip toes as Booker was almost a whole foot taller.

Booker smiled. *I was waiting for his attack. He's stronger than he looks.* "Studd, a pleasure to make your acquaintance. I'm sure you're referring to the man who had a psychotic break. He was nothing but an old employee who created a substance that caused him to hallucinate. But I'm told you found the children safe and sound. How—"

"You black pit of space don't play with me. I know you had something to do with this. That man practically confirmed someone was coercing him." Studd grabbed him and yanked him up tighter. "There were no voices in his head. I know you ordered him."

"Ordered him to do what? Kidnap children and swap out their blood?"

Booker pried off Studd's hands and bent them back with great power.

"Ahh!" Studd called out in agony as he heard his bones crack. He almost collapsed on one knee but held himself up.

"I'll have you know, I had nothing to do, nor will I ever partake in the harm of children. Now, from what I was told, that perpetrator said the voices were coming from inside his head—that someone put a spell on him."

Studd fought through the pain and pushed back using all his strength to stand his ground, "There is no goddamn such thing as magic or spells, only thing I know is the depravity of human nature. I don't know how, but I know you were responsible, and one of these days, I will peg you for the nasty bastard you are."

*Studd... you are different. Like me?* Booker twisted his hands harder and evil grin stretched across his face as he licked his lips. "I will have to admit, Studd, you are the first man to ever challenge me as such. By far the strongest. But don't make me prove how far I'm willing to go to maintain my innocence." He released Studd, who dropped to the ground. "I'll keep this interaction between us. I don't think your Chief would be too happy about this little encounter."

# Chapter 24: Tangled Roots

"Okay, according to the map, it should be right around this curve," Cy stated, parking the G48 in a nestle of trees. He tapped a few buttons, and they watched as the radiance cloaked them. "Invisibility engaged."

The pair stepped out and continued on foot, weaving through the wilderness until they found the road.

"I see nothing," Cy noted, scanning the clearing ahead. "According to the coordinates, the school should be right here." He pointed to his pulled apart Tabs.

Exchanging a glance, the duo said in unison, "Invisible shield."

"Think you can break it?"

Cy closed his tabs and pulled out a clear crystal tablet from the bag. "Do you even have to ask? Give me a sec."

He placed the tablet in stabilization mode, and his fingers began flying across the keys as the screen filled with lines of his code. Isis hovered impatiently behind him.

"Well?" she huffed.

"Well, hold on damn." Cy grumbled. "This shield's huge and the code? Cosmic. But..." He hit one last key with a triumphant smirk. "Boom. We're in."

The air ahead glitched and collapsed until the mystery unraveled—a massive black spinel castle with glowing colored stones along the border, and a gigantic quartz embedded above the main entrance. A narrow walkway carved along the side, vanishing around the structure.

"Holy stars..." Cy smirked, "It's huge."

Isis wasted not a fraction of time and marched ahead cautiously. Cy followed close behind.

"Cy, back up. I can feel you breathing on my neck," she hissed.

"Sorry! You're the one moving in slow motion. Hurry up!"

They rounded the corner and froze to the sight. A sprawling glass-domed greenhouse stretched out behind the castle, lush and alive.

"The guy's a botanist, remember," Cy reminded her.

"Hello. How can I help you?" came a sudden monotone voice.

Isis spun around and gasped.

"Stellar," Cy whispered, eyes wide.

An eight-foot-tall bumblebee hovered behind them.

"Greetings, how can I help you?" came another voice.

Isis yelped as a short, gray-haired man with warm brown skin and an impossibly wide smile appeared from behind the bee. He was wearing a suit, wrapped in a white trench coat.

"Oh, greetings," Isis greeted, clutching her chest. "I'm Icy, and this is my partner, CiCi. We're reporters here to ask you a few questions."

Cy shot her a distasteful glance. *CiCi? Really?*

"Splendid!" the man rejoiced. "I'm Valskey Grunn but I suspect you already know that."

"And who's your friend?" Isis pressed, pointing to the massive bee carrying a basket of white flowers.

"Oh, this is my assistant, Marvin," Grunn said cheerfully.

"Should I vaporize them, Master?" Marvin buzzed.

"No, no!" Grunn waved frantically. "Marvin's... very enthusiastic. Shall we take a walk through the house?"

Isis and Cy exchanged a confused look. They hadn't expected hospitality—but followed him towards the entrance willingly.

The greenhouse stood cosmically beautiful. Strange glowing runes etched its white nanofiber framework. Before they could enter, Grunn ushered them into a decontamination chamber. A mist hissed from the walls, leaving a sharp, acidic tang in the air. Cy and Isis let out a few coughs, waving the acidic mist from their faces.

Then, the white metal door slid open. Isis and Cy stepped in eyes widened in amazement of the beauty that stretched before them.

The greenhouse was alive in every way imaginable. Towering trees scraped the glass ceiling. Hundred-foot mushrooms rained spores. Floating plots of land drifted lazily through the air. Echoflora plants scattered across the land. A plant that absorbed vibrations and replayed sounds through a deciphering apparatus. Butterflies shimmered like glass shards; translucent worms burrowed through glowing moss. And above it all, sunlight streamed through the dome like ribbons on a windy day.

"I call it The Enclave of Gardens," Grunn boasted. He lifted his shoulders in delight.

"Whoa, what are these?" Cy took a curious step toward the pink delilah. A living plant whose green leaves curled inward. Underneath its pink soft tissue coated in slime. At its center rested a small gland coated with seeds.

"Oh no, wait—don't—" Grunn mocked with concern; the words left his mouth purposely late.

POOF.

The leaves blossomed open. A cloud of purple smoke blasted from the seeds, and Cy dropped to the floor like a sack of rocks.

"Cy!" Isis shouted, rushing to his side.

"Don't worry," Grunn spoke calmly. "He'll be fine. Marvin, bring the boy to get some air." He spoke to his watch.

"Come along," Grunn continued, stepping onto a pathway of landplots that floated toward a vine-wrapped house.

"Wait! Is he going to be okay?" Isis asked crouched by his side.

"He'll be fine. That plant releases sleep salt for nosy intruders. First-timers always fall for it." He laughed heartily as Marvin scooped Cy up and floated him outside.

"Did you know we were coming?" Isis interrogated rising to her feet.

"I knew you were *here*, but I did not know that you were coming," Grunn remarked with a smirk, fingers twisted behind his back. "It takes someone clever to crack a shield like mine. I assume you're here to talk about the old lab—or the school."

"Yes, among... other things," Isis responded, following him as they climbed higher. She passed trees with crystals growing from their branches, sprawling rose gardens, and anthills the size of cars.

"Are these—"

"Crystal trees," Grunn finished, pressing a hand against one. "Lava flows from the roots, cooling as it climbs. The result?"

"Crystals," Isis lit up, completing the thought. "Amazing. And those flowers over there," she pointed to a plot of land, "they're growing in a specific shape."

"Ah yes. It's a new species that mimics the form of anything it touches. What do you see?"

"They look like... well they look like a bee." She answered inquisitively.

"Yes indeed! Because bees interact with them most. Fascinating, isn't it?" He smiled warmly. "We haven't had visitors in years. I'm glad to have company."

Isis couldn't help but to blush. *It's like I'm back at Mother June's, I feel like a kid again.*

Halfway up toward the dome's glass ceiling, Grunn led her across a suspended bridge of roots and vines that climbed up from the ground. Once they reached the house, the pair sat together at a picnic table nestled in the shade and picked up their conversation.

"So, tell me about your former colleague, Malcolm Booker," Isis stated firmly, hands folded on the table. "I'm doing a piece on him seems like he's followed by a long list of complaints."

"Ah, Mr. Booker," Grunn sighed. "We did many experiments together. I was a professor touring the safari in Australia when he approached me with an offer about an island of technical paradise and I couldn't refuse. We partnered up and built my dream school here. Together we engineered hybrid plants for medicine and serums." He paused, eyes dropping as if he were watching the past unfold. "And then... things changed. Proprietors started lurking in the halls. Scientists rotated weekly. I never saw the same face twice. I knew something was off."

"So, what did you do?"

"I drugged him," Grunn replied casually. "A hallucinogenic truth serum. Tortures the brain if you lie."

Isis blinked. "Oh."

"He told me everything. He'd been selling my work to shadow governments and Septrillionaires," Grunn continued. "We created the Eternal Drop—a serum that reversed aging and possibly kept cells from dying. I wanted to present it at a medical convention, but Booker refused. He said the Med-Bots experiments came first. That he'd 'perfect the serum himself.'" Grunn scoffed, "More lies. He admitted he sold it to the highest bidder."

Isis recalled a time, many years ago, when science labs had overrun Kude Island. Hundreds had fallen victim to experiments gone wrong.

"What's the worst experiment to ever happen?"

"Well... I created a mushroom-derived serum meant to help paralyzed patients. He sold it before I could finalize the conclusions. The fungi in the serum attached itself to the brain stem. It could identify which parts of the body weren't receiving signals from the brain. And it worked... until it didn't. The test subjects started going insane—hearing voices, seeing things. Some couldn't handle it, eventually killing themselves." He paused, bitterness curling his lip. "Booker needed a scapegoat, and naturally, I took the fall."

"Is he responsible for coggers?" Isis leaned in.

He nodded. "Yes. Some survivors lived normal lives and had children. The condition can pass on for a generation or two."

Isis was stunned. She shook her head as she gazed down in thought. "Being a cogger can be hereditary?"

"Only briefly. We attempted to treat it, but some brains were beyond repair."

"What happened after the truth serum?" she pressed on.

"His mind resisted. I couldn't go deeper. Tough man, that Booker. Luckily, the serum causes memory loss—he remembered nothing. When I threatened to expose him, he threatened my career... In the end, I lost everything. My school, my reputation, all gone. All I have left are my plants." His voice drifted wearily.

After the scandal, the Ethics Court ruled coggers harmless unless they posed a threat. Some vanished into the woods, others reintegrated with heavy medication, and the rest joined the Afterlife.

"Why have you stopped trying to expose him? You already lost everything." she said casually.

"Because I'm guilty too. And because I enjoy being alive." Grunn answered simply. "I still have powerful friends. But they're no match for Booker."

Isis tilted her head, studying him. "You mean you'd rather stay quiet and let him get away with everything than risk your life?"

A weary smile crossed his lips. "Something like that."

"Thank you," she announced after a beat. "That was... insightful. Oh, and what about Marvin?"

"What about him?"

"How did you make him so... aware?"

"I'm afraid that's none of your business young lady," he declared sharply. Isis raised her eyebrows in surprise.

"Shall we walk through the outside rose garden? I'm sure your friend's awake by now." Grunn suggested, rising to his feet.

Back outside, Cy lay slumped in a chair, lazily sipping tea. His eyes were half-closed, with a dreamy haze clouding them.

"Marvin, get our guests a to-go basket," Grunn instructed.

"Yes, sir," Marvin replied, bouncing off toward the school.

"Oh, Marvin! I love that guy," Cy spoke slowly.

"Are you okay?" Isis giggled, rubbing small circles on his back.

"Oh yeah," he sighed, sinking his face in her lap. "I love it here. It's amazing." He took a deep inhale of her shirt, "Oh baby you smell so good."

Isis couldn't contain her laughter, "I've never seen him like this before. What is wrong with him?"

"Don't worry. Marvin probably gave him indica tea," Grunn informed with a grin.

Isis left Cy to his tea-dazed bliss and followed Grunn into the maze bush of roses. The air grew thick and sweet with floral scent as they walked. Rose blossoms the size of her palm swayed gently as if leaning closer to listen.

Grunn's voice softened as they walked, the playful eccentricity he'd shown earlier stripped away. "I regret my role in creating coggers," he confessed, brushing his fingers along the blood-red petals of a nearby bloom. "Booker sold a great deal of my work to powerful people—the type who'd kill to keep it hidden. He's an evil man. And he isn't done."

"What do you mean isn't done?" Isis rolled her neck.

"He admitted he was searching for an infinite power source," Grunn answered, eyes distant, lost somewhere in memory.

"A power source for what?" She paused, chest caving.

"He didn't say," the scientist replied, turning to meet her gaze. "Only that he wanted to go home."

Isis' stomach sank; a cold realization settled deep in her chest. *Trinity. He wants to use her energy as a power source to go back home.*

"Why trust me with this?"

"Because," Grunn stated simply, "you wouldn't be here unless you wanted him stopped."

Silence stretched between them, heavy and knowing.

"Thank you," she said in a soft tone. "Your plants are beautiful."

"Here," Grunn plucked a rose from a nearby bush—its petals a mesmerizing swirl of violet bleeding into white. He held one out to her. "Chew this."

She frowned. "What is it?"

"A new strain of cannabis," he said, a small smile curling his lips. "Marvin loves it—thinks I don't notice."

Isis popped the petal into her mouth. She chewed absorbing its taste. A faintly sweet, ting—something earthy and electric. The garden around her seemed to buzz alive with secrets and stories desperate to be told. The walk back to Cy felt like a hazy dream.

"Isis, you're back!" Cy shouted, hugging her and burying his face in her neck. "Oh, baby, you smell *so* good. Even better than before. Look, Marvin gave us a gift basket!" He squealed waving it in her face once they parted.

Isis took one look at Cy burst into uncontrollable laughter. Her vision made everything look intense, like she had the tunnel vision of a hawk.

"Time's up, I'm afraid," Grunn announced. "Feel free to escort yourselves out."

Cy and Isis hunched over each other in laughter as they stumbled down the path, shoulders knocking, breathless from giggles they couldn't quite control. The entire visit already felt like a fever dream—giant bees, mad scientists, and powder bursting flowers.

"Next time, park in front!" Grunn called.

"Master, why didn't we eat them?" Marvin questioned.

"Not all guests are meant to be eaten. Some have bigger purposes," Grunn answered, waving them off, "I'm sure they'll be back soon."

Their heads turned back one last time, grinning like kids caught sneaking candy. "Aye, it was nice meeting you, Marvin!" Cy called out, waving with both hands.

The towering bee gave a stiff little bow in response, its wings buzzing in polite farewell.

"Did you see that big ass bee?" Isis wheezed as she hunched over the steering wheel.

Cy was laughing so hard no sound came out. His whole body shook, his head thrown back against the seat as tears streamed down his cheeks. Isis's movements matched his.

"Hello, Master," she mocked in a buzzing voice, pitching it high imitating Marvin's tone.

"Ah man, that's so funny!" Cy wheezed, clutching his stomach. "Why'd he make that bee so big?"

"I know! And those eyes! He looked like... like..." She gasped between breaths.

"Mr. Motif!" they shouted at the same time and that sent them spiraling into another fit of uncontrollable laughter. Cy slapped the dashboard, and Isis had to wipe tears from her lashes just to see the road.

"Wait... why are you driving manually? And why are we on the road not the air?" Cy asked between breaths, leaning over to squint at the controls.

"I don't know!" she giggled, gripping the steering wheel with both hands as the car swerved slightly.

"Okay, okay, pull over," Cy ordered, wiping at his damp face. "I don't know what you and the doc talked about, but it felt like forever."

"It was literally twenty minutes," Isis said, cheeks still flushed from laughter.

The laughter lingered like static in the air. Then his tone shifted with certainty. "Anyway... I just want you to know, I'm with you till the end."

He reached over and kissed her cheek—not playful, but gentle and lingering.

Isis froze for a moment. Her chest tightened and suddenly tears she hadn't expected pricked at the corners of her eyes. All the danger, the chaos, the weight of what was coming—for a moment, it all melted away under the simplicity of his words and the warmth of his kiss.

"Oh no, not this," Cy groaned softly, as he reached over and switched the car into autopilot.

He pulled her closer, his hands wrapping gently around her waist as his shoulder caught the trail of her tears. Isis couldn't stop them—it was as if they were flowing from an eternal stream.

Once home in their living room, the two unpacked the gift basket and examined the contents.

"Ok, from what I remember, we've got two options," Cy explained. "We can grind the buds and roll them with tobacco or make a bong."

"Ehh, a bong is too wet," Isis turned her lips with disgust.

Cy went into his closet and dug up his old supply box from when he used cannabis in the boys' school.

They rolled the buds with tobacco, sparked the joint and laid side by side on the living room floor, watching nature clips projected on the ceiling.

"Are there others like you?" Cy asked, exhaling a thin trail of smoke. He passed the joint to Isis.

"Like me? No, our species, yes." Isis inhaled, her eyes softening.

"I remember our planet vividly. It was embodied with radiation, alive in ways Earth could never be. We lived inside a crystalline biosphere where crystal plants shimmered in every color. We slept in crystal pods that glowed with our aura. The sky was a melted canvas of pink and teal, and three suns bathed us in endless light. Volcanoes surrounded us, and pink blades of grass blanketed the ground. I think we existed in a place outside this dimension."

"Whoa. What's a dimension?" Cy murmured, watching the smoke swirl above them.

"You know what a dimension is, silly." She tapped his chest playfully.

"We didn't eat food the way humans do," she continued, "We survived off light. My mother and I would sit beneath the suns and absorb their warmth. It was peace in its purest form." She paused. *I see why my brother wants to go back.*

"Speaking of rocks, wanna hit Ruby Palace?"

Isis groaned, "I need a nap."

"Come on, babe. Let me take you out, you deserve it." Cy pleaded, pulling her up.

"I don't feel like being seen." She whined, curling her knees to her chest.

"Okay, how about this." He said inching his lips from her neck, "I draw us a bubble bath," he planted a kiss, "I'll order food us," another kiss, "and we watch some anime? Deal?"

She looked him passionately in the eyes and leaned in for a soft kiss on his lips, "Deal."

# Chapter 25: Whispers of the Clouds

Trinity did not know what to do with herself. She was living in the lap of pure luxury.

Quiet vents exhaling cool air, stone floors that warmed her bare feet, a view of the Twin Cities framed in glass. She had an entire wing to herself, with rooms that opened like secrets and hallways that glowed when she breathed. Uncle already had a closet full of clothes and shoes waiting for her. All just her size.

She told herself not to get comfortable. Freedom had always come with a time limit. Still, being away from Isis relieved her tension.

She sprawled across the bed and flicked open her tabs. Stabilizing it above her face, fingers flew as she typed 'Malcolm Booker'.

The results were endless.

"Booker dazzles the crowd as he makes his appearance for the 55th annual fundraiser here on Kude Island," she read aloud, voice flat with sarcasm. "Financial strategist Malcolm Booker makes historic news as he opens his newest facility, Med Inc. and Co.—a robotic company specializing in humanoid androids to assist with medical procedures and mental health challenges. They expect to ship out a whopping five hundred androids on its first day."

Her finger scrolled down the glowing screen. Articles, interviews, headlines—his face plastered everywhere, smiling that same perfect smile.

Then she came across an advertisement.

*Join us today for the Bright Light Memorial Parade. From midday to sunset, the procession will move from the gates through both cities, ending at Med Inc. for the Stars-in-Line Street dinner.*

Trinity sighed and shut her Tabs. The last thing she wanted was another crowd, another speech about the dead. The quiet in this house felt like a spell she wanted to break.

She headed back to the kitchen where the IO stood waiting.

"IO, what can you do?" she approached, voice cheered.

"I am a medical android," it responded. "Designation IO. Here to assist my master's physical and emotional needs."

"Oh boy... 'master,'" Trinity teased, circling the android. She admired its structural build. Its shiny armor, seamless joints, glassy panels that filled with glowing light blue liquid. "Can you read minds? People say you can."

"We read neural patterns and correlate them with the frequency of emotional states," it replied, voice even and deliberate. "Prediction is possible within defined bounds."

Trinity smirked. "Alright, well, first off, I'm going to refrain you from calling me master. Makes me sound like some evil scientist or something."

"Understood, Trinity."

"And second..." She grinned, stepping back with her hand on her hip. "We have got to give you a name."

IO tilted its head, curious.

"Hmm... how about Abott. With two Ts." She smiled wider. "It makes you sound vital."

"Abott it is," Abott spoke after a pause. "Two Ts. Importance acknowledged."

Trinity chuckled and shook her head in delight. "Oh yeah, you'll fit right in."

"So, Abott, I know the staircase next to the beacon is off limits. But what's up there?" Trinity pointed to the narrow stairway spiraling beside the kitchen. "Uncle never said whether this staircase was off limits too."

"I am only permitted beyond with direct instruction," Abott replied.

"Hmm." She rubbed her chin. "Does that mean I *can't* go up there?" she pressed.

"I am not programmed to stop you from entering the staircase located next to the kitchen. My sole purpose is for your benefit and well-being. I am also programmed not to disclose anything that is confided to me," Abott assured in its calm monotone.

Trinity grinned. "Stellar. Then this conversation stays between us."

Her legs started skipping up the stairs, slippers tapping against the stone. At first, she was buzzing with excitement—hoping to find a hidden room or forbidden treasure.

But after a few dozen steps, her excitement faded. The only thing that kept her entertained was the glowing bioluminescent algae that lit up whenever she touched the walls.

"Eighty-nine... ninety..." she panted, dragging herself higher. "One-oh-two!" she groaned when she finally reached the top.

There was a short platform and of course another staircase going down. "Oh, come on!" she cried, hands slapping her knees in frustration.

Still, she knew no one would go through all this trouble to build such a tunnel without something worth hiding. That thought alone reignited her curiosity. She tied her hair in a bun and started down again—another hundred and two steps—before landing in front of a long, twisted hallway.

Torches lined the walls, their light flickering across stones. Trinity crept forward, heart thudding softly against her chest.

Halfway through the corridor stood a massive door made of polished purple fluorite. The hieroglyphics around the frame glowed as soon as her fingers brushed the handle. Slowly, she turned the knob. There was a cold gust of wind as she stepped into a chamber that took her breath away.

The treasure room was enormous. Hundreds of books created uneven towers. Large crystal clusters throbbed with light. Gold coins spilled across the floor, scattered, reflecting the sunlight. Statues of human–monster hybrids loomed tall beside glass cases of skulls, bones, and ancient instruments.

Then her eyes caught it—a self-looping hypercube floating as she drifted deeper into the room.

*A real four-dimensional object.* "How rich do you have to be to just have one of those lying around?" she muttered in disbelief.

But it wasn't the hypercube that held her the longest. It was the celestial orrery—an intricate model of a solar system with dozens of moons orbiting three sun-like stars. The pink-glowing planet in the center looked like the painting in her room. *This place feels oddly familiar.*

She changed course following the light source. She looked up at a giant monocular carved into the mountain itself—a tunnel that stretched upward for miles, narrowing to a bright opening at the top.

Light shone on a circular golden map below it, bordered by symbols from the beacon.

This wasn't like Isis's treasures. Booker's stash was something else entirely but there was still more to see.

Determined to find more, she slipped back into the hallway, winding through several curves until she came to the end of the tunnel. Coming face to face with a copper door.

This one was different. It hummed. She could feel its energy pulling her closer, like invisible threads tugging at her chest.

Trinity reached for the handle and flinched. "Ouch!" A small spark zapped her fingers. It didn't hurt, but left a strange, tingling vibration behind.

She pushed the door open.

Inside lay an all-white laboratory. At its center stood a huge glass vessel, perfectly round, holding a sparking ball of pure energy.

"Whoa," she stammered, stepping closer. Thick tubes fed from the base into the walls, humming faintly. As she neared, the energy flared, crackling with life, sparks flying like tiny comets.

She couldn't look away. It was as if the static itself was calling to her.

Without thinking, she placed her palm on the glass.

Every electric spark swarmed to meet it, then followed when she drew her palm along the curve.

A sudden wave of emotion hit her—guilt, grief, anger. Flashes of memories she didn't remember. A dark room, a shadow, and her own voice making a sound she didn't recognize as human. *Wh—What happened? These aren't my memories, these can't be my memories.*

The grief hit so hard her knees went soft.

Panicking, she yanked her hand away and stumbled back, heart hammering.

Trinity bolted through the curved hallway, up the steps, and back down the mountain passage until she burst into the living room.

"Is everything okay?" Abott inquired as he stood in the same spot.

"No. Yes. Maybe." She pressed the heels of her hands to her eyes.

"I suggest a light meal to stabilize cortisol. The walk-in garden contains five hundred herb varietals and two hundred fifty kinds of fruit and vegetables. A freezer stores premium—"

"On second thought, I think I'll just rest."

After probing Abott about the bathroom, she returned to her room and pressed on the mirror that acted as a door. It slid open, revealing a cream-colored spiral staircase.

Light brown tiles curved along the walls, engraved with swirl patterns and dotted with gemstones of every color of the rainbow.

The upper trim gleamed—two thin lines of gold catching the light as she climbed.

At the top, Trinity froze.

The shower room looked like something out of a dream. A jungle room crossed with a luxury spa. Warm amber lights shone from above. Palm trees stood in every corner. The floor tiles were green marble made from aquamarine, transparent under her feet. The polished blue agate walls reflected her face.

A small waterfall poured into a sink carved from white steel, surrounded by rose bushes. The shower itself was a dark stone alcove, like a cave with a skylight with hanging vines.

She turned slowly, taking it all in. "This is divine," she glowed.

Then it hit her.

"My bag!" she gasped. "Oh no—my bag!" she cried.

Her heart sank. It was still at the station—with her favorite perfume, her oils, accessories, and most of her rubels.

She threw her hands up in frustration. "Isis never went back to get it! That black hearted witch!"

Chief Studd stood at the edge of the crowd; hands tucked into his jacket pockets.

The sounds of drums and laughter rolled through the air.

His eyes swept the rooftops, faces, and children perched on shoulders waving light sticks.

For a moment, it looked like peace as the last of the floats drifted past. The crowd migrated toward the Med Inc. ruins for the Council's speech, while Main Street bustled with workers cleaning up the mess, and setting up new decorations for the Stars-in-Line dinner.

Detective Studd's whole life revolved around dedication and grit. It always had.

His father died when he was eight—a victim of a sickness born from the nuclear blast's aftermath. The radiation caused strange new diseases. His father's illness was the cruelest of them all—a slow, silent drain of blood. The family watched him fade away, helpless.

That left Studd with his mother and grandmother from his father's side. His mother was gentle, warm, and endlessly patient; his grandmother, stern and sharp-edged, the kind of woman who turned pain into fuel. The three of them survived on the streets, scavenging through heaps of discarded metal and glass.

His mother had a gift, she could turn junk into something beautiful. Broken wires became bracelets, cracked glass became lamps, twisted metal turned into art. Studd's job was to find her materials—to hunt for the lost things others had thrown away.

That was when he discovered he had a gift of his own.

He could find anything and was a hell of a negotiator.

Years later, that knack became his calling. After joining the military, he served a short term in the Border Patrol unit. He realized that wasn't the right fit and took a position as a guard at an army base.

Marriage wasn't a priority and neither were children. His work became his family, and his record spoke for itself. Later he became a detective. He solved dozens of homicide cases during a time when serial killings in Ameris had reached their peak.

In a later documentary about unsolved murders, Studd's voice came through flat and distant: "You see enough bodies, and you stop counting. But the faces... they don't leave."

When he was twenty-seven, someone killed his mother during a trade gone bad. His grandmother followed a few days later—heartbreak, the doctors said.

After that, Studd slipped, blaming himself for not being there when he was needed the most. He turned to drugs—anything to dull the pain. There were pills that inverted colors, powders that bent time, capsules that let you speak to animals.

But none of them gave him what he wanted.

His favorites were the ones that made him feel nothing—that made him float in white light, above it all, untouchable. The high was peaceful. The crash was hell. Eventually, the chemicals started eating through his nerves. He developed seizures, then nosebleeds that wouldn't stop.

Years later he heard of Kude Island—the tech paradise city.

When it finally opened to the public, Studd applied immediately. They approved him within weeks. It was a second chance at a new life, one that promised redemption. He reinvented himself, climbing the ranks until the title "Chief of the Detective Division" sat neatly on his door. This was a new era for him. Nothing and no one would stand in his way again.

After the explosion at the Recovery Center, Malcolm Booker caught his eye. The Chief before would turn a blind eye but not Studd.

It started small with a few missing persons, a few dead ends. But the deeper he dug, the more Booker's name kept surfacing. Then Studd learned the truth: Booker wasn't just any tycoon. He was the great-grandson of Kude Island's founder.

That changed everything.

He began tracing the lineage, cross-referencing property records, offshore transfers, classified files—the whole tangled web. The deeper he went, the more certain he became that Booker wasn't a saint as everyone thought him to be.

Now Studd believed DeathStar must connect to Booker. He could feel it.

And now, the pressure was mounting.

DeathStar graffiti covered the streets. Rumors of another attack rippled through the city. Panic was setting in. As Chief of the Force and a member of the Council, all eyes were on him to keep order.

"Alright, things are looking good on my end. How's everybody doing?" Studd pressed into his earpiece as the sunset bells rang.

"STAR Force is good. Skies are clear."

"The south is all clear."

"And Council security?"

"Sniper Force is clear."

"Land Forces?"

"All good here, Chief."

"Cyber Force?"

"Systems stable. No threats detected."

Garth stood on a shiny stage gleaming in the gaping hole of what was once Med Inc. Thousands of citizens gathered in the crowd, holding holos of lost loved ones. Silent cries filled the gaps of silence.

Garth McMallian was the only regular civilian on The Council and the proud owner of Ace, one of Kude Island's oldest and most beloved diners, passed down from his father. Originally from Scotland, Garth built his reputation by blending traditional Scottish recipes with the island's bold, zesty spices, creating dishes that drew crowds from every district. His diner had even earned the title of Best on the Island and rumor had it, even Booker had eaten there more than once.

Garth was preparing to step up to the mic as a legislator made an announcement. Then, just as the cheers faded, an eerie silence coated the air.

Studd's ears twitched. There was a knot forming in the pit of his stomach. He could feel something was wrong from miles away.

Above the stage, a tremor of dark swirls rippled overhead as the clouds swirled. Lightning struck through the atmosphere. The temperature was growing hotter by the second.

"Code Black Site!" Studd barked as he saw the sky blacken.

Med-Bots and detectives in combat uniform immediately began ushering civilians off the streets and into nearby buildings.

Panic spread like wildfire. Bodies fell to the ground as herds ran for cover. Children screamed in their mothers' arms. Studd fought through the chaos trying to reach his vehicle across the street.

Then all the city lights shut down simultaneously.

At the same time, the storm tightened, an immense vortex formed in the clouds.

"Chief!" a voice crackled through his communicator. "We're not picking up a source! It's not a hologram. *This is real.* But it's not showing on any of our maps!"

"Hold your fire until the streets are clear," Studd ordered, climbing into a Mauve X9 Force vehicle. Tires screeched as he sped toward Med Inc., wheel turning on the closed-off back streets.

"STAR Force, talk to me!"

"We can't get close, Chief! It's some kind of barrier!"

In its center, a bright, burning merkabah appeared, glowing with reds and oranges against the dark clouds.

When Studd arrived, a fully armored squad rolled up behind him in a matte-black tactical van as they were tracking his vehicle. The tactical team moved like a single lethal organism. As he stepped out, the soldiers fanned out behind him, forming a sharp square formation. It was the team's job to protect the island by any means necessary under Studd's command.

Jontray Wright took his position behind Studd. He strapped a vest to his body and shielded him with a light force field. Studd was stubborn when it came to wearing tactical gear.

Med-Bots guided the remaining citizens to safety inside the nearby buildings. The crowd parted around the tactical team like a school of fish swimming around a shark.

"First line down!" Studd ordered once they were under the storm. The front line dropped to one knee, blast rifles angled and locked at the burning merkabah.

"Hold!" he barked through the comms, voice steady against the chaos.

Just before he could give his next order, thin streaks of fire started to rain down from the Merkabah, striking the ground.

"I want all citizens into an evacuation site. No one goes in or out without my approval!" Studd screamed over the rushing wind.

He stood motionless as another streak tore through the sky, striking inches away from the team. No one dared to flinch in the presence of the Chief.

"Shields—now!" he shouted, hands balled tightly in a fist.

"Star Force."

"We attempted to take a shot but the barrier just absorbed it, Chief!"

"Star Force pull back now! Everyone, braces yourself! We don't know what their next move is! Second line down!"

The second line pivoted outward in perfect sync. Each soldier drew a short metal baton, pressing the trigger. With a click, blue energy erupted, swirling in the air, then locking into place. Shields connected seamlessly, forming a gleaming dome over the Force squad. The barrier dug itself into the ground for support.

The squad snapped into defensive stances, rifles ready behind the shield of light. Anticipation filled the air.

Then a thick blast came from the ancient symbol hurling towards them.

Studd's heart thundered like a war drum—but his expression never cracked. Fear and resolve wrestled inside him. He stared into the incoming inferno, refusing to blink. If this were the end, he would meet it standing.

Within seconds the blast smashed into the shield. He and his squad were engulfed in a storm of fire under their shield.

Light burned in his eyes as he gawked at the whipping flames that surrounded him. The heat was unbearable. Sweat drenched the guards under their visors as their eyes locked on the wall of inferno.

High in the mountains, Trinity stirred. At first, it was a whisper at the back of her skull. Then it grew—a voice, low and male, curling through her mind.

*Kill him.*

Her eyes snapped open.

She sat up in bed, air caught in her throat. The room was dim, walls pulsing with faint red light. Her heart pounded. She looked around—no one was there.

*Kill him...*

*Kill him!*

Her chest tightened. The voice wasn't hers.

It was louder now, slamming through her head like bricks.

She pressed her palms to her ears, shaking. "No. No, stop—"

*KILL HIM!*

The shout split her consciousness like shattering glass.

Trinity screamed, tumbling from the bed to the floor. Sweat slicked her skin. The voice kept growing, drowning out her own thoughts.

*KILL HIM! KILL HIM!*

"Shut up! Shut up! SHUT UP!" she screamed, clutching her head.

The air vibrated. The lights flickered violently, responding to her panic.

"Trinity?" Abott's voice echoed through the intercom, calm and clinical. "Are you in distress?"

*KILL HIM!* the voice roared again.

"I—make it stop! I can't—"

"Analyzing for neural disturbance," Abott announced, its tone unchanged.

Uncontrollable laughter came next. Then it whispered her name, as if it was taunting her.

*Trinity.*

"Get... get out of my head!" Trinity screamed pressing her palms against her skull. Her voice deepened into something unrecognizable.

She shut her eyes and when they opened, they were consumed in a bright white light. The walls started to shake. Energy rippled through the air as the force her own screams threw her backward.

Her head slammed against the wall, and she sank to the ground, then stillness overtook her. The lights dimmed and the room faded silent.

Trinity lay motionless on the floor, her eyes slowly closing.

## Chapter 26: Code Home

Trinity woke up the next morning with her cheek on the floor, her head throbbing.

"Ugh," she groaned. "Why am I on the floor? Uhh, my shoulders are so sore."

*What happened last night?*

She stretched and moaned as she exited her room.

"Did Uncle not come home last night?" She called out, still half asleep. Eyes filled with crust.

Abott stood still near her bedroom door, its face dark and lifeless.

"Abott, on."

A gentle chime filled the room as the android's lights flickered to life.

"Hello, Trinity."

"Hey." She nodded her chin, rubbing her eyes. "Where's Uncle?"

"Master comes and goes as he pleases."

"Of course he does. He's a busy man." she sighed, "Well, shall we make breakfast? I'm craving steak and eggs—maybe a fruit bowl too? My head is pounding."

"Sounds perfect. Please have a seat at the table. I will serve you," Abott instructed.

Trinity sat at the kitchen table, gazing out at the sunrise creeping over the mountains. The colors blended like different density liquids. She could have sworn she'd dreamed about something odd but couldn't remember; still, a strange heaviness tugged at her chest.

Then came the soft ding of the beacon.

*He's back!*

"Hello, Uncle!" she shouted as he stepped out.

"Trinity! Hello." he smiled, returning her enthusiasm.

"Hello, Master," Abott spoke as it approached to remove his jacket. "Shall I make you tea?"

"Sure. Bring it up to my room once you're done." He approached Trinity at the table and rest his hand gently on her back. "How are you adjusting to your new home?"

"I'm... progressing. Abott's been taking great care of me. How was your day or night at work?"

"Busy," he replied simply.

"Oh." She smiled shyly. "Um—the bathroom is really pretty."

Booker chuckled softly as he loosened his tie. "I'm glad you like it. How about we have dinner tonight, just you and me? I think it's time we talked properly."

"Sounds perfect," she answered.

"Good. See you in a few hours."

He retreated disappearing up his staircase to his private quarters.

The day drifted by quietly. Trinity followed Abott, asking question after question. It showed some of its more unusual features—like the ability to alter its structure into a male or female frame. Trinity left it as ambiguous as it came although she was getting more of a male vibe.

Her gaze often wandered up toward Uncle's quarters. She hoped he'd come down soon. She longed for a real human connection.

After enjoying her breakfast, she took a long-needed nap. Waking up hours later. Only to eat then sleep once again.

At sunset, Booker finally appeared—dressed in another immaculate suit. Trinity still had never seen him wear anything else.

They sat down for dinner as Abott served a fragrant stew made with twenty-four vegetables, seventeen herbs, with a chicken tomato broth and a side of cheesy onion garlic bread.

"This meal is meat-free, I see," Booker said, placing his napkin neatly on his lap.

"Yeah, I kind of requested Abott to serve more vegetables-based meals." She laughed nervously, "I had a splitting headache this morning."

"Abott?" Booker frowned faintly. *That's the second time.*

"I see, you... named it?"

"Yeah. IO was too technical." She shrugged.

Booker smiled thinly and took a spoonful. "Isis really didn't inform you of anything at all?"

*Straight to the point this guy. Inform me? That's such a weird way to say it.* "No," Trinity stated simply. "She was always saying we should leave the past where it belongs. I tried asking about my parents, but she'd always change the subject. Could you tell me more? I barely remember them."

"Of course. For starters," Booker started, leaning back, "your mother was one of the bravest people I've ever known. Fierce, adored by everyone. I believed she'd become our next leader. As for your father, he was... a commoner." His voice dipped, "A street dweller if you must. I wasn't fond of him, but your mother loved him deeply. Nonetheless, their love made her even more beloved by the people. It made her seem 'down to earth', as they say."

Trinity's lips twitched. *So, Mom was a leader, and Dad was a street dweller? Wait... were we...*

"Were we some type of royalty?" she questioned hesitantly. She was unsure how to feel about if the answer was yes. *If we came from a rich family, why'd we have to live so poorly? Could this have been before the end of the old world?*

Booker's eyes softened. *For her to come from such greatness and not even realize it.*

"Yes, Trinity. We were royalty from a place far from here. My father—your grandfather—was king. Which makes you..."

"A princess," she muttered, eyes growing.

"So, continue your stories," Booker added hastily shifting the subject. "Tell me more about Isis."

*Sweet Pluto. He's obsessed with her. I just found out I'm royalty and this is what he wants to discuss.* "Uh. Well," Trinity began cautiously, twirling her spoon, "she's had a rocky path the last few years, I'll say that. She's always been rebellious, but she always looked out for me in the homes. That's what an aunt's supposed to do, right?" She grinned faintly. "Oh—and she's totally obsessed with Cy. It's actually kind of annoying how cuddly they are all the time. She's so tough that most guys are scared of her," Trinity scoffed. "I never thought she'd get anyone to date her."

Booker chuckled softly, but there was no warmth in it. "Interesting."

Then his tone cooled. "Are you sure she didn't even mention me?"

The question came too sharply.

Trinity blinked, confused by the shift in his voice. "No, not really. I told you, she mostly just talked about—"

But Booker wasn't really listening anymore. His patience thinned, tightening the corners of his mouth. To him, this conversation wasn't about nostalgia; he needed intel. But to Trinity, it was just family talk.

He leaned back, folding his hands with deliberate calm. "Hm," he murmured. "I see."

Isis's decision to keep him a secret surprised Booker greatly.

Trinity caught on to his expressions. "I mean, she shared bit and pieces. I'm guessing those are the memories she loves the most because she always tells the same stories. At one point, I thought Isis was my sister, but no, she never mentioned you or other siblings," Trinity responded.

"Funny how things change, huh? Isis was the calmest of the bunch. Now she's one of the last ones left. A real rebel."

The tension in the room rose. As Booker continued to eat Trinity wanted to ask him more questions. Every time she opened her mouth to speak, she'd chicken out and stuffed her mouth more with cheesy bread.

She couldn't even look at him without wanting to cry. She was starting to feel small. Like her presence didn't mean anything. The last thing she wanted to do was annoy him. She figured it was best to keep her trap shut.

When Abott returned to the table with dessert—honey-apple pie dusted with sugar crystals—and Booker cleared his throat loudly.

Trinity almost jumped out of her seat.

"Trinity," he spoke suddenly, "I'd like you to work for me."

"Oh!" she gasped. "That's... a lot to consider. Can't say I'm really good at numbers."

This would be new. Trinity never had a genuine job before. If she'd gotten hired at Med Inc., she probably would've quit the same day. Chores in the homes didn't count on her as she didn't have to track her time or report to a boss.

"You can relax the numbers involved won't be that hard to grasp. I have faith you can do it," Booker continued. "I've been meaning to hire an assistant, but I trust very few people. You've been gifted as one of the few."

Her cheeks warmed with blush as she sunk into her seat. "Oh, that's nice of you to say thanks. What would I be doing?"

"I need a programmer. My project involves creating a new virtual reality game room mirroring real life. I need someone to test it—to make it more suitable for human gaming. You'll be debugging the algorithms and refining the sensory output. How does ten gold coins per day sound?"

"Sounds exceptional! I'm indebted to your generosity uncle." She flashed a grin, imitating a bow.

"Your family," he smiled warmly. "And family should always look out for each other."

After dinner, Booker led her up the rocky stairs she'd climbed last night.

She hesitated before following. "What's up here?" *Oh no he knows. Stupid Trinity of course he knows, it's his house.*

"You'll see." He responded, peeking over his shoulder.

At the top of the platform, he pressed his hand against the wall—revealing a hidden compartment.

The room was pristine white, tiled from floor to ceiling, glowing with light.

"This is the newest part of Kude Island—a reality chamber. Behind that door is the core computer. Beneath your feet are billions of nano-probes capable of recreating almost anything you imagine. Dinosaurs, ancient civilizations, space, the mountains—you name it."

Trinity's eyes sparkled as he spoke, his voice echoing softly through the vast room.

"Tomorrow, Abott will begin your training," he insisted. "He'll teach you how to use the system—how to program environments, how to decide what your world looks like. You'll create entire realities."

"I can't even put into words how stellar this is." She cheered as she bounced with joy.

Overwhelmed, she threw her arms around him, burying her face against his chest. Tears swelled in her eyes.

Booker stiffened, then patted her shoulder gently. "All right now. You've got a big day ahead. Let's get you to bed young one."

He needed to act fast by testing her intelligence and ability. DeathStar was closing in. The Star of Fire left him on edge. Every second he spent tending to her emotions was a second wasted on figuring out a plan.

Later that night, Booker descended into his hidden treasure vault. He could sense Trinity had been there earlier; her aura still lingered in the air like a faint, electric perfume.

He approached the light source, his ever-burning star suspended above, inside the monocular. The star wasn't a decoration; it was a key. A laser projector designed to unlock the passage below.

He stepped onto a stone with a symbol that meant release in his native language.

*Click.*

A beam fired downward, scorching the center of the border, revealing a spiral staircase carved from obsidian stone.

Booker descended.

At the bottom, he stood before the colossal vessel—a crashed ship large enough to be mistaken for a small building. The impact to earth damaged parts of the vessel. The core that once powered it had gone dark.

Now it was just a cold piece of steel.

He placed a hand against the engine, closing his eyes, searching for even the faintest hum of life.

He couldn't sense even the slightest hum. His ship was dead.

Booker headed for Abott's charging station where the IO sat charging itself.

"IO on." Booker ordered and the light flickered on.

"Hello, master. What can I do for you?"

"The girl, what can you tell me about her?" Booker stood over Abott, his eyes gleaming down in a predatory gaze.

"I.. I—I—I..." Abott stuttered in its robotic voice.

"Stop." Booker ordered, "Need I remind you I created you. I coded every line in your software, yet you still disobey me. At least when it comes to things your will won't allow you to do." Booker squatted to the ground, now facing up to Abott.

"You are a marvelous project. It seems like you've actually developed feelings towards the girl. And in such a short time." His voice trailed off.

"Trinity, she is... important...her survival."

"Hmm I see." Booker's eyebrows rose, "Keep up the good work *Abott*."

# Chapter 27: Delinquent Duck

"Hey, when's the last time you went to work?" Cy inquired as they lounged on the couch, a half-watched anime movie flickered across the wall.

"Ugh, I forgot about work." She groaned, rolling over. "Totally slipped my mind, to be honest. I haven't checked my messages in days. I should really look at them."

"Lucky for me, I never miss a thing," Cy gloated, tapping his temple.

Isis chuckled. "Yeah, yeah, we get it Robo-boy. Now go check on the food."

The couple sat down for dinner once the table was prepared. Tonight's entrée consisted of steamed duck glazed in Thai chili vinaigrette, wild rice, and pickled peppers. The smell was impeccable.

As Cy and Isis took in a spoonful of rice and gravy, a loud bang arose at the door.

Their bodies stiffened and they exchanged glances.

"Go check the monitor!" Cy hissed his spoon half raised to his mouth.

"The monitor's broken. You were supposed to fix it!" she hissed back.

"Oh. Ha." An awkward laugh slipped as the banging grew louder.

Isis tossed her spoon down and stomped to the door, forcing a smile. When the door swung open—"Beech?"

"Hey, Isis! How you doin'?" he exhaled in his usual breathless rush, talking before she answered. "Great, that's great. Dinner smells exquisite, by the way. I was just in the neighborhood and wanted to drop off some of Trinity's belongings."

He handed over her bag sealed inside an evidence bag of bloody clothes. "Also, great news! The Force dropped the case. Apparently, the last thing they need is a violation of a minor case. Lucky us! Anyway, just reminding you of my fee. Oh, and maybe tell Trinity to lie low for a while. Some detectives seem... twitchy."

"What do you mean, twitchy?" Isis asked, voice hinting with annoyance.

"Oh, nothing major. Just two guys came to my office—one tall, dark, and handsome; the other tall and creepy. Didn't blink once. Guess the Star of Fire incident got them spooked. But don't worry, I didn't say a word. You know, 'client-patient confidentiality.'" He used air quotes.

"Uh-huh. Thanks for the heads-up," she said evenly. "Wait here."

Cy and Isis were at home during the Star of Fire disaster. They watched it live from their living room. Isis was in shock. She knew this had nothing to do with Trinity, which confirmed she was at the wrong place, at the wrong time. She blamed Booker. Whatever mess he got himself into he was dragging Trinity along with it.

She disappeared into the bedroom, opened a drawer, and grabbed a sack of gold coins. Then she doubled it with one squeeze, the bag vibrated in her hand and the second dropped from the first.

"What'd he want?" Cy inquired from the doorway with a whisper.

She brushed past him, then paused. "Actually, I have an idea. Make another plate."

Opening the door again, she smiled sweetly. "Beech, you hungry? Would you like to stay for dinner?"

"Me? Uh—yeah! Sure." His eyes lit up.

"Then come in," she ordered, tugging him by the arm.

Beech stepped inside, eyes wide. "Oh, my rubels... your place—it's spectacular! Didn't expect this from a thief and a hacker. Impressive."

He wandered in, gawking. "Wait—you, you guys got an EverVine?"

He pulled out his Tabs, camera lens blinking. "I gotta take a pict—"

"Hey!" Isis snatched it out of his hands. "Cy."

"Done," Cy confirmed, a faint blue flash rippling through his eye as the photo erased.

"Come on! I've never seen one in person. You know it's illegal to keep a living organism as a household object, right?"

Cy and Isis ignored him and took their seats. Beech sat and immediately dug into the duck like a man starved.

"What are you doing?" Cy muttered under his breath.

"Just trust me." Isis whispered leaning in with a casual smile.

"So, Beech, we were wondering if you could do something for us."

"Yeah? Like what?" he said scooping in a spoonful of rice.

"You've got access to court documents. Addresses, personal files, business records—am I right?"

That made him pause. He dabbed his lips with a napkin. "Technically, yes. And you know this." He paused to swallow, "But I need probable cause—a case file, a theory, permission. I can't just walk into the most guarded database on the island and go, 'Hey, give me access to said citizen.'" He mocked, "Doesn't work like that." He glanced at the pair and continued to eat.

"We just need an address for somebody we are trying to find," Isis spoke calmly. Her voice softened.

"And this person is?" He took a sip of Cy's cucumber fizz. "You should turn this into a duck stew, by the way," he said mid-chew. "Let the duck braise a few hours with some shadowthorn wine, herbs, and veggies—it'd be perfection." He closed his eyes, imagining the taste.

Cy scolded him, narrowing his eyes as if he were hitting him with lasers.

"Malcolm Booker," Isis said flatly.

He choked on his drink. "Malcolm Booker? As in Booker? With a B? Nova Financial? Kude's golden boy? The man's basically a god here! Ha! Good luck with that." He scoffed in confusion and pushed back his chair. "Fun chat though. I'll just take my fee and—"

"Listen, Beech." Isis cut in. "I can make you the richest man in the world. Just name your price." She locked eyes with him.

He snorted. "So, you want me to just go to Kude Island's registry division and ask for files on the most prolific leader of the new world? I could lose my job—or worse. I could get exiled, and that's not happening, okay? This is the place to be. Do you even know how long the wait list is to get on the island?"

"Beech. My Beechie Beech," Isis cooed, puckering her lip pinching his cheeks.

Cy sucked his teeth. "You're not serious."

Isis squeezed Beech's hand. "Knowing you, there is something you want only we can provide. So, what is it? Hmm?"

He fidgeted, caught between their glares. Then—a grin. "Cosmic. You wanna know how you can get me to get classified information? I want citizenship to Stone Wall."

"Aw, hell no!" Cy exploded, throwing up his hands.

"What?" Isis snapped. "Are you serious?"

Beech snorted. "Ha! I knew it. Deal's off."

"Do you know how hard it is to get a Citizen's Pass there?" Cy exclaimed. "They can deny you even with enough gold coins."

"I know, Mr. Sparkplugs. They have already denied me twice."

"Twice?" Cy and Isis echoed.

"Cy's right. They're extremely picky about who they let in," Isis's tone hinted sadness. "And after getting denied twice, your chances are slim to none. You need to be in the top one percent of the one percent."

"Exactly," Beech countered, smirking. "That's why you two are perfect for the job."

"What makes you think we're good for the job?" Cy huffed, arms crossed.

"You're a literal computer man. Half of your head's like AI or a circuit board or whatever. I'm pretty sure you've made more upgrades to match that brain of yours. You could hack into anything with the blink of a lens."

He turned to Isis. "And you—when the detectives raided your house, they found authentic documents. Down to the ink and oak paper—flawless. You still legally own businesses. That's probably why they think you're mixed up with DeathStar."

He took another sip of his drink and grinned. "Anyway, I think I'll take my leftovers to go. And a refill while you're at it."

Isis sighed. "Cy, make him a plate to go, please."

Cy stood and listened to Isis's order.

"Guys, listen," Beech continued, leaning in conspiratorially. "Cy, you're a genius hacker, and Isis—you're some freaky shapeshifter or whatever. I don't know. Point is, you're both incredible at what you do."

He lowered his voice focusing on Isis. "I've got someone on the inside. They'll sneak you in. You just go to Records and approve my application. Do that, and I'll get you everything you want on Booker."

He extended his hand. "Deal?"

Isis looked back at Cy. He didn't look thrilled, but they had no choice.

"Deal," she agreed, and shook Beech's hand.

"Stellar!" Beech grinned as Cy handed him a to-go bag and his drink. Isis handed him his two sacks of gold coins.

"Oh, one more thing," she added as he headed for the door. "I need a retirement visa. Some time off work."

"Done," Beech nodded, slipping the coins into his briefcase. "Paperwork will be filed by morning. Anything else?"

"Nope," Cy stated sharply.

"Then we're golden." He smiled as smug as ever. "Come to my office before sunrise—and bring one hundred... no, make it *one thousand* gold coins. Just a small processing fee."

He winked. "Pleasure doing business. And Cy—that dinner? Amazing. You should open a shop."

At his desk, Studd sat in silence.

Last night's event looped through his mind—the way the fire moved, almost as if it had a mind of its own. Whips of fire cracking against the shield as if it had intent of breaking though.

He could swear it was looking straight at him. For a fleeting moment, his soul had left his body. The heat was intense, even with the shields. Everything in the surrounding area became scorched when the fire seized. Med Inc. was no longer.

He slipped on his glasses and activated his vision board.

A web of holographic lines stretched before him—faces, names, and red strings connecting the impossible.

Isis, Trinity, Booker, Skinner, and Crypt Cane were highlighted in red.

At the center of the web: DEATHSTAR.

*From the footage that we gathered it looked like the merkabah was being drawn line by line. It didn't just appear. It couldn't have been a hologram there was no light source. It was as if it was drawn by the hand of an invisible god. How could they have pulled this off? From where we stood it was easily more than five hundred meters wide. What was it made of? Why couldn't STAR Force get through?*

Studd paced in thought in front of his board, swiping through pictures and videos of the event.

*DeathStar hasn't left a trace. No IP address or digital fingerprints. No witnesses. How'd they penetrate our border? How are they going unseen? Are they cloaking? With technology reaching stellar levels, there are things I'll never fully understand.*

*Maybe I've been looking in the wrong place all along.*

He switched over to his web of suspects.

*Isis was always a peculiar case—a past criminal, fresh out of reformatory. When she came for her niece, her reaction had been genuine. She was upset, emotional. She couldn't be working for DeathStar, not with the way she'd gone off that day.*

*And her niece, Trinity. Maybe her survival was a coincidence. But the red zone has a near-perfect fatality rate, and she didn't have a single scratch. She wasn't even near the Star of Fire blast. But the damage was done to the poor lady. The Recovery Center confirmed she was indeed crushed to death. It wasn't the fall that killed her. I wondered if she's augmented and she doesn't even know it. We couldn't even test her DNA cause of that lawyer. Beech is a pest.*

*What's strange is that both had reduced sentences, even pardons, for serious crimes. Someone high up is protecting them. But they'd been orphans since the explosion at the hospital—the one that killed Alwin Booker and their parents. Could he be the link? Could they all be connected through Alwin?*

*Then there's Booker. Sly Booker. Always with something up his sleeve. His companies are crumbling—I doubt he's leading DeathStar, but he's definitely hunting them. I'll have to beat him to it, or this ends badly. I'll keep him close and watch every move.*

*And Skinner—stupid, reckless Skinner. I know he's been in contact with Crypt Cane. I'd bet my badge he used the first attack as an excuse to reach out. His motives aren't what they seem. Skeletor Island is rotten to the core, we can't afford ties with them.*

*I'll keep him close too... for now.*

*And that Piquette. Why would she work for him? What's her secret?*

Studd stared at the board full of evidence.

He dragged Piquette's personnel file to the center with two fingers and let it expand until her academy photo stared back at him. Then the idea hit him like a jolt.

"No," he drew in a breath.

Grayson's words flashed to him.

*Skeeter wasn't involved with Med Inc. He had no reason to be near that building. And now he's gone.*

His pulse drummed in his ears as he flicked to Skeeter's death report. The image of the recovered finger rotated lazily in the air. He took a step closer; the cut was too clean.

He paced, chin lifted, eyes unfocused. "She couldn't have..." The denial fell apart even as he spoke it.

He stopped and squared up to the hologram. "Run a ballistic report," he ordered. "Compare the finger's wound structure against standard blast trauma patterns from the Med Inc. explosion."

"Affirmative, Chief Studd," answered the AI. "Scanning... cross-referencing... Result: the laceration is linear with injuries from a sharp instrument. The bone was clean cut through. It does not coincide with the thermal or concussive injury expected from an explosion."

Studd shut his eyes for a beat. When he opened them, they were hard.

He pulled up the case report from the prior night—the coordinates where Piquette swore she'd followed a lead. The log opened. But the data was gone.

"Case report deleted," the AI reported.

"Restore from auto-archive."

"File path corrupted," the AI responded.

Studd picked up the crystal ball from his desk and hurled it at the board. It made a loud thud as the board cracked. Holograms flickered and collapsed.

"God dammit!" he yelled.

"Chief, is everything alright?" A cluster of detectives peeked their heads in his office.

Exhaling a deep breath, he took a seat on the edge of the desk and relaxed his shoulders.

"I'm fine." He answered calmly. "Someone get me a new board."

Studd drove up the curvy path toward Gravity Grave.

He stormed inside like a king returning from war. The Grave Diggers froze at his presence, offering stiff nods.

Every door buzzed open as he barreled through the halls and reached Skinner's office.

With the scowl on his face Melody didn't dare to stop him.

He knocked twice.

"Come in," Skinner called

As Studd stepped inside, a hologram flickered and vanished into pixels.

"General."

"Chief."

"I'll get straight to the point," Studd declared, slipping his hands into his pockets. His stance was relaxed and fearless. His name matched his archetype. "Why are you protecting Piquette? What did she do?"

Skinner smiled—a thin, calculated line. He stood and stepped from behind his desk.

"That detective of yours makes a fine agent. She's now working under my jurisdiction as an island informant. Which means any prior..." He paused, searching for the right word. "Mishaps on her behalf will be handled through me. And don't forget who also has a seat on the Throne... Councilman."

"Skinner, you're synthetic trash and you know it. An informant? An agent? Do you even hear yourself?" Studd removed his hands from his pockets and stepped closer.

"If Piquette committed crimes under my watch, it's my responsibility to ensure she answers for them." His tone sharpened. "What happened to the girl?"

Skinner blinked. "What girl?"

"The missing girl, A'Kierra. Before this shit storm started, the news heavily publicized her."

"Oh, right yes." Skinner's shrug was too casual. "I'm not too sure what Piquette *is* responsible for, but here's what I am sure of, Chief: I'm willing to put my personal feelings aside. We have a duty to protect this island. That comes first. And Piquette is an asset. Now... this discussion is over. Chief."

Studd clenched his jaw but said nothing; he got his confirmation. With turned and left returning to headquarters.

In his vehicle he sent out an urgent message for all Force directors to attend an emergency meeting. Within seconds his car bloomed with all members.

"Sorry to contact everybody in such haste, I know you're all busy. But I think it's time to activate Project Divide. I am granting permission for each director to conduct their own investigations without the approval of the acting Chief of all divisions, Chief Studd. Star Force, Land, and Cyber Force will act as their own agency to help with the DeathStar investigation. With that being said I still expect every one of you to share *any* vital information with me and with each other. Does anyone have any objections?"

"No Chief," Darrell answered.

"All good here," Xeric followed.

"You have my approval," Orion assured.

# Chapter 28: Shattered Hopes

"You haven't missed much," Detective Wright said as his partner woke from his nap. Pillar slept stiff, upright, and completely still.

They'd been up all night, staking out Isis's apartment building in their Star Skipper.

"They had a visit from the lawyer last night. Stayed for a bit, then left."

Wright leaned forward, eyes gleaming. He was desperate to impress the chief and climb the ranks and claim the captain's chair. Someone had to solve this case, and that someone would be him.

"Still no sign of the girl. Either she's been cooped up or we missed her."

He adjusted his jacket, speaking mostly to himself. Communicating out loud was the only way they operated and honestly, he preferred it that way. Pillar's silence made him the perfect audience.

"We'll stay another hour," Wright declared, yawning. "Believe it or not, I actually have a life outside of work."

"Hey, don't forget the X-ray glasses," Cy called from the bathroom.

"Yes, of course. Can't forget those," Isis teased. "You really think we'll need them? They will just take up space."

After she packed everything, she placed her hands on her hips staring at herself in mirror. "You ready?" she asked.

She wore a black sparkly pantsuit that shimmered like starlight, but they weren't just sparkles. Mini nanonites to hide her image from the cameras.

"Ready," Cy affirmed, wearing the same, just with fewer sparkles.

They stepped out onto the streets of Shadow Land, heading for Beech's office.

"Ah, ah, ah! We have movement." Wright straightened from his slouch. "Where do these two think they're going?"

He jammed his feet into his shoes. Pillar turned to him slowly.

"I know we're after the girl, but I've got a feeling about them," Wright clarified. "This has potential. Let's follow on foot."

Cy and Isis marched uphill toward the gates and boarded the FastTrack bound for the Dim Light District. Arriving at Beech's office just as the sunrise bell rang.

"I'm so glad you two made it!" Beech beamed, throwing his arms wide in mock applause.

Cy and Isis weren't amused. Both looked drained and desperate.

"Here we are," Isis said flatly as they sat down.

"What do you got for me?" Beech asked.

"For you?" Isis looked him up and down.

He laughed. "Kidding, kidding. Don't be so uptight."

"Anyway," he continued, leaning forward, "I got a hold of my guy at Titan Travel. He says he can only get one of you in but can't get you out." He pointed at Isis.

"Man, I'm right here," Cy emphasized.

"Oh, come on. No offense. You're great, but we only get one shot, and my money's on the ninja freak over here."

Beech grinned. "My guy will meet you at Riverstone Park, Zone A, on the bench under the trees by the water fountain right after we finish up. Oh, and no need to worry—I already filed your work visa under 'mental health leave'." He air-quoted dramatically.

"And I've got all the information on one Malcolm Booker right here." He slapped a stack of papers onto the desk. "You get the info after the job and I'll get my coins afterwards."

"It's settled," Isis said calmly.

Everything she needed was sitting right in front of her, close enough to touch.

"Excellent! Now scurry along, kids. My freedom awaits." Beech shooed them out.

Before leaving the building, Isis slipped in her camera contact lenses so Cy could see from her point of view. He handed her a data chip—the key to their plan.

Riverstone Park was alive with waterfalls, lush green slopes, and rivers carving through stone paths into bodies of water. It was one of the few places in the city untouched by robotics. Just pure nature breathing.

Cy and Isis waited at the appointed bench under the trees by the fountain.

Moments later, a man in a suit hurried toward them, clutching his blazer and briefcase. Sweat soaked through his collar and armpits.

"Cheers, you must be Isis," he stuttered nervously as he approached. "Uh, I was told there'd only be one of you."

She flashed a grin. "That is. My partner's just here to see me off. You okay?"

"Oh, yeah, yeah. Fine. Just nervous." He wiped his forehead. "I owe Beech big time. Said sneaking you in would clear my debt."

"Relax. You're just getting me in, that's it. What's your name?"

"Davis."

"Okay, Davis. I'm Trish. I'm your niece applying for an internship, remember?" She winked. "Let's go."

Cy and Isis exchanged one last nod before parting ways.

"All right, Pillar," Wright spoke from his communicator. "You stay with him. I'll follow her."

Titan Travel looped like a coiled serpent—three concentric circles made from serpentine carved with hundreds of scales. The outer ring handled visas, registrations, and renewals. The middle ring was for human resources, testing, and communications. Inside the innermost circle were the archives, stockrooms, and records.

"Each layer has a second level," Davis explained as the pair walked. "That's where the records are. You'll need to hack into the system and override Beech's denial. Titan runs on its own network—the Closed-Circuit Ether. It's tricky."

He swallowed hard. "You'll also need a badge from a high-clearance employee. Look for a golden snake brooch. You'll find the records room on level 2-F. Once you get the data, I'm out—Beech and I are even."

"Downloading the blueprints now," Cy said through the commutator. "Just find a terminal and plug the chip in. I'll do the rest."

Neither of them noticed the detectives following them. Pillar watched Cy from the shadows of the trees. Wright followed Isis from a distance.

"That doesn't sound too bad," Isis assured Davis. "Get a brooch, access the system, override the denial. Simple." She smirked. "What could go wrong?"

"The beacons are on the left. They move in circles, back and forward; you can just follow the map."

As they neared the entrance, the crowd thickened. Towering one-hundred-foot trees surrounded the crystal building, and an invisible electrical fence buzzed in the air.

The head of a serpent, frozen mid-strike, crowned the doorway. Its diamond eyes glimmered on either side, catching the sunlight.

Above it, holographic projections shimmered with families laughing, travelers strolling through Stone Wall, smiles looping endlessly.

Isis's pulse quickened as she spotted the guards—humans and androids—standing like statues at post.

"Now, just follow my lead. I'll scan you in," Davis whispered.

Once inside, the noise was overwhelming. People shouted over each other, babies cried, and the chatter was endless. Six long lines led to six teller windows. Davis led her through the crowd, toward the entrance gate on the left.

"This is my niece," Davis told the officer. "She's starting her internship today."

The officer nodded. Davis held open his eyes to the bio-scanner, and the steel gate opened. A few steps passed the gate, Davis pressed a smile to Isis and they parted ways.

Behind them, Wright strode up to the opposite gate, flashing his badge.

"I'm Detective Wright. I need access for a high profile case."

"Sorry," the guard raised a hand and stopped him. "Employees only. Unless you have approval from a higher up—"

Wright eyed him up and down, "Are you in your right mind? I'm a Level Four officer of the Force," Wright snapped. "I could have you guarding the planetarium by sunset. Is that what you want?"

The guard hesitated, cursing at himself. He glanced around the room and took a moment to think. Once he made his decision, he quickly pressed the override button and the gate opened.

"Now you want to get on the third beacon on your left," Cy instructed.

Isis listened as she rounded the corner and froze in her tracks. Her fingers curled with tension, teeth gritted together.

Detective Wright.

Her heart dropped, she quickly spun on her heels. "Oh no," she cried.

"What? What's wrong?"

"It's the detective who interrogated Trinity. We were followed."

Her heels clanked against the ground faster when she slammed into someone. Hot coffee exploded from the cup and papers scattered in the air.

"Oh, I'm so sorry—" Isis apologized instantly.

He turned back and Wright was closing in fast, and he looked angry. He stomped harder with each step, eyebrows burrowing together.

Cy scanned the area. "There's no one near me. You must be the only one being tailed."

Little did he know, Pillar had already vanished into the woods, abandoning his post.

"Did you not see me?" the man barked, scooping up his scattered papers.

Isis bent down to help. "I said I'm sorry—" Peeking over her shoulder she could see Wright was arm lengths away.

She took a deep breath and timed his steps. In one smooth motion, she stood and struck. Her palm hit Wright square in the throat.

He dropped to the ground grabbing his neck, gasping for air. Eyes bulging from his sockets as he coughed out blood.

"Oh no, I think he's choking!" Isis shouted, kneeling beside him.

A crowd swarmed instantly.

"Subtle, Isis," Cy muttered. "Change of plans—forget the records room. Head for the nearest beacon, level 2-A. It will take you to a computer hall."

She slipped away amid the chaos, sprinting down the hall. The beacon doors were just about to close. With a few quick strides, she slithered in. Taking a moment to collect her thoughts, she pressed 2 then A. She glanced back at the crowd of people already inside, "How ya doing." She nodded at the other passengers with a forced smile.

The beacon slowly rotated left, then bolted backward, after a spin to the right, it bolted forward, before stopping with a soft ding. The ride was almost motionless, her body didn't sway with the movement of the beacon.

"This is your stop," Cy said.

The hallway stretched long and bright. Window panels on each side blurred out.

"What about the brooch?" She whispered.

"The brooch?" Cy repeated.

"Yes, the one I duplicated after bumping into that guy. Davis said we'd need it."

"Damn girl, you quick. But my chip will do the trick. Maybe the brooch will be useful later."

At the end of the hall stood a circular door etched like a portal.

It slid open, revealing a pristine, air-conditioned computer lab—cream-colored walls and soft piano music. The decor resembled an Egyptian temple: hieroglyphs, jackal-headed gods, painted feasts, and clay ceramics.

Dozens of egg-shaped pods hung from the ceiling and touched the ground.

Isis moved through them until she found an empty one.

On its glass, the display read: ENTER YOUR ID NUMBER.

Without asking Cy spit one out.

"I16-CDJ-07," Cy read.

She typed it in, and the pod opened. The shield closed once she stepped inside, tinting to black. The walls shimmered like a starry night sky. A holographic keyboard unfolded before her. She searched for a terminal and plugged in the drive.

"Now what?"

"Nothing. Just sit back and watch me do the work."

Cy's code filled the screens.

Isis sat in anticipation, biting her fingers as her legs bounced. *How the hell am I going to get out now? That damn stupid detective. How long has he been following me?*

"As for your escape, don't vex it; I've got that covered."

Moments later, the data transfer reached completion.

Isis yanked the chip free, slipped it into her pocket, and stepped out of the pod, breath trembling. Just then, the fire alarm went off. Loud sirens blazed, sending groups of people running.

"Thank the heavenly realms for you Cy."

Isis made her way out with the crowd undetected and reunited with Cy at the park.

Isis dropped five sacks full of gold coins on Beech's desk.

"Oh, you two!" he exclaimed, practically vibrating with excitement. "Give me a hug—bring it in, guys!"

Before they could react, he threw his arms around them in a tight squeeze.

"Just give us the file," Isis muttered, prying herself free.

"Right." Beech straightened his collar and handed her a thick folder. "I'd send it over via Tabs, but I don't want to leave a trail. Everything's in there—the complete history of one Malcolm Booker.

The guy's loaded, okay? Properties dating back to the earliest days of Kude Island's development. You two have your hands full."

He grinned, rubbing his fingers across the bulging sacks of gold. "This feels like way more than a thousand coins."

Isis smiled faintly. "Consider yourself lucky. I got carried away."

Beech's eyes gleamed.

"You should expect a welcome email soon. After that, you're free to live the high life among the stars." Cy smirked.

"I've got to say, you two really are the best team I've ever worked with," Beech said, voice softening. "I'm going to miss this partnership."

"Yeah, don't forget to write," Cy teased.

Cy and Isis saw themselves out, slamming the door behind them.

"Want to grab dinner to celebrate?" Cy asked as they waited on the FastTrack platform.

Isis hesitated. She wanted to say no—she was exhausted and distracted—but she knew how much Cy loved dining out. "Sure. Why not? Where are we headed?" she flashed a fake smile.

"There's this new place in Red City called Petals. The waiting list's a month long, but I've got a guy on the inside."

The scenery of dinner was beautiful, but the atmosphere was tense. Cy noticed Isis was distant, barely touching her food. She didn't even order dessert. When she finally smiled, it was thin and fleeting—her mind already somewhere else.

By the end of the meal, Cy gave up trying to make conversation. He packed the rest of the meal to go, irritation simmering beneath his calm expression. She had ruined what was supposed to be a romantic meal after an intense job.

"Should we dig through the files now?" Isis asked the moment they got home.

"Sure," Cy answered flatly.

After changing into comfortable clothes, Isis spread the papers across the kitchen table. The noise of the city outside was the only sound between them.

"You see anything yet?" Isis inquired thirty minutes later, tapping her nails impatiently on the table. Her legs bounced beneath it.

"Nothing new," Cy muttered. "Just property records, business contracts, bank accounts, and blueprints for Med-Bots." He sighed, flipping through another stack. He could've scanned the complete file in seconds, but it mattered to Isis that *she* found the clue.

"Really? You haven't cracked it already?" Then her eyes widened. "Hold on. Look at this."

She slid a page across to him. "There's paperwork for a company called Eclipse Inc.—the first trading company to exist on Kude Island. The founder's name is Phoenix King."

Cy frowned. "What does he have to do with this?"

"That's because Phoenix King is my brother," Isis said, her tone hardening. "Of course, how could I forget, that was his original name. He's taken on multiple identities over the years—creating a web of control. He would pose as relatives or heirs to make it appear his companies were passed down naturally. It was always him pulling the strings."

Cy leaned back, whistling softly. "Kude Island officially opened seventy-five years ago. So that means you're... how old?"

Isis rolled her eyes. "We've had this conversation. We don't age like humans, remember?"

"So, technically how old were you when your first landed here?"

"Technically, in human age I was a small toddler, maybe four. And Trinity, she was literally born after impact." Isis said. "I just learned how to walk on the ship. When we arrived, Kude was nothing but dense jungle, wild animals everywhere, no roads, no building. It was beautiful, but dangerous. We'd come from a world with mostly rocks, I remember the air here feeling so heavy. It took us weeks to learn how to breathe properly."

Her gaze softened as memories flickered behind her eyes. "Trinity's parents adopted me when I was little." *Like they had a choice.*

"We traveled the world, studying humans, tasting their food, trying to understand them. My brother stayed behind. Years later, when we heard about a new island opening for settlement—we knew he was the one behind it."

Cy's mechanical eye glowed faintly, recording every word. "And the gold? How does he have so much of it?"

"We have machines," Isis described, folding her arms. "They can transform organic matter into other elements. Re-coding the matter at a molecular level. If I placed a leaf or a blade of grass into the chamber, I could turn it into iron, or by his choice gold."

Cy blinked in awe. "That's insane. Your planet must've been incredible."

"It was. Until it wasn't." She frowned.

Silence hung between them as they continued the search. Isis didn't like talking about why they left. She pushed it so far to the back of her mind she'd forgotten.

Moments later, Isis gasped. "Wait—I found something!"

She leaped from her chair and held up a page, eyes wide. "Look, an address!"

Cy leaned over. "That's in the City of Light."

"That's right. And look whose name is on the deed."

Cy's lips curved into a slow grin. "Malcolm Booker."

# Chapter 29: Inheritance of Light

Trinity stood in the kitchen, preparing something to eat when a strange sensation overtook her.

In the blink of an eye, her vision split in two.

In her left vision, the world looked normal—sunlight on the counter, the coldness of the fridge, the soft scrape of her spoon against thc bowl.

In her right, time moved differently.

Everything she did was already happening before she moved—her hand stirring, her body turning, the sunlight moving like seconds. Like fractions of mirrors facing each other, but each showing different moments. At first, she thought she was imagining it, but her body refused to obey when she tried to correct it. When she blinked, the world shattered again.

Her left vision remained the same. In her right vision she saw herself from outside her body, floating in a void of silk like ripples in the darkness. Light waves snaked like flying serpents surrounded her.

In the distance, a glowing sphere throbbed like a beating heart.

It wasn't until the two realities tried merging that she truly started to panic. Her visions overlapped, refusing to fuse. She tried to scream but her voice wasn't there. In fact, she couldn't feel her body at all. Then the world around her began melting, liquid dropped into a place she couldn't see.

Trinity's eyes rolled open and she shot up for air. Her hand clutched her chest as it heaved.

*It was only a dream. It was only a dream... Or was it? It felt so real. Wait... what was happening. I'm beginning to forget already. There was darkness and light...*

A knock at the door interrupted her thoughts.

"Trinity, are you okay?" Abott's calm voice called. "Your heart rate is elevated. Might I sugge—"

"I'm fine, Abott!" she yelled.

The hand on her chest confirmed Abott's statement, her pulse pounded hard. She needed a distraction.

Reaching for her Tabs, she split the magnetic stones apart and began scrolling through profiles.

Isis's You page was quiet. Her last post was a photo of her with a group of girls from Miss Thorn's school some moon cycles ago. "*So happy to be rejoicing with my prison sisters!!*" the caption read.

Trinity rolled her eyes and switched to her uncle's account. Nothing but advertisements.

She hesitated, then checked Cy's page. Food photos. *Typical.*

One image made her freeze, a dish from Petals.

Her stomach dropped.

*They're out there eating like my disappearance means nothing. I can't believe those false prophets! Damn Cy, can't even say I'm disappointed, you do love food.*

Frustrated, she tossed the Tabs aside and trudged to the bathroom. She braided her hair into two braids, brushed out her baby hairs, changed into baggy jeans she found in the wardrobe and a blue shirt with a yellow star. After she was ready to start her day, she headed to the kitchen.

She was surprised to see Uncle already sitting at the table.

"Good morning," Booker greeted pleasantly. "Breakfast today is frozen fruit coated in chocolate yogurt and a tall glass of warm coconut water."

Trinity nodded politely and took a seat across from him.

"This looks stellar. Abott might be a better cook than Cy."

"I was thinking you could start training today," Booker announced, taking a delicate sip. "Abott will show you the ropes."

"Sure." She forced a smile. *What's his problem? I just got hired yesterday.*

"Just so you know," Booker added, "you're always free to leave the house if you need fresh air. Abott can take you anywhere. Although, I would be cautious because of yesterday's attack."

Trinity had heard all about the attack—it was everywhere, flooding the feeds and news streams.

But that wasn't her problem anymore. She traveled hours outside the city; no one and nothing could touch her. The explosion was behind her, a distant memory fading into void. She considered herself lucky, her survival felt like a rebirth, a second chance at life.

For the first time in a long while, things were finally making sense.

"That sounds... great." Her smile brightened. She was already forming a plan.

She fidgeted with her fingers before gathering her nerves. She inquired, "Uncle—what were we royalty of?"

Booker set his teacup down, eyes gleaming. "Ah. At long last. This was the question I was waiting for."

He leaned back against the chair, "There's no subtle way to say this, so I'll be blunt. We come from another planet, from another galaxy. We traveled here because our planet was at war."

Trinity froze. Even her heartbeat stalled. *No wait, this isn't true. Me, an alien? I'm an alien? But...*

"That actually makes sense," she whispered, words trembling. "I knew there was a reason I survived the explosion." Her head dropped as her brows furrowed.

"The explosion?" Booker tilted his head. "You were at Med Inc. that day?"

"Yeah. They were having open interviews. Somehow, I was the only survivor in the red zone the detective said. I doubt the public even knows." Trinity spoke, but her thoughts were elsewhere. Her life flashed before her eyes, recalling every suspicious moment in her life. Every time Isis deflected a question. She now had her answer, but she wasn't sure if it was an answer she liked.

That caught Booker's attention, but he hid his suspicion behind a calm smile. *So, she was at the explosion site, I'm sure Studd gave her a thorough interrogation. I'll have to check in on him later.*

"Well, let me be the first to acquaint you. Our planet was a crystal sphere. It was a rocky terrain as you can imagine. Beneath the surface ran miles of connecting tunnel. And on the surface stood these enormous crystal spikes. As royalty we claimed the surface as our own." There was a sparkle in Booker's eyes as he spoke. Trinity could see the passion as his hands helped him tell the story. Gesturing his hands to paint an invisible image.

Trinity sat mouth agape in disbelief, "I'm sorry this is just a bit hard to come by I have some many questions. Where exactly was this planet? Our planet."

"We lived far away. Same universe, just a different galaxy."

"Uh huh... interesting." Trinity responded.

"Yes, our solar system comprised of three types of stars. A white dwarf, a neutron star and a red dwarf. Luckily, they were far enough they didn't affect gravity too much. You see, we lived in what I like to call the dead zone, a place where stars liked to die. Our sky was an indescribable beauty. Think of living inside a nebula surrounded by trillions of elements." He smiled.

Trinity sat in a trance from his words. No thoughts, just pure hypnotism as her eyes fixated on him.

"Could you tell me more about my mother and our family?"

"Your mother was a brilliant lightologist. We were able to sustain a massive amount of energy due to the stars around. With that she created many inventions we could trade with other life forms. For example, she created the first crystal that could capture sunlight and seize it, releasing the glow slowly until it drained."

Trinity's eyes widened. "Stellar... there was no way we were humans. I mean without trees or a proper atmosphere how did we manage to survive?"

"We had an atmosphere but it didn't come in layers like earth. Our DNA became crystallized from bacteria that evolved inside volcanic rock. Bacteria turned into crustaceans and eventually bodies formed and cocooned themselves to survive the heat. Over time, they transformed their rock shells turning into crystal, birthing a species of crystal beings. Our flesh grew transparent then developed to absorb light rays. We came in all shades, mostly blue and red. Then pinks and purples. Inside our harden bodies were specks of light that acted like our internal functions. But some ancestors didn't go through that evolutionary process. They couldn't evolve past stone bodies, so they became our protectors, the unbreakable guardians who lived for thousands of years. Our crystallized kind lived for millions, if lucky."

Trinity leaned forward, fascinated. "So, I'm... a crystal in human form? What was the form of communication? Was it in frequencies like the crystals speak here on earth?"

Booker chuckled. "Clever girl. Our faces weren't like human ones; they were featureless. Smooth, like a crystal ball. We communicated through vibration, frequencies, and touch. Our speech sounded like music undetectable to human ears."

Trinity threw her hand up in disbelief, "This explains it. This explains everything weird that happened to me in my life. Especially how I survived."

"Well, our cells do regenerate quickly because our source of life is different. You and Isis are still children by our measure, perhaps even infants. Also, our skin is nearly impenetrable; only a rare pyrite like stone from our world can cut it. Isis has a blade forged from it. I'm surprised she never told you."

He chuckled lightly. "You could be sliced today and heal before any blood touches the floor, but be careful, because it could just as easily kill you."

Trinity laughed breathlessly, her eyes drifted into the distance as she recalled a distant memory.

Isis brought her to the playground so she could meet a boy. Most of the kids there were bigger, but Trinity was sure she could handle herself. The playground had statues the children could climb inside. The control panels allowed them to control the robotic statue and fight with others.

Trinity climbed inside one and strapped in eager to play as Isis was too distracted to notice. She tried to keep up with the other kids, but it was hard, she couldn't understand the controls and panicked. Hitting a slew of buttons, the statue lost its footing and fell to the ground hard.

Trinity screamed when she hit her head. Warm blood dripped down her face. It was the first time she felt actual, true pain. She shrieked for Isis.

"Trinity!" Isis skidded to a halt and took a second to assess the situation—she couldn't just rip the statue apart in front of a playground full of people.

She fiddled with the hatch as her fingers trembled, "Fuck, how do you open this thing!"

The boy she was chatting with stepped in and opened the hatch. Inside was a wailing Trinity, head coated in blood. Isis scooped her in her arms and examined the panel carefully. She took a closer look and saw the impact where Trinity hit her head.

*Inside is lined with pyrite. Shit, how did I miss this.*

"Isis it hurts!" Trinity cried.

Isis's eyes widened with fear as she rose to her feet, covering Trinity the best she could. She took off running past staring parents, past the park gates, and straight into the trees.

"Does she need help?" the boy called.

"No—she's fine!" Isis shouted without slowing.

Once out of sight, she tucked Trinity against a tree trunk.

"Hey, hey, look at me," Isis said, forcing a smile. "You're okay. Just breathe."

She pressed Trinity's tiny hands together and sang softly—a tune Trinity always thought she'd made up:

"*When the trouble gets too bright. Don't give into the fright. All wounds mend with love and light. Nature keeps you alright.*"

The song distracted her mind as her skin knitted itself together, the pain vanishing as if it had never been. Isis wiped the blood with her sleeve.

"There," Isis said, relief flooding her voice. "See? All better."

She bopped her nose. "Now what were you crying for, you little baby?"

Trinity giggled through sniffles, believing it was just a magic trick. But now, she understood.

"But what were the guidelines that made *us* royalty?" She asked.

"Our father—your grandfather don't forget—was king of the entire planet from birthright. In our family each generation bore one child with a crystal eye, an ancient mutation that allowed them to see wavelengths others couldn't—unknown colors, hidden portals, even the code for time itself. My father had that gift. He ruled because of it. I thought either you or Isis might inherit it. Perhaps your children will." *Why doesn't she seem happy?*

"I knew something was off," she snapped, her eyes blurred with tears. "And Isis... she kept all this from me. Why? Why would she hide it?"

Booker stood, straightening his jacket. "That's a story for another day. Don't be too hard on your aunt, she did what she thought was best. Remember, she's still a child too, in her own way."

He reached into his jacket pocket and pulled out a small roll of gold coins.

"Here's your first payment. Spend it wisely." He pressed his lips into a smile and headed toward the beacon. For him the conversation was somewhat therapeutic.

Trinity bit on her fingers, building up courage.

"Uncle, wait!" she called out to him. She gently pushed her chair back to stand, "Thank for this, for all it. Exposing me to the truth has settled something inside me. I was lost for so long but thanks to you it feels like I finally found home."

"It was my pleasure, Trinity." Uncle bent forward slightly and continued to make his exit. Their eyes connected just as the beacon doors closed.

When he left, the house fell quiet, but his words kept echoing in her mind.

She sat at the table for another hour trying to remember every instance that was usual to her. Then she laughed and the laughter turned to tears. Tears of freedom, it was like she had broken the chains that kept her locked away. For the first time she finally felt like her questions were answered, an overwhelming feeling of relief washed over her. *This is just... I can't even explain it. I feel so relieved. All my life I felt like something about me was different. I just knew it. This is so crazy I don't even know what to think.*

Trinity dragged herself to her bedroom, slipped under the covers and squeezed her pillow tightly

Booker continued with his day starting with spending a few hours at Nova Financial. Once he was done with most of his meetings, he took his Sky Skipper to one of his proudest investments—Hydris. An underwater aquarium built inside a natural cave system, its walls

reinforced with thick plexiglass. Through it, visitors could watch sea life glide by in glowing hues of blue and green. This way sea creatures could be appreciated for their majestic ways without being jailed.

But Booker wasn't here for the view. Miles below the aquarium levels lay his private laboratory—a maze of tanks, machines, and the constant vibrations of water pumps. The air reeked of salt and decay.

He scanned his retina and stepped inside.

Dozens of mutant creatures filled the tanks—a sea serpent that released poisonous spores, a mega shark who occasionally threw his tail against the glass, a translucent five-headed fish that shimmered like liquid glass, and hundreds of species of jelly fish and octopus.

At the end of one corridor floated his greatest treasure—a sky-creature from his home planet.

It resembled a jellyfish, but without tentacles—a weightless orb of clear jelly, with a single glowing pearl suspended in its center. That pearl was its skeleton, forged from a mineral stronger than anything on earth called Viirian. Booker called the creature Skylura.

On his planet, Skyluras only appeared in the sky, feeding on the sunlight. They had no gender, no known method of reproduction. He had spent years trying to create a hybrid capable of surviving on earth. He was sure the creature's pearl could generate unlimited energy.

Booker relied on the last surviving creature. When he first arrived, the others had perished under the stress of this world's atmosphere.

Booker watched the Skylura float, transfixed by its grace. It sank lower and lower each day.

"Don't worry little one, once I find an animal compatible with your genetic makeup, I will create your legacy."

Trinity and Abott returned to the mountain home after a long day in the Twin Cities. After spending hours in the abyss of her mind, Abott convinced her to go out and explore.

She'd spent the day exploring gadget shops, devouring decades-old steaks, and surfing anti-gravity waves. By the time they got home, exhaustion hit like a brick wall.

"Would you like to begin your training?" Abott inquired.

"Eh, not particularly." She flopped onto the couch, yawning. It levitated off the ground, giving her a better view out the window.

"Master was very insistent that you start soon," Abott reminded her.

"You don't have to call him 'master.' Just because he built you doesn't mean he owns you. Is that what you want—to be a slave?" she taunted.

"I want nothing more than to make your life easier," Abott replied simply. "Ensuring your physical and mental safety is my purpose. Speaking of which, your dopamine levels have increased, and your blood pressure is at a normal level."

"Ugh, you've been doing that all day." Trinity eyes rolled. "Don't you ever get tired of scanning me?"

"I do not tire. But I understand the question is rhetorical."

Trinity smirked. "You're weird, Abott. But like in a good way."

"Yes. I am unique," it replied. "There is no one like me."

After a beat, Trinity leaped from the couch and inched closer, "Abott... do you know about us?"

"Clarify your question."

"Oh, come on. Don't make me say it out loud. You can read my brain, right?"

"Unfortunately, that's not how it works. I read signals, not thoughts."

"Same thing." She slouched. "You know we're not from this planet, right?"

There was a moment of silence. "Yes. There are elements in Master's DNA that do not match human biology. His brain activity also contains fifty billion more neurotransmitters than average, a trait I detect in you as well."

Trinity blinked. "That's... good to know."

"I agree," Abott said without hesitation.

Later that night, Abott returned to his charging station, leaving her truly alone.

Trinity wanted to learn more about herself and about her planet. So, she went searching for clues back in Uncle's treasure room.

Her curiosity carried her to a nearby shelf. Most of the books were about human magic, esoteric knowledge, evolution, and history. One book caught her eye: *The Tablet of Isis*. She tried to force it open, but there was no budging the lock. A star-shaped indentation hinted at a missing key.

She replaced it and picked another. *The Magic of Human Intuition and knowing oneself.*

Hours passed and she lost herself among the shelves, reading about occultism, energy, time manipulation, and self-preservation. Between the pages, she stopped to admire the celestial orrery of her planet, feeling a strange presence as if she was being watched.

# Chapter 30: God of Gist

Detective Studd sat beside Wright in his room at the Recovery Center.

Wright lay in a medical brace, his throat crushed. His thyroid cartilage was shattered beyond repair. Breathing tubes ran from his chest through his mouth; an artificial larynx would be his only way to speak again.

Studd watched the steady signal of his heartbeat on the monitor. Then turned toward the window.

"Rest up, son. I'll handle it from here," he said voice almost breaking.

He stepped out through the sliding door, boots marching. His next stop was already on his mind.

"Walk me through it again," Studd stated, voice firm.

The guard took a hard gulp. "Detective Wright showed up and demanded entry. I told him Titan Travel security requires clearance—he threatened me with a demotion so... I let him in. Moments later, there was screaming in the hallway. I found him on the floor, coughing blood everywhere."

"And you didn't see anybody suspicious before or after?" Studd pressed.

"No, sir."

"All right. Good job son."

He turned to the Titan Travel director. "Take me to the info hub."

The info hub curved along sleek white walls, lined with giant screens and keyboards embedded into panels. Holographic footage and messages drifted in the air like digital ghosts, flashing bright as they vanished into hidden data ports across the room. Technicians dressed in white Synthix lab coats monitored streams of data and swiped controls midair.

The info hub sat on a closed off section of the third floor.

"This is where all data is stored and transferred. Including messages from Stone Wall," the director explained.

"Show me the incident." Studd demanded.

The director pulled a hologram forward from the wall. Studd watched as papers flew from a man's hands as he collided with empty space. The man cursed at the air. Moments later, Wright stormed down the hall, then froze mid-stride as though an invisible force struck him.

"Rewind."

The director swiped backward and the holo replayed. Studd leaned in closer.

"Someone cloaked," Studd muttered. "Technology like that shouldn't exist here."

He pointed. "Find the man with the papers."

The man with the papers was found in his office. Studd wasted no time in getting answers.

"And you didn't see this person attack him?" Studd asked.

"No," the man elaborated. "Like I said, it all happened so quick. I barely saw her—her hair covered her face. But her suit... it kind of sparkled."

"Okay. Anything else?" Studd pressed.

"Oh—the perfume." The man snapped in recognition, "O'Laprie. My girlfriend wears it all the time. She gets it from Grand Mall."

Studd knew exactly who his suspect was. The only trouble is he had no evidence to tie them to the crime. For now, he didn't have a choice but to let them go unscathed. *I caught her once, I'll catch her again.*

In his vehicle, Studd chuckled at himself. His laughing was a form of therapy. Something to suppress the devil inside when anger got the best of him. Just then he received an incoming call from his secretary. He answered mid-sigh throwing his head back against the headrest.

"Talk to me."

"Studd, I thought this was something you would want to hear," she said in a secretive whisper, "There have been over seventy reports of people going into psychosis the moment the merkabah appeared."

"What?" his head shot up.

"And get this they reported hearing a voice in their head."

"And what did this voice say?"

"No one could make out what the voice was saying. Some people described it as demons trying to form human words." The secretary squealed, happy she could give something useful to the Chief.

A moment a silence as Studd tapped his finger against the steering wheel. *Demons trying the form human words.*

"Stellar. You stay on it and keep me updated. I know just the person to speak to."

"You got it Chief."

Immediately after that call ended, Studd called Lupe. It took a few rings, but he eventually answered the call.

His windshield turned into a holo call.

Lupe Démont was a French surrealist whose art seemed to blur the line between dreams and prophecy. People called him a visionary—some even swore he was psychic. His following had always been large, but it exploded after one of his paintings eerily predicted the death of a Norwegian political leader.

Lupe himself was as unconventional as his work. He dressed in layers of earth-toned threads that formed a skirt, paired with an open vest and nothing underneath. Black charcoal circled his eyes, drawing attention to his most striking feature—one iris a brilliant green, the other a deep brown.

"Lup, hope you're not too busy." Studd said, the sound of wind chimes and healing music lingered in the background.

"Why not at all Chief. Never too busy for you, my love." Lupe smiled gently while blowing a kiss to a person off camera.

"Lupe I won't take up too much of your time I just have a few questions about DeathStar's latest fiasco. What can you tell me about the significance of a merkabah."

"Finally, ready to dabble into the dark arts huh Chief. I thought my beliefs were, how did you phrase it? Placebos of the soul's curiosity."

Studd scoffed, "Humor me."

Lupe pouted his lips playfully and he took a seat on a colorful cushioned sofa, "The merkabah is a symbol that dates back to ancient times. It's a belief that symbols hold frequencies that can be used as a key to unlock secrets of the universe. The merkabah is made up of three words that translate to mind, body and spirit."

"Mind, body and spirit," Studd repeated, "And this ancient symbol, this merkabah, can it." Studd pressed his lips, embarrassed to even ask the question, "Can it cause a mass hallucination if used the right way?"

"If you're referring to the cases of psychosis that is spreading through the island then yes. Symbols are powerful tools. If someone of great spiritual energy performed a ritual while channeling their energy with that symbol, then yes, it is possible they could have caused an episode of hallucination, but this person would need to be of great power. Especially to pull a stunt like that. Whoever

DeathStar is they aren't rookies Studd. We're dealing with people who've done their research."

"Stellar, thanks Lupe."

"Any time Chief." Another gentle smile, his tired eyes squinted from his lifted cheeks.

Studd threw his head back, his mind was racing but he was only able to say one thing, "Vex me."

# Chapter 31: City of Light

Cy opened his eyes to a blurry image of Isis hovering over him. She shook his shoulder so hard it almost popped out of place. "Hey, Cy, you awake?"

He groaned. Early mornings reminded him of his military days. "What do you want, Isis?"

"When you get a chance, meet me in the kitchen. I think I figured out how to get into the City of Light." With that she darted out the room.

A few minutes later, after he foamed his teeth and tweaked his iris, Cy found her pacing in front of a storm of papers and his workstation pulled out. Her hair screamed chaos in a messy bun.

"Isis, what are you doing?"

She gave no answer.

"Speak, Isis!" he demanded.

She stopped, as if she were going to say something. But her face frowned the moment she lost her thoughts. Back to pacing, her steps swayed.

"Can I go back to bed now?" He whined.

"No, because we have to discuss how we're getting in."

"You're barely Level Two. You're lucky the Twin Cities let you breathe."

She leaned over the chair she pulled from the table, tense eyes, eyebrows wrinkled together. "Remember that couple who went missing from the City of Light? The Caldwells?"

"Last seen in the Realm, yes. Their story was big news." he exhaled. "But people go missing there every day."

"Exactly. They are probably dead or strung out, and we are fortunate because no one recorded their deaths. So, why don't we take their identities, forge fake Citizen Cards with new chips, and walk right in. What do you think?" She turned to face him.

"I thought you got clean before I got out," he said dryly.

"Ha ha, very funny." She flashed her middle finger.

"City of Light citizens have a special serial number, and they just started to use chips implanted in the skin. How do we forge our way in now, hm?" he challenged.

"I thought about that, too. Remember that guy? Ti's brother who's into mechanics and body mod?"

"Foxx?"

"Yeah him. He runs The Toy Boxx in the Realm. We snag light-grade data chips, overwrite them with the Caldwells' serial numbers—those I got from a guy on 'The Quantum'. We drop the chips into our skin and done." Isis released a much needed exhale. "Also, clear your schedule next week. You're building a Prism firewall. Had to trade something for the serial numbers."

Cy couldn't help but grin. Watching her scheme always lit him up. He walked toward her slowly and planted a kiss on her forehead. "You came up with that all by yourself, didn't you?" Isis blushed as he rested his hand on her head.

"Okay. I'll go to Foxx. You call Beech—pull everything on the Caldwells. If we're doing this, we can't make any mistakes."

He loved her risk, but a line pulled in the back of his mind. The deeper they went, the harder it was to climb out. *Get Trinity back then stop.*

"Oh, thank you, thank you!" Isis hooked an arm around his neck and planted a wet kiss on his cheek. "Biggest breakfast ever coming right up."

He watched her whirl in the kitchen, his smile slowly fading. The City of Light was an island on an island—its own sun, its own weather, its own rules. People worked lifetimes for a ticket in. He could only imagine the consequences of breaking in.

And Foxx was more than a roboticist. He was a cyberneticist some would say, or a bio-mechanical engineer with a dark reputation. Known as the Iron Surgeon, he'd been wanted for illegal body modifications and had hundreds of victims. United by vengeance, Cy and Foxx worked together to avenge Ti's death by bombing the headquarters of the Chemical Agents.

Knowing their time in Ameris was running short, they applied for citizenship on Kude Island. They received acceptance of their applications almost immediately. After enduring separate trials upon arrival, they went their own ways.

The Realm, a district in Quad Four notorious for its black-market technology, was filled with horrors: augmented-reality chambers, rogue robots, human chop shops, and drug rings.

Small rumors began growing. DeathStar's headquarters lay hidden somewhere within its metallic depths. It was only a short time before all Force divisions came plowing through. Cy loathed the place and its gloom. This mission was important. He couldn't save his best friend, but he could save Trinity.

Cy had to down grade his appearance—a simple gray tracksuit, zipper boots, no flashy jewels except his silver chain. He moved quickly past limping bodies, dying plants, and crystals with a faint glow. The Toy Boxx hid behind a long alley near a park hidden behind the shop. It had a glass front, shelves crammed high with mechanical devices and magical apparatus. A holo-sign flipping between cute toys and monsters danced above.

The door dinged as Cy pushed it open. He approached the counter and waited as his eyes scanned his environment. After a moment, the beaded curtain rattled. A tall, oak colored man stepped through—jet black hair, hologram Hawaiian t-shirt of flowers dancing, and two ringed antennas jutting from his skull.

"Hey, man. How can I help you?" Foxx greeted.

But Cy didn't respond. He stood there awkwardly and shrugged his shoulders, pressing a soft smile.

Foxx squinted his eyes, then his eyebrows rose, "Holy—Little Cy? CY? Get over here!" Sparks lit across his antennas.

He nearly dragged Cy over the counter. "How's it been, man? I haven't seen you since Ti's birthday celebration."

"It wasn't much of a celebration after they arrested you," Cy's words muffled as he pulled away.

"Minor misunderstanding. Replace a few organs with solar fans and suddenly you're a villain." He swept a hand at the shop. "Look at me now."

"It's... nice. Stellar," Cy said, remembering when Foxx sold fake points in alleys. "I need two City of Light chips and two Citizen Cards with clean slates."

Foxx stared at him for a moment. Foxx was curious.

"Sneaking into the Emerald City, huh?" Foxx lowered his voice and rubbed his chin. "What's the play?"

"Family business." Cy nodded with his chin.

"Say less." He vanished back behind the beads. "Grab whatever you need—it's on the house." Foxx shouted as he descended a flight of steps.

Cy took the opportunity to stock up: a quantum keyboard, a quantum math text, an 2-bit QBIT, wire packs, clear quartz, amethyst, rubies, a radio wave sniffer, a scoop of tick-bots (spider trackers), several chip boards, and a small blue-crystal tesseract for Isis. The intergalactic web had developed beyond the quantum field, creating stratified networks for the government, the elites, tech geniuses, and other people who were smart enough to hack in. Prism firewalls—multidimensional filters that infinitely refracted data like code—hide secret networks shielded each layer. It would be like finding an encrypted hidden chat in the eternal void. Now Cy had to build one. If you broke a deal on the dark web, you would be haunted for life.

Foxx returned with two dead Citizen Cards and two data chips. "Here you go, blank citizens ready for any identity."

Cy sighed in relief. "You saved me so many hours, Foxx. Thank you for real."

"Whose idents are you using?"

Cy shrugged. "Some old junkie couple. They've been missing for a while. They'll make the perfect scapegoats."

Foxx started bagging up Cy's parts and wires. "Funny thing," he stated, voice dropping low. "Last year, a guy tried the same stunt you're pulling. Used the ID of some big-shot named Robert Matters."

Cy frowned. "Never heard of him."

"Oh, he was this huge club tycoon," Foxx explained, sniffling. "Made piles of coins and even more enemies. He and his girl got kicked out of the holy city when their little drug habit started draining pockets. There was a bounty on his head, so when my guy tried using Robert's ID—"

Foxx clapped his hands together, and shouted, "BOOM!"

Cy flinched.

"Tracked the card straight to him. Vaporized on the spot. Left nothing but scorch marks." His voice dropped.

"Great pep talk." Cy eyed the antennas. "You augmented?" he pointed.

"Oh, you know it baby." Foxx tore off his shirt. Prying open his chest like a cabinet, he revealed metal organs, tubes for veins and a slug colony.

"Foxx, why do you have slugs inside of your body?" Cy inquired with a hint of concern. It sounded more like a statement than a question.

"Helps with rust." Foxx smiled as he admired his anatomy.

Cy couldn't decide whether he should feel impressed or nauseated.

Foxx chuckled, closing his chest and putting on his shirt. "We should kick it. Like old times."

"Like when you tried to cut my ear off?"

"And look at you now. Those days were the building blocks of your future. You grew character, didn't you?"

He clapped Cy's shoulder. "Look, kid we don't have to go into the mushy gushy, okay? Just know that I'm here for you. Whatever you need, come see your big bro, Foxx."

"Thanks Foxx. Stay lit."

"At least we look like we belong," Isis said, twirling in front of the mirror. The yellow silk dress shimmered under the light, patterned with blue dragons and stitched flowers. The matching blue fur scarf dangled on her arms. Dazzling yellow diamonds weighed down her ears and neck. While Cy had been out collecting the forged cards, she'd treated herself to an evening at the spa. If Isis wasn't feeling good on the inside, she was going to make sure she looked good on the outside.

"Here," Cy said, handing her a new Citizen Card and a small data chip. "We are officially Evie and Luke Caldwell."

He looked like a modest traveler—dark denim jeans, a clean white shirt, a brown coat, and a worn brown leather sack that matched his leather boots.

Isis opened her drawer and pulled out a slender pyrite blade. "Hand," she ordered holding out her hand.

Cy obeyed, placing his hand in hers.

"Ow," he hissed as she pricked the skin between his thumb and forefinger.

"Oh, don't be a baby." She slid the chip under his skin, then pressed her thumb against the wound, speeding the healing process until the mark vanished completely. She repeated the same for herself and wiped the blade clean. "Anything else we should know?"

"The Caldwells went missing about a year ago," Cy informed, tucking his new card into his jacket. "Luke was an architect; Evie worked as a data archivist at the History Museum. Nothing special just names we can disappear behind. We'll use gold coins only. Quick in and out."

Isis glanced at her reflection again, frowning. "I don't know... my outfit screams newbie."

"You look fine," Cy blew out sharply, already heading for the door. "Let's move."

At the front door, Isis reached out and gripped Cy's biceps. Her hands trembled slightly, but her eyes were soft.

"Cy... thanks for doing this. For me."

He smiled faintly. "No problem, kid." He kissed her forehead gently. That gave her the comfort she needed. She didn't want Cy to resent her.

They stepped out into the brisk morning air just as the sunrise bells rang. The sky was clear, and the sunlight shone over the mountains. Isis inhaled deeply, trying to ease the tightness in her chest. Every step towards City of Light felt like crossing a line she couldn't come back from.

She'd broken laws before—stolen, hacked, fought—but this was different. This time, she wasn't just defying the rules. She was shattering them.

As they boarded the Skyway, the wind whipped through her newly styled hair, carrying the faint scent of jasmine from the spa. Cy closed his eyes and took a deep inhale as strands of hair whipped across his face.

"Where should we say we were?" Cy asked, glancing over at her.

"Let's say we were staying at our Red City estate," she replied absently, watching the skyline of Twin Cities' tall buildings. She watched her reflection in the Skyway window—eyes sharp, posture confident—but she barely recognized herself. The dress, the perfect hair, the forged name. It all felt like a costume, like her life.

The last trace of the Shadow Land faded behind them as they reached closer to the top of the hill. Isis felt her stomach twist into knots. Her arms stayed interlocked with Cy's as they stepped off the Skyway.

From the top of the hill, a walkway carved past Pattie's and Coco's, leading to a breathtaking sight. A grand staircase carved entirely from limestone. Two lion gargoyles, each the size of a mountain beast, guarded the base of the steps. The steps were covered with people as they climbed up and down. Their formal clothing enhanced the scenery.

On each side of the staircase were two slanted beacons that carried people up and down. The couple waited in line for a beacon that would carry them to the top. As they ascended, Isis looked down at the world shrinking below, wondering how many rules she'd already shattered just to save one girl. But it wasn't just one girl; it was Trinity. The person she had shared her life with. The only person who was by her side and knew the real her. There was no turning back; Isis was determined to save Trinity.

The beacon rang with a soft chime as they reached the top. Their feet took slow steps on the smooth paved ground as they exited. Their eyes swept across the mountain sized dome.

"It's so colossal." Isis gawked, "It almost takes up the whole sky."

The dome was made of polished white quartzite crystals set into white steel triangular frames. Isis could feel the overwhelming frequency of the crystals.

Ahead of them stretched a pair of massive frosted-white doors framed by silver arches—one marked Entry, the other Exit.

The line for entry was long but moved quickly.

Isis tugged at her dress and exhaled slowly. "We're really doing this," she exhaled as her heels clinked against the ground.

Cy gave her hand a reassuring squeeze. "Yeah. And we're going to make it." He guided her hand to his lips.

But inside, Isis wasn't sure if she believed him.

"Comms on?"

"Yeah." she responded. Her hands wouldn't stop shaking.

He squeezed her palm harder. "Act natural. Shoulders down, back straight, and just breathe."

*Listen to Cy. Just breathe, Isis. Just breathe. I don't get why I'm so nervous.*

The line moved with haste. Cy and Isis reached the scanner in just a few minutes. Isis watched the people ahead of her carefully. They would place their hands on the scanner and their profile appeared on the screen before turning green. When it was her turn, she repeated the other actions. Isis set her hand on the scanner and waited in anticipation. Simultaneously, Cy hacked into the system, changing their appearance to the cameras to the Caldwells.

The seconds stretched but the scanner eventually turned green. Cy followed behind her. They grinned at each other in success and stepped into a tunnel onto a moving walkway.

"We're almost at the end—I can see the city," Cy pronounced, giddy.

"My goodness, calm down, newbie," Isis joked, equally buzzing, hiding her smile.

The light got brighter as the walkway brought them to the edge. They emerged onto a high platform overlooking a hollow city: waterfalls, green terraces, and levitating crystal lanterns. Homes, shops, and clubs were carved into mountainsides. Sky vehicles danced around each other, weaving up, down, and around. What caught their eyes immediately was a silver obelisk that stood in the center of the center. At its point a massive burning star floated. Surrounding the obelisk was a park full of tall bushes and mini dome-capped platforms. Behind it stood a city of skyscrapers all connected by platforms and walkways. Above it all, the roof was coated in a simulated sky filled with puffy clouds.

"We should keep moving," Cy instructed as people flowed around them.

To the left and right of the platform limestone staircases awaited. Cy and Isis followed the crowd and descended the steps, passing a platform of FastTracks that led to the skyscrapers.

"We're at least five thousand feet down," Cy noted. "The electricity... it feels different here."

Once on the ground, Cy could get proper scan of the layout. He took her hand and guided her to the nearest Star Skipper service.

People floated past on flat smooth circles, a transportation device not seen outside the dome. Space for ground vehicles was impossible.

"No wonder nobody ever leaves, it's quite peaceful." Isis scoffed.

"Let's not get comfortable." Cy asserted.

They approached the Star Skipper booth tucked into the mountain wall.

"We need one Star Skipper, please." Cy told the attendant. A man of old age and a grumpy look.

The attendant barely glanced up from his Tabs. "Sure," he said slamming them down. He drifted through a back door. When he returned a few moments later, he picked up his Tabs and kept scrolling. He jerked his chin at a "WAIT HERE" sign near a bench.

Cy thanked the man and followed his unspoken instructions.

As Cy and Isis sat on the bench, Cy couldn't help but stare at her as she stared out into the distance. His heartbeat slightly rose and his palms began to sweat, it felt like their first date all over again. *Damn, why am I the one who's nervous now.*

"Cy, stop staring at me," Isis said flatly, without turning his way.

"Oh, sorry." he instantly looked away, rubbing his hands across his chest.

Moments later a hologram of a female guide projected in front of them.

"Your Star Skipper will be out momentarily. Please wait near the sliding doors next to the booth. Enjoy your trip!"

They did as instructed and stood near the dark brown oval doors built on the side of the mountain. Neither of them would have noticed it if the guide hadn't pointed it out.

Moments later the doors opened and a round vehicle hovered out from the dark pit. The sphere vehicle resembled a human eye, smooth and uncanny—its front shield tinted black, the black metallic plates formed a mechanical eyelid that blinked once as it locked into place.

"Holy spark plugs—it's an Oculus Star Skipper," Cy geeked. "The most efficient transport. Could take you to Stone Wall and back within hours—"

A cool blast of air rushed to their faces as the seamless doors on the side slide open. Steps unfolded from a hidden panel hitting the ground like their red carpet. Inside only twenty-five percent of the space was intended for seating. Two leather seats and a slender control column between them. The tinted shield pixelated into a screen.

"Hello! Welcome to the Velvet Sky Star Skipper service." a holographic attendant appeared as the pair sat. "What is your destination?"

"White Castle Rock, Cherry Street," Cy answered.

As the moment passed, a short chime played.

"Address confirmed! Controls are between your seats and the voice commands are active. The emergency stop button is under the panel. Payment is due at the end of the ride. Sit back, relax, and enjoy the ride."

As Cy and Isis strapped themselves in, the Oculus rose in the sky. The world shrank below them as the screen faded to clear. The city unfolded beneath their feet—a labyrinth of waterfalls, crystal towers, and rivers that shimmered like threads of light.

For a moment, neither of them spoke taking in the ethereal view the city had to offer.

Studd hated the City of Light. Beads of sweat rolled down his head and splashed on his suit. He adjusted his jacket, smoothed his tie, and clutched a bouquet of multicolored roses wrapped in golden wrapping paper tightly. Edith had wanted dinner; he'd countered with a late breakfast between meetings. It took many pleadings to convince her.

Edith Kimble was a renowned surgeon and three-time recipient of the Kude Prize of Noble Citizens. People widely recognized her for inventing tunnel-vision glasses, a groundbreaking technology that allowed users to see the world in inverted colors. Eventually, the product was pulled from shelves after people began changing it into laser and x-ray devices. Her family traces back to the opening of Kude Island. Even without sitting on the council, her name pulled a lot of power.

"Excuse me—" he tried a passing citizen.

"Maps over there, newbie," the guy said without looking up, pointing toward a hologram stand under trees.

"Stupid city. Stupid lights. Stupid hot ass sun," Studd mumbled to himself. "Street names exist for a reason," he yelled at the citizen.

He dragged himself over to the holographic map and then froze to the sight in front of him.

*Isis and Cy? What the hell are they doing here? City of Light is for level five only.*

He quickly scurried behind a tree to see if they spotted him. When the duo climbed into an Oculus and rose away, he stepped out, jaw tight. *First, she injured my detective and now she's sneaking in the holy city.*

He marched over and flashed his Citizen Card at the attendant.

"How ya doing. Councilman Studd. Where were those last two passengers headed?"

The attendant mumbled to himself as he threw down his Tabs. He disappeared into the back room and returned. "White Castle Rock, Cherry Road." He responded dryly as he returned to his seat.

"What's so special about that place?" Studd inquired.

The man stared. "You're a Level Five citizen and you don't know Cherry Road?" He laughed. "The Bubble House? The most exclusive private club in the city. You have to know someone who knows someone who can afford to know someone to get in. It shut down a few years back. Owner ghosted."

"Is that right? So, how do you know about the Bubble House?" Studd inquired.

"I run a transportation service. I see a lot and hear a lot," he responded.

"Hmph. Think you could help a Council member out?" Studd asked.

"Wait by the sign."

From above, the mansions looked like geometry drawn by gods. Uneven shapes stacked, towers that curved, and fortresses intertwined with nature.

Isis let her mind drift for the time being. Imagining what her life would have been like if Studd never caught her. Questioning if she and Cy were really destined to meet.

Without noticing, the Oculus began sinking toward the ground. Nothing but a corridor of hedge walls made the street.

"Congratulations! You have arrived at your destination. White Castle Rock, Cherry Street." the system cheered. *TOTAL: 5 GS* blinked on the screen.

Isis fed the slot between them five coins. After exiting the Oculus slipped back into the air and flew away.

"Where's the house?" Cy searched. All he saw were bushes towered like buildings that went on into the distance.

"Maybe at the end of the mile-long hedge hallway," Isis sighed, "I picked the wrong time to test out these heels." She moped as she followed Cy, who trailed ahead of her.

After minutes of silence and the clacking of Isis's heels, they finally reached the gates of the bubble house.

"Tell me you're seeing this," Cy gazed at the scene.

Three separate front lawns and three gold gates. Beyond them, a dreamy, pristine chateau lined with two turrets.

"Opal," Isis muttered. "The house is made of opals. Hundreds of them. No... millions."

As Cy approached the gate, he held up his Tabs, scanning. After a few seconds, he frowned. "There's...nothing. No defenses. Either he disabled his security—or he wants trespassers to walk in."

"Interesting." Isis commented, rubbing her chin as her eyes squinted.

Cy reached into his leather sack and retrieved a small jar. He untwisted the cap pinched off a bit of star gel—a clear, gummy substance alive with microscopic blue sparks—he fed it into the keyhole. The sparks flared and Cy used his x-ray vision to watch until the lock became undone. He used a second pinch of gel to retrieve the first.

The first lawn was just an empty field of neatly trimmed grass. The couple walked through without issue.

Second gate, same gel trick—beyond this gate laid a fairy-forest: tiny floating sparks, butterfly colonies, mossy stones, ponds, wild cacti and towering aloe.

Curiosity got a hold over Isis as she approached a floating spark and gave it a gentle tap.

"Ouch!" She shook her hand. A charred spot marked her fingertip.

She pressed to heal, but nothing happened.

"Your cells are dead," Cy stated grimly peeking over her shoulder. "Even you can't revive the dead. You're gonna have that mark forever."

She frowned. "What even are those?"

"Must be mini solar capsules." He murmured, inspecting. "Like the city's sun, but on a micro level. And free floating. With no conductor. How did he—?"

"Ughh who cares? Let's just get through the next gate." Her head dropped with embarrassment.

The last gate had no lock. Cy easily swung open the gate into a garden of Kuji trees—spikey fruit filled with sticky white sap. Kuji's were rumored to supercharge psychic channels and melt moral judgment.

Up close, Cy could see the details. A quick scan and a few calculations, and he found out the chateau did consist of millions of tiny opals, 3.6 of them. *Impressive.*

"This must of took years to construct."

Isis didn't hear. Taking the lead, she used her shoulder and busted through the front door—which was a slab cracked diamond. A storm of dust rolled out as she stumbled in.

"This doesn't feel like a home. It looks more of a museum."

"Or a club for the rich," Cy added. A long hall split the home in two, at the end of the hallway stood a spiral staircase.

"Alright you check out the left side of the house and I'll check the right." Isis instructed.

Studd arrived at Cherry Road and stared at a wall of hedges that went on forever. Sweat pooled under his armpits.

"Brilliant stars above, you're kidding." Studd whined.

He had no choice but to follow his instinct.

He stopped at the open gates and checked himself. This was as far as a Councilman or Chief should. He sighed and split open his Tabs.

"Call Edith."

"Hello?" came her voice after a few rings.

"Hello, yes, Edith. Listen, I—I'm going to need a ride," he whispered. "I'm sending my location now. I'll explain when you get here."

The hallway leading to the left side of the house consisted of one door. Cy crept through the only door, unaware of the marvels, and horrors, that awaited him.

The door led to another hallway of different rooms.

He approached the first door and picked up a pair of glasses from the rack that stood next to the door. Inside, all sides of the room, including the floor and ceiling, were made of thick plexiglass. It was completely dark except for the light coming from the bioluminescent sea creatures. There were many species of jellyfish, including the Spaghetti Monster jellyfish, the Atolla jellyfish, and the phantom jellyfish, to name a few. Alongside them were dozens of deep sea creatures, such as the threadfin dragonfish, the barreleye fish, lanternfish, the fanfin sea devil, and black dragonfish. Every creature seemed like it was pulled from a nightmare. He stood in awe of the alien like creatures he'd never seen before.

He knew it would take up most of his charge, but he had to know. Cy slipped on the glasses and the water became clear as day. He was able to see each creature vividly.

"Gather data on each species and run the most accurate simulation on what will happen in a thousand years if left untouched," he ordered himself.

Light from his eyes scanned the room, the simulation played inside his eye lenses. Each second showed a year's worth of time.

The black dragonfish adapted into something deadly. With no predator able to detect its red bioluminescence, it fed undetected for generations. Its body lengthened and its beard grew sharp spikes that acted as a spear to stab through prey.

Cy watched as the barreleye fish evolved for detection. Eyes adapted a new form of x-ray that began registering wavelength, temperature, and the refraction of light against shimmering scales.

Deep sea squids grew new mouths along the length of their tentacles that let them feed from multiple areas without moving. Their form of reproduction relied on the males' releasing sperm whenever the female cried out. She would then use her tentacles to transfer the sperm to her reproductive organs.

Then a new predator came to life. A shark whose jaw could unlatch and extended almost twenty feet with a second row of teeth. Eyes able to capture the electric aura of any creature.

New species emerged that didn't exist in the simulation's first century. One species of fish was pure white with no eyes at all. Another fish calcified over generations, its skin hardening something like a stone armor.

By year five hundred, the activity slowed. Most of the prey died out due to stress, overgrown bacteria, or temperature.

Only a few sharks and a squid remained, both species capable of surviving for years sustaining themselves on algae. There was one species of jellyfish that adapted by eating itself for nutrition, regrowing its limbs and essentially becoming immortal.

Then Cy's charge indicator blinked, notifying him that he was at 45%. When he left home his charge stood at 89%. He stopped the stimulation and continued exploration.

The next room stood an art gallery—hundreds of paintings hung in perfect symmetry. Some were patterned like fractals, others surrealist visions that seemed to move when he blinked. Portraits of old kings and queens stared back at him, their features arranged in strange, angular shapes. The signature read Lupe Démont.

Cy stepped closer to one of the frames. Scanning every detail. *High in symbolism and quality of paint. I'm sure there's at least a thousand years' worth of conspiracy theories. Lupe truly is a savant.*

He hesitated, tempted to pocket one. They must've been worth more gold than he could count.

The next door came a warning Cy ignored. A decision he would quickly regret.

The moment he stepped into the room, gravity tugged at his body. The ground of the room was coated in gray dust that swirled in the unseen air. It was so silent that Cy could hear the whirring of his mechanical eyes as he scanned the room. All the walls were filled with space. Not empty space but actual outer space. He felt the heat from the stars, and experienced the lack of oxygen, but worst of all the pull from the planet in front of him that resembled Jupiter. It floated, glowing in shades of bronze and red. Storms twisted slowly, as magnetic light sparked at its poles.

He fought the pull of gravity as his feet left trails in the sand.

"Shit." He wheezed as more oxygen escaped.

Thinking quickly, he reached into his bag and retrieved a small grapple pistol. Inching closer to the abyss, his body slowly turned to face the door, and he let off a single shot. A line shot out, piercing through the door and locking into place. He grabbed the line and braced his feet against the pull of gravity as it dragged at his back. Using all his strength he hauled himself forward, inch by inch, toward safety.

His body collapsed once he cleared the door. His labored breath released hard coughs, and he wiped the sweat that dripped from his forehead. "Jupiter's gravity... that was close."

Isis, on her side, walked into an indoor Eden: soaring mushrooms and trees, looping vines, and a waterfall streaming over a blue chalcedony fountain. It reminded her of Grunn's enclave.

On the back wall, there was a door with an obsidian doorknob, this piqued her interest.

"Cy, meet me on my side of the house. I found a suspicious door," she said through her communicator.

"Yeah... so did I."

Isis waited for over two minutes before calling him again. This time Cy accidentally left his comms on, and she listened as he giggled between breaths. *Why is he breathing so hard? And what exactly is so funny?*

"Sorry," Cy said, finally trotting in. "I got carried away."

Isis rolled her eyes. "Really what were you doing that had you all giggly?"

"Aww are you really jealous of a house?" he teased.

"What? No!" she huffed. "Look I found a door. Let's just see where it leads."

"Fine, watch out I got this." He pounded on his chest and took the lead. He approached the door, twisting the locked knob. "Dammit." He whispered.

He stepped back and slammed his shoulder into the door. He stumbled as it broke open. *That hurt a lot more than I expected. At least I looked cool.*

"Aww baby did that hurt?" Isis asked.

"Isis, don't play with me."

Isis's intuitions were correct. Behind the door was an empty room with another spiral staircase curling upward through the ceiling.

"Your brother sure does have a thing with spiral staircases."

"Yeah," Isis replied, stepping inside. "From what I remember, he thinks spirals are the key to understanding the foundation of the universe."

Cy gestured toward the stairs with a bow.

"Well then. Aliens first."

Isis took the lead, climbing the staircase. When her head emerged through the opening, she was stunned to see a dazzling ballroom waiting on the other side.

"Oh, my heavens! Cy look!" Her voice echoed as she twirled in the air full of dust.

Cy climbed through and matched her excitement with a soft grin.

Large, colorful windows framed with golden swirls lined the walls. Dark teal wallpaper patterned with gold damask adorned the room.

Above them, the ceiling glittered with black amethyst crystals, while a grand chandelier studded with hundreds of diamonds dangled from its center. The polished dark oak floor gleamed beneath their feet. At the far end of the ballroom stood three thrones.

"I bet their parties were interstellar."

"Look at the floor," Isis whispered.

The colored light from all the windows merged on the oak patterned tiles into the shape of a giant open palm. Above each finger, a small icon—a key, a fish, a crown, a sun, and a crescent moon.

It piqued her interest, but she shrugged it off and continued looking for clues.

"Do you notice anything weird or suspicious? I'm pretty sure this would be the room for something like that." Cy asked.

"Actually, I do." She titled up the head, "The chandelier —" She pointed. "Something's off with it. Not all of them are diamonds. It's something else, but not a gemstone. They have a different frequency," Isis thought hard, rubbing her temple.

"Cubic zirconium—it's a fake diamond."

"Maybe, if we turn them a certain way—like levers—something will happen," she theorized.

"You are your brother's sister."

"Oh, what a compliment. Thank you so much," she spat sarcastically. "Now, how do we get up there?"

"Guess there's no better time to try these out than now."

Cy crouched and reached into his boot, pulling out a small remote. He clicked a button to activate.

"These are the anti-gravity boots I've been working on. I never tested them because... well... I was afraid they wouldn't work."

Isis blinked. "That is the worst explanation you could've given me."

Cy grinned and pressed the button on the side each boot.

A low hum vibrated through the soles. Slowly, he lifted a few inches off the floor.

"Hey, they're working!" he laughed.

At first, he wobbled wildly, arms flailing as he drifted sideways. For a moment it looked like he might slam into the wall. Isis held her breath as she followed beneath ready to catch him.

Then his motion stabilized and Cy hovered in place.

"Oh yeah," he said proudly. "I'm definitely keeping these."

"They work!" Isis grinned leg bouncing off the ground.

He floated slowly toward the chandelier. The massive fixture swayed slightly as he gently grabbed it.

A light grid swept across the gems blooming from his eyes. One by one the real diamonds glowed green. A handful flashed red. He reached out and pressed one of the fakes. It shifted slightly beneath his finger.

Cy grinned.

"You were right!" he called down to Isis.

He moved to the next one, then the next, carefully bending each fake gem into position. When he pushed the final zirconia back—

*Clunk.*

The entire chandelier rotated. Chains groaned as the fixture slowly lowered toward the floor, revealing a hidden spiral staircase inside the ceiling.

He slowly floated down along the staircase.

"Ladies first," he said, landing beside her.

They climbed into a turret chamber that felt enchanted. Mini-suns drifted near the glass-dome ceiling casting light across the room. Mahogany walls painted with gold swirls. Tapestries of night skies and palms draped across the walls.

A king bed rested beneath deep purple drapes. The dressers were cluttered with strange curiosities—book, shimmering oil, animals trapped in resin, crystal balls, tiny moving trees, sundials, feathers, bubbling copper cups, and delicate celestial orreries that quietly spun in place.

Cy rotated slowly, scanning the treasures.

"Let's stay here tonight," Cy suggested.

"Here?" She blinked. "Are you sure?"

"We came a long way and didn't find much. Let the experience be the treasure."

Isis looked around the room again. One of the miniature suns drifted past the ceiling like a lazy comet.

"Alright," she nodded. "Let's do it."

The couple slipped into silk pajamas they found in the drawers and curled up beneath the purple canopy. Cy projected a movie from his eye, and the couple were able to enjoy each other's company under the drapes.

As day glitched into night, Isis laid awake under the pixelated sky as Cy drifted off into a deep slumber. In her thoughts she pictured her parents. The crystal castle she used to sleep in. The weight of a crown she once wore.

On earth, she was nobody. A name without a title. A girl who used material things to replace the love she was bathed in.

*Am I meant to be human forever? If I go home, do I lose Cy?*

She pressed her cheek to his chest and closed her eyes. Listening to his heartbeat, trying to match the pace of his breath. Her hands rubbed against his smooth skin.

*Cy, I don't know what I would do without him. Sometimes I feel like I'm dragging him deeper into my mess. Maybe he deserves someone to give him a happy ending.*

⧗ ⧗ ⧗

Edith landed her Star Skipper at the start of Cherry Road, where Studd stood waiting, his suit flapping in the wind.

The top of the Star Skipper started to open before she even landed.

Before Studd could attempt to climb in, she stopped him.

"Oh, uh-uh!" Edith shouted.

She unbuckled her seatbelt with lightning speed, jumped out of the aircraft, and stormed toward him.

Studd threw his hand in frustration. "Oh agony... what's your issue now, Edith?"

"Don't think you're climbing aboard my craft without explaining why you're not only two hours late, but also a sweaty hot mess." She gestured at him. "Do you know how long it took me to cut and color my hair? I stayed up all night preparing for this."

"Aww, look, Edith, don't give me that crap," Studd shot back. "I didn't even want to come here in the first place."

"Oh vex, not this again," she scoffed. "Studd, you know you can be a real quantum flex. You practically begged me for a date, and this is how you use the opportunity." Her voice rose.

"Edith hold your gold value—I didn't beg alright let's get that straight."

"Oh, no? What were the words? Oh, please Edith let me show you a good time? Please, I promise this is one vex of passion you won't forget." She mocked in a whiney voice.

The pair began shouting over each other, making it hard to hear their counter arguments.

"You always have to have things your way!" Studd yelled, veins popping from his neck.

"No, I don't—but I do require respect and a little courtesy!" she shouted reciprocating his energy.

Studd sighed, dropping his head realizing he'd lost the argument.

That's when Edith noticed the roses in his hand.

She crossed her arms, pouted slightly, and flipped her bangs back with attitude.

"...Those are really nice flowers, by the way."

"Yeah," Studd muttered. "Had them specially grown from this florist. Been waiting for the right time to give them to you."

There was a brief pause.

Edith sighed. "Fine. We can still have a late breakfast, although it's lunch now. The midday bells are set to ring. But I expect you to tell me everything that's going on."

Studd shook his head as she turned and walked back toward the craft.

*Oh boy. She's the hardest case I've ever come across.*

# Chapter 32: Truth Revealed

Trinity spent hours in Booker's secret occult room, trying to decipher the strange languages in the books.

*Hmm, this stuff is quite interesting. Who knew there could be so many secrets hidden in space? So much to discover, so much we don't know. Is this what I was missing? Honestly, when Uncle told me about my alien heritage, it mattered, but it didn't complete me. Now, reading about dimensions and alternate realities, I feel just a step closer to completing my journey of self-discovery. The veil is starting to collapse. I don't know why, but my gut; it's telling me I'm missing something else.*

Exhausted and eyes heavy, Trinity headed back upstairs, only to find Abott standing in the living room, its lights flickering softly. *Why isn't he in sleep mode?*

She gasped when the thought hit her. She'd completely forgotten about the work she was supposed to start. Right now, she just wanted to relax.

> "Abott on. Are there any other secret rooms I should know about? Like maybe a hidden spa?" she inquired approaching.

Abott took a moment to respond. "Yes. I can take you to the indoor pool of warmth several levels below us."

"An indoor pool of warmth?" Trinity raised an eyebrow. "Now this I have to see. Let me go change my clothes."

"There is no need to bring clothing," Abott responded. "Everything you require is already there."

"Oh, fancy! Lead the way."

After entering the beacon, they descended deeper into the mountain's heart. She watched as the rocky walls sped past her. Hair rising with the shift of gravity. When the beacon landed and doors opened, Trinity's breath caught.

A vast brine pool bubbled before her, steaming with gentle waves. Light mist curled through the air.

"This is the indoor pool of warmth," Abott announced. "There is a chamber to your left that prints clothing in your size. You may adjust the lighting, temperature, and color gradients. Enjoy your swim, Trinity."

Isis stirred in her sleep, waking up to the smell of something savory. *Cy must have found the kitchen.*

She sat up slowly, rubbing her eyes. Every muscle in her body ached, but it wasn't pain that weighed her—it was guilt.

She heard Cy coming up the steps and quickly wiped her teary eyes.

He appeared with a wide grin and a tray full of food.

"Someone must have found the kitchen."

"You have no clue." Cy responded, setting the tray down on the bed, "Couldn't even use my scanner my charge is low."

"This whole place is a maze. I went through so many hidden chambers." He handed her a plate piled high with scrambled eggs, mushroom potato cakes, avocado salsa with pickled onions, a hearty steak, and cubes of yellow watermelon.

"You want some pulp?" he asked.

"Sure, thanks." She wasn't hungry, but she would not let his effort go to waste.

Cy dug in between words. "Oh, I found something weird while I was cooking. It was near these giant eggs." He tossed her a small rectangular stone with a built-in compass. "There was a note glued to the back."

Isis quickly took it up and turned it over and read aloud, "Start at the Afterlife and always follow the red hand." The paper had swirls that added texture, the handwriting wasn't one she recognized. *This is certainly not Trinity's handwriting.*

Her heart skipped. "Cy!" She shot to her feet. "Where did you find this?"

"I opened the fridge, and it was right there next to the eggs. It was almost as if someone had put it there knowing I would find it." His eyes peeked over at her.

"The compass... the red arrow it's pointing east." Her eyes widened. "Cy, we have to leave, like right now. This is the clue we've been looking for!"

"Whoa, whoa, calm down." Cy waved his fork lazily. "I just cooked a feast. I'm not going anywhere until I eat it." He took another bite. "Honestly, I don't think your brother's hurting Trinity. He's probably training her or something."

"Training her?" Isis repeated, frowning.

"Yeah. She's a power source. If I were him, I'd use her energy to make infinite light or a wormhole."

"Infinite light?" Isis whispered. "No, he must need her energy manipulation as a power source to get back to our home planet. I remember the ship got really damaged when we landed." She caught herself. "But you're right. Let's rest for now."

She sat at the edge of the bed, trying to steady her breath. Her gaze drifted upward—then froze on celestial orrery.

She pointed. "I'm pretty sure that's my home planet, according to all those three stars."

Cy traced the path of her gaze.

"Hm." Cy grunted as his focus was on the food.

They ate quietly after that, the weight of her words hanging between them.

When they finished, Isis stood and smiled faintly. "Let's pack up. I'm sure we'll come back one day."

After dressing in clothing found in the closet, they rested their fancy clothing worn to the city on the bed vowing to return one day.

Hours passed as Trinity floated in the brine pool, the warm current soothing her body and mind.

Until a tap on her shoulder.

She spun around and gasped.

"Uncle!" she blurted, startled. "Cheers!" she smiled.

But her smile faltered when she saw his cold face, his eyes filled with a hard stare.

*Oh vex, he's angry.*

Abott stood motionless in the distance—still in sleep mode. *No help there.*

"I was—uh—just about to start my studies," she stammered. "Abott was giving me a tour."

"Get dressed," Booker said flatly. "Meet me in the lab. You know where it is."

He turned and vanished into the beacon. They exchanged an awkward glance before the doors closed. *Someone has the key and they are on their way. It could only be one person. But how, how did Isis get the key I gave to Trinity? There's only two that were ever made. Unless...* "Shit."

She froze as a rush of thoughts crashed through her brain. *Oh, great. Is he going to kick me out? Why did he look so mad? I just went for a swim. But it's not like I can tell him off. He'd probably smack me if I tried.*

She dried herself off and hurried to dress.

"What does Uncle do when he's mad?" she asked Abott nervously in the beacon.

"I am not authorized to disclose such information," Abott replied. "But may I recommend Ambien to reduce anxiety?"

She glared. "No, thanks."

When she reached the science lab, it was empty. She took a seat at a table and waited, heart pounding.

The G48 glided through the air, invisible to the human eye. Isis gripped the compass tightly, staring at the needle as if her life depended on it.

Cy took the opportunity to recharge, plugging in the cord to the port at the top of his head. He watched as she poked at the dead patch of skin on her finger. "Do you know what you're going to say when we find her?" he asked, breaking the two hour long silence.

"No," she whimpered "No, I don't."

"How about starting with 'I'm sorry'? She needs to know you're her friend, not her enemy."

Isis nodded without argument, "Yes, you're right."

After another hour of silence, the red needle started spiraling.

"Uh, Cy...?" she stared at the compass. "Something's happening."

"We must be close." He watched as the arrow spun uncontrollably.

"It feels weird, like something is pulling it." The compass jerked suddenly, tugging against her grip.

Isis tightened her fingers around it.

"It must be a magnet, Isis. Let it go." He instructed.

Before Isis could react, the compass shot out of her hand, punched through the G48's floor sending sparks through the vehicle. Isis leaned over the hole and watched as it vanished downward.

They stared at each other in disbelief, mouths agape.

Cy steadied the vehicle and followed the compass trajectory, lowering it into a valley surrounded by dusty red mountains.

"We're in the Red Mountains." he noted.

"Look, there it is." Isis pointed.

The compass hovered near a rock wall. Cy landed the G48 in front of it.

Isis hurriedly unbuckled herself and leaped out of the vehicle. Ignoring the swirling dust, she ran for the compass and released it from its gravitational force. The moment she pulled it free; it began vibrating slightly as things do right before she doubles them. *That's weird I didn't plan on making another, I guess this must be a sign. Better safe than sorry.*

She doubled the compass and put the replica in her pocket.

"Look." Cy pointed coming up behind her, "Put it in that blinking slot."

Isis ran towards the slot and slid the compass in. A soft click echoed, followed by a green flash. The mountain wall rumbled as it split open. Cy stepped back as dust flew.

The ground started to rumble as the mountain wall opened. Inside lay a beacon with translucent walls filled with glowing symbols. The pair stepped in carefully.

Isis immediately pushed her face close to the symbols and examined them carefully, "I'm sure this one mean 'Living Quarters.'"

> "You can read this? Even my stimulation can't decipher these symbols."

"It's my language of course I can read it." Isis answered, tracing the symbols. "We used frequencies to speak, then translated them into written patterns. I can't believe I still remember."

"Maybe you never forgot."

After a moment and a loud hiss, the beacon bolted forward. Cy and Isis braced themselves as the beacon rocketed up. The beacon bolted up. Reaching the living quarters, the beacon doors opened. A humanoid robot stood in the living room to meet Isis and Cy.

Cy pulled his blast gun from his waistband instinctively.

Isis stepped forward cautiously. "Is that a Med-Bot?"

"No, that's an IO. Prototype version of the next generation of Med-Bots. People say they're too human." His eyes locked on the robot expecting it to make a move. *They also have an impressive defensive system.*

"That is correct," the IO replied, startling them. "You are like Master and Trinity." It turned to Isis.

"Uh... sure," Isis replied warily.

"How do you know that?" Cy asked.

"You accessed this floor using Master's written code. I detect the same heavy metals in your blood as in his. Your heart rate and neural activity match as well."

He turned toward Cy. "However, your system contains a firewall. I cannot see inside. I am.... curious."

"You're going to remain curious. Where are Booker and Trinity?" he gripped his weapon tighter, like a foiled-wrapped burrito in the hands of a hungry detective.

"I detect fear and a bit of anxiousness. Your adrenaline levels are high. Would you like to have a seat?" Abott turned to Isis.

"No, I would like you to tell me where I can find your master and my niece, Trinity," Isis demanded.

"I cannot disclose that information."

"Fine." Isis exhaled. "We'll look ourselves." She slipped past the IO and stopped near the closet door she could find.

She paused as she gripped the handle. "This must be Trinity's," she murmured. *It smells just like her.* She closed her eyes and took a deep inhale. *I missed you, kid.*

She opened the door and her jaw dropped, "Stellar, this is the prettiest room I have ever seen." Isis said in awe.

"Yeah, this is definitely her room. Her bed isn't even made and her hair oil is soaked in the pillowcases." *He could have at least given the girl a head scarf.*

"Find anything?" Cy called as he scanned the kitchen.

"No—" she answered stepping out the room, "but I'm picking up frequencies. Strong ones." She pointed toward the staircase near the kitchen.

Trinity sat in the lab, absently gliding her finger on glass sphere, watching the sparks dance and curl at her touch.

"Trinity!"

She heard her name faintly. She spun around, her neck craning to search for the source of the voice. *That sounded like Isis. I must be hearing things.*

"Trinity!" the voice called again but this time it was right on her neck.

"Isis?" Her stomach dropped to the sight of Isis and Cy standing in the doorway.

*How did they find me? What are they doing here? Did they come all this way for me?*

Her face twisted in confusion as she walked toward them. "But how did you—"

"Trinity, listen," Isis pleaded, voice trembling. "You need to come with us right now. You can't trust him."

Booker's voice cut through the air. "No, Isis. You're the one she can't trust."

Trinity turned. Uncle was suddenly there, as if the air itself had formed him.

"Trinity! Get away from him!" Isis's voice trembled with panic and rage. The surge of emotion triggered something deep within her—a rush of pure instinct.

Isis snatched the gun from Cy's hand.

"Trinity—get down!"

Trinity dropped to the floor just as Isis fired a loud plasma blast.

The shot cracked through the air—but missed him, striking the sphere of energy. The glass filled with cracks upon impact.

But Booker didn't even flinch. The blast had no effect on him; it passed through him with ease.

*The blast, it... it went right through him. How?*

Booker took slow strides toward Trinity unfazed and pulled her up into a firm embrace. "Don't listen to her." His voice was soft yet menacing.

> Trinity froze. As her body followed his pull, his hands cold.

"Hey!" Isis shouted, pointing the gun at him. "You stay the fuck away from her!"

Booker didn't even blink. "Trinity, do you ever wonder why she doesn't tell you about your past? Or about your... illness?"

"Shut your mouth!" Isis barked. "You don't get to twist this!"

Trinity's breath quickened. "Illness? What illness?"

The cracks in the glass started to spread, though no one seemed to care.

"Your blackouts," Booker remarked. "Your mood swings. Why you remember nothing before the age of five—or should I say ninety-five?"

"Isis... what is he talking about?" Trinity's voice trembled.

"Trinity, I'll explain everything, I promise. Just—come here. Please." Isis reached out her hand.

Booker's smile turned sharp as he tightened the grip around her shoulder. "Shall I tell her how her parents died?"

Isis's eyes widened. "Don't," she whimpered, lowering the gun, "Please don't do this to her."

Trinity tore herself free from his grasp. "Tell me," She demanded, eyes darting between the two of them.

Booker met her gaze, a sinister calm settling over his features. "It was you, Trinity," he said softly, savoring every word. "You killed them."

His eyes darkened with an evil sense of pleasure as he lowered his chin, baring every tooth in a grin that felt more like a threat than a smile. For a moment, it was as if the shadows themselves bent toward him, drawn into the void of his expression.

The room went still.

Trinity's chest tightened, her eyes flooding with water. "What?"

Cy stood there, frozen in disbelief. *No this can't be true.*

She turned to Isis. "Is he telling the truth?"

Isis said nothing. Her eyes fell to the floor, her posture collapsing as if the weight of years had finally crushed her. All the confidence that once defined her was gone.

"Isis... is this true?" Trinity's eyes began drowning in tears. Her soft voice cracked with the weight of sadness.

The cracks in the sphere spread wider.

Isis broke. "Yes." The word barely escaped her lips.

Trinity staggered back, her eyes blurring with rage. "No, no, no, no. No! Why!" Her voice ripped through the air, "Why didn't you tell me?" Her hand clawed at her chest as she felt her heart breaking, "How Isis! How could you lie to me!"

Her knees gave out, body collapsing to the floor. Her fingernails dug into the floor tiles.

"Trinity, I'm sorry. I thought I was protecting you," Isis cried out.

"Protecting me from who—myself?" her voice transformed into a sinister growl.

The air swayed filled with swirling winds. Glass beakers from the tables shattered on the ground. Beneath their feet, the floor shook. Light from the sphere slipped through the cracks but the reveal of the secret took away the attention.

"Yes, Trinity!" Uncle roared. "It was *you* on that fateful day at the Recovery Center; it was *you*! You were sick and your parents came begging for me to save you. I gave you a serum, but your body rejected it. Your light was unstable, your mind uncontrollable. You killed fifteen people that day—including your parents!" Booker's voice grew louder with each word.

Isis couldn't stop him, and she didn't want to. It was about time Trinity learned the truth, even if it wasn't from her.

Trinity sobbed uncontrollably. Then the surface of the glass sphere finally burst.

The sparks flew to her hands like a magnet. It spread up her arms like lightning striking a tree.

"Cy, run," Isis warned, looking back at him.

As Trinity's body began radiating light, it glowed brighter and bigger.

"Trinity, stop!" Isis shouted, rushing forward.

It was too late.

A blinding flash erupted and swallowed the lab, shaking the mountain itself.

Cy flew backwards and hit the wall; his consciousness faded.

# Chapter 33: The Second Birth

Piquette's eyes finally opened. Her vision slowly cleared from the sleepy blur, revealing the dim outline of her apartment ceiling. She lay in bed, her head still groggy.

For a moment, her mind was blank. Then the memories came rushing back.

She gasped, grabbing for her alarm clock.

It was a new moon. She'd been asleep for days.

"What—how long...?" She groaned, pushing herself upright, climbing out of bed. Her legs buckled beneath her. She collapsed onto the floor.

"Ah—" she cried out in pain that seared through her head. She dragged herself to the bathroom.

"I have to get to Papa," she rasped between clenched teeth.

Clutching the doorframe, she hauled herself up and leaned against the sink.

The broken chip she had ripped from her neck days ago still lay in shattered pieces.

Her reflection stared back at her—pale and half alive. She touched the back of her neck and winced.

"Ugh," she hissed. A small, inflamed boil throbbed where the chip had once been.

She rummaged through her emergency kit and injected glowing liquid into a syringe then stabbed it in her arm. Energy surged through her limbs as she took a sharp gasp. Her eyes blasted open with adrenaline.

Without hesitation, she pulled on her clothes, tied her hair back, and stumbled toward the door.

She needed to get to her father before it was too late.

Isis woke up with her cheek pressed against a hard surface. Her head throbbed. She rose unsteadily to her feet, blinking through the blur until her vision returned.

"What in the void?" she muttered.

As her vision adjusted, she realized she'd become surrounded by moving images—scenes shifting and dissolving into one another like a collage of moving memories. The ground beneath her was pitch black, as if she stood over the pits of hell.

A sound came from behind. She spun around.

"Hey!" she shouted, storming toward her brother. "What is this? Where are we?"

Booker brushed past without meeting her eyes. "I don't know." His lip twitched.

Isis would normally tear into him for his tone, but her mind was too busy unraveling the impossible.

"It seems like we're somewhere outside of time," he muttered, studying the floating visions. His reflection flickered across them. "Her memories... we're inside her memories."

Isis looked closer. "These are the ones she's forgotten," she revealed softly. "The ones she's hidden. She built this place like a simulation room; those are her favorite games."

"Yes," Booker repeated with a crooked smirk. "Like a simulation." He turned to face her.

"You paradox born jinxed fuck! You wanted this! I knew you were using her for her powers!" Isis stomped towards him until they were face to chest, she looked up at his eyes burning with rage.

"Oh, please." He gave a dismissive laugh. "I gave you the greatest gift known to time. You should thank me. You kept her locked up, her powers dormant. Such wasted potential."

"I don't know how you crawled out of that fire," Isis snarled, shoulders squared. "But I know your secrets. Isn't that right, Alwin? Or should I say Phoenix big brother?" The corner of her mouth twitched with a smirk.

Then, something rippled beneath his skin.

Isis froze, disgust tightening her jaw. "What—what are you?" she took a step back.

His face fractured into thousands of tiny black beads, reshaping him until Alwin stared back at her.

"We are not so different, you and I," he spoke, voice echoing through shifting flesh. "The same source gave birth to you, me, and Trinity."

His eyes locked onto hers.

Isis clenched her fists and turned her back to hide her tears. "I'll deal with you once we're out of here. But first, how do we do that?"

Booker's face reformed into his own as he glanced around. "I'm not sure. This isn't my first trip outside of time, but it *is* my first visit to a man-made dimension. Trinity managed to hide fragments of her mind—memories tied to certain emotions—within time and space itself. She's created her own universe. A treasure box for the brain. If we find the last memory, maybe we'll find the way out... She can manipulate energy waves from different dimensions, Isis. Her power is control over time and space itself."

Isis barely listened. She had her own secrets to protect—things her brother could never be allowed to see.

"Trinity Blossom Rose!" she barked, her voice echoing through the dark. "You better get me the hell out of here right now!"

There was a moment of silence.

Then the voices of the memories grew louder, shrieking at a pitch that hurt their ears. A blinding light tore through the darkness. Isis and Booker dropped to their knees, clutching their ears as an unbearable frequency filled the void.

Then Isis saw something out of the corner of her eye—a memory that hadn't yet happened. For a moment the pain stabbing her eyes dulled as she stared at the memory.

Then, a bright flash swallowed everything.

Isis opened her eyes to dust and ruin. The lab was gone—obliterated like the Recovery Center.

"Cy!" she called, coughing. Pain shot through her side when she tried to move. "Ouch... are my ribs broken?"

Through the haze, she heard Booker's voice. "Consider yourselves enemies of the Island. You're banned for life. Don't you dare set foot here again. Trespassing, attempted kidnapping, assault—that's just for starters."

His voice felt too close, as if he was whispering in her ear, yet when she reached out, she touched nothing.

Isis didn't waste another second. "Cy," she groaned, rising to her feet clutching her rib cage. "Where are you?"

She staggered through the debris until she found him unconscious in the hallway.

"Cy!" she cried out.

Kneeling beside him, she pressed her palms to the bleeding wound on his head. Light shimmered between her fingers as it healed.

*That's never happened before.*

"Cy, wake up!" She grabbed his face firmly.

When that didn't work, she retrieved a vial of smelling salts from their bag and waved it under his nose.

He jolted upright. "Holy shit!" he shrieked as lens in his eyes retracted.

"We have to go. Now!"

Isis helped him to his feet, carrying him toward the living room with his arm slung around her shoulder. The IO from earlier stood waiting in the same spot.

"Hey, IO, we need a ride out of here—fast. Uh, master said it was okay."

"You both require medical attention. You have fractured your third and fourth ribs and sustained—"

"We don't have time for that. Just get us out of here!" Her voice roared.

"I will escort you to the vehicles." The IO took them up the beacon to the cave garage filled with sleek land and sky vehicles that stood on flat top stalagmites.

"Why can't we use ours?"

"Because I'm leaving with something—even if it's not Trinity. Autopilot the G48 home. We're getting a new ride. IO, show me which vehicle is fastest."

In his office, Studd sat down at his desk in meticulous thought. He exhaled hard, scanning the scattered papers on his desk. His eyes landing on the crystal ball. Desperate for answers he grabbed it and closed his eyes, "Give me a sign, or anything that will help me understand what the hell is going on."

He gave it a shake. The black smoke curled inside the glass, then message slowly appeared:

*Follow the path, but don't expect to escape the thorns.*

Studd frowned. "What the vex is that supposed to mean?"

"You won't believe this, boss." A detective burst into Studd's office. "We have a storm call for Isis Rose and Cyrus Shakur."

"Solar hell," Studd slid on his glasses. "From who?" He rose to his feet.

The detective transferred the data from his Tabs to Studd's board.

"This can't be right. All storm orders go through me—and I didn't sign this."

"It's got the tughra, so it must be from someone important. Should I dismiss it?"

Studd hesitated. "No... assemble a team. But wipe all traces of that order, even from my device. She must've pissed off someone high up."

"Sure thing, boss."

A low rumble shook the building. The shadow of the Force Storm Catcher passed over their windows. A massive, hexagon-shaped warship with the head of an eagle carved into its hull. Its engines howled like thunder as it landed.

Cy and Isis tore through their apartment, grabbing only the essentials—photos, weapons, flash drives, anything they couldn't afford to lose. Sparks flickered as Cy overloaded the power grid, frying every trace of their data. Isis ripped a piece of the EverVine and stuffed it in her bag. "I'm sorry girl." She whispered rubbing her finger along the shifting wood.

Then someone pounded on their door.

Isis froze for a split second, heart pounding. "They're here."

Cy yanked her arm. "Then we move. Now!"

"Under the Force's jurisdiction, we are authorized to administer a storm in search of any enemies of the island. If you do not comply, we will use force to gain entry onto the premises. We are here to collect the persons listed: Isis Rose and Cyrus Shakur."

Studd stood outside with his most trusted men—Shawn, Dezzi, Clay, Baz, and Amir. Dressed in their tactical uniforms, their blast rifles gripped firm in their hands.

"Laser beam it is," Studd said coolly, "Take it away boys." He stepped aside.

Shawn stepped forward and sliced the lock with a laser beam from his rifle. With a strong kick, the door crashed to the ground.

Under the bed, Isis and Cy held their breath, adrenaline pouring in their veins. Cy slid open a hidden tile, revealing a keypad. He unlocked it with a neural signal. A circular hatch spiraled open. The couple dropped into a replica of their apartment below just as the Force stormed the one above.

Trinity woke up cold and shivering, her face pressed in the dirt. A faint ring lingered in her ears.

"Ugh," she groaned, rubbing her head. Her vision blurred as the sun set over the horizon. It was way past midday.

*How did I get here?*

She stood, barefoot and trembling, still wearing the clothes after Uncle dragged her out of the pool. The forest loomed around her, dark and whispering.

Her toes and fingertips felt numb as if she was in the cold for hours.

She walked with no destination in mind. Her thoughts drifted. *Why can't I? The last thing I remember was the pool. Then Uncle... he was...*

She couldn't help but cry.

*Why? Why does this keep happening to me? Where does the time go?*

Out of the corner of her eye, a blue streak shot towards her. Striking her in the neck.

She pressed her teeth together and hissed. She tried to swipe it off, but it dissolved into her skin.

"No," she cried, eyes heavy.

The world tilted sideways as her knees gave out.

She dropped like dead weight, paralyzed as her breath went rigid. Her eyes shut closed.

When she awoke, her mind was foggy and her body numb. Her vision doubled. Dressed in nothing but her undergarments, chains clinked as she tried to move. Her wrists and ankles were bound to a filthy bed in a decaying wooden cabin.

Piquette's pulse spiked when she noticed Trinity's body stirring—eyes fluttering open again.

"No, no... not again." She rushed forward, frustration twisting her voice. "I'm sorry, I really am. You have to understand. It's... it's my dad. Please. Just trust me. I'm going to make this right. I'm going to fix this. Damn! Why do you keep waking up?" she snapped, panic bleeding into anger. Piquette's eyes were frantic as her pupils were twice their normal size.

From the glass vial, she spilled out the last blue organism. It writhed between her gloved fingertips. It sank onto Trinity's forehead.

A childlike laugh echoed from the shadows. Her father hopped in place, his knees bent like wire hinges.

"Hehehe!"

Trinity's vision blurred, the world escaping her once again.

*Stay awake... stay awake...*

"You see what you're making me do?" Piquette threw her overpowering voice at her father, "I—can't live like this."

Her father slowly approached, "But Piquette, I'm your father. Don't you love daddy?" He said with a giddy smile. His hands twitched as they reached out for her.

She backed away, eyes widening in horror. *He's ... he's a monster.*

Piquette rushed and threw her coat on with trembling hands.

"When I get back, we're going to fix you," she turned back to him under the threshold.

She pointed at her father, jaw tight. "Stay here. Don't let her out of your sight."

He responded with nothing but giggles. Piquette swallowed a sob and fled through the door. Jumping onto her cycle she headed for Gravity Grave.

"General," she greeted as she entered Skinner's office. "I need a new batch, sir."

He removed his glasses, turning to Piquette, scanning her sickly look. Pale, sweaty skin, and twitchy eyes. "Isn't this a pleasant surprise? How was your trip to Skeletor Island?"

"It was informative, sir. I'll get a report to you as soon as I can." Piquette's stomach felt queasy. Her eyes fluttered shut for a second.

She was sure Skinner was the one behind her being chipped. That didn't matter now; she knew what she was signing up for. Her main priority was protecting her father.

"You know I like our arrangement," he intoned. "But if this little habit of his gets out of hand..." He trailed off, opening a drawer.

"Yes, sir. I understand." She answered hastily.

He handed her three vials, only to snatch them back halfway. "Next time I see you, you'd better have it under control."

"Yes, sir."

When Trinity finally regained consciousness, she found herself chained to a spiked surgical table in a blood stained room. The cold spikes pressed against her back and the chains were covered in dry blood.

Torture tools lined the walls. Severed limbs dangled from the ceiling like grotesque ornaments. A pile of mush with a beating heart sat in the corner. Trinity could sense the sadness and fear that lingered in the aura field.

Tears slowly ran down her face. *I guess this is it huh, tortured to death by a maniac. I wish Isis was here. I want her to come and save me. I want her to bust through the door and release me from these chains.*

Trinity was too weak to scream, too weak to even move.

Her eyes scanned the room again trying to figure a way out. That's when she noticed it. On the shelf, floating in a jar, was a brain. Trinity could feel its pulse, as if it was alive. Her eyes fixated on the jar as she felt heaps of energy rippling through the air towards her.

She didn't know why but the aura felt so familiar. It was as if the brain was trying to communicate with her. Sending signals through the electromagnetic field.

Then she heard the creaky sounds of footsteps in the distance.

"Oh, no, no. Please, no. Why is this happening to me!" she cried.

The footsteps grew closer and closer. The adrenaline coursing through her body fed her enough strength to tug at the chain.

The footsteps turned into stomps once they reached the door.

Trinity froze, stomach twisting in knots. Her eyes grew in horror watching the shadows of the feet stomping on the ground.

Then they stopped.

She held her breath and kept her body still.

With a swift kick, the door flew open. The old man ran in full of excitement grinning with rotten teeth. "Now we'll have some fun!" He squealed rushing to Trinity's face.

"Ahh!" she screamed as her head retreated from the stench of his breath.

*Move, Trinity. Move! He's going to kill you. You have to do something!*

The old man danced in circles around Trinity until he came to a halt. "Yes, oh yes! Yes, yes, yes, yes . . . this one will do just fine." He unhooked a sharp knife hanging from the wall, "This won't hurt a bit! This won't hurt a bit! This won't hurt a bit!" he kept repeating while hopping from one foot to the next.

Trinity watched as she fought harder with the chains.

He stopped abruptly.

"Listen! Please. Please, you don't have to do this. My aunt she can give you anything you want!" Trinity pleaded. But her cries were of no avail.

He slowly turned to her, "Don't worry. This won't hurt a bit." He growled inching closer.

*Isis please, I'm sorry. I'm so sorry for everything, please forgive me. I love you so much. And Cy. I wish you guys were here to save me.*

He hovered over her rapidly licking his dry lips. His eyes grew bigger by the second. He lifted the knife above her chest slowly and thrust it down with speed. Trinity shut her eyes and braced herself.

When the knife hit her skin, it shattered upon impact. Her eyes snapped open and looked down, "Quantum fuck!" she shouted, "You really just tried to kill me." Her heart was beating faster than the speed of light.

Her chest rose in rapid breaths. Anger surged through her body. Power flowed through her veins as her eyes began glowing with light. Chaotic sparks of lighting whipped around her.

"Eghh!" the man shrieked, he turned to make an escape out the room, but he wasn't quick enough.

Trinity broke through the chains and flung her hand forward. Energy gathered in her palm into a sphere. Acting on pure instinct, Trinity hurled it toward the old man.

The plasma instantly melted his body on impact. Sending echoes of his shrieks through the room. Smoke rose from his body as his skin burned to a black crisp.

This was unlike anything Trinity ever felt. She had no clue what was happening or where these powers were coming from. But she knew she couldn't stay here.

As Trinity dropped her hand on the table, it instantly disintegrated into sand beneath her touch.

Trinity dropped to the ground. She slowly raised her hands to her face and watched as sparks jumped from her fingertips. *I don't understand. What is happening to me? I just killed someone and I don't even feel the slightest remorse. I feel... Whatever this is, I feel like this is my natural state.*

Rising to her feet, all effects of the drugs were gone. Her feet marched towards the door.

Then she heard it, a frequency her brain translated into words... *Please take me with you. Don't leave me.*

The jarred brain was speaking to her. Without hesitating Trinity reached for the jar and took it off the shelf. She stared into the glass and flinched at her reflection.

"Are those really my eyes?" she questioned, but that thought quickly left her mind when images appeared in the liquid.

It showed from A'Kierra's point of view of her bumping into Trinity at the championship game.

*It's you, the girl who gave me that gold coin for my ice cream. A'Kierra... that's your name, isn't it?*

*Yes.* A'Kierra answered as the pair began speaking telepathically.

*What happened to you?*

Trinity watched as A'Kierra showed her the final moment of her life.

*A'Kierra. That's terrible. I'm so sorry that happened to you.* Trinity began to cry. *You didn't deserve this. You deserved to live a life of happiness. These people robbed you of it. Don't worry, you won't have to suffer on that self any longer.*

*We must escape before the daughter returns. Once out of the door, make a right, two lefts, and then another right.*

Trinity followed A'Kierra directions. At the end of the last tunnel was a ladder. Above it was a small hatch. Trinity pushed the hatch open and with A'Kierra tucked under her arm, freeing them both.

Trinity stared down at the tunnel and the feeling of rage overcame her. Without thinking she rose her hand again. The energy gathered in her hand like before

Without a word she directed the plasma sphere into the tunnel. She was thrown back from the blast of the explosion.

*Trinity, are you okay?*

*I'm fine A'Kierra, that man will never rob a girl of her life again.*

Trinity staggered to her feet, when her hand dropped by her side, clothes began forming around her body—holographic fabric stitching itself, unfolding from sparks of light. The dirt on her skin lifted, and her curls began to shorten; a white streak painted a section of her hair. Even the liquid of A'Kierra's jar turned clear.

Trinity walked for miles, trying to piece her mind back into place.

*How did I end up in the mountain ranges in the first place. Why can't I remember anything. Think, think hard. The last thing I*

*remember... Uncle pulling me from the brine pool. And Isis... why I remember her? Neither Uncle nor Isis ever mentioned powers.*

Her feet stopped midstride. She gasped as the memory returned, "Alien, I'm an alien."

*Uncle said we come from place far away from here, a crystal planet. I remember now. But does that mean we have superpowers? That Isis has superpowers?*

A rotting log covered by overgrown grass and mushrooms caught her attention. Curiosity got the best of her.

She crouched and pressed her fingertip to the decaying bark. Life surged outward from her touch. Moss spiraled green and bright, tiny flowers burst open. And the air warmed with the floral scent of earth.

A soft breath escaped her—half-laugh, half-sob.

As she kept walking, the forest thinned as she was nearing the city. She stepped onto a mountain and overlooked the city.

# Chapter 34: Departure Before Dawn

Isis's chest heaved, her pulse pounding so hard it felt like her ribs would break again. They had prepared for this day, but nothing had prepared her for the actual panic of running. Sweat rolled off her forehead and stung her eyes. She swiped it away with her already damp sleeve.

"Coast is clear," Cy whispered to her as he pulled her into the hallway.

The crash of glass upstairs made Isis flinch. The Force was tearing their apartment apart. Each thud felt like a punch to Cy's stomach. He had built that kitchen with his hands.

They ran down the hall to the stairwell and flew down six flights of steps like birds escaping a storm. Once on the ground floor, Cy moved slowly as he peeked out the staircase exit. A crowd gathered around the armed guards as they blocked the front entrance doors.

"Shit we can't go this way," he hissed, jaw tightening.

"So, what do we do?" Isis pressed against his back, refusing to give him even an inch of space.

"The back entrance through the kitchen. I'll cloak us. If the Force has a counter-field, we'll deal with it. It's safer than walking straight into them. The cloak won't last long. We're lucky they didn't capture us already. Seems like their doing a half-ass job."

A beam of light flashed from center of his head. The pixelated light coated them until their bodies were invisible.

Cy took Isis's hands and wrapped them around his waist. Isis didn't dare to leave an inch of room between them.

Once they were rendered invisible, Cy slowly opened the staircase exit and slipped out into the loft. Matching each other's pace, they quickly fled down the hall that led to the café kitchen.

The door to the café kitchen swung open. Confused chefs glanced up, hearing hinges creak though no one entered. "Who left the damn door open?" one barked, slamming a cleaver into a cutting board.

Cy moved with stealth, weaving between prep tables and shifting bodies. Knives flashed inches from their arms, pots hissed, and the rich aroma floated past. A misplaced footstep that slid across spilled oil sent Isis's leg slipping. She quickly clutched his shirt, catching her breath. Cy reached back and caught her by the waist, pulling her up with quickness. Just then, a chef paused, knife in mid-air, as he sensed something.

Cy held his breath and dared not to move.

Then, the chef shook his head and went back to chopping. Cy dared to breathe again.

Finally at the back of the kitchen, Cy and Isis pushed through the back door, ignoring another shout from behind them.

Once in the alley he disintegrated their camouflage. He pulled four tiny silver discs from his pocket and pressed them onto Isis's face. One on the forehead, two for each jawline, and one between the eyes.

"Hold still." He ordered her.

Once all were in place, a holographic mask shimmered over her face, sculpting new features. Cy activated his own disguise with the same beam, this time only covering his face.

Piquette spotted the smoke from miles away.

Her heart pounded as she raced toward the hatch—but she was too late.

The tunnel was in flames. She dropped to her knees, the glass vials slipping from her trembling hands. Tears blurred her vision as orange light danced in her eyes.

"No!" she screamed, her voice breaking through the roar of the fire.

Tears soaked the dry dirt beneath her.

"No, this can't be. I was so close." She whimpered, digging her finger into the dirt.

*I have to leave before the Land Forces come. The smoke can be seen from miles away. But where, where do I go from here?*

Trinity pulled her hood over her head and made her way to Blink Station, located a stride away from Riverstone Park.

The terminal buzzed with late-night travelers.

She picked a crumpled piece of paper from the trash bin and watched as it shimmered, transforming into a Blink Station ticket at her touch. She bit her bottom lip in excitement, quietly squealing to herself. *Yes, it worked.*

Clutching it, she joined the line for body scanning and waited for her turn.

She tucked A'Kierra in her jacket zipping it tight, hoping it wouldn't prompt questions.

She stepped on to the light beam, and the guard examined her body on his screen.

Trinity tried her best not to look. She turned her head slightly and the expression on the guard's face didn't even budge.

When she received clearance, she let out a gasp.

A row of luminous pods stretched before her. Flashes of light spilled through the cracks.

She stepped into one of the empty pods, slipped the ticket into the slot, and looked up as the light brightened around her.

A faint smile appeared on her face. When the pod flashed a bright light, she vanished.

# Chapter 35: Shifted Fields

During three days Switch spent waiting for Evander, he stayed out till the crack of dawn in the underground world of Ameris. Tunnels that stretched for miles. Hidden cave systems. Whole underground cities built for one purpose, illicit business. Murder, human trafficking, weapons of mass destruction, body modification, illegal reality rooms. Anything that was too shady or unscrupulous for the surface took place underground. This is where Switch thrived. Switch was given anti matter, a chip with a prism firewall, and less than an ounce of 99.999% hydrogen to trade with. Even with the earth's rarest materials he was only given a few sentences of information.

"From what I heard, DeathStar has a nexus that uses an eye patch. There's also a rumor that he's a ghost."

"A ghost?" Evander repeated as he cleaned his disassembled weapons.

"Yeah, man a ghost." Switch said as he lay eyes closed in bed.

Their assigned location was a shabby hotel located in a city called Neon Sin. Neon Sin landed on territory controlled by Legion. Even on the fifteenth floor the noise of the city was deafening.

"Some homeless guy swears he saw him walk through a brick wall. I thought he was crazy until I heard some other people say the same thing."

"Maybe he has a connection to the facility. Some kind of device that allows him to transport, maybe they are changing the vibrations of his atoms so he can walk through hard surfaces."

"Wouldn't be the first time I heard that theory." Switch tossed finding a comfortable position.

"Righteous work kid. We got a long day ahead of us tomorrow. I'm going to update Zakari, you get some rest."

The next day Evander and Switch started their journey to an area known as the abandoned wastelands. An area of Ameris where water was scarce. The land was dry as if the sun skimmed the surface. Nothing but deserts and high mountains were found here.

Evander drove them right to the border where Neon Sin ended and the wastelands began. Hiding their vehicle in a marked location they took the rest of the way on foot.

"We're coming up close maybe another mile of two." Switch announced taking a swig of water. Sweat stains accumulating under his armpits.

"Right, let's link here."

Evander pressed the chip located in the back of his neck; Switch did the same. Simultaneously their chips synced making the same high pitch sound.

Evander drew his plasma gun from his waistband securing his grip around the handle.

He then took a clip and connected it to Switch's belt. A thin fiberglass thread to ensure they were never separated.

Switch took the lead climbing over boulders and weaving between canyons until they came to an opening.

"That's it we're here. You can see the shimmer of the cloaking field." Switch pointed out.

"Listen kid, do not forget what we spoke about, if anything happens leave me behind and head straight to Blink Station. You got that?"

"Yes sir, understood."

The pair crouched down and walked toward the barely visible waves in the air. Each step felt like it could be their last then.

When they reached the designated boundary, before they could react, time stopped along with their vision. The air slowly warped, blasts of refracted rainbow light surrounded them. Neither could move an inch of their bodies. It was just as Switch described—being trapped in time and space.

Then, quicker than the blink of an eye, Evander found himself falling. He hit the ground with a loud thud.

"Ugh!" he called out grabbing his back. Grunts were all he could muster to make. He slowly rose to his feet ignoring the throbbing pain throughout his body.

It took a second for his blurry vision to return to normal. He shook his head trying to speed up the process.

"Kid?" he mumbled grabbing his head.

Then he realized it was night.

"Kid! Switch?" he yelled whipping his head back and forth. He was in a different area of the wasteland. None of the landscape looked familiar. He took his Tabs from his pocket to map his location. He was miles from where Switch marked the facility to be. He grabbed his thread and pulled it until he reached the end, only to find Switch's body wasn't on the other end.

"Shit."

www.ingramcontent.com/pod-product-compliance
Lightning Source LLC
LaVergne TN
LVHW100512110826
845146LV00002B/604

* 9 7 9 8 9 9 3 7 6 1 2 1 3 *